THE MOURNING WOODS

The Tome of Bill

Part 3

RICK GUALTIERI

Edited by Megan Harris at www.mharriseditor.com
Cover by Mallory Rock at www.malloryrock.com

Published by Westmarch Publishing
www.westmarchpub.com

ISBN: 978-1-940415-05-5

Contents

For Dick and Diana, you are always remembered and greatly missed.

Special thanks to my fabulous beta readers: Alissa, Solace, Jenn, Melissa, RJ, Matt, and Bucktooth Bob. You helped add that extra layer of story polish and for that I am grateful.

Tis better To Have Loved and Lost

"WHAT DO YOU mean she quit?!" The question came out ... well okay, it came out far *less* harshly than I had intended. I had really meant to scream a massive string of obscenities into the phone. Sadly, even I had to admit that yelling, "What the fuck are you talking about you balding little middle management douche of a shit?!" probably wouldn't have been particularly diplomatic, especially considering that I was speaking to my boss.

"I know it's abrupt," replied Jim, my manager at HopskotchGames, "and believe me, I'm as upset as any of you, but we'll just have to handle our own paperwork for a while. Don't worry, I'll start interviewing for a replacement next week."

My roommate and coworker, Ed, hit the mute button. We were seated in his bedroom/office for the weekly conference call. He knew me well enough to know when a tirade was incoming, one it was probably best to spare Jim from – particularly if we wanted to avoid the unemployment line.

Jim's voice continued to drone, moving on to whatever topic of "importance" was next on the agenda. I didn't hear a single word he said. For all I knew, he could have been telling us that he had just won the lottery and was currently getting a blowjob from a thousand-dollar hooker.

"Calm down," Ed said preemptively.

"Paperwork?" I spat, ignoring him. "He thinks I'm worried about *paperwork*? The only woman I've ever loved has just walked out of my life, and he's concerned that he has to print his own fucking spreadsheets."

"Being just a tad melodramatic, aren't we?"

"No. I mean, I know we've only been dating for a few months, but..."

"Dating?" he interrupted. "You've gone out for coffee maybe three..."

"Four!"

"Fine, *four* times. And didn't you say it was Dutch each time?"

I glowered at my friend, letting my fangs extend menacingly. He stared right back, nonplussed. I'm a vampire – an immortal terror of the night – and I couldn't even get the humans I shared an apartment with to tremble in fear. My God, life was just not fair.

"Are you done pouting?" Ed asked.

"This is not pouting. It's supposed to be threatening."

"You might want to practice that in the mirror some more." He stood up and stretched. "Anyway, as I was saying, you're overreacting just a bit."

"Like you would know?"

"As a matter of fact, I do. Growing up, my older sister used to force me to watch Disney movies with her. Trust me. Four non-dates do not a fairytale romance make."

"There was more to it than that and you know it. Sheila and I..."

"Had nonstop, mind-blowing sex?"

"Well, no..."

"Played multiple games of tongue-hockey?"

"Not exactly."

"Spent every waking moment together?"

"Okay, I get the point!"

"Christ, did you ever even hold her fucking hand?"

"Well, once I brushed up against..."

"Exactly," he stated. "You pined for her for years and that's it. I had a more intimate relationship with my grandmother."

"Thanks for the visual, dude."

"Do you guys have any questions?" the voice from the speakerphone asked.

"Huh?" Ed and I both replied in unison. Oh, yeah, we had forgotten all about Jim. Hopefully, he hadn't been saying anything important.

Ed quickly un-muted the phone and said, "Nope. I think we're good."

"Awesome," Jim replied. "Then I'll let you guys get back to work. Keep me updated on your projects."

"We will," I answered, having no idea what he was talking about. A moment later, he cut the call off from his end. Oh well, I could always tease the info out of him later with a carefully worded email. Besides, Jim was so far from the top of my priority list right then that he barely even existed.

"Goddammit!" I cried and brought my fist down. The cheap folding table that served as our "conference room" immediately buckled, sending the phone clattering to the floor. Crap. Sometimes I forgot our furnishings weren't built to withstand vampire-level abuse.

"I can see that you're having a moment, Bill," Ed replied nonchalantly, stepping over the debris. "Coffee?"

"Sure. Blood and cream, if you don't mind."

"No prob. Regular or Baileys?"

"The latter. It's gonna be one of those days."

He nodded and walked from the room, leaving me alone with my rapidly darkening thoughts.

I swear, when life decides to kick you in the balls, it sometimes wears metal cleats. It seemed like that had been my existence for the past year, one big haymaker to the nuts after another. Oddly enough, that timeframe coincided just about perfectly with when I was turned into a vampire.

Don't get me wrong, I'm not about to get all weepy and angst filled. I'll leave that shit to Anne Rice. No, the reality of being a vampire isn't about sitting around for millennia, writing shitty poetry while you pine for your lost mortal existence. It's actually far more like being stuck in high school again, except this time it's

4

for all eternity. This is fine if you happen to be one of the jocks. It's not nearly as much fun if you're in the vamp equivalent of the nerd herd. The main problem was that, instead of growing up, the undead assholes running the show never matured past that stage and just ended up becoming bigger assholes as the centuries flew by.

They're not the only ones, either. In the past year, I had learned that there's an entire supernatural underworld that exists just outside of plain sight. Magic, monsters, and whatnot were all real ... and almost all of them were dicks, too. I know people say that absolute power corrupts, but they don't know the half of it.

It wasn't all bad, though. I had good friends and powerful allies. I'm the leader of my own coven of vampires. Heck, I'm even told that amongst the undead I'm special – and not in a short bus kind of way either. Still, it's been a rough road. Most days, the plusses have been just barely enough to keep me from opening up the curtains and embracing the sunshine.

That's where *she* came in.

Sheila is ... err, was ... an administrative assistant at my job. I first met her about four years prior, on the very day I first interviewed there. How I actually managed to get hired, I have no idea. I spotted her when I entered the office and, it was as if everything else blanked out for me. To this day, I'm surprised that my paychecks are actually made out to William Ryder, as

I'm fairly sure whatever I wrote on the job application was an incomprehensible scribble.

Unfortunately, whatever powers dictated the concept of "love at first sight" were likewise also assholes – big surprise, huh? It hadn't been mutual. Therefore, I spent the next few years of my mortal life barely being able to say "hi" to her. All the while, she hardly acknowledged my existence.

Amazingly enough, my rebirth as one of the undead was actually the catalyst that helped propel our "relationship" out of the rut it was in – and probably would have stayed. No, I didn't tell her that I'm a vampire. No bullshit *Twilight* love story for me. Generally speaking, announcing the existence of vampires to humans was considered a no-no, at least, if one didn't want to find themselves on the business end of a wooden stake. Sure, my roomies, Tom and Ed, knew about it. A few of my other friends did, too. I mean, hey, even Bruce Wayne had a few people who knew that he's Batman.

Anyway, through a series of events that ended with me getting my ass thoroughly kicked – by vampire assassins and a douchebag wizard/marketing VP – I momentarily forgot about my many insecurities and wound up asking Sheila out for coffee. Sure, it wasn't much, but it was practically earth-shattering progress compared to what I had managed before. Imagine my surprise when she actually said "yes." It was amazing. At my darkest hour, she was there like a beacon of hope.

But now, she was gone, and I couldn't help but feel that it was my fault.

* * *

Our fourth, and apparently last, non-date had been just a few weeks prior. On a Friday night, we had met at a café in the Village section of New York City. Normally this would've been a little out of the way for me. For starters, I lived in Brooklyn. Since I'm a vampire, things like working in an office during the day tended to be difficult. It's generally pretty hard to get any work done when a stray beam of sunlight could turn you into a smoldering pile of ash. Fortunately, thanks to my doctor friend, Dave, I was able to work from home. He wrote a bullshit medical excuse that allowed me to permanently telecommute. That being said, my coven was headquartered in SoHo and I'd usually end up there on the weekends anyway...

Oh, who am I kidding? Fuck the coven! I would've walked barefoot across the Sahara to spend five minutes with Sheila. If she had told me to meet her at the top of the Empire State Building at sunrise, I'd have been there in a heartbeat –metaphorically speaking, anyway.

I had let her lead the conversation, as I usually did. Even though I'd gotten past that first hurdle of actually asking her out, I didn't trust myself to say too many sentences in a row without stammering like a retard. Still, as our coffee encounters continued, I was pleased to find myself becoming more comfortable in her presence.

That night, the conversation had turned, as they often did with twenty-something-year-olds, to our hopes and dreams for the future. I sputtered something to the effect of enjoying what I did and hoping that the world didn't stop needing programmers anytime soon. It was a lie, but it was better than going off on some rant about being surrounded for all eternity by a bunch of immortals that looked and acted like spoiled underwear models.

After I had finished, she stared at me for a few seconds. Sheila had the most stunning eyes, a soft grey color. I don't think I could ever get tired of looking into them. After a brief pause, she replied, "I'm glad you're happy. I don't think there're too many things better than earning a living off of something you enjoy." *Oh, I could think of a few.* "For me, though..."

"What?"

"Well, I think it's pretty obvious I'm not exactly in my dream job."

"Has Jim been cracking the whip?"

"No," she replied dismissively. "Don't get me wrong, I like working for him. I just want ... I don't know ... something more."

"That's no surprise. Besides, what you do is just a stepping stone to something bigger."

"Maybe... I just don't know if I have what it takes for whatever that something might be."

I laughed. She narrowed her eyes at me in response, causing me to almost choke on my latte. I quickly added, "Sorry, I'm not laughing at you. It's just funny."

"What is?"

"You do all this stuff for Jim, me, and the rest of the team. You put together the presentations, you handle all the HR crap, and you update all of our project schedules ... hell, that's not even half of it. You keep the department running. Without you, we'd all fall flat on our faces."

"I doubt that."

"Are you kidding?" I asked incredulously. "Remember when you took those sick days last year?"

"It was a bad flu season."

"If you think you had it bad, you should have seen *us*. Jim was practically a basket case without you. Ed and I weren't much better off, either. Nothing got done that week. I mean it. *Nothing*! So no offense, but to hear you question yourself is a little silly."

"Really?"

"Really," I echoed, meaning every word of it. She threw a smile back at me that made me want to run through the hills singing the theme from *The Sound of Music*. I gave my head a quick shake so I wouldn't get lost in the moment. Nothing more jarring than to be talking about work when suddenly the bozo across from you started screaming, "GOD, I LOVE YOU!"

Instead, I somehow managed to continue with the conversation at hand. "I've seen you work. You get things done where the rest of us wouldn't have a clue. They couldn't replace you if they tried."

"You think so?"

"I *know* so."

"Thank you, Bill."

"No thanks necessary. It's the truth and, deep down, I think you know it."

She looked thoughtful for a moment. In retrospect, I wouldn't have been surprised if Future Bill had picked that exact moment to appear from out of a time machine and beat the ever-living shit out of me. If I had any part in her decision to move on, it's there that those seeds were sown.

Finally, she answered, "Maybe you're right. I guess I just needed to hear it from somebody else. I have all these ideas, all these things I want to do, but sometimes it's hard to believe in myself. When I lie awake at night, I have all these doubts about whether I really can do better."

"My mother always says sometimes we're afraid to believe in ourselves until somebody else does it first." Well, okay, I don't recall my mom ever saying that. At the time, though, I was trying to sound supportive. Sue me for making up shit on the spot. "Just for the record, I believe in you. I believe you can do better."

"Seriously?" she gave me a dubious eye just in case I was joking.

But I wasn't. Sure, I might've been a little biased. Emotions can do that to a person. Hell, if she ever said, "Bill, your roommates annoy me. Can you please kill them?" I would probably gleefully walk home and go on a bloodthirsty massacre.

Still, there was (love struck) sincerity in my voice when I answered, "You know what I see when I look at

10

you?" *Besides the most gorgeous creature to ever walk the face of this planet?* "I see someone with the talent to do anything she puts her mind to. I have no doubt that you could move mountains if you decided to."

Again, she looked thoughtful. Her eyes got a faraway look for a few moments. Oh, if only she would wear that expression when she thought about me. For that, I'd gladly suffer an eternity of the minions of darkness using my nuts as croquet balls. Hell, I'd even tolerate Sally, my vampire partner in crime, being the one to swing the mallet. Fortunately, Sheila spoke again before that particular imagery could further solidify.

Her eyes regained their focus, and maybe it was just me, but I could have sworn I saw a glimmer of determination in them that wasn't there before. She nodded her head once and said, "Maybe your mom's right. Either way, you've given me a lot to think about."

The rest of our little pseudo-date was spent talking about considerably less heavy topics, or at least I think it was. My brain had given its all just to get those thoughts out. I had no idea what I said or did, other than making puppy dog eyes at her until we went our separate ways. Sadly, I didn't have a clue as to how separate they were about to become.

It figured. I'd survived multiple brushes with death in the past several months, most of them at the hands of creatures far more lethal than I. Wouldn't it figure that at the end of the day I would be my own worst enemy?

God, I am such an asshole.

Late For My Own Funeral

THE THING I'VE always loved about programming is that it's purely logical. While having a passion for the job helps, at times one can shut down their emotions and type away, android-like, to get the job done. Pity I wasn't very good at doing that. Fortunately for me, though, I had a few spare keyboards in my closet. I needed them.

The next few hours found me trying to do my job and mostly failing. I'd be typing away when suddenly something like, "FUCK FUCK FUCK!" would come screaming out of my mouth, followed by me turning my keyboard into a mashed pile of plastic. Oh, well, at least they were cheaper than monitors.

Ed, for the most part, left me to my misery. He realized I needed a little "me time" to cool off. As late afternoon approached, my sharp vampire ears picked up his voice from out in the living room. I couldn't hear both sides of the conversation, but from what I could tell, he had phoned my other roommate, Tom, to let him know that it was probably not a good time to invite his girlfriend over. Ed doesn't usually like to show it, but he can be a hell of a good guy when he wants to be.

Sadly, the truth was, there really wasn't such a thing as a good time for Tom to ever bring Christy over. See, she's a witch, a real one. That in itself didn't bother me. It was the fact that she wanted me dead that put a damper on our relationship. She and her mentor, Harry Decker – the aforementioned VP/wizard from my company – had this loony theory that I was the harbinger of doom for wizard-kind.

They, along with all the vampires I knew, referred to me as the "Freewill." Apparently, I'm this rare breed of vampire that can do things the others can't. As such, there were all sorts of bizarre myths and legends surrounding me. Harry and Christy believed in one in particular that involved my existence somehow heralding the return of these other legendary creatures called Icons. Supposedly, if these Icons showed up, they'd destroy all the magic users ... yadda yadda, and other assorted bullshit.

Personally, I couldn't have cared less about any of that. All I knew was that Christy was the fucking Wicked Witch of the East Coast. That girl had some scary mojo about her, and she wasn't afraid to use it against me. Tom, my oldest and dearest friend, but also a fucking idiot, decided that the best way to handle this was to make her pinky-swear not to kill me in our apartment.

Needless to say, because of those little details, my relationship with Christy was a bit strained. Pity, because she was kind of cute.

What? Sharks are deadly, too. Doesn't mean they're not fun to look at in the aquarium.

Speaking of things that were both pretty and deadly, I was interrupted from eavesdropping by the ringing of my own cell phone. I didn't need to look at the caller ID to know who it was. The specific ringtone, the theme from *Halloween*, gave it away.

I answered with a sigh. "Hello, Sally." It was unusual for her to bother me in the middle of the week. Typically, she was happy to let me live my life – not that I had much of one. While I was gone, she was left in charge of the coven. Hell, even when I was there, it was pretty obvious that she was calling most of the shots. For the most part, she was a competent, if scary, person to leave in charge. However, occasionally her psychotic side got the better of her and she would do something that made me want to shove her out into the sunlight.

"Aw, what's the matter, Bill?" she replied with her typical snide tone. "You don't sound like your normal chipper self."

"I'm having a bit of a day," I said, using my free hand to massage my temples. Talking to Sally had a habit of bringing on the migraines.

"Well that's good, because you're going to have a bit of a night, too."

"What do you mean?"

"What I mean is that I think your 'penance' is about to be paid."

Oh, crap. "How so?"

"Boston called. They said we should expect company."

"Who?"

"They didn't elaborate."

That wasn't good. Boston was the center of vampire-related activity on the East Coast. They didn't often get involved in the day to day operations of the covens under their jurisdiction, but when they did, you could be certain shit was about to hit the fan. In my case, I was pretty sure a pile big enough to smother an elephant hung over my head.

"Did they say...?"

"No, they didn't. Colin sounded pretty agitated over the phone, though. I think you'd best get your dumpy ass over here as soon as sundown hits."

Colin was the vampire currently in charge of the Northeast. It was a temporary position. However, since his boss, James, was missing, it was looking more and more likely that his would be a permanent promotion. Pity, as Colin was a little suck-up of a weasel. If he could have, he would have gladly glued his lips to the asses of the elder vamps who made up the First Coven, the vampire ruling body more affectionately known as the Draculas.

A sheen of perspiration broke out on my forehead. "Oh, shit."

"Said with your usual eloquence," Sally quipped. "So, are you coming?"

"Do I have a choice?" Silence on the other end. "Sorry, stupid question. Yeah, I guess so. They can only kill me once, after all."

"Not really." As usual, she was doing her best to make me feel worse. "See you in a few."

I hung up. This did not bode well for me. Three months ago, some serious shit had gone down. It had all started as a joke. Sally had shipped me to China, supposedly at James's behest. Notice I didn't say it was a *funny* joke. When Gan, a three-hundred-year-old spoiled vampire brat, decided she was in love with me, her father was *displeased*. Unfortunately for me, her father was the Khan, a member of the Draculas. Even less fortunate, his way of voicing displeasure was to send a trio of his best assassins to cut off my head. Not only had they failed, but the whole mission had turned out to be a fatal mistake on his part.

Unbeknownst to me at the time, he and his people were attacked while this debacle was going on. His forces depleted, the Khan's coven was overrun with nary a sign of any survivors.

The rest of the Draculas subsequently pinned the blame on me. Word had come down from them that I was expected to make things right. The only problem was they didn't specify *how*. I had thus spent those three months constantly looking over my shoulder.

At last, it seemed I was finally going to get my answer. Oh, well, at least I would know and, according to GI Joe, that's half the battle right there. Pity the rest of it would probably be slightly less fun.

Anticipation is a Killer

BOTH OF MY roommates, bless their still-beating hearts, insisted on coming along after I filled them in on the news. Part of it was their friendship to me, of which I was grateful. As for the rest, well, I wasn't entirely stupid. I knew morbid curiosity when I saw it.

While I was in China, James had absentmindedly dropped the name *Alma* to describe their enemies. An Internet search had revealed that Alma was the Mongolian name for *Bigfoot*. To say that my friends, Tom especially, were excited about the prospect of a vampire/Sasquatch showdown would've been an understatement. Hell, if I weren't the one in danger of becoming a casualty of this grudge match, the eternal geek in me would have been pretty darn stoked about it, too.

Still, their willingness to stand by my side was welcome. Unfortunately, as I explained to them, I couldn't bring them to my meeting with Sally. Normally vampires and humans mix about as well as people and nacho platters. As the leader of Village Coven – a stupid name if ever there was one – I had decreed that my friends were off-limits. Even Sally had to agree with that one, as they had helped us both out on more than one occasion.

Unfortunately, whoever was coming to see us wasn't a part of my coven and weren't beholden to my rules. If they were parched from their journey, then my roommates would make handy refreshments. I couldn't let that happen. Thus, to all our chagrin, I had to turn them down and take a solo trip on the N-train toward Manhattan.

Well okay, I wasn't entirely alone. I had dozens of potentially horrific demises running through my head to keep me company. Lots of fun, I tell you.

* * *

The center of my undead "empire" was a place we simply refer to as the Office. My coven rented out a few floors in a building close to NYU. We had lots of places both in and under SoHo (sewers may stink, but they tended to be free of pesky things like sunlight). However, currently a lot of that space was empty. A while back, roughly half of my coven ended up permanently dead thanks to a combo of the Khan's assassins and this little spat we had with another coven from Queens. Since then, despite Sally's constant nagging, I'd been hemming and hawing my way out of replenishing our ranks.

I'm sorry, but I have a conscience about these things. For starters, I had no desire to refill my coven with the current types that dominated it. When I first "joined" the ranks of the undead, Village Coven was entirely populated by two types: uber-hot, but entirely vacuous, females, and pretty-boy douchebags. Sally was the lone exception. She was as hot as they come but could think circles around the rest. Hell, I'm not exactly an idiot myself and I'd still think twice before going against her in a battle of wits.

As for recruiting people more like me, that had its own problems. I had little doubt I'd be able to find a small army of comic book geeks who would gladly join the ranks of us night stalkers. But did the city really need a population of dorks suddenly thinking they're superheroes? Trust me, I've been there. Vampire powers or not, it doesn't work out well.

I pushed all those thoughts out of my mind as I arrived at the Office. As much fun as it might be to imagine myself as the leader of a group of vampiric X-Men, it wasn't the time for such distractions.

As usual, the stairwell was empty, so I was able to run up to our floor at a pace that would have left an Olympic sprinter wheezing. Just for the record, not all parts of being a vampire suck. I might not be much to look at, but being a vampire had its advantages for *anyone,* regardless of whether they looked like they're allergic to exercise equipment.

Also, as was typical, I felt a shudder of revulsion pass through me as I walked in. The desks up front were manned and going full force. Rather than let the coven hunt for prey openly, Sally had instituted a half-assed suicide hotline to lure in victims. It kept the coven's larders full while ensuring that most of the humans we harvested were those who wouldn't be missed. Sorry, her words, not mine. Personally, I found the whole thing to be so evil that Satan himself would probably step back and say, "Whoa!"

At that moment, though, I had other things with which to occupy my mind. I strode past the rows of desks and went straight toward the back corner where Sally had commandeered an over-sized executive suite. She definitely didn't believe in suffering for the cause.

Seated at a desk outside of her office was Starlight. She was a strikingly beautiful African-American woman. Though in her forties, she was eternally stuck in the body of a twenty-one-year-old fashion model, but what a body it was. Unfortunately for her, Starlight was a genuine sweetheart, just not an overly bright one. Both of these traits meant she was easy prey for manipulation, and Sally was a grade-A manipulator. She had continually coerced Starlight into acting as her personal secretary ... so much so that I had given up trying to do anything about it. There were far worse fates.

"Hey, Bill," she said, seeing me approach. "You can go right in, Sally's expecting you."

I smirked. Technically speaking, I was in charge. I could go wherever and whenever I pleased ... at least as far as the rest of the coven were concerned. To them, I was this fearsome predator, a beast of legend even amongst vampire-kind. They all afforded me respect that far outweighed what I deserved. Sally, however, knew the truth, and though she kept up appearances for the others, I had to tread lightly around her.

"Thanks, Star." I walked in, shutting the door behind me.

I half expected the room to be full of hooded figures hissing at me to kneel while they proceeded to dole out my punishment.

Instead, I found myself alone with Sally ... and she was *naked*.

Well, okay, she was only naked in my mind. But then, she always was. In actuality, she was seated – fully clothed, sadly – behind her desk where she dismissively motioned for me to sit while she continued chatting on the phone.

"Wednesday? Sorry, mornings don't work for me," she said casually into the receiver. "How about the evening? That'll work. No, it doesn't have to be here. We can do this over drinks. Great. I can't wait to see the layout. You, too. Talk to you soon." Her tone was disturbingly chipper as she hung up.

She turned to me as I sat there looking at her expectantly. "Sorry about that. *The Village Voice* is running a story on the hotline and wanted to know if I was available for an interview."

"I'm so happy for you," I replied coldly.

"I know, isn't it great?"

"Oh, yeah, killing off the city's poor and defenseless ... real great."

"You have no head for business, you know that?" she sniffed.

"I couldn't care less as long as I get to keep mine." I looked around. "So what's going on?"

"You're early, I guess. Nobody's here yet."

"Great. I love getting extra time to stew in my juices right before being executed."

"They're not going to execute you ... at least, I don't *think* they're going to."

"How reassuring."

"Listen." She leaned over the desk toward me. Her new angle afforded me a generous view of her ample cleavage. Noticing where my eyes were headed, she quickly added, "They don't talk back ... especially not to you. Eyes up here while you still have them."

"Sorry."

"Bullshit," she replied offhandedly. "As I was saying, I doubt execution is on their minds."

"I got one of the Draculas killed."

"*Supposedly* got one of the Draculas killed," she corrected. "There's been no proof, at least none that I've heard of. The Khan is missing until proven otherwise. Besides, you didn't do it on purpose. Stupidity is not as serious a crime as treachery."

"Thanks ... sorta."

"What I mean is, the Draculas aren't known for dicking around. If they had wanted you dead, that would have been it. You would have been dusted before we ever got a chance to talk about it. Trust me, these guys are big on making examples of people."

"Maybe because of this Freewill crap, they..."

"It wouldn't matter. Legends or not, if they wanted you dead, that would be it. Think about it. The Khan's people gave you tons of 'chosen one' bullshit, right?"

"True."

"And yet it still didn't stop him from ordering your death just because his little bitch of a daughter decided she wanted to elope with you."

I winced a little at the memory of Gan. I had no doubt there was still unfinished business there, at least as far as she was concerned. "Gan aside, I think I get what you're saying. Prophecies or not, the Draculas are the big dogs in the room."

"Yep, and they'll piss all over you without a second thought."

"I've noticed."

"Which means," she went on, "that they have something else in mind."

I couldn't help but visibly shudder at the implication. It might be something else other than death, but I had little doubt it would prove to be equally unpleasant.

Unexpected Company

SALLY AND I bantered back and forth for about an hour, at the end of which I didn't feel any better. She had a ton of useful skills, but her pep talks left a lot to be desired. She was in the middle of trying to give me an update on the hotline when she suddenly stopped mid-sentence. She raised her head and sniffed the air. "No way."

Since Sally's older, her senses were more finely attuned than mine. I had barely enough time to spurt out a quick, "What?" before the door to her office was pushed open from the outside. In strode a very familiar face – one I had been convinced I would never see again.

"Holy shit, James!" I said, rising to my feet.

"Dr. Death," he replied with a quick grin, using my old coven name – the one I'd been given by our former leader, Jeff AKA Night Razor. If James was pissed over what had gone down in China, he was doing a good job of hiding it.

I didn't know what to think. On the one hand, he had my eternal gratitude. He was the reason I was still walking around as opposed to lining the bottom of an ashtray. The flipside was that he was over six hundred years old. That put him at a power level that far eclipsed mine. If he suddenly decided that a little revenge was in order, my options would be limited to whining and taking it like a bitch.

For the moment, though, he didn't seem interested in bouncing me off solid objects. He met Sally as she came around her desk and gave her a quick hug. "A pleasure as always, Sally."

"It's great to see you," she replied with a genuine smile. Sally had been James's confidant during my early days, which had eventually led to my rise as coven master. "We all thought you were..."

"Dead? Yes I know."

"Guess that explains why Colin was so pissy on the phone," she said.

"Ah, yes. My overly ambitious assistant. Well, he may yet get what he desires," he cryptically stated. As far as I was aware, Colin wanted James's job, i.e. jurisdiction over all of the Northeastern covens. However, now that James was back, that would mean things would return to the way they should be. Wouldn't it?

I didn't get a chance to ask, though, as he then said, "We have much to discuss. But, perhaps we should find more suitable surroundings. Sally, my dear, would you happen to know if that café I favor is still open? I could very much go for one of their marvelous espressos."

* * *

26

To say that things felt a little surreal would be an understatement. It was like déjà vu. Less than a year earlier, I had been seated at that very same café with the very same company and the conversation, though of a different nature, had been of the same gist: namely, my fate. At the time, I had gradually come to learn that both of them had been in favor of my continued existence, despite my initial reluctance to believe Sally. Since then, I had come to trust ... well okay, *mostly* trust, her. James was now the X-factor, though. Something nasty had gone down in Asia, and I was the one he was most likely to blame.

Still, it was hard to feel too condemned sitting there watching him down his third espresso.

"Absolutely fantastic," he said with a sigh of contentment. "While the selection of tea in China, forgive my pun, is vastly superior to what can be found here, they simply don't have anything that can hold a candle to this." He held up his cup. "Alas, it was one point on which my sire and I could never see eye to eye."

"You mean the Khan?" I asked, testing the waters.

"Yes," he replied, his eyes somewhat distant.

"How is he?" Sally asked conversationally. She could afford to be casual. It wasn't her ass on the line.

"Sadly, I shall never get a chance to convince him otherwise." He placed his cup down on the table. "The Khan fell in battle with our enemies."

"The Alma?" I blurted out.

"They go by many names," he replied, "some of which are not to be used lightly. Names carry power, even collective ones."

"Uh, okay," I said, having no idea what he meant. "Listen, James, I'm really sorry about what happened. I had no clue Gan..."

He held up a hand to cut me off before I could start rambling. "Be at ease, my friend. I don't blame you for what occurred. Gansetseg may be impulsive, but she gets it from her bloodline. My sire over-reacted, and I even told him such. The Khan, however, was not one to be swayed once his mind was made up."

"But still..."

"But still *nothing*. Our enemies attacked us en masse. Nergui's presence would not have made much of a difference," he said, referring to the chief assassin the Khan had sent. "They had a specific goal in mind: to get our attention. In killing a member of the First Coven, they have most certainly gotten it."

"Goddamn, the war against the Feet," Sally said with a sigh.

I looked up. I had heard that phrase before, months back. Sally had been specifically coy about it at the time. "What about it?"

"Ah yes," James replied. "It's a vulgar simplification that many of our stateside brethren use."

"Maybe, but it fits," she said, then turned to me. "In case you haven't figured it out yet, Bill, and since you're a little slow on the uptake, I'll assume that's the case."

"Get to the point, Sally," I snarled.

"Bigfoot, or Bigfeet, if you prefer the plural. I don't know much. I am a city girl, after all, but I know we've been locked in a cold war with them for like forever."

"Forever is not too far from the truth," James replied.

"Okay, let's back up for a second," I said. "I figured out the Bigfoot part already. Ed googled Alma and that's what popped up. But you'll forgive me if I say that makes no fucking sense."

"Oh, please." Sally gave me one of her trademarked eye-rolls. "Like you have any clue as to what makes sense."

"Maybe not," I shot back, "but I do know that vampires versus Bigfoot..." I sputtered to a halt as James shot me a warning glance. I turned my head to see our waitress approaching. Thinking quickly, I added, "would be a hell of a movie to see on the SyFy channel. I hear Roger Corman is producing it."

* * *

Once our waitress had walked away, taking with her an order for yet another espresso, I continued. "I'm not following. Why the hell are vampires in a war against a bunch of giant smelly apes?"

"Like you're one to talk about hygiene," Sally quipped.

"Children, please," James said, once again echoing the conversation from nearly a year ago. "I'm sorry, Dr. Death, but you are greatly over-simplifying matters. Were these Bigfeet, as you seem insistent on calling them, merely apes, then there wouldn't be an issue. You don't see us warring against the mountain gorillas of Uganda, now do you?"

"No. Or at least not that I've heard of."

"Trust me, we're not. The creatures you are referring to are far more than giant primates. They are ancient forest spirits, and their somewhat brutish forms are simply how they choose to physically manifest themselves."

"So they're like ghosts?"

"Not quite," he explained patiently. He seemed to think about it for a moment. "They're more akin to human stories about brownies, pixies, or gnomes ... just a tad larger."

"And meaner, too," I replied, remembering how one had chucked a bowling ball sized rock at me with enough force to almost crush my ribcage.

"Quite so. Even the least of their kind possesses the physical strength of a vampire several times your age."

I considered this. I had seen James in action. The guy was practically Superman compared to me. The Khan had been older, thus it stood to reason he was even stronger than James. That being said, the Khan hadn't exactly been a prime physical specimen. Hell, that was being generous. The guy was a big fat fuckhead of a vampire, probably tipping the scales at five hundred easily. I looked like a Calvin Klein model next to him. Ancient vampire powers or not, I just couldn't envision him moving with the same grace or speed I had seen James use. Still, that didn't mean he wouldn't have been a formidable foe. For all I knew, he could've been the King Kong Bundy of the undead world. If these monsters could take him down, what kind of chance would I stand against them?

The thought of the Khan reminded me that I was probably being a rude asshole. At the very least, I could be considerate toward James. This guy was his vampire dad, so to speak. "My condolences."

"Eh?" he grunted, taking another sip of espresso. Across from him, I could see Sally rolling her eyes again.

I wasn't a heartless bitch like her, so I continued, "I'm sorry about the Khan. He was your sire, after all. How are you holding up?"

To my surprise, he actually chuckled in response. "Thank you, Dr. Death. You're actually the first person to ask me that. I have to admit, though, once you reach my age, feelings such as regret, remorse, or grief just don't have the same punch as they used to. Ogedei Khan's passing is regrettable. He was a piece of living history. Regardless, my dealings with him have been limited as of the past few centuries and, truthfully, we were never really close to begin with."

"What about Gan?" Sally asked. I knew for a fact that she despised Gan. No doubt she was asking because she knew the topic would make me squirm. Sally and I had an interesting relationship, to say the least. No matter how close we might or might not be, she always took perverse pleasure in annoying the shit out of me.

"Suffice to say, I think Gansetseg will get over it quickly," James replied. "She's been in her father's shadow for three hundred years. Whatever grief she might feel has been eclipsed by the opportunity it opens up. When last I saw her, she was consolidating her father's power base beneath her and being brutally efficient about it as well. Oh, by the way, she sends her love." He directed that last part to me, a smirk working its way into the corners of his mouth.

I sighed and glared daggers at Sally, practically daring her to make some sort of asshole comment. She threw me a saucy grin in return and changed the subject. "So where have you been? Didn't this all go down three months ago? That's a long time to play dead."

"Nothing escapes you, does it, my dear?" he commented. "A fair question. After the Khan's coven fell, I found myself trapped behind enemy lines. For weeks I was forced into the position of guerilla, pun notwithstanding. I'd bury myself in the desert sands during the day and do my best to avenge my fallen brothers during the night. Eventually, I made contact with Gansetseg's forces and was able to get back to friendly territory."

"And that brings you back here?" I asked.

"Not quite. As with any war, there is diplomacy involved. I was summoned to Europe to meet with the remaining members of the First Coven and discuss options. Open warfare is in neither of our species' best interests. The world has changed so much since the last time we clashed."

I listened in rapt interest. This was starting to get good. I was always up for a good monster versus monster yarn. Unfortunately, Sally had to play story cock-blocker.

"What about the Draculas?" she asked. "With the Khan dead, there're only twelve of them. They have any replacements in mind?" The tone of her voice implied that she knew something I didn't. Not that it was surprising. Sally seemed to be at the center of the vampire gossip circles. She collected information like ... well, like my roommate, Tom, collected toys. The only difference was that her holdings were often worth something.

"As I said, nothing escapes you," James replied. "What I am about to say is not public information, but I am told I am up for consideration as a new member of the First Coven."

"WAY TO GO, JAMES!" I shouted and held up my hand for a high-five.

"So much for not making it public," Sally said with a huff. This time, even James sighed. Seeing their reaction, I lowered my arm.

"Your enthusiasm aside," he said dryly, "it's not as cut and dry as that. There are other candidates being considered as well. With the specter of war currently hanging over us, this little competition comes at an ill-advised time. If I didn't think it would constitute an insult of the highest degree, I would gladly back out of consideration."

"Competition?" I asked. "What, do you all have, like, thirty days to see who can rack up the highest body count?"

"Nothing quite so simple, I'm afraid. Ultimately, the First Coven will make the final decision. However, as is often the case with multiple hopefuls, it would not be uncommon for a few of them to drop out of the running *permanently*."

"I see."

"Therein lies the problem. The First hold vampires of my age to a high standard, but even they are forced to admit that trying to avert a bloody conflict while continually looking over my shoulder is a daunting task. That, Dr. Death, is what brings me here tonight."

Oh, crap. I had gotten so caught up in James's drama that I had completely forgotten that I was also in the Draculas' crosshairs. That did not bode well. I remembered back to my time in Asia. Gan had been sputtering off some nonsense about how the Freewills of old used to lead the vampire armies against their enemies. Fuck! I could barely keep my D&D party from getting ambushed. I was about as far from being West Point material as they get.

Seeing the panicky look starting to appear on my face, Sally did as expected. She sat back, took a long pull from her coffee, and smirked. Bitch! One of these days I was going to ... oh, who was I kidding? Chances are I'd have some Sasquatch wiping me off the heel of its foot before I had a chance to even think of something appropriately Sally-worthy.

Instead, I decided to ignore her. I turned to James and said, "I know the Draculas are pissed at me for what happened to the Khan, but they're making a massive mistake if they think that appointing me a general in some half-assed army of darkness is going to..."

I was interrupted by him spewing espresso at me. Ewww. He choked for a moment and then dissolved into laughter. Glad to know I was so amusing.

Finally, after a few moments, he got himself under control. "Oh, that was rich," he said. "I do thank you for the laugh. It's been a while. I'm sorry, but the thought of *you* standing at the head of our forces ... well, don't take this the wrong way..."

"General Patton, you are not," Sally finished for him.

"Quite true, my dear. Alas, that was never the First Coven's intention. They can be ruthless leaders, but they aren't insane. Your status as the reborn Freewill grants you certain liberties, not the least of which is that our ruling coven would prefer not sending you forth a lamb to the slaughter."

Their mockery of my abilities aside, I breathed a sigh of relief. "Well, that's good to..."

"I'm not finished," James interrupted, wiping his chin with a napkin. "Your status as a Freewill comes with certain downsides as well. I heard from Gansetseg about your altercation with the wizard. If they're aware of your existence, it's reasonable to assume other factions of the supernatural world are as well, including the Alma."

"Is that why they attacked when I was over there?"

"No. Otherwise you would have been a prime target. I believe that was just a coincidence. Still, it is prudent to assume they are aware of you by now. This is where you come in."

"I'm all ears," I replied with a complete lack of enthusiasm.

"The Alma are a caste based society. They place great weight upon one's station in life. Their chieftains are given all the trappings of royalty. So, too, are the rankings of enemies given much consideration. The slaying of the Khan was a great moment for them. Much honor has been heaped upon those responsible."

"Yeah, but I'm just a..."

"We know," Sally quipped.

James ignored her and continued. "The Alma are a highly spiritual race as well. Great heroes and others who their legends speak of are afforded the same honors as their highborn. Once again, so too with enemies."

"I'm not even remotely following you."

"The First Coven has reached out to the Alma in an attempt to avert a war. The Alma in turn have shown themselves to at least be open to discussion. However, due to their victory against the Khan, they see themselves as having the upper hand. They're willing to talk, but they insist on setting the rules for this engagement. Their first demand was that these talks take place in person between the upper echelons of both sides."

"I see where this is going," Sally chimed in. "The Draculas, not being stupid, aren't about to waltz right into the lion's den."

"An over-simplification, but essentially true," James confirmed. "Being that Dr. Death is the long lost Freewill of vampire legend..."

"Oh, no fucking way!" I cried, standing up. As they stared at me, I noticed the eyes of the other patrons in the café likewise turning in my direction. Thinking quickly, I added, "Ten bucks for a cup of coffee? Wow, this place is expensive." Several piteous glances came my way, but soon enough, people turned back toward their own business.

"Way to work the crowd, Bill," Sally commented, sipping her drink.

I sat back down and lowered my voice. "So let me see if I'm hearing this right. The fucking ape-men consider me to be on par with our leadership, correct? So, being that the Draculas see me as important ... yet still oh-so-expendable ... I get to go sit down with these monsters and hope they don't eat my fucking face. Does that sound about right?"

"Said with your usual eloquence, but in a nutshell, yes," James replied.

"You do realize that growing up I couldn't even convince my neighbors to keep their dogs from shitting on our lawn. I don't know what kind of treaty you're expecting me to negotiate."

"Believe me, I am all too familiar with your somewhat unique way of communicating," he said. "You won't be going in alone. This isn't a one-on-one affair. You'll be there as a figurehead at most."

"You should be used to that," Sally said out of the corner of her mouth.

"This will be more of a summit than anything else. There will be negotiators there with you, as well as bodyguards. I wouldn't be surprised if other factions wished to make themselves present as well. In short, you will be there to preside over our side, but ultimately others will be doing the work."

"And if I refuse?" I asked, knowing full well that wasn't really an option.

"If you refuse, then I daresay the First will find some other sort of duty for you. It's a fair bet that whatever they choose will make this seem like a vacation in paradise, comparatively speaking."

Ringside Seats

THE CHECK CAME and suddenly I found two sets of eyes looking at me expectantly.

"What?" I asked.

"Coven hospitality," James replied, a grin on his face. "It's tradition."

I turned toward Sally, who gave me her best innocent expression before replying, "Don't look at me."

"You handle the coven's finances," I protested.

"True, but I left my purse back at the Office."

Grumbling, I pulled out my wallet to cover the tab. Vampires were immortal, arrogant, and powerful ... I made a mental note to add *cheap* to that description.

"Some of us still have to work for a living," I griped.

"Then win the lottery," she cooed. "Oh, wait ... you get to work with me, so you already did."

Trying desperately to keep myself from stabbing her with a fork, I changed the topic back to business. "So what next?" I asked James.

"For now, just wait. The details are still being hashed out, participants are still being considered, all of that."

"Do I get any say in this?"

"Of course. You are perfectly welcome to bring along your own contingent. They'll be figureheads much like yourself, but as the honored Freewill, you'll be expected to have your own band of supporters."

"Awesome," I said and then quickly added, "I nominate Sally as my first choice."

"WHAT?!" she cried.

"You heard me," I replied with a sly grin. "You got me into this whole mess. If I'm destined to get corn-holed by Sasquatch, you get to be next on deck, *partner.*"

Ultimately, that was true on many levels. Sally had gotten me into just about every mess I had found myself in these past several months. She was the one responsible for my becoming a vampire. Through her machinations, I became the leader of Village Coven. Finally, she was the primary reason I had wound up in Asia to begin with. All roads led back to Sally. It was about time I got a chance to "repay" her.

"But what about the coven?" she stammered.

"Starlight can watch over things for a few days. It'll be good practice for her."

"James..." Sally said, turning to him.

He, however, just chuckled in response. "I'm sorry, my dear. But, alas, it is his choice. He is *officially* the coven leader. There *is* certain protocol to be followed here."

She glared flaming, poison-tipped daggers at me. Oh, well, when one plays with fire, one does tend to occasionally wind up with burnt fingertips.

"Now, if we're all finished here," James said, ignoring the swordfight Sally and I were waging with our expressions, "I have a car waiting. I need to get back to Boston and continue working on things from my end. You'll be contacted with details soon enough."

"Thanks, James," I replied, albeit there wasn't much gratitude in my voice.

"Just one last question," Sally said. "Why'd you come all the way down here? I mean, if you were giving Bill a death sentence, that would be one thing (*thanks, Sally*), but you could have said all of this over the phone."

"True enough," he countered, and then added, "But then I wouldn't have been treated to such a wonderful evening of discourse."

"In other words, you came for the espresso," I said.

"Of course. One must have one's priorities straight."

* * *

I departed before Sally could corner me. I had no desire to be chewed a new asshole. Also, it let me leave on a smug note. If we had started talking about things, I probably would have let slip that my desire for her to come along was only half motivated by dickish pettiness. The truth was, when push came to shove, she was one hell of a person to have watching your back. Sure, she practically jumped on every chance to piss me off but, over the past year, she had more than made up for it. I didn't need to be reminded that she had almost gotten killed defending me against the Khan's assassins. She had even lost a hand in battle with them. Sure, it had grown back, but it was the thought that counted.

If there was the possibility of shit going down during this peace conference – and let's face facts: I've seen enough episodes of Star Trek to know these never went smoothly – then I wanted her there beside me. I had called Sally my partner as a dig to her, but the truth was, I believed it. The only downside was that I was going to have to listen to her bitch about it all ... and she would, probably to the point where I would start looking forward to whatever horrific death was waiting around the corner.

Speaking of bitching, I returned to my apartment to find my roommates engaged in their typical type of conversation.

"There's no way the Galactica could take out a Star Destroyer, end of conversation," came Ed's voice as I walked in the door.

Right on cue, Tom replied with, "Two counterpoints, dude: nukes and FTL drive. They jump in, blast the shit out of the Empire, and jump out before Darth Vader is even aware that he's now floating in the cold vacuum of space."

Before I could add my opinion that the Enterprise E's quantum torpedoes would fuck up anyone's shit, they both turned toward me.

"Since you're here," Ed asked, "is it safe to assume that the words 'immediate execution' didn't come up?"

"Thankfully, no. In fact, it wasn't so bad. I thought they were sending some vampire goon squad. Instead, I wound up spending the night sipping espressos with James."

"Ozymandias?" Tom asked, referring to the pseudonym James used back when my coven was still run by Jeff.

"The one and the same."

"I thought he was missing in Mongolia," Ed said.

"Not anymore. He's back and up for a big promotion, too."

"Awesome," Tom replied. "It never hurts to have friends in high places." If anyone understood that concept, it was him. He worked over in Manhattan's financial district. As he was fond of telling us, it was a game of kissing ass and gaining favor with the higher-ups. He'd once told me, "You just pucker up, apply some super glue, and latch on."

"I'm assuming he didn't drive in just to tell you about his new executive parking spot," Ed said.

"You assume correctly."

"Spill, dude," Tom said.

So I did. I spent the next half-hour telling them about how I was supposed to be the vampire nation's new peace envoy and how my status as the Freewill of vampire legend afforded me this high *honor*.

"And if you happen to get snuffed in the process," Ed surmised, "these Draculas can just sit back and say 'too bad, so sad.'"

"That's about the size of it."

43

"I think that settles things," he said. "You've been putting *it* off for too long."

It took me a second, but then I got his drift. "No way. It's too dangerous. Who the hell knows what'll happen?"

"What'll happen is it'll save your life if those Sasquatches decide to make you their sacrificial lamb."

"We don't even know if it's controllable," I protested. "It only happened those two times. For all I know it was just a fluke."

Ed gave me his most condescending look, the one he reserved for when he thought I was acting like a stupid child, but I held my ground. I wasn't quite ready for what he was suggesting.

See, being a Freewill came with a few other perks above and beyond what a normal vampire could do. For starters, there's the ability for which it was named: the power to resist the mind control of another vamp. I was glad for *that* ability. Nothing worse than some asshole giving you a compulsion and having no choice but to follow it through, no matter how demeaning it might be.

Of somewhat more practical use was the ability to somehow leech another vampire's strength. Most vampires weren't able to drink another vamp's blood. Something about it is incompatible with their systems, violently so. In our tussle with the Khan's assassins, I had seen Sally take a bite out of one of them. The effort had saved me, but reduced her to a retching basket case for the next several hours.

It's different with me, though. Not only could I drink vampire blood, but doing so temporarily turbo-charged me with their power. I could go from zero to hero with just a swallow. The more powerful the vampire, the more power I absorbed. The only downside to this was that I had to get in close enough for a bite, something that most weren't exactly keen on letting me do.

Unfortunately, though, that's almost the extent of my knowledge. I'm the first of my kind in over half a millennium, so the records weren't exactly up to date as to what else I could do. There's more, though, and some of it was frightening as all hell. Twice, during my ordeal from a few months back, I lost control. The first time I recovered quickly. The second time, Sally had been near death. The rage I felt had pushed me over the edge. I don't know what happened next except that something about me changed and I could suddenly take on two vampires whose power both eclipsed mine by many times over. Take your pick of either Bruce Banner or Dr. Jekyll, but either way I had something similar in me. The only question was *what*?

Since then, I hadn't been in any utterly enraging situations, nor had I given in to my friends' insistence that this was something that needed to be tested. I had nothing against a power boost, but not at the risk of waking up to find myself ankle deep in the blood of my buddies.

"Not worth the risk," I stated adamantly.

"But..."

"No! Not going to happen. It's one thing for you two to continually stab, slice, and set me on fire to chart my powers, but this is just too dangerous. We've all seen enough movies to know that the 'we'll stick you in a cage while you transform' scene always ends badly."

Ed considered this. "I get what you're saying, Bill. But still, this whole scenario has a bad vibe to it. If things turn to shit, you're going to need every advantage you can get."

"That's why I'm bringing Sally. She'll be there to watch my backside."

"But who's going to watch hers?"

"Us," Tom chimed in. Ed and I stopped speaking and turned to him questioningly. "We'll be there watching her ass, amongst other things."

"Hold on just a sec..."

"Didn't you just tell us that you were allowed to bring a contingent of supporters?" he asked. "Well, who else is going to support your sorry self better than us?"

"No fucking way..."

"My point exactly," he stated. "No fucking way are we missing a possible vampire/Bigfoot death match. Not happening. Even if you weren't my bud, I'd still be sneaking along just to see that shit."

"He does have a point," Ed said. "A couple of them, actually, which is probably a new record for him."

"It's settled, then!" cried Tom jubilantly.

I tried protesting some more, but I could tell my words were falling on deaf ears. *Great! Now, not only do I get to die, I get to do it with my friends cheering me on.*

Friends Don't Let Friends Drink and Dissect

THE FIRST HALF of the weekend was surprisingly pleasant. I went over to the coven, as usual. However, Sally was nowhere to be seen. She was apparently still miffed at me. Oh, well, she'd come around. I knew deep down she would eventually see things my way. We were partners, after all ... perhaps for all of eternity. She'd never admit it of course, but when push came to shove, I had (almost) no doubt she'd be there backing me up.

Still, it was nice to spend some time looking at the eye candy of the coven without her harping in my ear about something or other. Being king is only good so long as you don't have a bitchy prime minister continually spoiling your fun.

Sunday was game day. No, not *that* game. I had little interest in whoever was going to be kicking the Giants' asses on that or any other weekend. I meant my weekly Dungeons & Dragons game. I left the coven while it was still dark to head toward scenic Newark, New Jersey. The game didn't start until late morning, but heading over while the sun was shining wasn't a particularly smart move for one such as I. Fortunately, I knew my game master, Dave, would already be up and waiting.

Dave was a third-year medical resident. He was also one of the few humans, outside of my roommates, who knew that I was a vampire. His plan was to go into pure research after he finished with his residency. It wasn't for any altruistic reason, such as helping mankind. No, it was because he pretty much hated everyone he saw on a day to day basis. Probably a good call. It's safe to say that most of us preferred to put our lives in the hands of people who didn't openly despise us.

I had told Dave my secret because I needed his help to become a permanent telecommuter. In return, he had been almost giddy as a schoolgirl. He saw me as his ace in the hole. In return for his help, I agreed to give him tissue samples to use in his research. His plan was to eventually come up with some sort of miracle drug, based off of vampire DNA, that would set him up for life.

We had to keep things on the down low, of course. Letting humans in on the secret of our existence was generally frowned upon. It wasn't too hard to assume that human experimentation on vampires was probably an even more massive no-no — one that, if discovered, would most likely result in me, Dave, and everyone we knew being wiped off the face of the Earth with extreme prejudice.

That concept in and of itself made me nervous enough. That Dave had begun to exhibit signs of turning into a mad scientist likewise started to worry me. I had little doubt he conducted his research while giggling maniacally to himself. Still, he was my friend, no matter how nutty he was becoming.

Little did I know he was preparing to ratchet up the crazy, although I should have suspected. Let's face facts: when I stepped into a shit-storm, it rained down upon me with all the fury that Mother Nature had at her disposal.

I knocked on his door just as the first rays of sunlight began to peek over the horizon. As expected, he was waiting for me.

"Come on in. I have a few new tests this morning."

I just stood there looking back at him expectantly. "Hi, Dave."

"Sorry. Hi, Bill. How are you this fine morning?"

"I'm fine. How are you?"

"Wonderful. Now get the fuck in here before I kill your character."

Yep, that's Dave, straight to the point and not afraid to use threats to get there.

During my short tenure as a vampire, I had been poked, prodded, lanced, and burned so many times, I almost didn't notice it anymore ... *almost* being the operative word. That's a bit of bullshit from Hollywood. You see, in most movies, Dracula will stand there, being pelted by bullets and laughing as his cold, dead flesh absorbs the damage.

Unfortunately, while real vampires may technically be just as dead, there's nothing wrong with our nerve endings. Somehow, those work the exact same way as they always did. While I could definitely absorb a hail of gunfire, that didn't mean I wouldn't wind up huddled in a fetal ball, crying. Apparently when we got turned into vampires, our bodies didn't get the memo to stop transmitting the ouchies to our brains.

Sadly, when asked if this was something he could look into during his research, Dave responded with, "Suck it up like a man." Some days it was tempting to find new friends who were more human and less asshole.

I followed him in and shut the door behind me. Fortunately, his place was vampire safe during the day. The guy kept his apartment as dark as a cave. It was perfect for both gaming and not bursting aflame. Being that we still had a few hours before the rest of the party arrived, I followed him to the back room where he kept a makeshift lab.

"How's the research going?"

"Same as usual," he said with a bitter sigh. "Until I get some corporate backing, I'm stuck using whatever shit I can purloin from hospital storage."

I laughed. "You're like Dr. Evil ... if he shopped at Walmart."

"Tell me about it. I've been working on this stuff for the better part of a year. Figured I'd have some breakthroughs by now."

"Still nothing?"

"Almost. I mean I've isolated some bizarre protein strands in your blood, but I'm fucked if I know what they do. Originally I figured it was some sort of virus in your system..."

"Like in Blade?"

"Yeah, but no such luck."

"Oh well, you tried," I said, turning back toward his living room. I can't say I would be too sorry to see this end. I couldn't help but feel like a lab rat around Dave as of late.

"Not so fast." *Damn!* "It doesn't mean I'm giving up. I think it's time to refocus my efforts."

"Define 'refocus.'"

"I need to take this back to square one, watch what happens during the vampire turning process."

That caught my attention, and not in a good way either. Yeah, Dave was definitely starting to get a Dr. Frankenstein vibe to him.

"I really hope you're not suggesting I bite someone just so you can watch them go from living to undead. That'd be kind of fucked up."

He shot me a withering glare. He must have been taking lessons from Ed. "Do I look like I want to go to jail? Let's be serious here for a second. I want a nice comfy research grant, not to wind up some convict's bitch."

"Then how..."

"Did you learn nothing in college? When science wants to test something, we turn to our four-legged friends." With that, he pointed out a little tank sitting off in a corner of the room. Inside was a bunch of white mice.

"You want me to put mice in my mouth?"

Dave chuckled in response. "If I was going to do that, it would be to post the pictures to Facebook. No, while the thought of you chewing on rodents is amusing, I'd prefer to obtain a venom sample so I can test it under controlled conditions."

"Venom?"

"For lack of a better word, yeah. Since I can't seem to isolate a virus, it stands to reason there's something else in a vampire bite that causes the change. It might be saliva, but I'd be willing to bet it has to do with those nasty canines you're sporting."

I rolled my eyes (guess *Sally was starting to rub off on me*). "Did you ever think that maybe it's beyond knowing ... supernatural and all that crap? Maybe it's just *magic*."

Dave gave me a look that suggested his opinion of me was rapidly being downgraded. "In the Middle Ages, people thought the sun was magic. Hell, if you showed your cell phone to certain tribes in the Amazon today, they'd either worship you or burn you at the stake. Magic is just a bullshit term for stuff we haven't figured out yet. I, for one, intend to figure it out."

"Okay fine, I'll humor you. So how are we going to do this?"

"The same way they milk snakes."

"Dude, I know you work long hours and don't have much time for a social life, but no way are you *milking* me."

"Would probably be the most action you've gotten in a while," Dave replied with a chuckle. "But let's not be stupid here." He grabbed a cup from a shelf. The top was covered in a plastic membrane. "Here, bite this."

To say I was somewhat less than impressed would be an understatement. "You do realize how batshit insane this is, right? I mean, outside of the stupidity of *milking me* for venom, you're planning on using it to make vampire mice? Seriously, tell me that's not a low-budget horror movie in the making."

"I have it covered," he insisted. "I have welders' gloves for any handling that needs to be done. The tank is reinforced Plexiglas, and it's sitting right next to the window. All I have to do is open the blinds."

"And if one should escape?"

"I bought three dozen mousetraps and a pound of raw, bloody, chop meat."

I blinked in surprise at that last one. "Well, okay that is pretty fucking clever."

"Thank you. Now bite," he commanded, handing me the glass.

I sighed. Oh, well, in for a penny. I extended my fangs then also blackened my eyes – hey, might as well make a show of it – and did as asked. About a minute later, he said that was good enough and took back the glass. I don't know if it was venom or just my drool, but there was definitely something collected inside of it.

"Just one more thing." He placed it to the side and began rummaging in a nearby desk.

"Let me guess, more blood samples," I groused, starting to roll up my sleeve.

"Not quite." He turned back to me holding a pair of garden shears. "Take off your shoe."

"Why?"

"I need a more extensive tissue sample so I can continue testing your regenerative abilities."

"More extensive?"

"I figure one of your little toes should work. I'd ask for a finger, but I know you do a lot of typing."

I held up my hands and started backing away. "Whoa there, Hoss!"

"Oh, don't be such a baby. It should grow back before you even leave here today. Didn't you say that other vampire's entire hand grew back?"

"Sally."

"Whatever. It's not like I'm asking to cut off your dick. It's just a little toe. Evolution-wise, they're not even necessary anymore."

"I don't care. I'm not letting you prune my digits, no matter how *unnecessary* they are."

"Pity. I was planning on dropping a vorpal weapon into the game. Doesn't Kelvin use a saber?" he asked, referring to my character.

"Not gonna work." That lasted all of two seconds before I blurted out, "What kind of plusses are we talking about?" Damn my weakness for treasure.

"Four at the least."

"I don't know..."

"Oh, and did I mention that the lovely Princess Sheila was looking for a royal concubine? You did save her from those giants, after all."

"That's low, dude."

"I'm not above bribery. So about that shoe..."

"No. No fucking way. Not going to happen. I don't care if you throw in the armor of the elder gods, too. There is absolutely nothing you can say to convince me."

* * *

Ten minutes later, there was a knock on Dave's door. It was the cops. Guess his neighbors got a little freaked out by all the screaming. What a surprise. It's amazing just how many nerve endings are contained in one little toe.

Diplomatic Immunity

OUTSIDE OF A citation for disturbing the peace, the rest of the game was fun ... especially my ill-gotten gains. I could tell the rest of the party were miffed that I seemed to be the golden boy this week, but oh well. I didn't see them offering up any digits in the name of science.

Dave was right, too. By the time I got home and took off my shoe, stuffed full of blood-soaked bandages, my foot was whole again. One wouldn't have known that just a few hours earlier, in a fit of apparent insanity, I had voluntarily let my so-called friend dismember me. Why did I have a feeling all of that was going to come back and bite me in the ass? Oh well, I'm sure that's a horror to contend with for another day.

Little did I know that other horrors were now awaiting me ... and it was just the first day of the goddamn week.

* * *

I was sitting on our living room couch, still marveling at the fact that I had ten toes again, when our front door opened. Tom walked in, but before I could voice a greeting, his girlfriend, Christy, entered as well. Wonderful. Just how I liked to end the weekend – in the company of my would-be murderer.

I started humming the refrain from Rob Zombie's *Dragula*, specifically the part about burning through the witches. I found myself doing that a lot lately while in Christy's presence. For some reason, it was soothing. Go figure.

Tom took her coat and put it in the closet. Great, that meant she would be staying for a while. I was just getting ready to stand, intent on retreating to the relative safety of my bedroom, when she walked over and sat down next to me. That was surprising. Christy and I had a bit of an unspoken agreement about not being in the same room together for extended periods of time.

Thus, I was caught even more off guard when she said, "Hey, Bill. How's it going?"

I did nothing but blink for a few seconds, most likely looking like a moron. She and I had said maybe ten words to each other in the past few months, and most of them were inarticulate grunts of begrudging acknowledgement.

I opened my mouth, not really sure what would come out, although expecting something like, "Hey, yourself. Eaten either Hansel or Gretel lately?"

Before I could say anything, though, Tom jumped in. "Want a beer, Christy? How about you, Bill?" he asked, rummaging through our fridge.

"No thanks, hon," she cheerfully called back.

"I'll take one." I had a nagging feeling I'd need it.

"So," she started, "Tom told me about the peace conference."

What? Christ, I really needed to stop telling him everything. The guy had a big fucking mouth, especially when it came to women. He's one of those people for whom it did not take a lot of effort to fuck their brains out.

My eyes narrowed at Christy, but I answered pleasantly, "Excuse me for one second." With that, I grabbed the TV remote, turned, and chucked it at Tom, hitting him square in the side.

"Ow!" he yelled while I turned back to Christy.

"Now, what was that?"

She replied as if I hadn't just assaulted her boyfriend with a hunk of plastic. "Tom filled me in on the conference. I talked it over with my coven (*the assholes stole the idea from us vampires*) and they think we should go, too."

I'm glad Tom hadn't retrieved my beer yet because I would surely have choked on it at that moment. "What?"

"Well, at least Harry does," she said. Harry Decker was the leader of Christy's coven, the VP of marketing at my company, and a complete nutcase. He was a firm believer in some dumbass prophecy proclaiming my existence heralded the end of wizard and witch kind. Thus, through faulty circular logic, he concluded that if I were to die, then this magic apocalypse wouldn't occur. He had come pretty close to making good on the threat, too.

At the end of things, though, I managed to live and he wound up with a bloody nose. Since then – outside of a petty attempt to get me into trouble with our HR department – he had been lying low. However, I knew it was only a matter of time before he became a thorn in my side again. Guess it was springtime, because it looked as if that flower was blooming.

"Really?" I arched an eyebrow at her, Spock-style.

"Yes," she replied conversationally as if we were discussing shades of paint rather than vampires and Sasquatches.

"Why?"

"Because this has potential repercussions for us all. If this goes badly, it could have a ripple effect for all of the races, fae and demonic alike."

"You're shitting me right? Fae?"

"Fairy kind," she explained.

"I always suspected there was a bit of fairy in Bill," Tom commented, walking over and handing me a beer.

"Don't make me look for the remote," I warned. He sat and I addressed Christy again. "So let me get this straight. This meeting between the vampires and a pack of shit-flinging monkeys has dire consequences? As a result, your coven, a group who doesn't exactly have my best interests in mind, wants to tag along?"

"I already told you, the prophecy is nothing personal."

"Sorry. I tend to take being killed somewhat personally."

"That aside, the Forest Folk are not to be..."

"Forest Folk?" Tom and I asked in unison.

"Yes, the creatures you've upset with your..."

"Hold on there. I haven't upset shit. Your kindly 'Forest Folk' were the ones who tried to put a kindly forest rock through my sternum."

"Regardless of what happened, open warfare is simply not an option here."

"Be that as it may," I said, "you're still not invited to ... wherever the hell it is."

"That's not for you to say. My master has already reached out to your people in Boston."

My eyes opened wide. Holy shit! Not only was this bitch hell-bent on frying my ass, but now she was going over my head, too. Talk about sticking it in and breaking it off.

"You talked with Boston?"

She nodded in response.

"The same Boston that's aware of what you guys did while Gan was over here?"

Another nod.

"And they didn't freak out, threaten you with death, any of that stuff?"

"No. They were quite cordial, actually. This one vampire my master talked to -Colin, I think his name was – he didn't seem to like you very much."

Motherfucker! I put my face into my hands while I absorbed all of this.

"Really?" Tom asked. "I would've thought the vampires wouldn't be too big on you guys."

"My people aren't at war with the vampires, just..."

"Me," I finished.

"Pretty much," she confirmed. "Besides, we reached out to them diplomatically. There are protocols around these types of things."

"Jesus Christ, does everyone know these protocols except me?"

"Yeah, it does seem you're always the last to find out about these things," Tom said, echoing my sentiment. "Maybe you should get Sally to keep you in the loop a bit more."

I shrugged in return and took an extra-long pull on my beer. The way this was going, I might need a chaser of significantly higher proof.

While I did so, Tom said to Christy, "Cool. I guess we get to take a vacation together on the supernatural world's dime."

"It's not really a vacation, dear," she chided. "We're going to be in different parties and we'll be traveling there separately. Technically speaking, we shouldn't even fraternize during it."

"Not at all?" he asked, a mock-frown on his face.

"Well, I guess we could sneak away for a little..."

"I don't need the details," I interrupted.

"Oh, yeah, speaking of details, did the vamps tell you where this was all going down?" Tom asked.

"No," she replied. "That's still being worked out. We should know in a week. They said, once that's decided, they're flying in a special envoy to work with Bill."

"They are?" I asked, looking up.

"Let me guess," Tom surmised. "They didn't tell you that part either."

Hell's Hair Salon

BY WEDNESDAY, I couldn't take it anymore. I couldn't get anyone in Boston to return my calls. James was apparently busy and Colin was being a prick. I hadn't heard anything from Sally, either. Between that, the stress of not knowing, and the added agitation of being certain that the love of my life had left for parts unknown, I was getting absolutely nothing done at work. Fortunately, my boss was too busy trying to figure out his own paperwork to bug me much. Gotta love downtime.

After the sun had set, I decided to head over to the coven. Maybe someone there could fill me in a bit more about this ancient war with Bigfoot. At the very least, the women of the coven were distracting eye candy. A little T&A wasn't exactly a bad way to kill a few hours. Hey, I never claimed I wasn't shallow.

I made my way first to the Loft. It was located right in the middle of SoHo. Back when I was alive, you couldn't have paid me to hang out there. There's only so much vacuous smarm I could take without retching. As luck would have it, though, I just so happened to be in charge of a group of vampires headquartered there. Yeah, life sometimes had a funny way of telling you to go fuck yourself. Anyway, the Loft was where it all started for me, it being the place where I was turned. It just so happened to also be one of the coven's more popular hangouts. Sally in particular had a fondness for it, often using it as her home when not at the Office. If she was lying low, there was a good chance it would be at the Loft.

Alas, no such luck. I found a few coven members milling about a dead body, a not uncommon sight. Seeing no sign of Sally, and not really wanting to know much more about the circumstances around their kill – I lost enough sleep as it was – I decided to try the Office instead.

Much to my surprise, Starlight, still in her conscripted role as secretary, told me that Sally was in. I started toward her office, but Star held up a hand. She hooked a thumb and pointed it toward the back. Upon my questioning glance, she smiled sheepishly and made it a point to get back to typing.

Okay, whatever that meant. I turned toward the rear of the floor. There was a changing area, complete with full shower facilities at the back. It was a handy thing to have for vampires. Unlike me, a good deal of the coven preferred their food alive and squirming. That ensured things tended to get messy. Stain resistant carpets, French drains, and places to clean up were necessities for any facility owned and operated by vamps.

Perhaps Sally had just returned from a hunt. She definitely had no problems with taking live prey. Considering how she looked – petite, blonde, and absolutely gorgeous – she didn't often have much problem attracting her next meal. On the upside, if she was in the back room, that meant I had a chance of sneaking a peek at her in the shower. It would probably get me slugged – and Sally could pack a hell of a punch for her size – but it would be worth it. No question there.

As I got closer, my sensitive vampire ears began to pick up sounds from ahead. There was definitely water running, although it sounded more like one of the sinks. That wasn't what caught my ear, though. I picked up heavy, content breathing complimented by the occasional sigh of pleasure. I stopped walking, but continued to listen. Sure eavesdropping was rude, but fuck that shit. Being the head of a vampire coven meant never having to apologize.

The sighs continued. It sounded like ... holy shit! Was she getting it on with someone? Here, I was struck by a moral dilemma (*something rare in the vampire community*). On the one hand, Sally was allowed her privacy. She was my partner in the coven. Hell, she had saved my ass on more than one occasion. She deserved it. On the flipside, when was I going to get another chance to see her getting plowed? Oh, yeah, that decided it.

But still, I hesitated. Something didn't feel right about this. After a moment, I pulled out my cell phone and turned the camera on. *Now* it felt right.

Holding it in front of me, I hit "record" and walked through the door.

"Don't mind me," I cheerfully called out. "Just keep on doing what you're..." What the hell *was* she doing?

Sally, wearing a silk robe, sat in a chair with her bare feet immersed in a portable foot bath. As for the rest of her, the chair was inclined and her head was leaning back in one of the sinks. A somewhat effeminate looking man, one I had never seen before, was busy washing her hair.

Upon hearing my voice, she opened her eyes and raised her head. She looked at me, then at my phone, cocking an eyebrow in the process. "Nice try, Bill," she said, leaning back again.

"What the..." I stammered. The man gave me the once over, sniffed, and then went back to rinsing her hair. "Who is this?"

Without moving, Sally gave another sigh of contentment. "Bill, meet Alfonzo. Alfonzo, Bill."

"Alfonzo?"

"He's my stylist," she explained as if that answered anything.

"Stylist? You can't just bring a person..." I stepped forward and took a breath. I smelled shampoo, conditioner, Sally's expensive perfume – damn, she smelled nice, not that I would ever tell her – and something else. My senses weren't as acute as an older vampire's, but at Sally's insistence, I had been practicing. For a moment, I was confused, but then I realized what it was. Alfonzo wasn't human.

"What the hell did you do?" I snapped.

Alfonzo, thinking I was speaking to him, replied in a nasally accent, "I am accentuating her highlights in preparation for..."

I tuned out the rest. Jeez, I hated to stereotype, but this guy sounded just like I would imagine an overpriced SoHo stylist. We're talking a grade-A, bad Inspector Clouseau imitation here.

"Not you. In fact, would you mind giving Sally and me a moment?"

"Impossible!" he spat in a prissy tone. "The color must be managed down to ze' precise..."

"*GET OUT!!*" I commanded. Compulsion was another thing Sally had been bugging me to practice. I hadn't thought much of it before then, as I hadn't met too many vampires younger than myself. Still, I immediately saw how it could come in handy.

Though my compulsion wasn't nearly the strength of some others, it had the desired effect. Alfonzo's eyes glazed over. He straightened up and, without another word, marched from the room, shutting the door behind him.

"Finally got that figured out?" Sally asked conversationally from where she still reclined.

"Thanks to you. Now, if you'd be so kind, can you please explain Alfonzo?"

She raised her head to meet my gaze. "I already told you. He's my stylist. He's been doing my hair for years. Oh, the things that man can do to a scalp."

"Fascinating, I'm sure. And has Alfonzo always been a vampire?"

"No."

"So you turned him?"

"Yep. That's typically how it works."

"WHY?" I snapped.

She looked at me innocently before answering, "I've been stressed and Alfonzo's salon has been all booked up."

"So you turned him into a vampire?"

"Seemed like a good idea at the time. We're still short on members and he does great work. You really should let him give you a manicure. Your nails are looking a little ratty. He is heaven with a file..."

"I don't need a manicure. And who the fuck gave you permission to recruit new members?"

She just arched her eyebrows at me. In front of the others, I was in charge. Behind the scenes, though, she was on equal terms with me ... maybe even slightly more than equal. Her look told me she wasn't about to be intimidated.

Trying another tactic, I changed my tone. "Besides, weren't you the one who told me that only the coven master could recruit? That there were rituals that needed to be respected?"

She appeared to consider this for a moment before blithely answering, "Yeah, but you said it yourself ... those rituals are stupid."

Damn, she had me there. There were formal rites that were supposed to be performed when one was accepted into a coven, but they were idiotic, not much better than a fraternity initiation. I had told her as much on more than one occasion, not considering that she would probably use my words against me. I should've known better. Sally was a rattlesnake in a size-four dress and three-inch heels.

"Besides, I thought you wanted to branch out from the typical muscle heads that Jeff used to recruit."

Again, she had me. Jeff had been a spoiled, pretty-boy, douchebag asshole. As such, all the other males in the coven had likewise been of similar caliber. They and I had proven to be a bad mix. Thanks to the Khan's assassins, however, there were now far fewer of them to contend with. That aside, though, I had been putting off active recruitment for the coven because ... well, it just seemed like such a fucking evil thing to do. Sure, there were plenty of Goth weirdos who would jump at the chance to be moody for all of eternity, but I had envisioned a coven populated by a more normal, well-adjusted crowd. The problem was, how did you approach someone like that with the offer of, "Hey, can I kill you so you can join my army of the undead?" Apparently, Sally wasn't concerned with minor details such as this.

"Yes," I said. "But that didn't mean you had free rein to make someone your eternal slave just because they happen to do a passable job of covering up your roots."

"I'll have you know I'm a natural blonde."

"Yeah, and I look like Johnny Depp," I countered.

"You might look more like him if you let Alfonzo give you a makeover."

"I'll pass on the Queer Eye for the Straight Guy treatment for now. I think we have more pressing matters to discuss."

"Fine. Pull up a chair, but can you let Alfonzo back in first?"

"Why?" I asked.

"Because if I wind up with streaks in my hair, you aren't going to live long enough to let a Sasquatch kill you."

The Dude with the Crazy Eyes

I DON'T KNOW why I ever bothered talking to Sally. It almost never made me feel better. Well okay, the sight of her cleavage often made me feel better, but it was superficial compared to the pounding migraines I usually ended up with.

Case in point, as the coven's newest recruit continued to tend to her hair with more care than I've seen most parents show to a newborn, Sally blithely told me about how she pretty much knew everything I had come over to talk about. Somehow, I wasn't surprised.

"You know about the special envoy they're sending?"

"Of course. I keep tabs with Boston."

"And you didn't tell me because..."

"As I said, I've been stressed. It slipped my mind."

"Well, did you know we're going to be having company, as in company that just so happens to use magic and wants me dead?"

"Yep, heard that, too. Pity they're going to be under a flag of truce. Otherwise, I'd say it'd be a good opportunity to make them disappear." She said this last part conversationally, her eyes closing as Alfonzo continued to work her scalp. "Oh, and before you ask, yes, I know that your roommates are coming, too."

"Boston knows about *that*?" I asked. Were the assholes spying on me now?

"No, but let's face facts: they follow you *everywhere*. It's like you live with two lost puppies. Speaking of which, remind Ed to bring his shotgun ... just to be on the safe side."

"I'll remind him to bring a box of condoms and some penicillin, too ... *just to be on the safe side*."

She sniffed at the dig. Some months back, Ed had asked her out and she had agreed, much to my surprise. They hadn't gone on a second date, but I suspected that had a little to do with the fact that I completely freaked out upon learning of the first one. Since then, they had both asked about each other a few times, leading me to believe there was probably some unfinished business between them.

Truth be told, I wasn't jealous of them developing a relationship. Well okay, I wasn't *that* jealous. Don't get me wrong. If given the opportunity, I'd happily bang Sally. You just don't say "no" to a piece of ass that fine. Nevertheless, I had my sights set elsewhere. I was more against their relationship out of fear for Ed. Sally was the femme fatale that James Bond had nightmares about. If the mood struck her, she could use Ed, break him, and then treat him like a Happy Meal without a second thought.

"Just make sure Tom leaves at least some of his stupidity at home," she added.

"As if that's even possible," I replied with a grin.

* * *

I found myself back at the Loft on Saturday. Boston had informed Sally that preparations were nearly complete. Our *guest* would be arriving that night to fill us in on the details. We were also informed that the information about to be imparted to us was for *our* ears only. Apparently, knowledge of Sally's status as my silent partner wasn't as silent as we had thought.

We decided the Loft made the most sense for this meeting. It was easy enough to tell the rest of the coven to find somewhere else to be for the night. Sally also didn't want to meet at the Office and run the risk of having to shut down her precious hotline. God forbid the city be allowed one night where its people weren't being harvested like cattle.

I arrived early and had to listen to her go on and on about the fabulous job Alfonzo had done with her hair. The changes were pretty subtle – some layering and a little extra body added (*did I actually just think that?*). That being said, some people pulled off subtle far better than others. Sally's one of them. However, letting her know that wouldn't be any fun.

"So what did he do?" I asked innocently. "Clean out any excess lice and rat droppings?"

A few minutes later, she was distracted from trying to break into the bathroom – where I was hiding – to answer the door. Saved by the bell. And *yes*, it was totally worth it.

As she disengaged the multiple heavy-duty locks, I slipped out and assumed a casual position on the couch. I was fairly sure the elder vampires already had a relatively low opinion of me. I saw no reason to exacerbate it further by letting them see Sally and me acting like ten-year-olds.

She slipped me a sour smile and then opened the door. While she did so, I indulged in a little fantasy involving a sword swinging through the open doorway and decapitating her before she had a chance to make even a single snarky remark.

Alas, no such luck. Instead, a voice said, "Hello, my name is Alex. I believe you are expecting me."

Sigh. What was it with the formality? Did vampires above a certain age become allergic to contractions?

Sally stepped aside and made a welcoming gesture. As our guest walked past, I could see her sizing him up, and not entirely in a sisterly manner either, if you get my drift. She looked up from his ass just in time to meet my questioning gaze. Realizing she had been caught, she quickly turned to close the door.

As usual with the vampire world, the person who stood before me was nothing like I expected. This guy was supposed to be a specialist, hand-picked by the Draculas. As such, I was expecting some Nosferatu-looking dude in a severe black and white suit. Sure, I had never actually seen a vamp who looked like that, but still, this guy had flown in from Europe. I had figured that maybe over in the old country they still respected tradition, or at least the tradition established by multiple Christopher Lee movies.

The newcomer was a few inches shorter than me, but his shortcomings ended there (*figures*). He was broad shouldered and obviously had a strong build beneath the unassuming leather jacket he wore. Jeans, a t-shirt, and a laptop bag rounded out his look. Hell, the dude looked like he could have just driven over from some construction site in Jersey. It seemed the Draculas weren't big on giving their minions a hefty expense account for wardrobe purposes.

Moving on to the rest of him: he had wavy dark blond hair and a smooth complexion. However, what stood out most of all were his eyes. An intense gaze met my own, one that was augmented by the fact that two different colored eyes peered out of his head: one a bright green, the other brown. Hell, I thought Huskies were the only ones like that.

Thus, instead of saying something non-idiotic like "Hi," I instead asked, "Contacts?"

"Excuse me?" he answered in a slightly accented voice.

"Your eyes," I said. Hey, in for a penny of stupidity... "Are you wearing colored contacts?"

I heard Sally sigh. No doubt I was breaking some established protocol for visiting dignitaries. However, being that our guest looked like he had just gotten off a motorcycle, I figured I was justified for not dropping to one knee and looking for a ring to kiss.

If Alex was insulted by my question, he didn't show it. "You have a unique way of introducing yourself," he replied in a bemused voice. He held out a hand and repeated his initial greeting. "My name is Alex. I am here as a representative of the First Coven to assist you, and this is my natural eye color. Any other questions?"

I smiled back, half amazed. Though I had met only a small subset, my dealings with the vampire world had led me to believe it was mostly populated with self-absorbed, humor-deficient assholes. Thus, to meet a vamp who obviously had some rank behind him (*the Draculas were rumored to be very picky about who they hung out with*) yet wasn't immediately oozing with douchebag vibes was a pleasant surprise. I reached out my hand and shook his.

"I'm Bill. Pleased to meet you, Alex."

"Likewise, Freewill," he said, indicating my status as a one-man vampire freak show. "And I presume you are Sally." He turned toward her. "I was told you were quite stunning, but I daresay the reports did not do you justice."

To my surprise, she actually blushed – quite the feat for someone lacking a pulse. Damn, Alex was a playa.

He gave her an appraising look. "I hope you did not go through a lot of trouble to make yourself presentable just for my arrival."

"Oh, this? I just threw on something real quick," she replied as if she hadn't spent the greater part of the week under Alfonzo's care. Now it was my turn to eye-roll.

I had to admit, Alex was one smooth character. No wonder the Draculas employed his services as a diplomat. He had disarmed both Sally and me within seconds, the former accomplishment being something I had yet to master.

"We all have a lot to discuss, so we should get started right away ... as soon as I make use of the facilities, if I may."

"Sure," I replied. "Make yourself at home." I pointed him toward the bathroom.

He stopped at the doorway, no doubt noticing the numerous dents in the door and newly splintered wood in the frame. He turned back and gave us a questioning look.

"Oh, don't mind that," I said. "I was combing my hair earlier and Sally had a burrito for lunch. When you gotta go..."

He gave a sheepish smile in reply and then entered.

As the door clicked shut, I yelled to him, "There's some air freshener in the cabinet if you need ... OUCH!" Damn, Sally could hit hard when she wanted to.

* * *

Alex returned to find us sitting on the couch waiting for him, me still rubbing my arm. The phrase "hits like a girl" definitely did not apply to the saucy little blonde in the room.

Ignoring whatever had occurred during his brief foray in the restroom, Alex sat in a chair opposite us and opened his bag. He pulled out a ruggedized laptop and proceeded to boot it up. Apparently, ancient scrolls written on parchment made from human flesh was passé these days. Nobody believed in setting the proper mood anymore.

"Care for a glass of blood before we get started?" I asked, trying to be cordial. My thoughts regarding the Draculas aside, if this guy held favor with them, then that probably meant he wasn't exactly a spring chicken. The older the vampire, the stronger. I didn't see any need to get on this guy's bad side and discover just how quickly he could kick my ass.

"No thank you," he replied, typing on the keyboard. "I had a light snack on the way over."

I didn't ask him to elaborate. Knowing vampires, I wouldn't be the least bit surprised to read about some missing cabbie in the morning paper. Friendly or not, I needed to remind myself that Alex was probably a top notch killer. It was best not to get too enamored of him, especially since his primary job was to prep me on how to be the Draculas' fall guy.

Seeing that the small talk was rapidly fizzling out, I proceeded to sit there and wait. Sally, too, was unusually quiet. Our normal banter aside, it was starting to sink in just how serious this was ... or more precisely, just how deep the shit we were both standing in was.

After a few more moments of uncomfortable silence, Alex pulled his eyes away from the screen. "Before we begin," he started, "I should point out a few nuances of your situation. Both of you are far too young to have

RICK GUALTIERI

had any serious dealings with the First Coven." I opened my mouth to say something, but he held up a hand. "I am aware, Freewill, of your dealings with the Khan. Suffice to say, that circumstance was anything but typical."

"Thank God," I muttered.

A look very close to amusement passed through Alex's freaky eyes. "The first thing I shall say is that you should both consider it an honor. It is almost unheard of for the First to have dealings with any of our kind less than a century in age. The First are not particularly tolerant of *children*." He put a heavy emphasis on that last part.

Thinking back to Gan, my mouth decided to have a mind of its own. "I don't blame the Draculas. Kids these days," I said with a laugh, only to realize I was the only one in the room grinning.

Alex had a look of mild disapproval on his face, while Sally's eyes were wide open in shock. "Yes, about that," said Alex. "I should warn you that the First are not particularly fond of that nickname. Their agents have been given authority to make liberal examples of offenders."

"You're one of their agents, aren't you?"

"Yes."

"Way to go, Bill," Sally quipped quietly.

Again, Alex smiled. "I think, considering the circumstances, we can forgo the formalities of this offense for the time being. However, you should know that the First are not particularly known for their forgiveness."

"Point taken."

"Good. Now, is it correct that the Wanderer filled you in on some of the details as to why you have been chosen?"

"The Wanderer?" Sally asked.

"James," I replied to her. As I had learned in China, the dude had a lot of nicknames. He apparently got around. I then said to Alex, "Yeah, he brought us up to speed on the whys. I'm to be their proxy to this event because ... THEY'RE A BUNCH OF PUSSIES AND I'M OBVIOUSLY FUCKING EXPENDABLE!"

Well, okay, that's what I *thought*. I really finished with, "because I'm the Freewill and thus considered to be highly honored."

"Essentially correct. The Grendel demand that..."

"Grendel?"

"Yes," he replied. "Our adversaries at the table..."

"You call them the Grendel?"

"They have lots of names."

"So I'm learning," I said. "Isn't 'Grendel' a little insulting, considering how Beowulf kicked its ass?"

"Very astute of you," Alex replied with a hint of approval. "Yes, it is. Therefore we don't call them that in their presence."

"Cool. So Beowulf was a vampire?"

"Not quite. He was one of the Shining Ones."

Seeing our confused looks, he added, "Sorry. I sometimes forget that name has fallen out of usage in recent years. I believe you refer to them as Icons."

There was that word again. Apparently, many of the famous monster slayers of old were actually these so-called Icons. From what I had been led to believe, they were actually a bunch of egomaniacs. Even so, somehow their belief in their own badassery actually made it so. They were able to empower themselves with faith, a form of magic that's not too compatible with vampires or other supernatural creatures, wizards included.

These guys got around back in the day, and by that, I mean kicked everyone's asses. According to the wizards, supposedly my *birth* meant they were returning too. Hoo boy, shit was definitely going to start getting real. Assuming, of course, I managed not to get my head ripped off by a pack of apes with lots of names – each stupider than the last.

Yes, This is One of Those Exposition Chapters

"ARE YOU STILL paying attention?" Alex asked.

"Of course," I lied. He had been droning on about politics and places at the table for over an hour. He lost me about halfway through, going on about the supposed high honor bestowed upon me by Bigfoot.

"Then you understand the significance of signing this treaty anew?"

"Well..."

"Anew?" asked Sally. "I keep hearing that. So what happened to the old treaty?"

"Yeah ... what she said," I unhelpfully added.

"Very well," Alex replied. "I suppose a little history is in order. Although keep in mind what I am about to share with you..."

"...is First Coven business, for our ears only, blah blah blah."

He stopped and stared at me for a moment. Again, a smile broke out on his face. "You certainly are a refreshing individual compared to those I usually deal with."

"Thanks."

"Pity most of the elders would not see it in that light. It could get you killed one day."

"I'm more concerned about not getting killed by the Alma, Sasquatch, or fucking Forest Folk in the here and now." I should've been watching my tone, but Alex's easygoing attitude was a bit disarming, so I found myself speaking more and more freely.

"Either way you look at it, Bill's not exactly building a huge friend list," Sally chimed in. Guess she was feeling the same about him.

"Very well. Probably a wise attitude, to be concerned with the present," Alex replied. "As for your question, Sally, our original treaty with the Grendel stretches back over five thousand years."

"Holy shit!" I said. "We're talking cradle of civilization here, aren't we?"

"Very much so. The rise of man triggered the first great war with the Grendel."

"Why?"

"Well, this was a long time ago and records are a little sketchy, but from what we know, it was all about encroachment. As human civilization grew, it also expanded. The Grendel, being nature spirits, took offense to this. They considered it an affront, that mankind had begun to defile the lands with their continued expansion."

"Kind of like druids in D&D?" I asked. As expected, that drew an eye-roll from Sally. Alex, however, just looked at me with a confused expression. Jeez, was I the only vampire on the planet who was into role playing? "It's a game," I explained.

"I see," he replied in a tone that suggested quite the opposite. "Alas, what we are talking about here is no game. Insulted and feeling threatened, the Grendel launched an all-out war against humanity."

"So where do the vampires come into this?"

"An excellent question. Before humanity's rise, we were different than we are now ... or so I am told. In fact, we were not entirely dissimilar to the Grendel at the time. However, something happened. Whether accidental or not, I do not know. What I do know is that we somehow became tied to the human race. Our spirits coexisted with and amongst theirs. It was the beginning of our kind as we know it today."

"I think I see," replied Sally. "So when the apes began killing off our supply of junk food, we took offense."

"It goes deeper than that. In linking ourselves with humanity, as they thrived, so did we. We had no choice but to enter the fray against the Grendel. If human civilization had perished, we would have followed. Thus, for a time, we fought side by side with humankind as brothers."

"So what happened?"

"Mesopotamia became a blood bath. At first, the Grendel were both stronger and more numerous. However, humanity spread quickly and learned even faster. They mastered tools and weapons. They built impregnable city states. In time, some mastered the use of magic as well. With our strength added to theirs, the sides became evenly matched."

"And?" Sally and I both asked, now entirely engrossed.

"And it continued that way for a millennium until eventually all sides grew weary of the constant slaughter."

"All sides?" I asked.

"Yes, for by then nearly all aspects of both the natural and unnatural world had been drawn into the fray on one side or the other. It was truly the first world war. Even human history, which is a dreadfully forgetful thing, remembers bits and pieces of it: the great flood, the destruction of Sodom and Gomorrah, stories of the Nephilim, et cetera."

"So they worked it out?"

"In a manner of speaking, yes. There was a great summit between the powers of the world, not unlike that which we are preparing for now. After nearly a year of deliberation and debate between the parties, the Humbaba Accord was signed."

"Humbaba?" I chuckled. "Sounds like some bizarre sexual position."

"Not that you would know," Sally countered.

"Bite me."

"Not even if I was up to date on my shots."

"Eh hem!" Alex cleared his throat, distracting us from our banter. "Thank you. Humbaba was the name of the Grendel leader at the time. It was he who originally proposed the terms of the treaty."

"So what were these terms?"

"The entire treaty was several dozen scrolls in length. The main gist of it, though, was a dividing line. The Grendel would get the forests while our kind would stay within the confines of the cities. Humanity would be allowed to continue to build their civilizations as long as certain areas of spiritual significance to the Grendel were considered off limits."

"So in other words," I offered, "vampires became the cool urban types, while the Bigfeet became the rubes."

"I am not sure I would put it quite that way, but essentially correct. The treaty was signed in blood, and aside from occasional isolated skirmishes, it has been respected ever since."

"So what changed?"

Alex sighed. "Humanity. They have forgotten the lessons of the past. Creatures such as ourselves have been forced to step back and fade into the realm of superstition."

"So? It's not like Bigfoot is exactly considered real either."

"That is not their concern. Perception is irrelevant. All that matters to the Grendel are that in the past few hundred years humanity's forward march has gotten ever more aggressive. Forests are being cut down. Fields are paved over. The jungles are being burned away."

"Which has *what* to do with us?"

"It has *everything* to do with us. We dwell within and amongst humanity. As they expand, so do we. Though relegated to the shadows, we have continued to thrive as humanity has grown. The Grendel are aware of mankind's short memory and have been mostly tolerant of them. We, however, are immortal. They consider the fact that we allow humanity to grow unchecked to be a blatant disregard for the Accord. Ever since the Industrial Revolution began, there have been rumblings that some amongst the Grendel are actively accusing us of being in abeyance of the treaty."

"Oh."

"'Oh' does not even remotely cover it. The attack on the Khan was not just the latest in a series of clashes between us. It was meant to convey a message. By striking out at one of our ruling council, they have declared the treaty null and void. Open warfare could be declared at any time."

"And if that happens?" I ventured, already having a sneaking suspicion that the answer would not be good.

"If that happens, then the veil will be lifted. All of humanity's darkest nightmares will be revealed as reality. The world will become a battleground."

Vacation Daze

I COULDN'T HELP but have doubts about Alex's sense of impending doom. Even if what he said was true and Sasquatches suddenly came charging out of the woods en masse, I had a hard time imagining the plot from Rise of the Planet of the Apes becoming a reality. I voiced as much to him.

"You are correct at the most basic level," he admitted. "The world has changed a great deal in five thousand years. Humanity's capacity for destruction has grown exponentially. Many humans would die, but if it were only the Grendel waging war, then perhaps things would not be as dire as I make them out to be."

"Well then..."

"But it is not only the Grendel. The old alliances are still in place. If the Grendel declare war, then it is possible that other factions could once again join the fray. Believe me, when I say there are powers far beyond what you could possibly comprehend out there. Some would be eager to make the world remember their existence."

"Such as?"

"I very much doubt the citizens of this city would be too appreciative if Marduk and Tiamat were to suddenly do battle in Times Square."

I did a mental calculation of both their stats from the latest edition of the Monster Manual. Hmm, not cool.

"Not to mention," Sally added, "how long do you think it would be before the humans brought out the big firecrackers?"

"Nukes?" I asked.

"Bingo."

Alex nodded somberly. "Yes, there is that to take into consideration, too."

"How the hell did we get from Bigfoot attacking vampires to Mad Max Beyond Thunderdome?" I asked skeptically.

"I will admit," said Alex, "that is most likely a worst case scenario. But still, it is in all our best interests to get up to the Northwest Territories and make sure that it never gets a chance to escalate to that point. If we do not, then our alternatives are..."

"Wait a second. Did you say 'Northwest Territories?'"

"Yes."

"Where the fuck is that?"

"Isn't it in Canada?" Sally asked.

"Yes," Alex replied. "Northern Canada, to be precise."

"Why the fuck are they having peace talks in Canada, of all places? Couldn't they pick somewhere more ... relevant?"

"It *is* relevant to the Grendel. Ever since the First Coven reached out to discuss parley with our ancient enemies, the Grendel have been in active competition for a place to host the event."

"Competition?"

"The Grendel are a spiritual race, thus they demanded the talks happen at a place that holds significance for them. However, they are also a caste-driven society that places heavy significance on both birth as well as strength of arms. Not only are the Territories home to one of the larger populations of the Grendel on this continent, but it is also the location of the Woods of Mourning, an ancestral burial ground that holds the remains of many of their fallen warriors. I don't know exactly what transpired, but the chieftain of that area came out victorious. The honor is his to..."

I started to chuckle.

"Don't do it, Bill," Sally warned.

"If I may ask..." Alex started.

"Morning wood!" I let out, cackling. "Oh, that's great. I bet their ancestors got a *rise* out of that one."

"I am afraid I do not..."

"I'll be sure not to let any *boners* slip during the peace conference," I continued, still laughing.

Alex turned to Sally, a confused look on his face. She replied, "Don't ask. Just assume Bill is a retard. It's easier that way."

Still looking confused, he simply replied, "If you say so."

Yeah, I think it's safe to say he was starting to have doubts about sending me.

* * *

It was only later, after Alex had departed for his hotel, that I realized what deep shit I was in.

I turned to Sally. "Didn't he say that the last treaty took a year to hammer out?"

"Something like that."

I slapped the palm of my hand against my forehead as realization hit. "Oh, fuck."

"What now?"

"I only have two weeks of vacation."

"After all of that, the thing you're most worried about is unpaid time off? We are so screwed."

* * *

"Canada?" Ed asked. "This is a peace conference to decide the fate of the world ... and they're having it in Canada?"

"Pretty much what I said."

"Why can't they ever do these things someplace nice, like the Bahamas?" Tom asked from his place on the couch.

"Well, just off the top of my head, I'd guess sunny, ninety-degree beaches aren't conducive to giant monkeys covered head to toe in foul smelling fur ... or vampires, for that matter."

"Guess I should start doing my research," Tom said.

"Research?"

"Yep. Time to start eating Canadian bacon, drinking Molson, and finishing all of my sentences with '*eh.*'"

That caused a chuckle amongst us.

After it had passed, Ed said to me, "Idiotic or not, Tom does have a point about research."

"I'm all for a few beers."

"Not that," he replied. "Well okay, not *just* that. I'm thinking we'd better start boning up on Bigfoot."

I started laughing again. When he questioned me, I told them about the whole Woods of Mourning thing. Soon we were all cracking up.

Finally, Tom said, "Well then, this should be easy."

"How so?"

"With Sally around, I don't think pitching a tent will be a problem."

I laughed. "Just don't let her hear you say that. She might break it off and feed it to Bigfoot."

* * *

"What the fuck are you doing?" Ed asked me two days later. He had barged into my bedroom/office to ask a question and found me staring at my monitor.

"Dude, try knocking first!"

"Please tell me you weren't jerking off to ... what *is* that anyway?"

"Research," I replied distractedly, unable to take my eyes from the screen.

"What the hell kind of research is this?"

"Well, I decided to look up some info on Sasquatch."

"Sasquatch porn?"

"Sasquatch *erotica*," I corrected.

"That's wrong on so many levels."

"I agree. But when dealing with an unknown enemy, one should study them from all angles."

"I'm not sure some of those angles are even possible."

"Tell me about it. I guess Bigfoot likes them nubile. What did you want, anyway?"

"For the life of me I can't remember," Ed stated. He sighed and then turned to leave. "Just wash your hands when you're done, you fucking perv."

"Will do. Hey, want me to email you the link?"

"Okay, sure," he replied, closing the door behind him.

* * *

Soon after I had finished my ... err ... *research*, my cell rang. Hearing the tone, I immediately picked it up.

"S'up, Sally?"

"Hey, Bill."

Hearing a bit of an edge in her voice ... well okay, more of an edge than usual, I asked, "What's the matter?"

"Alex just sent me our travel arrangements."

"It was only a matter of time. Did he take care of Tom and Ed, like I asked?"

"Oh, yeah."

"Cool. Then when's our flight?"

"About that..."

"Don't tell me I'm booked freight again, Sally. I swear to God, if that's the case I'm going to..."

"No, it's not that."

"Okay then, what is it?"

"There is no flight."

"Excuse me?"

"You heard me. There's no flight. We're not flying."

"Then how are we getting there, magic?"

"Car."

"Hold on a second," I replied, quickly calling up Google Maps on my PC. "You do realize that it's over two thousand fucking miles away, right?"

"Don't yell at me. Yes, I know that."

"Then can you explain to me why the hell we're driving across almost an entire fucking continent to get there?"

"Complain to the Bigfeet. It was their idea."

"Why?"

"According to Alex, since they're hosting this thing, they get to set some of the ground rules. Apparently, not only do they hate civilization, but they can't stand technology either. They consider it an affront against nature or some other bullshit. Stupid, shit-flinging assholes."

"Let me guess – airplanes are a great big affront to both nature and convenience, right?"

"Pretty much."

"That makes no fucking sense. What do they think cars are, horses disguised with wheel wells?"

"That was their concession to us. We're allowed to drive in. However, flying would constitute a great offense to their chief, blah blah blah."

I sighed and began to rub my temples. One would think that a positive side effect of being a vampire would be no more stress headaches. One would be wrong in that assumption.

"You do remember I don't have a car, right?" I asked.

"Of course. Kind of hard to forget your shortcomings."

"And I doubt Ed's piece of shit will make it even halfway to Canada."

"Also true."

"Then how are we supposed to get there?"

"I'm told they're taking care of that."

"Why doesn't that make me feel any better? Oh well, maybe it won't be too bad. I doubt the Draculas would make their special envoy travel in anything less than style."

"Alex isn't going with us."

"What?!"

"He said he'll meet us there. He has to leave early to get some of the preparations made."

"The fucker's flying, isn't he?"

"He didn't say, but if I were a betting woman..."

"Which you are."

"Well, I will admit to enjoying a good game of roulette ... Russian or otherwise. But yeah, we're getting fucked here and not in a fun way."

"Are you surprised?"

"With *you* around? No, not really."

"Well hey, it could be worse."

"I'm going to be stuck in a car with your idiot friend for a week," she replied, no doubt referring to Tom. "Pray tell, how could it be worse?"

"They could be sending us up via dog sled."

"Bill, I hate to point it out to you, but the last several hundred miles of the journey aren't exactly going to be jam packed with gas stations. We might just wind up getting there that way."

I sighed into the phone. This kept getting better and better.

Driving in Style

FORTUNATELY FOR ED and me, we had no lives. Thus, in addition to sick days, we both had about three years' worth of unused vacation time accrued – almost two months in total. That being said, most employers tended not to be too understanding when you called them up last minute and told them you needed to disappear for several weeks. Jim wasn't an exception. He pretty much flipped out, although it wasn't exactly surprising. When two members of your team both decided that they needed an extended vacation at the same time, it probably only meant one of a few things: we were quitting; we were affirming our long denied love for one another and running off to a state that supported gay marriage; or we were setting off for a massive peace conference between vampires, Bigfoot, and whatever other weirdness the supernatural world had in store.

Yeah, most employers probably don't assume that last one. Considering the fact that my crush on his former assistant was supposedly well known within the company, Jim was probably giving himself a near aneurysm over the assumption that we were probably jumping ship.

In an attempt to keep him from stroking out, we both offered to bring our laptops and at least attempt to get a little work done whenever we were within either WiFi or 3G range. Programming was really the furthest thing from my mind going into this clusterfuck, but we were going to be on the road for at least a week. There were doubtless going to be times when it was best to shut up and type, lest we face the possibility of Sally killing us all on the side of the road.

That covered Ed and me. Tom didn't work with us, though. Since the financial district wasn't particularly known for their tolerance of slackers who disappeared for weeks at a time, I expected him to have to bail out. It was regrettable. Sure, Tom was a sexist moron even on his best behavior, but he was also one of only a handful of people I trusted to have my back. Still, his staying behind wasn't a bad thing either. It would ensure that at least one of my friends lived to tell the tale.

Alas, though, that didn't come to pass. He came home the day before our journey was to start and announced that everything was taken care of.

"They're letting you take that much vacation?" I asked.

"Nope," he gleefully answered.

"So what then?" Ed asked. "Did they fire you on the spot?"

"Negative on that one, too," he replied in that same infuriatingly cheerful tone.

It was only after we threatened to beat the shit out of him that he finally relented and told us.

"I'm scot-free," he said. "I get to keep my job, not lose any vacation, and still come on this little getaway."

"How?"

"Christy," he explained. "Since this is a special occasion, the fate of the world hanging in the balance and all, she got her coven – who I might add are a hell of a lot more useful than yours, Bill – to work a little of their mojo."

"What did they do?"

"They cast some kind of spell for her. I'm not sure the specifics, but she said it's some sort of mass hypnosis. Since I'm an official part of this peace process, she got them to include me, too. For as long as the spell is in effect, people at the office will randomly see other workers as me."

Ed and I both looked at each other, confused.

"Say you're talking to Bob at the water cooler. Well, even though you're talking to him, you'd see me instead. Same with work. You hand an assignment to some other schlub and – poof – I get credit for doing it."

"Yeah, but the person who was supposed to be doing it gets fucked," I replied.

"Dude, this is finance. Someone is always getting fucked. It's par for the course."

Though of dubious morality, Ed and I had to admit it was pretty damn clever. Psycho though she may be, there were definite perks to banging a witch. That she was indirectly helping me by aiding her boyfriend was probably accidental. However, it was still a plus in my column. I'd have to remember that later. Should Christy run afoul of an angry Sasquatch, well, I still might not help her, but at least I wouldn't feed her to it. That had to count for something toward my karma ... maybe.

* * *

There was an additional bonus to dating Christy. She had given Tom a vial of some foul smelling powder. He was to pour it across the threshold as we left. It would act as a ward against any burglars during our extended absence. I personally wasn't too worried about that. For starters, we didn't live in a high crime neighborhood. Secondly, considering for how long we were potentially leaving, most everything that we owned of value was packed for the trip. Still, we'd been forced to redecorate the apartment a few times since I was turned into a vampire, thanks mostly to our dealings with some of the destructive elements of the supernatural world. Anything we could do to keep from having to spend more money at IKEA would be welcome.

So packed up and with our apartment warded, we lugged our suitcases downstairs in the hours before dawn to await our ride. The last time we went on a trip with Sally, she had shown up in a Cadillac Escalade, recently liberated from its formerly living owner. I didn't know what the Draculas were sending us, but I hoped it didn't smell like a crime scene.

A short while later, a vehicle turned onto our block. As it slowed and we began to make it out, I started missing the Escalade.

While it pulled in, Tom whispered to me, "Dude, did we suddenly step onto the set of Sanford and Son?"

I shrugged, not really knowing how to answer. It wasn't quite what I was expecting, although knowing the vampire world and their propensity for being assholes, I wasn't surprised.

Parked in front of us, with Sally behind the wheel, was an old, beat-up Jeep Wagoneer. Towed behind it was a U-haul container that had seen better days.

She turned off the engine and got out. The look on her face was anything but amused.

"You've got to be kidding me," I said. "This thing is older than I am."

"You're preaching to the choir," she replied. "But this is what they sent us."

"Normally," Ed commented, "I wouldn't condone doing anything that'll get us sent to prison for an extended period of time, but this piece of shit looks like it's on its last legs. Maybe we should grab something a little ... better."

"Apparently," Sally said with a sigh, "the fucking Sasquatches are also against all the computers and fancy gizmos in modern cars. That's why we got this fine conveyance here."

My roommates and I gave a mutual shrug and walked over.

"Put what you can in the trunk. Fit the rest in the trailer. Just be careful," she said.

I was about to ask her why, when Tom opened the trailer and we were almost overwhelmed by heavy fumes.

Gagging, I exclaimed, "What the hell?!" before looking inside. Taking up over half the available space, stacked from floor to ceiling, were gas cans. Judging from the smell, they were full.

"To get us there once we leave civilization behind," she explained.

"Only one problem," Ed said. "How are we going to get past the border with a couple hundred gallons of combustibles?"

"Leave that to me, champ," Sally replied. "For now, you just have one thing to worry about."

"What's that?"

"Driving," she answered, then tossed him the keys. "I believe you know the way to Boston."

* * *

Fortunately for us, we were allowed one modern convenience in our *luxurious* ride: heavily tinted windows. Without them, the trip would have quickly gotten a bit uncomfortable for those of us with a habit of turning to ash under the glaring light of the sun. After a couple of hours on the road, though, I was beginning to think that maybe getting dusted would be the kinder fate. Let's just say I'm pretty sure this car was built before shocks were invented.

While my ass continued to be assaulted by the rough ride, I thought to ask, "Why are we heading up to Boston?"

"Yeah, it is a bit out of the way," added Tom from the front seat.

"James said so," was all Sally answered before going back to the fashion magazine she had been perusing.

Five hours later, we pulled into the car wash that served as the aboveground facade for the Northeastern vampire headquarters.

"Let me guess, we wait in the car again?" Ed asked.

"Not this time," Sally replied. "Since you guys are part of Bill's entourage, you get treated slightly better than the blood cows you are. Besides, it's not like you don't already know enough about the vampire world as it is."

"Awesome," Tom said, stepping out and stretching his legs. "I have to take a piss. Vampires have bathrooms, right?"

Sally let out an annoyed sigh. "*Yes,* vampires have bathrooms. Although I'm not sure you can use them."

"Why?"

"Simple. There's both a ladies' and a men's room, but I think they forgot to install one for dipshits."

* * *

No doubt remembering my outbursts from our last visit, Sally turned to all three of us before we entered. "One word: *behave.* Bill needs to show up to this summit alive, but that doesn't mean there can't be any *accidents* along the way, especially if any of you embarrass the living shit out of me."

"So I take it that means no reenacting scenes from *The Walking Dead*?" asked Tom, referring to the zombies most likely awaiting us inside. That was one aspect of the undead life that never stopped surprising me. Zombies were real, but rather than lumbering across the countryside eating any hapless humans in their path, they essentially existed as clerical help for vampires. Go figure.

As answer, Sally gave us a look full of enough daggers to impale a rhino. Then she turned and led the way inside.

It was pretty much how I remembered. Vampires had excellent night vision, so that meant they tended to cheap out on the overhead lighting. The gloominess aside, though, the structure resembled nothing more threatening than any other office in corporate America. That being said, the cubicles that flanked us on either side were full of workers that weren't much different from the beaten down souls you'd see in any company. They were just somewhat less alive ... if only barely.

Sally's warning all but forgotten, my roommates and I exchanged bemused glances with one another as we passed zombie after zombie performing mundane office tasks.

"Can you imagine being someone's office drone for all of eternity?" I whispered to Ed.

"And you still wonder why Sheila quit?" he replied.

RICK GUALTIERI

I gritted my teeth. Yeah, he had a point, but did he really need to bring her up? I mean, I was just starting to enjoy myself. Great, now I'd have her on my mind for probably the entire trip to middle-of-fucking-nowhere Canada ... just in time to get my face stomped in by the Boggy Creek monster and all his cousins.

I sighed, then noticed that Tom was harassing a zombie pushing a mail cart. My God, sometimes he was no better than a fucking kid.

He was waving his hand in front of the office zombie and mocking it. "Ooh, look at me. Tasty human right here. Yeah, I bet you'd like to munch on my yummy yummy brains."

The zombie, in turn, was giving him a look that would've probably conveyed utter contempt, had half its face not been rotted off.

"Jesus Christ, Tom," I hissed at him. "Stop screwing around."

He turned his head and gave me a smirk. "Dude, chill. I'm just having a little fun. When am I ever going to get another chance to mess with a zom ... OUCH! The fucker bit me!" Tom yelled, pulling his hand back and cradling it.

In response, the zombie gave a half-faced grin, raised up one arm and flipped him the finger ... or part of one, anyway.

I took a step forward, when I suddenly realized that all sounds in the office had stopped. A quick look around confirmed that all eyes, living and otherwise, were turned in our direction.

Make that *almost* all eyes. Sally had stopped walking, but she still faced away from us. Unfortunately, even in the dim light I could see that her hands were balled tightly into fists – so tight that blood was dripping between her fingers.

Oh, crap.

Damn Nazi Vampires

I WAS SPLIT. On the one hand, Tom was now whimpering, "He bit me. I'm gonna turn into a zombie." On the other, I could see Sally literally shaking with rage. I wasn't sure which fire to put out first.

Fortunately, Ed was there to make that choice for me.

"Let me see," he said to Tom. "Oh for God's sake, you fucking pussy. He didn't even break the skin."

"But he bit me," Tom again whined.

That decided it. I turned toward Sally, quickly trying to think of something to distract her from the pummeling she was no doubt contemplating. Before I could sputter some lame excuse, though, once again I was saved.

"My dearest Sally," came a slick voice from the end of the hall, "you do realize we have a strict policy against bringing cattle to the office, don't you?"

I turned in that direction, already knowing whom I would see. It was Colin, James's would-be successor. He was, to put it mildly, a pompous prick. As far as I could tell, people like Colin existed for only two reasons: to kiss the asses of anyone who outranked them, and to be an absolute asshole to anyone who didn't.

All things considered, though, I was glad to see him. Sally and he apparently had history. What that history was, I didn't know. She wouldn't tell me, and I had a feeling that Colin would sooner demote himself to janitor than talk to me. Regardless, there was a definite aura of dislike between them. For now, that meant whatever venom Sally wanted to unleash upon me and my roommates, she'd most likely redirect at the well-dressed vampire lackey before her.

"I'm surprised to see you here, Colin," she replied. "I didn't realize your choke chain reached this far. With James back, shouldn't you be fetching him coffee or something?"

He tittered in response. "Sally, you do so amuse me with your lack of understanding for my station. Oh well, it's to be expected from one of your 'standing.' Assuming you do stand, of course. Personally, I wouldn't be surprised to learn you performed all your duties on your back."

Ooh, massive burn from Colin. I reached Sally just in time to see her eyes turning black. I put a hand on her shoulder and then stepped in front of her.

"Hey, Colin," I said in my best cheerful voice. "Long time no see."

"Freewill," he spat back, as if the word tasted bad.

Cutting straight to the chase before an office brawl ensued, I said, "James is expecting us, I believe."

He narrowed his eyes at me. "You're correct, and he is not a vampire to be kept waiting. Please follow me, and do pick up after your *pets*. We have a standard to maintain here, after all." With that, he turned on his heel and began walking.

I heard Sally utter a snarl behind me. I spun, looked her in the eye, and said, "One word: *behave*." Before she could knock me through a wall, I gestured for Tom and Ed to hurry up. I then turned and began marching after Colin, Tom's continued whimpering of "I can't believe he bit me" following in my wake.

* * *

The last time I was there, James wasn't around, so we got no further than Colin's desk. James's outer office was the one place there that seemed to conform to my expectations for an undead lair. Whereas the rest of the building was a typical office in most ways, this area had a much more sinister feel to it. I had little doubt it was on purpose. When one had rank, one often wanted others to know about it.

With the exception of a small waiting area, this part of the office looked as if it had been carved out of the rock around us. Considering we were underground, I realized that was likely the case. The tapping of our feet on the obsidian tiled floor echoed off the walls as we approached the double doors just beyond Colin's desk.

"Holy ... well, batcave, Batman," Ed whispered behind me, taking in the surroundings.

"Tell me about it," I muttered.

"He's expecting you," Colin said with a sour grin from behind his desk. Now that he had gotten in a dig at Sally, he seemed content with dismissing us. He reached under his desk, pressed something, and the doors to James's office clicked, letting us know they were unlocked.

"This should be good," I whispered back to my friends. I could only imagine what kind of medieval torture chamber awaited us. I was expecting to find something worthy of a James Bond villain. Perhaps there'd even be a shark tank in which to dispose of his enemies. That would be so fucking awesome.

I really need to stop psyching myself out, I thought once I had stepped through the doors. Whereas the outer chamber was decorated in early sixteenth century Vlad the Impaler, the inner sanctum couldn't have been more of a contrast. It was like stepping into an archeology professor's office. The room was well lit with a fairly simple desk at one end. Shelves and cabinets lined the walls, all of them filled with a variety of knickknacks, most of which looked a lot older than me – no doubt a testament to James's nickname of the Wanderer. Off to one end was a coffee table and a well-worn, but comfortable looking, couch. Upon it sat James, a cup of espresso in his hands.

He stood as we entered. "Sally, Dr. Death, a pleasure as always."

"James," I replied as way of greeting. "These are my friends, Tom and Ed."

"Ah yes." He turned to them. "Dr. Death's human friends. He's told me all about you. Especially you," he said to Tom. "You're the one with the fetish for ... what are they called ... transforming something?"

"*Transformers*," I clarified. Several months back, Tom had somehow imbued an action figure with a small portion of his life force, essentially turning it into a weapon against vampires, much like Peter Cushing might have used a cross in the old Dracula films. It had gotten broken during the course of that little adventure, something he never failed to remind me about.

"Fetish is such a strong word," Tom replied, no doubt forgetting that he was talking to a six-hundred-year-old vampire, one who could kill him as easily as he could a gnat. "I prefer the term *collector*."

"Kindly forgive my transgression," James replied amicably enough. He was truly an odd duck amongst the older vampires I had met. Somehow, through all of his centuries of existence, he had managed to hold onto his sense of humor. Most others of our kind hadn't mastered that feat. Hell, I doubted most of them had even tried.

The pleasantries aside, James walked to the door. "Colin, be a good chap and grab some coffee for our visitors. Perhaps some lunch, too. Send one of the thralls out to a local eatery, would you?"

Having given his instructions, he closed the door, although not before I caught a glimpse of Colin's furious expression. Heh, the fucker had just been sent on a food run. I was beginning to understand what Ed had been saying about Sheila. No matter what the station or setting, an assistant could become a glorified gofer at any given time.

James turned back toward us. "That'll assure our privacy for a few minutes at least. Alas, despite the formidable construction outside of my office, the doors are pitifully inadequate at keeping sound from carrying."

He pulled a few chairs from his desk over and we all sat. "I trust the First Coven's envoy has brought you up to speed?" he asked me.

"Yeah. Alex gave us the rundown on the Grendel," I replied, using his word for them.

"I haven't heard that term used in a while. Alex, you said, correct?"

"Yeah, you know him, right?"

"I'm afraid not. Sadly, even with my current standing, I am not privy to all of the First Coven's inner thoughts."

That was surprising to learn. Considering James was in the running to join their merry little bunch, you'd think they might've been slightly less dickish toward him.

"Well, he seems like a nice enough guy," I replied.

James nodded and said, "I'm sure he does. Nevertheless, I would highly recommend you keep your guard up around him at all times."

"You don't trust him?" Ed asked.

"As I said, I don't know him. I neither have reason to trust nor distrust him. However, what I do know is that he would obviously be a person of significant diplomatic skill. Otherwise, the First would not have chosen him. Such an individual would excel at coming across as likable."

"So you're saying he probably has his own agenda," Ed surmised.

"Undoubtedly. He follows the will of the First and their machinations remain their own."

"But we're all on the same side here, right?" I asked.

"You're almost cute when you're stupidly naïve, Bill," Sally commented.

"Her thinly veiled insult aside, Sally is quite correct. While I believe the First want this peace conference to be successful, there are no doubt nuances at play that will make it more or less successful by standards of which only they are aware. Should all other factors align in their favor, don't assume they wouldn't consider your loss to be an acceptable outcome."

Great! I so loved being cannon fodder. Nice to know that if the Bigfeet said they'd accept peace, but only if they all got to take turns sodomizing me, that the Draculas would be all gung-ho for that plan.

"I would highly recommend," James continued, "that you all watch one another's backs continually and assume that anything that is said to you is of dubious intent."

"Not to be rude or anything, but why are you telling us this?" Tom asked. "I mean, aren't you up for membership to this group of backbiters?"

James arched an eyebrow. I knew I should've made Tom wait in the car.

"Nice knowing you, jackass," Sally whispered from the corner of her mouth.

However, rather than eviscerating Tom as a lesson to the rest of us – a deserved lesson, in all honesty – James instead shrugged and replied, "Fortunately for you all I haven't ... what's the phrase ... ah yes, drunken their Kool-Aid yet. Besides which, I have grown fond of Dr. Death here. Irrational of me, I know."

"Cool," I replied, trying to steer the conversation away from Tom, lest he say something stupid again. "It's good to know you'll have my back, too."

James looked me in the eye and gave an apologetic glance. "Alas, that may be a problem."

* * *

"Define problem," I said in a calm tone, despite a sinking feeling starting to permeate my gut.

"Normally I wouldn't discuss this with outsiders present," James began. "However, since it is painfully obvious that you tell your friends *everything* that goes on in the vampire community, I see no reason to play mum."

I gave him a sheepish grin back. I didn't look at Sally, but had little doubt of the eye-roll she was probably making.

"As I have said, there are other candidates being given consideration for ascension to the First Coven."

"I remember," I interrupted. "That's the reason why I'm conducting this crazy train. You can't run the show and keep watch over your own backside at the same time, right?"

"Exactly. Unfortunately, it's become even more complicated than that. I have since learned that my chief rival is a vampire named François. He and I have a bit of history with one another."

"So what's the deal with this guy?" asked Sally.

"The deal is: much like I currently hold jurisdiction over the covens of the Northeastern United States, François likewise holds a sizable area under his direct supervision. Shall I give you a hint as to where his power extends?"

There were knowing nods all around the room, except from Tom, who asked, "Okay, what's the hint?"

Ed let out a heavy sigh. "Where are we going, stupid?"

"Canada," Tom replied uncomprehendingly for a second before adding, "Oh, I get it now."

"I highly doubt that," Sally spat.

"It leaves me in a difficult position," James said, ignoring the exchange. "François neither requests nor wishes for my involvement in this summit. Truth be told, there is little love lost between us. As someone who has had firsthand involvement with the Alma, by rights I can participate regardless of François's wishes. However, I must be careful. One false move and the balance of power could tip in his direction. That would be bad."

"For you?" Ed asked.

"For *everyone*."

Tom said, "I don't see the big deal. Bill's told us about you. It doesn't sound like you have much to worry about from some French surrender monkey."

James once again raised an eyebrow. "Despite your somewhat unique way of putting it, you're actually far more apt than you realize."

"He is?" Ed and I blurted out in unison.

"Yes. You see, under different circumstances, there wouldn't be much question regarding inclusion into the First Coven. Usually the oldest and strongest are picked. It's tradition. François is by far the oldest of the hopefuls, besting even the Khan by a quarter century."

"Then why isn't he already one of them?" Ed asked.

"There are safeguards in place to deal with unusual circumstances. You," he said, turning toward Tom, "mentioned the overused joke regarding the French and surrender. Well, François went much further than that. During World War Two, he was an active member of Hitler's SS."

"Whoa!"

"Indeed. He is a nasty character even amongst our kind. Supposedly, he bought into their rhetoric quite fully. Not only did he join, but he revealed himself to their upper ranks."

"So he was punished?" Sally surmised.

"Not for that, no. He was too old to be reprimanded for such a thing. If that were all he did, this tale would have a much different ending. François didn't stop there, though. Whether deluded or mad for power, he decided to aid their scientists' efforts to create a master race. As such, he allowed them to experiment on vampire blood. Even for one of his age, such a crime is considered quite serious."

I could feel pinpricks of sweat break out on my forehead. If they found out what Dave and I were up to ... oh boy.

"So what happened?" Ed asked.

"Near the end of the war, one of the First perished at Nagasaki. François was all set to ascend to the ranks of our leadership when his actions were brought to light."

"And that's when the Draculas brought the hammer down?"

"Exactly. François was too old and had too many supporters to be outright killed. However, he was passed over for membership, allowing my sire, the Khan, to ascend. As further punishment, he was removed from Europe and given his current post."

"Makes sense," said Ed. "How much trouble could he cause in the frozen tundra?"

A thought hit me. "Just out of curiosity, did the person who exposed François happen to be nicknamed *the Wanderer?*"

James smiled. "Very astute, Dr. Death. I will admit a little bias in seeing my sire ascend. It didn't exactly hurt my standing amongst our kind."

"Hold on," Sally interrupted. "I'm not getting the politics at play here. If this François guy was punished, why is he up for consideration now?"

"It's quite simple. He has survived and managed to stay out of trouble. For all intents and purposes, his sentence has been served. Regardless, due to the severity of his crimes against our kind, the others are leery of automatically promoting him. Rather than judge by seniority alone, the remaining twelve have decided to pick the new member based on accomplishments. François has many, do not get me wrong, but he has to prove to the elders that he has learned his lesson. If he can do that, he may very well ascend to their ranks."

"And this peace conference would be a major feather in his cap," I said.

"Yes it would."

"Is it just me," Ed asked, "or does anyone else find it a bit suspicious that the Khan, the guy who bumped François, got killed and then suddenly a peace conference is happening in this dude's backyard?"

"Without hard evidence," James replied, his tone stern, "it would be considered highly insulting within the vampire community to insinuate such."

"Sorry, I didn't mean to..."

"However," James continued, "as you are not a member of the vampire community, you may insinuate as much as you please."

"So that's why you have to tread lightly," stated Sally. "If you say anything, you look like you're trying to set him up and then you'll lose."

"And a French neo-Nazi nutcase suddenly becomes one of the most powerful vampires on the planet," Tom added. My God, he really did want to get us all killed.

"More or less, yes on both counts."

I let out a sigh and replied, "So what you're saying is I'm on my own ... as usual."

"Hey, I'm going to be there, too," Tom protested.

"Yep," Sally said. "As usual, Bill, you're on your own."

Four-legged Vampire Slayer

IT WASN'T ALL bad. Colin eventually returned with our lunch. Watching him set up a table for us went a long way toward making me feel better although, if I had to guess, I wouldn't doubt my glass of blood also had a generous dollop of spittle in it. Oh, well, it was a small price to pay to watch that monkey dance.

James said he would be joining us up north, but he'd be arriving later than the other participants and staying mostly in the shadows. While I wasn't too keen on putting my neck on the line just so he could get himself a big fat promotion, he had always been cool with me. There was also the fact that he had saved my ass a few times. I owed the dude and I was not one to welch on my bets. Well, okay, maybe I was, but not when the person in question could rip my head off and shove it up my ass with little to no effort.

We finished up, said our goodbyes, and resumed our road trip of the damned. Of course, once we were piled back in the car and everyone had a chance to collect their thoughts, Tom started in again.

"It probably all doesn't matter anyway, since I'm going to turn into a fucking zombie."

"You're not going to turn into a zombie," snapped Ed from behind the wheel.

"Easy for you to say. You didn't get bitten by the disgusting undead. No offense, Bill."

"None taken," I replied from the back seat.

"It's not like he chomped off your fingers, asshole," Ed said, "You don't even have any bite marks, so stop whining."

"But I can feel it tingling."

"Psychosomatic," I replied.

"Am I the only one here who watches the movies?" he protested. "A zombie puts its teeth on you and you're doomed. It's only a matter of time before I start craving brains."

"That would be a step up, if you ask me," Sally commented from behind a copy of Cosmo.

"Sally, can you tell this idiot that he isn't going to turn into a zombie?"

"Fine. You aren't going to turn into a zombie, idiot."

"There, see..." I started to say.

"Not that I would know," she added.

"What do you mean?" Tom asked, wide-eyed.

I turned to her. "I thought you knew about zombies, Sally."

"Yes. I know that a bunch of them work in Boston. So do you, congratulations."

"Don't you know how they got there?"

"Nope."

"What about how they're made?"

"Nada on that, too."

"Why not?"

"Because," she said, throwing him a look of bored contempt, "it never occurred to me to give a shit ... although now that you mention it, I still don't."

* * *

The next few hours were long ones. As we drove north through Vermont, I plugged my 3G modem in and attempted to get a little work done on my laptop. Ed continued driving while Sally put on a pair of earbuds and proceeded to tune us all out. As for Tom, he continued whining from the front seat, a continual stream of bullshit along the lines of, "I can feel myself starting to decay." Forget the vampires in the backseat, considering how white Ed's knuckles were turning around the steering wheel. I had a feeling he was beginning to contemplate reaching over and shoving Tom out of the moving car. After a while, I doubted I would have tried to stop him.

Thanks to our stopover in Boston and then some traffic, we didn't near the border until after sundown. Sally indicated, though, that actually was perfect timing.

As we got in line for the border crossing, Ed asked, "So what exactly are we supposed to say once they ask to look in the trailer? That we're traveling Exxon salesmen?"

"They're not going to," she replied blithely. "Pull into lane five."

"Lane five is closed."

"Not for us it isn't. Pull in and flash the lights three times."

Ed shot us a dubious look via the rearview mirror. No doubt, he was thinking we were all about to enjoy a nice long strip search at the Canadian border. Regardless, he did as told. He pulled into the closed lane, enduring a few annoyed beeps from the other cars in line. He flashed the high beams – which weren't all that high in this clunker – and, sure enough, the light in the lane switched from red to green. That elicited a few more angry honks.

"Watch and learn," Sally said, rolling down the back window.

We pulled into the booth and she leaned out. I could see by her profile that she had blackened her eyes and brought her fangs out. The border guard leaned over and spoke to her.

"Your coven?"

"Village from New York," she replied.

"Purpose?"

"Business."

"What business?"

"First Coven business. Do you *really* want to ask more?"

The guard's eyes momentarily flashed black, revealing his undead nature, although whether out of shock or annoyance I wasn't sure. He quickly composed himself, though, and looked toward the front seat, where Tom and Ed sat. He took a quick sniff of the air. "Technically you're supposed to declare any food you bring across the border."

"They're just snacks for the road," Sally replied.

"Speaking of which," the guard turned his head toward the cars which had followed our lead into the lane, "it is almost dinner time. Carry on. May the First smile upon you." He gave us a sort of salute and waved us through.

"What was that about?" I asked once we had pulled away.

"There're a lot of ass kissers out in the field," she said dismissively.

"Did he mean what I think he meant?" asked Ed.

"About what?"

"About the cars behind us?"

"Probably," she said with a smile.

"Serves them right," Tom commented. "Line cutters are assholes."

* * *

We continued north. After another hour, I took a turn behind the wheel. That lasted all of fifteen minutes before my companions demanded I pull over. Tom then got in the driver's seat.

"What?" I demanded. "The speed limit said ninety."

"*Kilometers* an hour, shithead," he said. "Even I know that."

"Besides, you were driving like an ass," Ed added.

"Was not."

125

"You were weaving in and out of the lanes."

"It's been a while since I've last driven," I offered as way of excuse.

"And it's going to be a while before you drive again," Tom said. He then adjusted the rearview toward Sally. "How much farther until we stop, Ms. Daisy?"

One corner of Sally's mouth turned upwards at the joke, but she stopped short of a chuckle. "Keep going. We'll find a motel before dawn."

"All night?" Ed asked.

"Yes, all night," she replied. "This is a vampire mission, thus we're keeping vampire hours."

Tom sighed. "Ugh, I'm going to need a coffee stop. Maybe a few."

"Fine. Just pull in at the next Tim Hortons you see."

"Too late," I replied, looking out the window. "We just passed one."

"Yep, and now we're passing another," she said. Sure enough, she was right. "This is Canada. Trust me, they have one on *every* corner."

* * *

"I want the bed tomorrow," I complained, stepping out of the motel room.

"Sorry, Bill, but it doesn't work that way," Ed said. "Tom and I are the ones playing chauffeur. Ergo, you get the floor."

"Screw that," I protested. "Guest of honor at the peace conference standing here. I show up all disgruntled from sleep deprivation and the world could end. Do you really want that to happen?"

"If it means not having to listen to you whine like a bitch, than yes. I'm cool with it."

"Why do we have to share a room anyway?" Tom asked.

"Sally said the Draculas only budgeted for two."

"Do you believe her?"

"Not even for one goddamned second," I replied. "But all of the coven credit cards are in her name."

"I don't see why she gets one all to herself," Tom sniffed.

"Because I'm special," Sally said from right behind us, causing us to jump. She was good. Even I hadn't heard her exit her room.

"Yeah, you're special, all right," I groused, opening the tailgate on the Jeep. I pushed aside some of our bags to get to the cooler. It was packed with pints of blood. "Want one?" I asked her, grabbing one for myself.

"No, I'm good."

"What do you mean you're 'good?'" I asked, an edge creeping into my voice.

"Exactly that," she said with a sniff. "You can suck down the bottled stuff if you want, but I decided to try the local cuisine."

My roommates turned a shade paler at that. I rounded on her, though. "Did you ever think that maybe, just maybe, it might not be the best of ideas to leave a trail of bodies in our wake?"

She gave me an easy shrug in response. "Wouldn't be the first time." She started walking toward the car before turning to say, "Come on, night time's a burning. We have a long way to go ... unless you'd like to wait around for the Mounties to arrive."

Bitch!

* * *

That's pretty much how it was for the next two days as we made our way further north. Eventually, the towns became fewer and much farther in between. When not driving, Ed joined me in trying to stay as busy as possible. Unfortunately, cell service was starting to become spotty in the long stretches of ... well ... Canadian nothingness.

Tom, for his part, continued to push himself further up Sally's list of people to kill. Despite looking absolutely fine, he continued to whine about becoming one of the undead. When I pointed out that both Sally and I were amongst that number and neither of us (especially her) looked worse for wear, it only increased the whining. "Yeah, but you guys are vampires, the undead elite. I'm going to be a disgusting corpse, forever in search of brains."

"When you finally find some, I hope they stick," Sally replied.

"Personally," I said, "I think you should be more worried about your dick rotting off."

"Seriously, Bill," Ed asked. "Do you think Christy would even notice?"

"Nah, probably not," I replied, eliciting laughter.

"That's right, joke about it now," Tom said morosely. "Just don't go looking for any mercy once the zombie apocalypse starts."

* * *

Eventually, we were forced to start using our fuel surplus. We stopped along the side of the road at the northern tip of Saskatchewan – or whatever the fuck they called it – to refuel. It was about midnight, cold as fuck, and utterly desolate. While Tom and Ed went to grab some gas from the trailer, I got out to stretch.

"Don't wander off," Sally said from still inside the car. She was bundled up in a parka and looked like the world's most expensive Eskimo hooker.

"Yes, Mom," I replied. Her warning aside, I started to walk toward the tree line. It had been a couple of hours since our last stop and "little Dr. Death" felt the need for a piss break.

As I walked, I glanced up. It was truly marvelous how the night sky looked when there wasn't any city around to muck it up. Even had my vampire night vision not been up to snuff, the stars were bright enough to make things passable. At least out in the open they were.

I entered the tree line and the gloom settled around me. Even though my vampire eyes cut through the darkness, the density of the brush made it difficult to see more than a few feet in any direction.

Once I was out of sight of the car, I found a suitable looking tree and unzipped to do my business. Ah! Few things were as reinvigorating as a good piss after a long drive.

I was almost finished when a sound caught my attention. Thinking it was one of my roommates, I called out, "Go find your own garden, guys. This one is already watered."

There was no response, save the crunch of more foliage. My thoughts immediately turned to Sally. She had been in the car as long as the rest of us. Maybe she needed a "rest break," too. While the thought of her squatting amongst the trees was definitely humorous, I had no intention of getting caught with my dick hanging out. I'm not sure what comment she would have, but I'm certain it wouldn't be kind.

I quickly zipped up, and that's when I heard another crunch. Whereas before the sound was hard to pinpoint, this one was close enough for me to tell it was coming from the opposite direction of the car. Another crack. Closer, and it sounded big.

I reminded myself that was probably bullshit. It was absolutely quiet out there. In such solitude, a fox could step on a twig and it would sound like cannon fire. I was probably psyching myself out for nothing.

There came a snort from directly in front of where I stood. Brush obscured my vision, but I could make out a shape beyond it and it was bigger than me ... a lot bigger. Oh crap. I hadn't even considered that I might run into the Alma, Sasquatch, Grendel, or whatever the fuck they were called. What if they were making a preemptive strike to take me out? I wouldn't put it past the filthy, shit-flinging fuckers.

I began to back up. I had gotten a taste of what these guys could do when I was over in China. I wasn't about to underestimate them. The shape in the woods matched me step for step. I began to crouch down in a defensive stance – learned from countless hours of kung-fu movies – when it stepped from the brush and I found myself staring into two large, brown, and not overly intelligent eyes. A set of antlers nearly four feet wide sat atop a large head. A fucking moose.

I breathed a sigh of relief and chuckled as it just stood there, dumbly chewing its cud or whatever the fuck moose chew on. Damn. There I was, almost shitting myself, and for what, an oversized deer? On the upside, it was the first one I had ever seen outside of a zoo. Now that the scare was over, it was actually kind of cool.

Figuring a photo would make for a neat souvenir, I pulled my phone from my pocket, aimed the camera, and pushed the button. The flash went off, causing the moose to jump in surprise. It made an angry snort and then, without further warning, charged straight at me. Oh, fuck! Forget what I said about Bigfoot. Being trampled by the equivalent of a freight train on legs wasn't particularly high on my list. I turned and ran. Judging by the crashing sounds behind me, the moose was following.

Thank God vampires were fast. Used to be I was the fat kid in high school who came in dead last in every single track event. Nowadays, though, there wasn't an Olympic sprinter alive who could keep up with me once I got going.

There were just two problems. For starters, this wasn't ideal terrain for me to go all out in. Secondly, my pursuer had both the home field advantage as well as an extra set of legs. I had just burst from the tree line, I could see the car ahead, when this deficiency became painfully clear.

I was mowed over from behind. It felt like a bus plowed into me. I went down, but was that enough for my moosey friend? Of course not. I felt a pair of hooves slam into my back. The air was forced from my lungs and I was pretty sure I could feel some of my favorite body parts cracking. Then the fucker did it again. It was stomping the shit out of me.

I curled up into a fetal ball as it continued trying to turn me into a puddle of vampire mush. Talk about embarrassing. In the past few months, I had come out on top against two master vampires and a trio of vamp assassins. Hell, I had even managed to survive Gan. Yet there I was, getting my ass handed to me by an animal with less brains than my nut sack. What a way to go.

I was starting to get a bit woozy from the continued attack. I heard my roommates' voices yelling for me. Hey, there was hope. Ed had his shotgun with him, maybe he could use it to ... oh, hell, by that point, I'd have been happy if he had used it to end my misery.

I was just thinking how embarrassing the epitaph on my tombstone was going to be, when there came another loud cracking noise and suddenly the assault stopped. A scant second later, there was a heavy thud on the ground next to me.

"Bill!" came Tom's worried voice. "Are you okay?"

"No," I replied, still face down on the hard ground.

A strong hand grabbed me by the arm and hauled me to my feet. I got up, surprised to find I could still stand. Thank goodness for vampire healing. It was already starting to patch up the worst of my beating.

I turned to find Sally standing next to me, the look on her face conveying slightly less than worshipful awe.

"That was badass," said Ed, walking up to us.

"Thanks," I replied. "It's not every day one survives a..."

"Not you," he corrected. "*Her.*"

"Huh?"

"While you were getting stomped, she ran past us, jumped on its back, and snapped its neck like a twig."

"Really?"

"Yeah, dude," Tom confirmed. "It was pretty fucking awesome."

"I'd say that sums me up nicely," she replied with a smirk.

I tried to play it cool, not an easy thing to do when you're covered in hoof prints. "I'm sure I'd have eventually..." I stopped as she raised an eyebrow at me. "Okay, fine. Thank you for saving my ass ... *again.*"

She smiled, which would have been tolerable except that wasn't the end of it from her. "It's turning into a regular habit, isn't it?" she asked, still grinning. "Although I have to admit, Bill, saving you from elder vampires is one thing, but an oversized cow? That's just embarrassing."

"It's a little more than an oversized..."

"It would be a damn shame if the folks waiting for us were to learn of this incident. The fabled Freewill, laid low by Bullwinkle."

I let out a sigh. This wasn't the first time I'd been blackmailed by Sally and probably wouldn't be the last. Sensing where this was going, I held up a hand. "Alfonzo can stay."

Her grin widened. "Great! You know, you really should let him give you a pedicure."

"Let's not push it."

"Your loss," she said dismissively, and then to Tom and Ed added, "Okay, meatsacks, show's over. Get that car refueled before I do the same thing to both of you."

My roommates both gave her a mock salute, then turned back to the car. After a few steps, Ed whispered to Tom, "She is so fucking hot."

My vampire ears easily picked it up, so I had no doubt Sally's had, too. The smug look on her face as we walked back confirmed it.

Along the way, I casually asked, "Have you ever tried moose blood?"

"Don't make me smack you."

Are We There Yet?

THE LAST HUNDRED miles took far longer than I would've liked. Thank God for four-wheel drive. Had the weather been any worse, I don't doubt we'd have had to find a village or traveling hockey team and trade in our wheels for a couple of dog teams.

At long last, though, we were driving through dense, dark woods, following a trail just barely wide enough for our vehicle, when the portable GPS finally told us we were close. It was about time. We had maybe one more tank of gas left in the trailer and our supplies were beginning to run low. I had been starting to wonder whether we should have drained that moose just in case. Another couple of days and I would've probably needed to start keeping an eye on Sally around my roommates. On the upside, Tom's constant zombie moaning and groaning had lessened considerably (albeit not entirely). So there was that. What can I say? I'm a "glass is half full" kind of guy.

Having arrived at the coordinates we'd been given, we all kept lookout through the windows for ... something.

"Jeez," I complained, "this is only a conference to decide the fate of the world. You'd think they'd at least have signs telling us where to park. Are you sure we're in the right spot?"

Ed turned and gave me his best withering glance. "We're in the middle of fucking nowhere. How the hell am I supposed to know if it's the *right* middle of fucking nowhere?"

"Don't get testy..." I started to say in a condescending voice, but immediately had to change my tone. "HOLY SHIT! STOP!"

He turned back to the trail and immediately hit the brakes. The car skidded to a halt just inches from the thing in front of us. It had appeared from out of nowhere.

"Is that what I think it is?" Tom asked excitedly.

From my vantage point in the backseat, I could only see the front of the car and a pair of hairy, heavily muscled legs standing in front of it.

"Well..." The question was answered as the owner of said legs bent down and peered into the windshield. The face that looked in at us pulled back its lips in a snarl. It was one hell of an ugly motherfucker. Take the creature from Harry and the Hendersons and then beat it with the ugly stick for an hour or two and you might be in the ballpark.

Sally, Ed, and I just stared at the gruesome visage in front of us. Tom, ignoring the basic tenets of sanity, lifted his cell phone and immediately started snapping pictures. The creature noticed him and looked none too happy about it.

I reached forward and smacked him upside the head. "What the fuck are you doing?"

"What?" he complained. "We just proved Bigfoot is real. These babies are going up on Facebook."

"Are you absolutely sure I can't kill him?" Sally asked.

I glared at her out of the corner of my eye. "Let me get back to you on that."

"*Get out.*"

"Huh?" I asked. "What, Ed?"

"That wasn't me."

"Then who..."

"*GET OUT ... NOW!*"

"Did that thing just talk?" Tom asked, echoing what the rest of us were thinking.

I turned to Sally. "They can speak?"

"How would I know?" she snapped back. "Do I look like Jane Goodall?"

"Weren't you supposed to ask Boston about these things?"

"How the hell would I even know to ask? The only apes I've ever seen are in the Bronx Zoo. Last time I was there, they didn't talk back."

"*NOW!*" the ugly face before us demanded again. This time, it brought one cantaloupe sized fist down onto the hood of the car. The entire vehicle shook from the impact.

I looked each of my companions in the eye. "I think he wants us to get out." Never let it be said I didn't have a grasp of the obvious.

* * *

"Uh, Ed, what do you think you're doing?"

"Not being stupid," he replied, stepping out of the car, shotgun in hand.

"Your funeral," I commented, likewise getting out.

Once we were all standing again, we got a true sense of scale for the creature looming before us. At over eight feet in height, it dwarfed my roommates and me. Sally was just barely over five-feet in heels, so I could only imagine that she felt like a Munchkin, assuming they had strip clubs in Oz.

The thing – Sasquatch, I guess – looked us all over. Upon seeing the gun in Ed's hands, it threw back its head and let loose what I think was a laugh. It was hard to say. Imagine trying to chortle while gargling gravel and you'd get an idea of what it sounded like.

While it did that, I felt Sally give my shoulder a nudge. "What?" I asked.

"Introduce us."

"Why me?"

"Because you're the star and we're just your entourage."

Some days I really hated being the vampire *chosen one*. Okay, if I was going to do this, I might as well try and act tough. Sure, the thing in front of me looked like the Hulk wearing a fur coat, but if so, I was

Captain Marvel ... yeah right! Even the most deluded sections of my subconscious weren't buying that one.

I took a deep breath, immediately regretting it. Now that we were out in the air, the smell of this thing hit me like a baseball bat. I doubted there was enough Febreze in the world to fix this guy's odor. How the fuck was I supposed to function with this stench assaulting my nostrils?

No. That was a defeatist attitude. I could handle this. I was a gamer, dammit. Ogres were bigger and nastier than this pile of shit and I had faced down dozens of them over the years. Sure, it was only on paper and with a twenty-sider, but same general principle ... right?

I stepped past my friends and looked up into the face of the brute. I smiled, fangs extended for a little bit of extra menace. "I am Bill, Freewill of the vampire nation. I believe you've been expecting me." Hmm, maybe I should have gone with Dr. Death instead ... way more badass sounding.

The creature stopped laughing and looked down upon me. I had a distinct feeling that the next words to come out of its mouth would be, "BIGFOOT SMASH!" followed by a pummeling that would make me look back longingly at my encounter with the moose.

For some reason, this thought struck me as funny. I don't know why. A painful demise wasn't something I normally considered to be chuckle-worthy. Either the surrealness of the whole situation was getting to me or I was losing my mind. Regardless, I felt the corners of my mouth curling up into a smirk.

Oh, well, in for a penny, I thought. I locked eyes with the creature – which I seemed to recall learning from National Geographic wasn't a particularly smart thing to do with gorillas – and continued speaking. "These are my companions. We're here to meet with your leaders."

"*And why should Grulg take you?*"

Grulg? What the hell's a grulg? Oh, fuck this! While I tried to avoid getting beaten to a pulp as much as possible, I was also of the mindset that if I had an ass-kicking coming, then I might as well deserve it. "Listen, Kong, I don't have time for your shit. I have business to discuss with your *betters*." At that, I heard multiple gasps of breath from behind me. Gotta love everyone's confidence in my abilities. Of course, how would I even know that this guy wasn't the one in charge? Oh, boy.

There was a tense moment of silence, during which I saw Ed raise his gun. Maybe we'd all get lucky and he'd just blow my head off rather than let me stick my foot any further into my mouth. Finally, though, the smelly-ass Sasquatch in front of me simply nodded his head.

"*You follow Grulg.*"

"Uh..."

"Oh, Jesus Christ," Sally spat. "*He's* Grulg, you fucking idiot."

"*Your concubine speaks with much fire*," Grulg said in a tone that sort of sounded bemused, although maybe it was just me.

"Concu..."

"Yes, Grulg," I interrupted before Sally's temper could undo what I had gotten lucky with. "That's how I like her ... *sassy*."

If Sally could have killed me with her mind, I'm sure she would have. However, Grulg merely gave what I took to be a shrug. "*Follow.*"

"What about our stuff, Grulg?"

"*Leave here. We bring Freewill's belongings later.*"

I exchanged glances with the members of my party that didn't want to kill me.

"Valet parking, Bigfoot style," Tom commented.

That made about as much sense as anything at the moment, so I turned back to Grulg and said, "Lead the way."

* * *

Had I known I was signing up for a wilderness trek, I would've invested in a pair of hiking boots. Grulg led us onward for what felt like at least a mile. I think we followed a mostly straight path, but the truth was, I had absolutely no idea. He could've been walking us in circles for all I knew.

Finally, he stopped next to a tree. It was large and old, and pretty much looked like every other tree we had passed, with the exception that it was covered in an intricate series of scratches about seven feet above the ground.

Before I could question what he was doing, Grulg lifted his head and let out a piercing howl. I have to admit, it was kind of freaky. I had seen enough movies to wonder if he was now giving the signal for an ambush. Any second now, a bunch of his hairy buddies would come rushing out to tear us apart ... not that Grulg looked like he needed the help.

No attack came, though. A few moments passed and then answering howls rang out in the night, but they sounded far away.

Once silence had again descended, I let my curiosity get the better of me. "Grulg, what was that for?"

"*Respect.*"

"For?"

"*For the dead. We enter Woods of Mourning now.*"

I heard a quiet titter behind me. "Excuse me for a moment, Grulg." I turned around. Unsurprisingly, Tom was standing there, a guilty look on his face. "Read my lips, *shut ... the ... fuck ... up*," I said as softly as I could and still be heard.

He continued grinning, but made a lip zipping motion. I sighed and turned back to our hairy escort. "Sorry, please go on."

Grulg gave me what looked to be a dubious glance. "*Many ancestors buried here. Mighty warriors. Their spirits rejoin the land. They all around us, listening.*"

"Mighty warriors?"

"*Yes. Many laid low by the T'lunta,*" he spat that last word. I had a sneaking suspicion what he meant by it, but I asked anyway. "*Undead,*" he answered with a snarl before once more turning to lead the way.

Oh, yeah, this was gonna go well.

As Primitive as Can Be

GRADUALLY WE BEGAN to see signs of life again. It started slowly – a shadow here and there, usually off in the distance. However, soon we started seeing more of Grulg's kind. Some paid us no heed. Others bared their teeth at us as we passed. Yeah, there was definitely no love lost with these guys. It was a pretty safe bet that the Twilight movies weren't a favorite at whatever passed for the local cinema.

Finally, we came to what I guess would be considered a village of sorts. I could see a series of huts spread out amongst the trees. Though crude, they were obviously built for the size of the normal inhabitants. They looked practically cavernous compared to my freshman dorm room. Unfortunately, they looked about as neat, too. They were mainly covered in leaves and moss, held together by what I really hoped was mud. In short, they were shit-holes. Guess I should've expected that we wouldn't exactly be staying at a Marriott.

As we entered the encampment, a voice called from off to our right. "I will take them from here, Grulg.

They are under my protection now." It sounded familiar. I glanced over in that direction and my eyes immediately went wide.

"Oh, shit," I muttered. Looking back toward the rest of my group, I saw that Sally's face held the same surprised expression. No wonder, in her case. The vampire who strode toward us was the very same who had casually lopped off her hand with a silver blade just a few months back. Judging by how he looked, he was every bit as well armed now as he had been back then.

"Nergui?" I asked disbelievingly as he came toward us.

He ignored me, instead walking up to the monster that had been our guide and locking eyes with it. A tense moment passed. Eventually Grulg bared his lips in a snarl and broke the gaze. He turned back to us.

"*You with own now. We begin tomorrow,*" he said, then turned to wander off, leaving me to wonder if I had a tomorrow. The guy he was leaving me with had every reason, and ability, too, I might add, to make sure I didn't live to see another nightfall.

As Nergui turned to us, I could almost feel Sally tensing behind me. Sure, we bickered like five year olds most of the time, but when push came to shove, I knew she would be there to back me up.

However, Nergui surprised me by bowing. "Greetings once more, Freewill," he said upon straightening. "It is an honor to serve you."

"Really?" I asked, completely taken off guard.

"Why would it not be?"

"For starters," Sally said, stepping up next to me, "you did kind of try to kill us both not too long ago."

"Yes. As I explained at the time to the Freewill, it was a misunderstanding."

"A misunder..."

I interrupted Sally before she could blow her top. "Yes, an unfortunate misunderstanding for *all* of us. Still, considering what happened afterwards..."

He nodded, and a brief flash of emotion shone in his eyes before his normal stoic demeanor took hold again. "Yes, the loss of my master is regrettable. If I could, I would gladly have given my life to save his."

"From what I've heard, it wouldn't have done any good."

"Yes, so too has the Wanderer told me. Perhaps, perhaps not. I cannot change what has occurred. I can only serve my new mistress with as much honor as my worthless self can manage."

"New mistress?" asked Sally.

"Gan," I answered.

"Yes, the princess. She now commands what was once her father's."

A horrible thought hit me. Oh, crap. The last thing I needed was that psycho little hellion coming after me like a hungry piranha. "Nergui, is Gan here?"

"No," he replied. If he noticed the sigh of relief I let out, he didn't acknowledge it. "My people need a leader now, and her place is there."

"So then why are you here?"

"When she learned of this gathering, she dispatched me immediately. The princess is aware of the possibility of treachery against her beloved" *ARGH!* "She has entrusted me to watch over you."

Despite her wariness of Nergui, Sally couldn't help but comment. "Aww, that's so cute. Gan is trying to protect her Billy-willy."

"Aren't there some lumberjacks around for you to proposition?" I spat out of the corner of my mouth.

Oddly enough, despite Gan's twisted reasons for sending him, a small part of me suddenly felt a bit better. I knew that Nergui's attack against us hadn't been personal. He was a product of his culture. He lived to serve. It just so happened that, at the time, the fuckhead he served had wanted me dead. Now the situation had changed. Though I had absolutely zero intention of returning Gan's affections, her interest in me had provided perhaps the first glimmer of hope I had seen so far this trip. Sally, Ed, and Tom were great, don't get me wrong. I'd trust them – well, Tom and Ed, anyway – with my life. Nergui, however, was three and a half centuries old. He could mop the floor with all four of us and still have plenty left in him to go a full twelve rounds.

"What about my friends?" I asked.

"The princess's orders were specifically for you, Freewill."

"Surprise, surprise," I muttered under my breath. "Perhaps," I said a bit louder, "but my friends are vital to my success in this endeavor." *Sorta.* "Their safety is my safety. I will accept your protection, but only if you agree to watch over them as well."

Nergui appeared to consider this for a moment. Finally, he nodded. "If your cattle and the wh..."

"Don't even think of *saying* it," Sally snarled.

I had to cover my mouth to keep from laughing out loud. *Whore* had been Gan's pet name for her.

"My apologies," Nergui said evenly. "If the Freewill's *advisors* are important to him, then so, too, shall they be to me. I offer my protection to you all."

"Did he just call us 'cattle?'" Tom whispered to me, followed by, "Oof!" as Ed elbowed him in the gut.

"We gladly accept," Ed replied.

"Awesome!" I cried. "I'm happy to hear I don't need eyes in the back of my head in case these monkeys decide to try anything."

"Be wary, Freewill," Nergui said in a low voice. "Treachery need not come only from the Alma."

"What do you mean?"

He took a quick look around and then simply replied, "It is not my place to speak further of this. I simply offer you the warning." With that, he turned and beckoned us to follow.

Great, as if I already didn't have enough to worry about.

* * *

Nergui led us across the crude village. As we walked, I could hear a bit of a commotion going on up ahead. One didn't need vampire ears to be able to pinpoint it. Standing in front of one of the huts was a tall, well-built man. He had dark hair and a pencil-thin mustache of the variety that had gone out of style with Prohibition. He was busy bitching out some others who stood around him. My command of languages other than English was somewhat less than stellar. However, I had seen enough Pink Panther movies to surmise he was speaking French.

"Let me guess," I said out of the corner of my mouth to Sally, "François?"

Suddenly his head swiveled in our direction. Oh, shit! I kept forgetting that older vampires likewise had superior senses. Since this guy was supposedly even older than the Khan, he could probably hear a fly taking a shit from a hundred yards away. He wasn't the most physically imposing creature I had ever seen, especially not with nine-foot apes wandering about, but there was something cold in his eyes. He hadn't even blackened them, yet they held a kind of darkness to them. I'm no psychoanalyst, but if I had to guess, I'd say Frenchy here was psychotically insane. How wonderful.

I didn't need to worry about Sally. She had more experience dealing with asshole elder vamps than I did. Instead, I threw a quick warning glance back to my roommates, Tom in particular.

As we approached, all of the vampires in front of the hut stopped what they were doing and turned toward us. Most of them were focused on me, which was fine. There were a few salacious glances toward Sally, no doubt undressing her with their eyes – also not a big surprise. What worried me, though, were a few nakedly hungry looks toward my roommates. That would need to be nipped in the bud. My friends were strictly off the menu.

Nergui stopped in front of the group and gave a curt bow, noticeably shallower than the one he'd given me. He then stepped to the side. "The Freewill and his advisors," he announced.

The one I presumed to be François stepped forward. This close, his presence had a decisively slimy feel to it. However, whereas Colin's greasiness radiated a massive inclination toward ass-kissing, this guy was far more ominous. I got a bad feeling in my gut that this was the sort of jerk who would literally do anything, no matter how depraved, to further his own agenda. Of course, that could all be bullshit and maybe I was just psyching myself out due to James's warning. Whatever the case, though, I had learned in the past year that a little paranoia wasn't exactly a bad thing.

He looked me over, shot Sally a sideways glance, and then gave a sniff, barely laying his eyes on my friends, as if they were beneath his contempt. "You are the Freewill?" he asked with just the slightest accent.

Since I had been raised to always put my best foot forward (*as Dad always said, let the other person be the asshole first*), I held out my hand and said, "Yep. I'm Bill."

He gave me back a sour smile as if I had just used that hand to wipe my ass. Ah yes, douchebag status confirmed.

"There are a few things you should be aware of," he said, ignoring my greeting. "Regardless of what you have been told, I do not care if you are the Freewill or the second coming of Moloch himself." Huh? "I rule here. Respect that and we will get along fine. Cross me, and I will stake you with your own spine."

Before I could even think about it, my mouth opened on its own. What can I say? My subconscious had an automatic defense mechanism against shit heads. "Eh."

"Excuse me?"

"You forgot the 'eh.' You said you rule here. Well, this is Canada. You should at least speak like a Canadian, *eh*?"

His eyes narrowed at me, but I continued drawing upon my lexicon of Canadian language, learned from multiple viewings of *South Park*. "We traveled all this way, eh. I mean, it's aboot time we arrived, eh. You'd think you hosers would be a little more hospitable, eh."

François's eyes darkened and I could see his fangs extend. Fortunately, two things stopped him from outright killing me right there. First, Nergui's hand flew to the hilt of one of his daggers. Secondly, flunkeys or not, a few of the vampires behind him chuckled at what I said.

He quickly turned his head and hissed at his lackeys. Silence resumed amongst them. Regardless, the moment was over. That was good. Considering François's age, I wasn't entirely sure even Nergui would be able to stop him. When François turned back to me, his eyes had resumed their normal color. To my surprise, a smile actually crossed his lips. That didn't exactly inspire confidence.

"Your reputation for having a quick, if somewhat crude, tongue is well earned," he said.

"What can I say? I like to make an impression."

"I can see that."

"This playful banter aside, I'm not here to make waves. I just want to do my part so we can hash out a truce with the Sasquatches. Once that's done, I'll go home and you can keep Canada."

"Yes, of course. We're all on the same side here," he replied in a tone that implied we weren't even remotely on the same team. God, what a creep. Even if James hadn't warned me about him, this guy would still be giving me serious douche-chills.

"Cool," I said. "Is Alex here yet? I'm thinking we should all sit down and discuss things. I want to make sure I know what to say and such."

"Alex?" he replied, raising one eyebrow.

"Yeah, the Drac ... err First Coven's special envoy."

"Interesting. I know of no Alex."

Hmm, that was odd. Still, this guy looked like the sort of stuck up prick that would barely notice anyone beneath him in rank.

"Okay then, what about the negotiators that were being sent in? Maybe Alex will check in with us later."

François's face took on a look of concern ... mostly. I'm not great at reading subtle expressions, but I'd have sworn his eyes were twinkling with laughter. "Haven't you heard?"

"Heard what?"

"The team that the First were sending never arrived. They simply vanished ... without a trace."

"Vanished?"

"Yes, it's quite tragic," he replied without a trace of remorse. "I suspect these beasts had something to do with it. Alas, I have no proof of their treachery."

"Then we're postponing the summit, right?" Sally asked from beside me. I was amazed. It was the longest I could remember her keeping her mouth shut.

"Child," François replied, putting extra emphasis on the word as if to imply *stupid child*. "This gathering is far too important to put off. Every day that goes by is another step closer to war. And it's not just us. The other delegations have all arrived. It would be an insult to cry foul and tell them to all go home. Believe me, there are beings present that are not to be trifled with."

Emboldened, either by the fact that I was still alive or by Sally, Ed spoke up. "So what is Bill supposed to do? He's not exactly a UN diplomat." When I turned to give him a glare, he replied, "Let's not fool ourselves here. You're not."

That's the thing with Ed. He continually ticks me off by being right. I sighed and turned back to François. "He has a point."

François seemed not to hear me, though. "You allow your food to speak for you? How quaint. I see James is letting discipline slip down in the States."

Now it was my turn to flash my fangs, albeit I imagine I was just a wee bit less impressive than he was. I may be strong by human standards, but to an elder vampire, I was probably about as frightening as a kitten. Still, I couldn't let him get away with treating my friends like an appetizer. "They're my friends, not my food. They're here to assist me and thus are under my protection."

"*Your* protection?"

"Yes. You've heard stories about Freewills, right? Care to see if any of them are true?" I won't lie. I was really hoping the answer was a resounding no.

"Silly boy. You'll find I've faced down far scarier things than *you*." His eyes momentarily flashed black then back to normal in no more than a blink of his eyes. Damn, I couldn't do it that fast. I actually had to concentrate to get that stuff to work. "Regardless, now is not the time. Alas, your *advisors* are moot here."

"How so?"

"Have you not been listening, boy? The First's diplomats are missing. The peace meeting must go on. Thus, as leader of this region, I have hand-picked my own team of negotiators to fill in for the First's."

"Your own team?"

"Yes. Entirely loyal to the vampire cause, I assure you." Yeah, right. "Your mission has not changed. They will hash out a treaty with the Sasquatch leader. You will go along with their suggestions as the figurehead you are. Were those not your orders?"

"Well..."

"As I thought. You will perform your duty as instructed. Once finished, you will leave my domain. *IS THAT CLEAR*?!"

I'm not sure if he meant to send that last part as a compulsion or if it just came out that way because he was pissed, but damn! The force of it sent me flying back into my roommates. Judging by the boneless way they collapsed under me, I assumed they had gotten a pretty hefty taste of it as well. Compulsion worked on humans, too, just not quite as well. It took a vampire of considerable strength to pull it off. Unfortunately, François definitely had a checkmark in that column.

As for me, my head was ringing. It felt like someone had beaten me senseless with the world's largest tuning fork. Even so, I was by far the least worse off. I saw Sally, Nergui, and all of François's vampires standing there with the same vacant, glazed look in their eyes. Each and every one of them was under François's spell. I was going to need a bottle of aspirin when this was over, but at least I was immune to his control.

I turned to my human friends. Both of them appeared to be knocked for a loop. Their eyes were rolled up into their heads, showing only the whites, but they were still breathing. Fortunately, within a couple of seconds, they both started blinking and groaning. They were coming out of it, hopefully with not much worse than a headache to show for their troubles. That was good because I didn't have time to tend to them. Vampires like François – which covered just about *all* vampires – were predators, and the last thing you wanted to do with any predator was show them weakness.

I stood up and casually dusted myself off, acting as if my head didn't feel like it had the New York Philharmonic playing in it. I walked up to Sally and quickly snapped my fingers in front of her face. No response. I turned back to François, smiling, and said, "Cute. But it doesn't work on me."

"I see that," he replied and then matched my grin with his own. "But it is painfully obvious to me that though I can't control you, I can hurt you." Oh, crap. Guess I needed to work on my poker face a bit.

I stood my ground and said nothing. François stepped forward, into my personal space, and continued. "Shall we try it again? I for one would be curious to see how many times it would take for me to liquefy your brain."

I was about to make a witty comment regarding his breath, but just then, the barrel of Ed's shotgun was laid over my shoulder, pointing directly at François's face.

"I don't know, but I'm willing to bet it would take just one bullet to knock that smile off *your* face, permanently," Ed's said from behind me. "And in case you're wondering, yes, they're silver."

I shifted my eyes to the gun barrel and then back to François, grinning even wider. "What's that you were saying about my advisors being moot?"

The smile dropped from his face and, apparently with it, his concentration. The vampires behind him began shaking their heads. I had little doubt Sally and Nergui were doing the same.

I could see out of the corner of my eye that we were attracting a small crowd of onlookers. Vampires and Bigfeet alike were starting to gather round, not to mention some other ... err ... *things* that I couldn't readily identify. Guess they weren't shitting me about there being other guests in attendance.

François was a cock-meat sandwich of the highest order, but he wasn't stupid. Whatever his agenda, he knew that the bullshit we were engaged in now wasn't going to help our position. Almost as if reading my mind, he suddenly started laughing. It almost sounded genuine.

"Well played, Freewill," he sang out in an exaggerated voice that everyone in the immediate vicinity picked up. "An excellent demonstration! With you at our vanguard, our enemies will think twice before trying anything."

I shifted my eyes around. Sure enough, the tension seemed to have gone out of the onlookers. Thinking this was a staged display, they quickly began to go back about their business.

"Slick," I whispered.

"Necessary," he replied, equally quiet. "Letting your oafishness give our enemies the advantage would be to all of our detriment."

"Are we done here?" I asked, at which point Ed finally lowered the gun. I was glad he hadn't been given reason to use it. Regardless of whether it would have done much to François, I didn't relish the thought of a twelve gauge shotgun going off right next to my head.

"For now," François said with a sneer. "The sun will be up soon. I will return tomorrow night for the opening talks."

"You're not staying here?"

"In this place?" he asked, the snooty Frenchman in him coming to the forefront. "I think not. Enjoy the accommodations." He spun on his heel, nodded to his companions, and together they began to walk away.

He turned his head back to us only once. "Remember my warning: you are a figurehead here. Nothing more." Before I could reply with anything snippy, he and his contingent strode away. That was fine with me. It gave me a chance to let out a large breath that felt like I had been holding for hours.

"Now there goes a true asshole," Tom commented, still looking a little dazed from the compulsion. "And no, I don't care if he can hear me."

"For once we're in agreement," Sally added. She then turned to me, and said in as serious of a tone as I'd ever seen her use, "We need to watch out for him, Bill. He's bad business. I don't think I've ever met another vamp as strong as he is."

"You don't need to tell me that. I'm not so sure his little threat about turning my head to mush would've been entirely idle. Thanks for the save, Ed. I owe you."

"Just one?" he replied with a coy grin.

We all chuckled. "Nice bluff about the silver bullets, by the way."

"It wasn't a bluff."

"No? Where the hell did you get silver bullets?"

"I gave them to him," Sally said. "Since that business a few months back," she gestured slightly in Nergui's direction, "I figured it was a good idea for you guys to have a little extra backup. So I had them specially made."

"You did?"

"Yeah, I gave them to Ed the last time we met for coffee."

"Sally gives the sweetest gifts," he said with an exaggerated grin.

"Hold it!" I interrupted. "What do you mean, 'last time you met for coffee?' I thought you guys only went on one date?"

"Well, technically, coffee isn't a date," Sally said with a huffy sniff.

"And neither of you told me *why?*"

"Well you kinda freaked out the last time," Ed replied.

"Oh, please," Sally said. "I don't require that you keep me up to date on *your* social life, nonexistent as it is."

"She has a point, dude," Ed added.

As we continued bickering, a small part of my brain couldn't help but notice that there we were, the fate of the world in the balance, and the most important thing on any of our minds was who was secretly dating whom – like some fucked up episode of Friends.

Goddamn, the world was so screwed.

Strangers in the Night

THE SHOW OVER – for now at least – Nergui showed us to our hut. Yes, they intended for us all to share one. None of us was particularly happy with that, especially Sally. When she found out, she opened her handbag and produced a very familiar looking weapon: a Desert Eagle. Technically speaking, vampires – at least those in New York City – weren't supposed to be armed. It was a clause in some back-alley agreement we have with the NYPD. Sally, however, wasn't one to let silly things like rules get in her way.

Brandishing the handgun, which looked comically large in her petite hands, she said, "I don't give warning shots, just in case anyone gets any funny ideas about stealing my virtue."

"Stealing? I was pretty sure I could buy it with a fiver." Before she could comment, or shoot me in the leg for my troubles, I added, "Jeez, am I the only one here who isn't packing?"

"I'm with you, Bill," Tom replied. "I'm more of a lover than a fighter anyway. Speaking of which..." He started waving toward the left. I looked in that direction and saw a small group of white-robed figures. One of them looked toward us, raised her hand in return, and then came running in our direction – Christy.

"When did you get in, babe?" Tom asked once she had reached us.

"A few days ago. We've been communing since then," she said, whatever the fuck that meant.

"Nice outfit," he said in a suggestive tone.

"We really should be sky-clad, but it's kind of cold."

"Ooh, sky-clad. I could get into that. Maybe we should do some communing of our own."

"Getting ready to puke here," Sally snapped.

Christy and Tom, being the overly cute couple that they were – she was cute and the addition of Tom made them a couple – ignored her.

"Sorry, hon. Remember the rules. No fraternizing."

"That sucks," he replied in a sulking tone.

"Although," she added, "If we just happen to bump into each other out in the woods..."

"*Really* getting ready to puke now!" Sally snarled. To add further emphasis to her annoyance, she cocked the hammer on her weapon with an audible click.

Not wanting to get in the middle of a gun and magic battle, I went over to Tom and grabbed him by the shoulder. "He'll meet you later, Christy. We gotta go get settled now."

If she was irked by this, she didn't show it. Instead, she blew her boyfriend a kiss, then turned to rejoin her own group.

160

I let out a sigh. Things were going to be difficult enough without having to worry about Tom sneaking off for a magical booty call.

* * *

The hut smelled every bit as bad as it looked, which is to say it smelled about as good as the creatures playing host to this clusterfuck. Comfort-wise, well I had passed out on my fair share of floors during my college years, so I could deal. Sally was another matter entirely. She convinced Nergui to find her something with which to partition off a little area for herself. After he had done so, she gave us one last warning to stay out of her side. Well, okay, she actually gave Tom and me a warning. Ed was conspicuously absent from her venom. Before he got any bright ideas, though, I gave him a quick, "That means you, too."

Our bags were unceremoniously deposited outside our dwelling a short while later. Thus armed with at least clean underwear, we all decided to turn in. The next day was most likely going to be a long one.

"Goodnight, boys," Sally said from behind the divider.

"Are you naked over there?" I called back, eliciting chuckles from my roommates. Her response was another dry click of a hammer being cocked. "Err, I meant, goodnight, Sally."

With that, we all settled in for some much needed rest. Uncomfortable though it might have been, I didn't have much problem sacking out. I had long gotten used to the idea of getting some shuteye in the face of impending doom. Thus I slept fairly well ... at least, until I was awoken by something covering my mouth.

* * *

I jolted awake and instinctively raised my hands to pry off whoever was attacking me, but they had me in a grip that felt like iron.

"Be quiet," a voice whispered.

I blinked and saw a hooded figure standing over me. I couldn't tell who it was. The darkness wasn't the issue, though. Unfortunately, I wasn't wearing my glasses, so the person's face was little more than a blurry blob. Damn the peculiarities of vampire healing. I could grow back lost limbs, but God forbid I got twenty-twenty vision out of the deal.

I stopped struggling and nodded. The figure released me and I quickly reached over and put on my glasses. "Alex?"

"Obviously. Now please keep your voice down."

I sat up and immediately felt a little woozy. I sniffed the air. "What..."

"A special incense to keep your friends asleep. Do not worry, it wears off quickly."

"Why?"

"The less who know I am here, the better. Regardless, we must still keep our voices down. I do not think I need remind you that we are surrounded by creatures with exceptionally acute senses."

The whole secrecy thing was feeling a little fishy to me. I eyed him warily as I said, "I spoke with both

James and François. Neither of them had any idea who you are."

"That is because neither of them has been told about my identity."

"Because?"

"Because the First do not answer to them. I am their agent and theirs alone. If they wish others to know about me, then they do. If not, then others remain ignorant of the fact."

"But I thought you were their special envoy for these talks," I replied somewhat accusingly.

"I was."

"Was?"

"Yes. I was to officially arrive with the rest of my party."

"The rest ... you mean the group that disappeared?"

"The same. Some of the finest negotiators this planet has ever seen, each one hand selected by the First."

"Didn't they have bodyguards?"

"Of course. Do not be foolish. Yet, escorted or not, the fact remains that they have met with an unforeseen fate."

"What do you think happened?"

"I am not sure we shall ever know. However, the details are not important. What matters is that they are in all likelihood dead."

"And François has conveniently replaced them with his own people," I added.

"You are not nearly old enough to be accusing a vampire of François's status of anything. You should know that before you open your mouth in front of other company. I will allow, though, that it is suspiciously convenient."

"Okay, but you're still alive. Why don't you introduce yourself and confront him?"

"I am afraid things are not that simple. We cannot afford to let any schisms show within our ranks. The Grendel would pounce upon that. Besides, I do not know what François is planning. If he is indeed behind the missing ambassadors, then I have little doubt he will attempt to have me meet the same fate."

"That sounds a lot like an accusation right there. I thought you said we weren't allowed to do that."

"No," he replied with a grin. "I said that *you* were not."

"Fine, so what then? Am I supposed to just go into this meeting and smile like an idiot while his team sells us out?"

"I very much doubt they will be *selling us out*. Then again, I also do not doubt that whatever is bargained will be in François's favor."

"Not to mention, if his own people successfully hash out a peace plan, then that pretty much guarantees him a lock on joining the Drac ... First Coven."

Alex's weird eyes opened wide in surprise. "You know about that?"

"I hear things," I coyly replied.

"So it would seem. You are correct in your assumption. At the moment, François is holding a very strong hand."

"So what do we do?"

"We stack the deck, of course. We put a joker in amongst the aces."

"Why do I have a feeling that I'm the joker here?"

"My apologies, Freewill, but it is a necessary evil."

"I seem to get that a lot," I said with a sigh. Oh well, it's not as if I expected this to be easy. "What do you need me to do?"

"You are officially no longer a figurehead."

"Huh?"

"You heard me. Your mission was to go along with whatever our people negotiated, but that was before any peculiarities transpired. As an agent of the First, I wield their authority. Thus, within these proceedings, by way of your status as Freewill, I say you are now officially in charge."

"Oh, no..."

"Oh, yes. As representative of the vampire nation, and chosen of the First Coven, your word is law."

"But..."

"Thus, if you choose to go against the recommendations of François's advisory staff, they will be powerless to contradict you."

"But I'm not a diplomat," I protested. "Hell, I can't even get them to drop the charges when I'm a day late returning a DVD."

"No, you are not. Based on what I have heard, though, along with my own observations, you are a decent person – a rarity in our world. Do you wish to see war erupt between our two species?"

"No. I mean, Tom might get a kick out of it, but..."

"And do you wish for our kind to be subjugated beneath the heels of the Grendel?"

"Nope, that would suck."

"There you have it. Aim for the first, but ensure you do not give up enough for the second."

"But what about..."

Again, he interrupted me. It was starting to get annoying. "I will be working from the shadows to uncover the treachery that has been wrought. If it can be brought to light, it could count toward a great deal. Rest assured, though, I will also be providing you assistance as I am able. Should you go too far astray, I shall be there to guide you back. You also have another you can call upon."

"Please don't say 'Sally.'"

"Sadly, I get the impression that diplomacy is not her best facet. No, I am speaking of another. The one called the Wanderer is expected to be in attendance for tomorrow's opening remarks."

"James? That's cool and all, but he told me he can't get involved."

"Correct. He cannot take a direct stance in these matters. However, he can openly advise you where I cannot. His wisdom is sound, make use of it."

"But..."

"But *nothing*! I speak for the First. I have conveyed to you their will. To do otherwise would..."

Now it was my turn to interrupt. "Let me guess: to do otherwise would end badly for me. Trust me, I know the drill."

Continental Breakfast

I SHOULD'VE ASKED Alex to leave me some of that special incense. Hell, I should've packed a few joints and a couple of liters of Jack for this goddamned trip. It's a good thing my vampire body required less rest, because I sure as shit didn't get back to sleep after Alex slipped away into the ... well, day I guess. Hope he was wearing some sunscreen under that hood.

As for me, I put my arms behind my head and just lay there staring at the ceiling, listening to my hut-mates breathing (*damn, who'd a guessed it ... Sally snored*), and wondering if any passing asteroids might be so kind as to come crashing in right about now. A fight to the death I could handle, but this night would bring a different kind of battle: a battle of wits. I usually didn't consider myself a slouch in that department, but then again, my usual war of words heavily consisted of suggesting the other party suck my dick. I'm pretty sure they didn't say that too often at the U.N.

* * *

At around four PM Eastern Time – aka whatever the fuck that translated to in Canada – my companions started to stir. I found it a bit odd, all of them waking at the same time, but then I remembered Alex's special incense. Guess it was wearing off.

I sat up and looked toward the flap of our hut. From the look of things, the sun was setting. Thank God the higher-ups scheduled this when the nights were longer. If they had gotten it wrong, we would have been royally fucked. It's hard for vampires to negotiate for peace when the day is all of one hour long.

"Rise and shine, you lazy fucks," I announced loud enough so that my roommates and Sally alike would hear it.

"Uh, I feel like shit," Tom complained.

"Me too," Ed agreed.

"Yeah, well, that's not too surprising," I explained. "You see, we had a visitor..."

"Don't say another fucking word!" Sally commanded, bursting through the ratty curtain dividing our space. All three of us were momentarily stunned into silence, not so much by her yelling – that was normal – but by the fact that she was wearing a short night shirt and not much else.

Seeing us all gaping, she gave a quick sigh and said, "Take a picture, it lasts longer. Seriously, Bill, not a word."

She quickly went back to her side. Tom, Ed, and I exchanged confused looks all the while. A few moments later, she reappeared, hastily dressed. She grabbed her coat, then stalked outside.

"What the hell was that about?" I asked.

"Maybe she's on the rag," Tom offered.

"Do vampires even do that?" Ed asked.

"How should I know? Hell, I kinda assumed Sally was permanently PMSing."

Her odd behavior aside, I quickly brought my friends up to speed on our visitor from the night before.

"So let me get this straight," Ed said, once I had finished my tale, "This Alex dude wants you to take charge of things, even if it means purposely pissing off the guy who knocked us all for a loop with just three words yesterday. Am I correct?"

"More or less."

"It's a good thing we came along then."

"Why? Don't you get it? We thought we were maybe wading into shit before. Instead we're dog-paddling way over our head now."

"Exactly," Ed replied. "Everyone else *thinks* Tom and I are your advisors. It looks like we really are now. Well, I am, anyway."

"What about me?" Tom whined.

"Sorry, but even you have to admit your snap judgments sort of suck."

Tom looked a bit crestfallen, but he also didn't protest either. I clapped him on the shoulder and said, "Don't worry. I still need you there, even if it's just to back me up."

"I'm here for you, man."

"Cool. Although I hate to say it, but you'll probably need to ix-nay any forest-side trysts with Christy for now."

"No prob, dude. Besides, it's pretty fucking cold up here. My dick would probably freeze and snap off anyway."

"Thanks for the visual," I replied, right before we all started laughing.

* * *

After getting dressed, I walked out of the tent in search of Sally. I didn't have to go far. She was standing a couple dozen yards away, facing the tree line.

"See any knotholes that you feel like competing against?" I asked, walking up behind her. Her response was a quick lifting of her arm followed by her middle finger. Ignoring it, I continued, "So what the hell was that back there?"

"Protection," she replied.

"For what?"

"Not for what, for who," she stated. "For *you* and those two fleshbags you keep around."

"I'm not following."

"Color me surprised," she mumbled before answering. "I'm here for you – well, okay, I wouldn't be if you hadn't dragged me into it – but since you did, I'm here for you. We are partners, for better or worse. But there's a problem."

"What?"

"François."

"I kinda figured he wasn't exactly on our side."

"No, you don't understand. You remember yesterday, that compulsion he threw out?"

I nodded.

"The guy didn't look like he put any effort into it, yet he bowled over both my and Nergui's defenses like they were tissue paper."

"You're afraid he might compel you to act against me?"

"Maybe, but if he did, you'd probably see it coming. A compulsion like that wouldn't be too subtle. What I'm more afraid of is him using me as a spy of sorts."

"Wouldn't I notice that, too?"

"Not if he just compelled me to spill my guts and tell him everything I know."

"Ah, I see. That's why you stormed off a few minutes ago."

"Yes. For right now at least, the less I know that isn't common knowledge, the better off you'll be."

I was touched. Sometimes it was easy to forget that in some ways Sally and I were every bit as close as I was with my roommates. She could be a caustic, bitter, sarcastic bitch, but when the shit hit the fan, it was always awesome to see her step up to the plate. Sure, some of it wasn't exactly altruism on her part. We both knew that she benefited greatly ever since I took over our coven. Still, she could easily have brokered favor with a higher ranking vampire like François by fucking me over. That she was going out of her way to do otherwise was pretty goddamned cool. If I didn't think I would get decked for the effort, I'd give her a big ole hug.

"Fair enough," I replied. "Just know one thing."

"I'm already aware of how tight my ass is."

"Besides that. If I start doing anything stupid in there today..."

She raised an amused brow.

"You know what I mean. If I do anything that seems to go against François's rules, just know that I'm doing it on purpose and not just to piss him off. Well okay, part of it might be to piss him off. I might as well enjoy myself while I can."

"Thanks for the heads up. Oh, and if I start getting that glazed look in my eye, you have permission to slap me back to reality."

"Really?"

"Yes. Just don't screw it up. Hit me when I'm not compelled and I'll strangle you with your own intestines."

Somehow, I suspected she wasn't quite joking on that last one.

* * *

My conversation with Sally quickly fell back into our usual bickering. She was in the middle of complaining about the lack of facilities (it was a fair bet that within a few days we were all going to be smelling about as good as our hosts), when suddenly a shadow fell upon where we stood. We both looked up to find a Bigfoot towering over us. As with the other day, it had seemingly appeared out of nowhere. How could something so big be so quiet?

"*We begin soon,*" the creature grumbled. "*Eat now.*"

"Eat?"

"*I leave food for you in hut.*"

"Thank you, Grulg," Sally replied. At that, he grunted and lumbered off.

"That was Grulg?" I asked once he was out of earshot.

"Yeah."

"How could you tell?"

"By scent. Each of these creatures has a *unique* odor," she replied, wrinkling her nose.

"Oh. I didn't think of that. Been mostly breathing through my mouth since we got here."

"You, a mouth breather? What a surprise. Oh, well, let's go see what our gracious hosts have left us for breakfast."

* * *

We returned to find Tom and Ed sitting at a makeshift table, several crude bowls in front of them. Ed was busy duct-taping a heavy duty flashlight to the barrel of his gun, while Tom was eating.

"I hear room service has been by," I said, walking over to them.

"Yep," Ed replied, finishing up his makeshift night scope. "Sadly, the breakfast buffet in this place leaves a lot to be desired."

"The nuts and berries aren't so bad," Tom commented, scooping up a handful. "Tastes kind of like trail mix."

"I guess so," agreed Ed, "but just between us, I'm going to pass on the grubs." He indicated a bowl in the middle, within which several fat bugs squirmed.

"Nice," I said. "Nuts and berries it is, then." I reached for the bowl in front of Tom, but he slapped my hand.

"Not so fast. *This* sumptuous feast is *ours*. They dropped *your* meal off in the corner there, or can't you smell it?"

I turned, taking a breath through my nose and then it hit me. "What the fuck is that?"

"Offhand," said Sally, stepping over to the source of the stench. "I'd say it was the world's unluckiest hiker."

Sure enough, she was right. Lying in the corner was a human corpse, all decked out in cold weather camping gear. Judging by the condition of the body, though, it wasn't exactly a fresh kill.

"Been dead for about three weeks, I'd say," she continued, adding a sarcastic edge to her voice. "So nice of the Bigfeet to stock their larders for us ahead of time."

"I'll pass," I said, stepping over to our cooler. I opened it and noticed just two pints of blood left. "Want one?"

"You keep it. You like the bottled stuff more anyway."

"You're not going to actually chew into that, are you?"

"Don't be stupid. I'm going to go out and wander around a bit. I'm willing to bet some of the other vamps here have brought along something a little fresher."

"Going to bat your eyelashes and convince them to invite you over?"

"Hell yeah," she said, walking toward the entrance. "If you've got it, use it ... and I've definitely got it." With that, she stepped back outside.

She had a point. I knew Sally was over fifty years old, although she was pretty coy about her exact age. Even immortal chicks were apparently weird about those things. Still, regardless of how old she was, I was fairly sure it had been a long time since she had stepped into a bar and paid for her own drinks. I had little doubt when next we met that she'd show up well fed.

So that left me. I downed one of the pints immediately. That would leave me good to go for the time being. Unfortunately, these talks were bound to last a while. No point in suffering needlessly. I looked again in the cooler and found a near-empty Snapple bottle. I finished off the contents, then poured the remaining blood into it. Remembering one of the primary lessons learned in college, I pulled out a pen and wrote "BILL" on the label. I didn't know if Sasquatches drank blood or not, but better safe than having one of those ugly motherfuckers backwash in my drink. That would just be nasty.

That done, I cleaned myself up as best as I could. When finished, I asked my friends, "So what do you think? Do I look ready to save the world?"

"If they're judging you by appearance," Ed replied. "Then I'd say the world is fucked."

"Works for me. If I'm going to plunge this planet into a global genocide, I'd prefer to be comfortable doing so."

Satan's Snack Cart

SALLY RETURNED A short while later looking fully sated. The smirk on her face was all the answer I needed as to whether she had been successful in her attempt to scam a meal.

It wasn't too much longer before a familiar guttural voice called to us from outside, *"Time is now."*

Thus summoned, we stepped outside as a group. Standing there, as expected, was Grulg. Next to him was Nergui, decked out in full battle armor, looking like some sort of samurai.

He gave us a quick glance as we approached, and I could have sworn something like disapproval passed through his eyes. My companions and I looked more likely to be the victims in a Friday the 13th movie than important delegates.

Grulg grunted and turned, beckoning us to follow. As we started walking, I asked Nergui, "You expecting trouble?"

"I am always open to the possibility, but, this," he indicated his attire, "is tradition. As your guard, I am expected to be armed for conflict. So too will my counterparts be. It is purely *ceremonial*."

Something about his tone told me that was only partially true. I could only imagine that, amongst supernatural beings with a penchant for violence, purely ceremonial could quickly turn into practical. Just great. Armor was fine for him, but if the talks suddenly devolved into combat, my winter coat wouldn't do much to protect me.

I knew Sally had her hand cannon, and Ed was openly carrying his shotgun. Tom was likewise unarmed, but I had little doubt his hell-spawn of a girlfriend would come to his aid if trouble broke out. That left me. Wonderful.

Perhaps sensing my discomfort, Nergui matched my stride. I felt him press something into my hand. I looked down, it was a sheathed dagger.

"Purely ceremonial?" I asked.

"Of course," he replied, quickening his pace again.

* * *

"Suddenly, I feel underdressed," I said, seeing the large group of vampires standing before us on the trail.

Whereas we looked as if we had just spent the night camping, which wasn't too far from the truth, the party before us could have stepped out of a Hollywood soiree. Crisp suits, overcoats, and polished shoes stood out like a sore thumb amongst the foliage. Great, now I had to worry about the undead fashion police, too.

I frowned as I recognized François and his contingent amongst the group. However, that frown almost immediately turned upside down as I finally saw a familiar face: James. He stood a bit away from François, their mutual dislike apparent even from a distance. Several vampires stood with him, a few of whom I vaguely recognized. He had brought some of his own people with him. Smart. Even smarter, I didn't see Colin amongst them. Good. I had enough to worry about without that little ass kisser trying to gum up the works.

Once we had arrived at the group, Grulg announced, "*Grulg go ahead. T'lunta enter when announced. No sooner.*" He gave us all a look of barely contained anger and walked ahead. Mind you, almost every look I'd seen him give us had practically screamed that, so maybe I was reading too much into it.

Fortunately, lest I start to miss them, François was right there to continue giving me hostile glances. He gave my friends and me the once over. "So much for us putting our best foot forward," he said with a haughty sniff.

"Sorry. I didn't get the memo about the dress code," I replied.

"I can assure you, it's quite all right," said James, walking up to all of us. "I sincerely doubt the Alma will be all too concerned with our attire."

"They will not be the only ones present," spat François, oozing disgust.

"I am well aware," James answered evenly. "Just as I am aware that the majority of the witnesses present will not exactly be mavens of fashion themselves. I for one will be quite surprised if the au naturale participants do not outnumber the clothed ones by a good many."

François narrowed his eyes, but James held his gaze. Though François was older, the two were of the same rank. In the vampire community, to show any sign of weakness was to acknowledge the other as your better. Fuck that! Hell, I was little more than a piece of shit compared to either of them, and I wasn't about to acknowledge some French Nazi dickweasel as my superior.

Finally, François turned to me, a sneer on his face. "It ultimately doesn't matter. Just do your job, Freewill. Sit at the head of the table, nod when you are supposed to, and let those far more qualified set the terms for this treaty."

"Right-o, chief," I said glibly, eliciting a chuckle from both my roommates.

He gave each of us a glare that said he would have gladly gutted us, and then turned on his heel. His lackeys ... err, negotiators immediately fell into step and began following him.

Once he left, the tension eased considerably. James walked over and gave Nergui a hearty clap on the shoulder. "It is good to see you again, my friend."

Nergui nodded. "Her highness sends her regards, Wanderer."

James must have noticed me wince a little, because he smiled before addressing me. "Welcome, Dr. Death. I am happy to see you made it. I'm told that others were not so fortunate."

"Yep," I acknowledged. "While still others seem to have benefited from that misfortune."

The smile dropped off his face and he got serious. "Yes, a most disturbing turn of events. I shall be monitoring things quite closely from my place on the sidelines. If François's men do anything to jeopardize the peace process, whether purposely or through their own ignorance, I will be forced to become more involved."

"Isn't that dangerous for you?"

"Yes, but I place the good of the whole before my well-being. For now, though, I will trust François's people to uphold the will of the First. However, should that change..."

"I have it covered," I said.

A look of something close to panic came over James's face. "No! Your duties have already been set in this matter. Do not overstep your authority. It would be unwise."

I gave Tom and Ed a quick glance. I opened my mouth to mention how there had been a change of plans, but then remembered Sally's warning. I'd have to bring James up to speed when she wasn't around. For now, I simply nodded.

"Good," he replied. "To do otherwise could be disastrous."

* * *

"There shouldn't be too much to worry about today, regardless," said James as we walked along the forest trail. "I expect little more than introductions, some posturing, and a setting of the ground rules. Even François's men should be able to handle that."

"Sounds pretty easy..."

"There is one issue of concern, though," he said.

"Just one?"

"A rather important one," he stressed. "You have no doubt noticed Grulg speaking in English, correct?"

"Kind of hard to miss."

"That is one concession they were willing to make for your benefit. You should know, though, that the Alma's natural language is quite different than ours. Not all of their words translate well."

"Okay and..."

"And, I cannot stress this enough, you must be utterly respectful to them, especially their leader, regardless of what they say."

I gave James a grin back. "Relax. We've all heard Grulg speak. I can handle a little broken English. Hell, I hear worse at some of the Chinese restaurants back home."

"I'm not talking about a little..." but I didn't hear the rest.

We stepped from the trail into a large clearing and well ... holy shit!

* * *

So maybe "clearing" wasn't the right word for it. Hell, I don't know what was. All I know is that despite being a vampire for nearly a year and having seen sights that would cause ordinary folks to piss themselves, I wasn't even remotely prepared for this.

"James Cameron, eat your heart out," Ed whispered from behind me. Sure enough, what was before us looked more like a scene from some summer blockbuster than anything else.

The trail sloped downward in front of us, into what appeared to be a shallow valley. The entire place was lit with dozens of torches. The sides had been carved into levels not dissimilar to stadium seating. Within each level, downed trees and rocky outcroppings acted as seats. That wasn't the extent of the weirdness, though.

It was the myriad creatures taking up the seats that threatened to blow my mind completely. A quick glance back showed the same wide-eyed look on my friends' faces. Hell, even Sally seemed in awe. Only Nergui, James, and James's contingent appeared to be taking it all in stride.

For a moment, I just stood there gawking. It was like the greatest effects people in Hollywood had gotten together and decided to have a kegger. Beings – for that's the best word I have for them – of all shapes and sizes stood, sat, and in some cases floated in the vast space before me.

It was only after a few moments that another bit of strangeness occurred to me. Though I could see several of them ... err talking, I guess, there wasn't any sound. Mouths opened and closed, flanges gestured, *things* rippled. We should've heard the commotion from a mile off, yet there was nothing but the silence of the forest around us.

I turned and looked at James quizzically. Whatever warnings he had been imparting to me were gone. In their place was a wide grin. "Courtesy of our magic wielding guests." He raised his hand and pointed. A short way off from us, standing at the top of the rise, a white robed figure – one of the witches from Christy's group – stood with her arms in the air, a purple glow enveloping her. Turning, I scanned the area and noticed three more beings, none of them human like the first. They were standing symmetrically to each other at opposite ends of the open area. All had the same glow about them.

"Look closer," James said.

I did, and for the first time noticed that the air in front of me had a slight shimmering quality to it.

"It's a fucking force field," Tom gasped.

"Not quite, but close," James replied. "After you."

I stepped forward, the shimmer becoming more pronounced. I looked back, shrugged, and stepped through. In for a penny...

There was a momentary tingling, and then suddenly the voices, hoots, hollers, and murmurings of the creatures filled my ears. Within the space of a second, things went from being a library to a high school auditorium.

I voiced my amazement, but I'm pretty sure nobody heard me over the cacophony of sound.

* * *

Stepping forward, I got a better look at the bottom of the valley. It was roughly the size of a basketball

184

court, oval in shape, and set apart from the ... err ... bleachers, for lack of a better term. A small platoon of Sasquatches stood at the perimeter of this space. Their purpose was pretty obvious: security. I found myself wondering whether I had stepped into a peace conference or a rock concert.

What stood in the center of the clearing, though, was no stage. At first glance, it appeared to be a large, rough-hewn table. As I got closer I could see that it looked organic, as if it were some weird conference table/tree hybrid. I had once run a druid in a D&D campaign, and supposedly they had all sorts of organically grown furniture like this. But to actually see it for real, whoa! It wasn't the prettiest thing in the universe, but I had little doubt it would be far sturdier than anything one could buy at Office Depot. Stumps surrounded the table, no doubt meant to be chairs for the participants of the talks. I immediately found myself wishing I had brought a pillow. Damn if they didn't look like ass-crackers to me.

Standing at the bottom of the aisle before us, looking quite impatient, were Grulg, François, and François's minions.

I turned to my friends, shrugged, and started forward.

I took one step, and that's when I heard Tom's voice from behind me. "Bill, watch out!"

* * *

An undulating ... *mass*, I guess, lurched out of the crowd toward me. It moved, much more quickly than its mucus-like body would suggest it was capable, to a spot directly in front of me. I stopped dead in my tracks, not wanting to see if the movie *The Blob* was based on reality or not. I stood facing it, wide-eyed. In turn, it made bizarre gibbering noises at me and began quivering its body. Within seconds, the noises became more urgent-sounding. I raised my hands in a questioning gesture and took a step back. It followed. Oh crap.

Instinctively – probably stupidly too – I drew Nergui's dagger and brought it up. The blob lunged forward and engulfed my hand. Gross! When I pulled it back out the dagger was gone. That wasn't exactly promising.

Almost immediately, Ed was by my side, shotgun raised. "Back off, slime mold," he snarled.

Fortunately, before the situation could further escalate, James stepped in front of us. He approached the thing and began making what sounded like slurping noises. Ewww! I hoped he wasn't planning on tasting that thing.

Whatever it was he *said* seemed to do the trick, though. After a second or two, the blob monster moved back into the crowd.

"Thanks for the save," Ed said, lowering the gun. "Not sure this would have worked against it."

"It wouldn't have," James replied. "However, it's a good thing you didn't fire. Things are tense enough without us starting things off by shooting a food merchant."

"What?!" I exclaimed.

"He was just trying to sell you some refreshments."

"Oh," I replied lamely. "Well, what about my dagger?"

"He thought you were offering him payment."

"But..."

"All things considered, I think it best to let him keep it as a tip."

I didn't argue the point. Our close call with Hell's hotdog vendor over, we walked down to join the others. Most of them were trying, poorly at that, to hide smirks. Even François's face held a bit of a grin, albeit it wasn't a kind one. Apparently, he enjoyed seeing me act like an ass. Well if he loved that, I could only imagine how much he was going to love me overruling his lackeys if the situation called for it.

But that would be for later. For now, the ceremonies were about to begin.

What's in a Name?

AS ONE, THE Sasquatches standing at the edge of the arena – I couldn't help but think it more resembled a coliseum than meeting hall – raised their heads and let loose with an ear-splitting screech. Fuck me! It sounded like someone had stuck a fork into the ass of every single monkey at the Bronx Zoo. It definitely got everyone's attention, though. Within seconds, the various noises coming from the crowd ended. All eyes were on the center.

"Okay, that was inter..." but I was interrupted before I could finish.

There came the crack of thunder – odd, considering the forecast called for clear skies – and suddenly a bolt of green lightning descended from the heavens, striking the conference ... err ... tree dead center. Rather than blowing it to smithereens, as lightning is wont to do, there was a blinding flash. When it cleared, the table was still intact and everything was as it had been ... oh, except that a glowing green ball of energy now floated above it.

"What the fuck?" my roommates and I sputtered in unison.

"WELCOME!" a booming voice sounded. It was loud, completely drowning out everything else. As it faded, though, I noticed something odd. There was no echo and my ears weren't ringing either. I was just beginning to wonder about that when I heard Ed from behind me.

"Was that in my mind?"

Holy shit! He was right. Whatever the fuck had just said hi to us had done so psychically.

"WE, THE GATHERED, ARE HERE TO BEAR WITNESS..." the voice began. It was hard to concentrate with it pounding away like a bass beat on my frontal lobe. I turned to James and managed to ask, "What the hell is that?"

He turned his attention away from the orb, and replied, "Neutral third party."

Oh, of course.

"...HAVE BEEN ACCUSED OF BREACHING THE TERMS SET FORTH IN THE HUMBABA ACCORD OF THE YEAR..."

Blah blah blah. Christ, supernatural ball of light or not, this thing sounded like my sophomore year history teacher.

"...RITUAL COMBAT WILL THEN ENSUE..."

Whoa. Hold on a second. What was that about ritual combat? God, I really needed to pay attention to these stupid monologues. I tried sending out a quick request with my own mind. *Would you mind repeating that please?* Unfortunately, the voice kept droning on. I guess it was set to send, not receive. Fucking asshole ghost orb.

"...HAND IN MARRIAGE FOR THE TRADITIONAL EXCHANGE OF..."

What? Goddammit! I was doing it again. Why couldn't they print this shit out in advance so guys like me could read it in peace at our own leisure? It's not like...

"...LED BY THE ONE CLAIMING TO BE THE REBORN FREEWILL."

Half the crowd erupted into what sounded like cheers. Freewill? Wait, that's me. I didn't realize I was so popular. Guess Alex was right about us having our supporters to...

"Go."

"Huh?"

"That's your cue," James said from behind me. "Go out and meet the other delegation."

"Oh, okay," I replied, really wishing I had paid better attention.

"Good luck," he said, sounding as if he truly wished he believed it. Talk about making a guy feel confident about himself. "And remember what I said."

"No, prob," I replied, walking forward, having no idea what I was supposed to remember.

I turned to find my friends following me. I looked at them quickly, each in turn.

"You did get all of that, right?" Sally asked.

I blinked stupidly back at her, but then replied, "Of course."

My group passed François, and his team of negotiators fell in step behind me as well. Guess things were about to start. I just wished I knew exactly what that entailed.

* * *

I reached the conference table, then turned to François's group. "Where should I sit?"

Apparently, these guys were all relatives of Sally's. They gave me an almost synchronized eye-roll. Finally, one of them, a prissily dressed vampire with salt and pepper hair, replied in a heavy French accent, "At ze' head of ze' table, but not now. We must greet our ... 'ow do you say ... counterparts." He pointed one well-manicured finger to a spot near the middle of the table. So that's where I walked, the others once again in tow.

As I did, the glowing ball of doom continued to drone on. I likewise continued ignoring it until I noticed that all of the Sasquatches in the valley had once again started hooting. Guess their big cheese was finally making an appearance. I looked to the far end and saw their contingent getting ready to step out. All of them were impressive looking, for disgustingly dirty apes at least, but the one in the lead looked like he had stepped straight out of a horror movie.

Nearly ten feet tall, he made Grulg look puny in comparison. Fangs, longer and thicker than mine, protruded from his lips. Strapped across his chest, like a primitive bandolier, were several skulls: some human, some ... well, who the fuck knows? All I knew was that if someone handed this guy a bowcaster he'd look like Chewbacca's bigger, uglier cousin.

Well, Alex had told me that the guy in charge of this place had won out over his rivals. I could see why. I was just starting to think that this monster would stand a chance of winning favorable terms on intimidation alone, when our moderator spoke again and completely trashed that idea for me.

"...THEY ARE REPRESENTED BY THE MIGHTY LEADER OF THE NORTHERN TRIBES, TURD."

Did he just say...? Nah. I turned back to my group. François's asshole buddies were all standing there stoic and straight-faced. Tom and Ed had the same questioning look as I, both of them straining to keep grins off their faces.

Sally took one look at me and mouthed what looked like, "Grow up." I was almost tempted to heed her advice when every Sasquatch in the area began to chant, "*Turd, Turd, Turd, Turd...*"

That did it. I could feel a smirk coming over my face and there was nothing I could do to stop it. I realized what James had been trying to warn me about, but it was too late. Some things just cannot be prepared for.

I turned and scanned the crowd. I saw James, François, and their various minions seated near the front row. Upon seeing my grin, James dropped his face into his hands. Gotta love his confidence. Well okay, it was probably deserved. I mean c'mon, the guy's name was Turd, for Christ's sake.

So Turd (*oh, God, that just kept getting funnier*) and his small group strode forward. With their size, they were upon us within seconds. He walked straight up to me, and I made the mistake of looking forward and not up. Due to his size, I found myself eye level with his Sasquatch-sized junk. I could sense the Bigfoot chieftain glowering down at me, but it didn't matter. What I found far more menacing was Turd's dick, which was just about a foot away from slapping the shit out of me.

"You finally get to live out your fantasy, Bill," Tom said, snickering softly.

It was quickly followed by Sally hissing, "Shut up!"

"THE LEADERS OF EACH PARTY WILL NOW GREET EACH OTHER."

Greet? Oh, crap. I was suddenly hit with an image of me reaching out and giving Turd's wang a friendly shake hello. I could feel the grin beginning to win out over my control. Fuck me! I was gonna plunge us into global Armageddon in the first minute alone.

"*Freewill*," came a voice from above. I looked up to see Turd's snarling mouth speaking. "*You are different than I imagined.*" I'm sure this last part was meant to be ambiguous, but the tone of his voice definitely implied a heavy insult. He needn't have bothered. For starters, I've been dissed by the best. Hell, I dealt with Sally on a daily basis. Secondly, the breath that wafted down at me was insult enough. Motherfucker! These guys might've hated civilization, but at least we understood the concept of mouthwash.

"*I look forward to challenging you,*" he finished.

Why did that sound like a threat? Probably because it was. Oh, well, fuck this shit. Alex told me I was in charge, so I might as well set the tone for things.

There was a pause, so I assumed it was my turn. I looked up and locked eyes with the big monkey. There was a grin of sorts (*I guess*) on his face. He knew how big and nasty he looked. The giant fuckhead probably thought I was too scared to speak. Well, he might've been right had his name not been Turd and had his dick not been swinging right in front of my face. Those two things combined activated my automatic asshole defenses.

"Oh, mighty Turd," I said, letting the grin win out. "I pay you great respect. I have seen much in my time, but know that you are the largest and most impressive turd I have ever witnessed."

A series of choking coughs broke out behind me. I knew that one would get Tom and Ed going. Amusingly enough, judging by what I heard, Sally was having a hard time keeping it together as well.

"In fact," I continued, "I would say, you are perhaps the greatest turd of them all."

A look of shock came over Turd's face. I was pretty sure I was about to get pummeled. Guess I laid it on a little too thick.

However, he surprised me. "*You pay great honor to Turd, Freewill,*" he replied solemnly, almost sounding I dare say *embarrassed* by his earlier insults. "*Turd will remember this.*"

I tried to keep it together. All in all not a bad outcome, considering I had just called him a gigantic pile of shit. Gotta love those language barriers.

* * *

The formalities over, we seated ourselves. Turd and I wound up at the head of our respective ends. Once we were seated, Nergui took a place behind my chair, whereas a Sasquatch, nearly as large and ugly as Turd, stood behind him – a massive club in one hand. Damn, I wouldn't want to get smashed with that thing.

I couldn't help but notice the discrepancies between us. There sat Turd, stupid name aside, looking every bit the warrior chieftain. Contrast this to me: a dumpy guy, just shy of six feet tall, wearing glasses, a ratty old winter coat and, oh yeah, a Snapple bottle half-filled with blood sitting in front of me. I could've probably been called a lot of things right then and there, but I doubted impressive was one of them. Hell, whereas Turd's bodyguard looked like he was there for show alone, I probably looked like I would hide behind Nergui at the first sign of trouble – which wasn't too far from the truth.

* * *

Fortunately, I needn't have worried myself, at least not for that first session. James was right. It was all administrative bullshit, several hours of it: what was to be discussed, what was not to be discussed, things that were off limits for negotiation, what data would be admissible, blah blah blah. After a while, I zoned out and let François's lackeys handle the details.

I wasn't alone in this either. Sally leaned back and actually began filing her nails. Ed nodded off, not being entirely used to keeping the hours of the undead. As for Tom, he kept making goo-goo eyes out to the audience. I didn't bother to look, but it was a fair bet he had found where Christy was seated.

Looking across the table, it was obvious even Turd was bored. He had one massive elbow propped on the table and was using that hand to support his ugly head. He definitely seemed the type who would favor all-out conflict over what was transpiring – hashing out a truce for what might be days on end. That made me curious. I had no idea of the inner workings of Sasquatch society, but there had to be at least some faction that wanted peace, otherwise we wouldn't be here. Of course, it was also possible that they weighed their chances in an all-out war and decided that they weren't very good.

Ugh! I shook my head to clear it. I'm no strategist. Hell, two Sundays ago, I couldn't even lead my party on a successful raid of an Orc fortress without getting spotted by every single sentry they had. It was probably best to leave such musings to those in a position, and with more of a mindset, to care.

My mind had just started to wander again when I was jolted back to reality by a commotion from the other contingent. One of the Bigfoot negotiators had stood up and was pounding loudly on the table.

"*No! We end this now!*" he yowled. End what now? I found myself kind of wishing I had been paying attention.

Almost instantly, all eyes were on him, including Turd's. I was curious to see what would happen. Would Turd reel in his dog or let things devolve? However, he just sat there with a contemplative (for a ten foot ape, anyway) look on his face as the other creature continued with its tirade.

"*Rise, my brothers! Rise and let us kill the T'lunta!*" He slammed both fists upon the table, then reared up and began beating his chest – ooh, Tarzan eat your heart out. "*No peace! NO PEA...*" He was cut off mid-rant.

A bolt of energy shot out of the orb still hovering over the table. There was a flash and when it cleared, nothing was left of the offending ape except a smelly pile of ash and some burnt hair.

"YOU ARE OUT OF ORDER," the phantom orb calmly said.

Holy shit! Most moderators will just beat a gavel. Whatever this thing was, it was a wee bit more effective. Fucking wonderful. Now not only did I have to worry about being clubbed to death by Turd's massive beef stick, but if I got up to protest it, I could get phasered by V'Ger here.

Even worse, the crowd went nuts over it, and I'm not just talking about our supporters either – not that I could tell them apart. I was right about this being an arena, and the crowd was apparently thirsty for blood.

Looks of shock went up and down my end of the table. They were mirrored on the other side, but there was quite a bit of anger there as well. Turd, however, was surprisingly calm. He simply nodded once and then went back to being bored. Suddenly, I was sure he had planned it. The motherfucker wanted to know what the boundaries were and what would happen if they were crossed. Goddamn! Turd was a real shit.

When You Gotta Go

FORTUNATELY, THAT WAS the end of the excitement, for the time being anyway. A replacement was called in to take the seat of the Bigfoot who was *out of order* then the negotiators tried to get back on track. It was obvious, though, that everyone – at least everyone not named Turd – was still rattled. After another hour, the moderator called for a recess until the following evening.

I stood, stretched, and then gaped as I watched the crowd disperse. Some simply walked (or slithered) away. Others vanished in puffs of smoke or flashes of light, and this one group of lizardy-looking things simply seemed to melt into the ground. Pretty freaky stuff, or at least it would have been had I not both lived in New York and seen just about every Sci-Fi movie ever made. Still, it was kind of cool.

As we left the table, Christy came walking over, still wearing her white wizarding robes. I momentarily found myself wondering if she was wearing anything underneath, but quickly quashed that thought. Cute though she may be, I tried to ix-nay any sex fantasies involving chicks who wanted me dead. Double that for ones who were banging my roommates.

"You were great!" she squealed, giving Tom a big hug.

"Great?" I scoffed. "He didn't do anything."

"True," he replied. "But did you?"

"Sure. I insulted Turd and didn't get my ass kicked."

"Yes, but I managed to almost not laugh while you were doing it."

"Fair enough," I grudgingly admitted.

"Come on," she said, taking his hand. "I'll introduce you to my coven sisters."

"Just don't wipe his mind or anything," I called after them. Oh, well, even if she did, was it really that much of a loss?

"Not bad, Bill," Sally commented, catching my attention. She walked up alongside of me as I headed toward the group of waiting vampires. "You managed to keep from getting us all killed on the first day. Looks like I owe Starlight fifty bucks."

"Your faith in me is astounding."

I was heading toward James, but François's arrogant mug stepped in front of me before I could get to him.

"Well done, Freewill," he said with a sneer. "Your antics with the Sasquatch leader aside, I commend you for following instructions. Continue to do your part *as told*, and we will surely achieve our desired outcome."

"*Our* desired outcome?"

François adopted an innocent tone as he answered, "Of course – peace. Is that not why we are here?"

"Of course," I echoed.

"Then we are decided. Sleep well this day, Freewill, for come nightfall, the true negotiations begin." With that, he nodded to his people and began walking away.

I waited for him to be out of sight, then padded a few extra seconds onto that before finally saying to James, "That guy is a serious asshole."

"On that we are agreed."

"Seconded," Ed said. "Now if you'll excuse me, I didn't realize the supernatural world wasn't big on bathroom breaks." He left us, heading back in the direction of our huts.

"Hold up, I'll go with you," Sally proclaimed, following him.

James watched them go. "Should you perhaps be worried about your friend? It was a long meeting, after all."

"It's not his blood I'm worried about her sucking."

A confused look momentarily came over James's face. "Whatever you say."

"Speaking of blood," I said, holding up my now empty bottle. "Would you happen to have a refill? We packed enough to get here, but suffice to say the room service kind of sucks."

He smiled and nodded. "I expected as much. Though the Alma have been accepting of these talks, we are still their ancient enemies. I wouldn't expect them to be particularly cordial with regards to the accommodations. I took the liberty of having one of my men restock your supplies while you were partaking in the opening talks."

"Really? That's super cool of you."

"There should be enough for both you and Sally for the next several days."

"For me, at least. She doesn't like the chilled stuff. She'd rather flash some leg and let the other vamps invite her over for breakfast."

"Hmm, I'll make sure my people have plenty of thralls around, then."

"You said that word before – thralls. Do you really have humans enslaved to your will? Is that even possible?"

James laughed. "Considering your friends, do you really want to know?"

I thought about it for a second. "No, probably not."

* * *

I arrived back at my hut with still a few hours to go until sunrise. I entered, debating how best to utilize the time, and then realized it was empty. That was kind of a relief. Though I had no reason to believe that Ed was indeed boning Sally, that didn't mean a small part of me wasn't half expecting to walk in on them doing just that. My roommates and I had a long standing rule against seeing each other's junk, and I'd hate to break it.

Pushing aside thoughts of Ed railing Sally like the dirty little bitch my brain insisted she was, I walked over to the cooler. I opened it and found that James was good to his word. It had been filled with pints of blood and a few ice packs to keep them cool. Awesome! Just what the doctor ordered, and I mean a sane one, not my buddy Dave.

I was reaching in for a drink when I heard a gun blast. I know what a shotgun sounds like, and as far as I'm aware, Ed was the only person in the area with one. That wasn't good.

I immediately headed for the door, thinking, *What have you done now, Sally?*

* * *

Thank God for vampiric senses. Between the sound of the shot and knowing what Ed smelled like (*and believe me, after several days in the car, I got plenty of good whiffs of them all*), I was able to immediately discern the general direction it had come from. I stepped from the hut and noticed several other vampires milling about, minding their own business, and pretty much ignoring the fact that someone had just fired off a twelve-gauge. Goddamn, vamps could be real assholes. Shit happened and they just sat around with their thumbs up their asses. And yet, I'm supposed to be on their side.

Oh well, there would be plenty of time to kill them all later, mentally at least. For now, I had a friend in need.

I left the clearing and raced off in the direction that my senses were telling me to go. I really hoped they were right. If not, I'd wind up lost in the Canadian wilderness, which wasn't exactly a small place. How fucking embarrassing would that be if they had to send out a rescue party for me ... assuming they even came looking. But, enough of those thoughts. I needed to trust my senses and hope they, unlike almost everything else, weren't purposely trying to screw me over.

A roar of anger from up ahead caught my attention. A moment later, a familiar ass-like scent came wafting to my nostrils – a Bigfoot. As I got closer, another sound carried to my sensitive vamp ears. It was Ed's voice.

"Back the fuck up! The next one won't be a warning."

Uh oh! It was usually pretty hard to rile Ed. To be fair, though, a half ton of giant gorilla about to kick your ass would most likely crack even the most stoic of veneers.

"*Defiler!*"

Oh, what the fuck did he do? Were he and Sally caught screwing on a Sasquatch burial mound? I'd expect stupid shit like that from Tom, but Ed?

I caught sight of a flashlight beam ahead. Ed's, no doubt. I got closer and finally saw my roommate. He stood beneath a tree, shotgun raised. A few feet away stood a massive (as if there was any other type) Sasquatch, and it did not look happy.

Both parties turned toward me as I came running up. I stepped in between them, probably not the smartest of strategies, and asked, "What's the prob..."

"*T'LUNTA!*" the creature snarled and immediately swung a massive backhand at my head.

Thankfully, numerous ass-kickings at the hands of other vampires had given me at least a few survival instincts. I managed to duck as a dinner-plate sized fist sailed over me.

"Okay, that's it," Ed said, leveling the gun at the beast's head. His heart was in the right place, but his brain had taken a temporarily siesta. I sincerely doubted he brought enough bullets to deal with the shit-storm of angry apes that would descend upon us if he killed this one.

"ENOUGH! We're under truce here, so back the fuck up!" I commanded the Bigfoot in a voice that almost sounded convincing. "As for you," I turned to my friend, "lower the damn gun before you get us all killed."

Despite my tone to him, I wasn't too worried about Ed shooting me, so I quickly turned back toward the creature. It had already taken one swing at me. No way was I giving it a freebie with my back turned.

Fortunately, I seemed to have gotten through to it. It took a step back, still angry, but at least it didn't look like it was about to attack again. Reminding it of the truce had been the right course. Turd had casually sacrificed one of his own troops to test the boundaries of the talks. He no doubt had imparted to his people that breaking the truce and causing an incident would get them thrown to the wolves ... maybe literally.

"That's better," I said raising my hands in a conciliatory gesture. "Now what is this about?"

"*Human defile sacred tree,*" it growled.

"Sacred tree?"

"*Ancestors buried beneath sacred tree.*"

I looked up. I'm no arborist. It just looked like another big, dumb fucking tree to me.

"So, this tree in particular is special?" I asked.

"*No. All such are sacred.*"

Okay, whatever the hell that meant. I turned back to Ed, a quizzical look on my face. "And you defiled it?"

"What? I had to take a shit."

"*Defiler!*"

Ignoring the agitated creature behind me, I asked, "Any reason why you chose this tree in particular?"

Ed's response was a glare that said his opinion of my intelligence was rapidly dropping. "Not really. I'm not exactly a connoisseur of fine trees to take a dump behind."

I sighed and said to the Sasquatch, "We humbly apologize. My friend didn't know what he was doing. It was an accident."

"*It is insult!*" it snarled. "*You come to Woods of Mourning, yet not learn of our ways. You spit upon my people.*" (Well, maybe spit wasn't the right word.) He bared his teeth and backed up another step. "*Turd will hear of this.*" He continued backing away. Within a few steps, he practically melted into the forest. Silence returned. It was pretty fucking freaky, like something out of *Predator*.

Then Ed had to go and ruin the mood. "So Turd will hear of my crap?"

I turned back to him. "Not funny, dude. Well okay, it is kinda funny. But not really."

"Sorry. I wasn't trying to cause any trouble. You know that."

"Yeah, I know. Where's Sally, by the way?"

"How the hell would I know?"

"I thought she followed you."

"For a little while. But like I said, I had to take a dump. It's not exactly a spectator sport."

"I heard the gunfire and thought she was..."

"Was what?"

"Well, killing you, I guess."

He smiled at that. "But what a way to go."

"True enough. Oh, well, we should probably go look for her. Unless, that is, you'd like to take a shit on anyone else's dead grandfather."

"Fuck you, Bill."

"Not tonight, I'm tired," I joked then began to turn back toward where the village was (hopefully). Suddenly a thought struck me. I stopped, looked around to make sure no hairy eyeballs were watching, then plucked a few leaves from the sacred tree.

"What are you doing?" Ed asked.

"I'm going to show these to James. Maybe he'll know why they're so special."

"It's not. It's just a maple tree."

I raised an eyebrow. "Are you sure?"

"I had them all over my yard growing up. Trust me, I raked enough of them to know."

"Hmm, so what you're telling me is..."

"That these guys are a bunch of fucking retards."

"Fair enough, although I could have probably guessed that already. I mean, c'mon, their leader is named after what you just dropped on their ancestors."

Keeping One's Priorities Straight

"YOU'VE GOT TO be kidding," I said, upon entering our "luxury suite." "You've been here all along?"

Sally looked up from where she was busy painting her toenails and let out a sniff. "Where else would I be?"

"We just spent the last hour walking through the woods looking for you."

"Oh. Well, I was here. I had some important business to take care of." She wiggled her toes to emphasize her point.

"I can see that," I replied snidely. "In the meantime, Ed and I were busy trying not to die."

"I see you were successful. Good for you," she said, going back to her feet.

"I assume you didn't hear..." Ed started.

"The gunshot? Yep, I heard it. Thought it might be you."

"And you didn't come to help, because...?" I snapped.

"For starters, I'm not the designated babysitter. Secondly, I knew you would go and check it out. But most importantly, because I fucking *think* these things through before I go off half-cocked."

That stopped both of us in our tracks. We shared a glance, then Ed said, "Explain."

"It's simple," she said, pausing to switch feet. While she did, I began tapping the table with my fingers. "Don't be impatient. If I rush, I'll get streaks." I was just starting to grit my teeth, when she started again. "As I was saying, it's simple logic. Did you see any other vampires rushing headlong into the woods?"

"No," I admitted.

"Do you know why?"

"Because they're assholes?"

"Well yes, that's probably true. No offense, Ed, but coming to the rescue of a human isn't going to be at the top of their priority list."

"None taken," he replied evenly.

She threw him a quick grin. "But that's only part of it. Remember, we're the enemy here. Don't think that we're not being watched every second of the day. We go rushing off en masse and the apes are going to notice and respond accordingly."

"But Ed was in..."

"Was he really?" She glanced up to address him. "Were you actually attacked?"

He thought about it for a second. "Threatened, yes – hence why I fired – but actually attacked, no."

"That thing took a swing at *me*," I said.

"Exactly," she replied, still giving her toes more attention than us. "You're a vampire. Worse, you're the semi-official vampire leader here – God help us all – their sworn enemy. Ed, however, is a human. The Feet aren't particularly big on humanity, but they don't put them on the same pedestal of hatred as they do us. Whatever he did out there, the fact that they didn't kill him outright tells me they were only sending a warning."

"And when I showed up..."

"You made it worse. Congratulations, Bill. As usual, the road to Hell is paved with your good intentions."

"Oh shit," I said, sitting down.

"An apt word, considering the circumstances," Ed commented.

"So what do you think will happen?" I asked.

Just then, as if on cue, Tom came walking in, hand-in-hand with Christy. "What the hell have you been doing, Bill?"

"You mean besides sitting here listening to Sally's rapier wit?"

"He's not joking," Christy said. "Word just reached my coven that the Forest Folk are up in arms."

"Let me guess," I replied, rubbing my temples. "The word Freewill was mentioned."

"Quite a bit, actually."

"What did you do?" Tom asked, a little more gleefully than I would have preferred.

"Don't look at me. Ed's the one who dropped a deuce on their forefathers."

"Huh?"

"Never mind," I said. "So what does the rumor mill have to say about things?"

Tom couldn't help himself. He grinned widely before saying, "Turd is having a shit-fit."

Lord help me, but even in the middle of all this, it was *still* funny.

"If I were you," Christy said, ignoring her boyfriend's idiocy, "I'd be prepared tomorrow. They're going to call you out on whatever it is you did, and I'm not sure they're going to accept an apology, being that they hate your kind and all."

"What if I apologize and explain things?" Ed asked. "Technically it was my fault, I guess."

I raised an eyebrow. "You guess?"

"It won't help," Christy said to him. "You're here as Bill's advisor, so they could claim that any insult you caused is automatically..."

"My fault," I finished.

"Something like that."

"Just wonderful. Guess the vacation's over." I stood, then turned to face Christy. "So where do you stand in all of this?"

"What do you mean?"

"Well, I appreciate the warning, but all the same, if Turd shit-stomps me into paste, doesn't that give you and Decker exactly what you want?"

"Speaking of which," Sally interrupted. "Where is that asshole? I didn't see him in the crowd."

"He couldn't make it. There's an executive retreat this week," Christy replied offhandedly before

212

addressing me once again. "A full blown war won't benefit any of us. Besides which ... oh, never mind."

"A retreat?" I asked, "They never invite me to any ... wait a second. Never mind what?"

Christy didn't immediately answer. However, that didn't stop Tom from doing so.

"You're starting to grow on her," he said brightly. "Isn't that right, honey?"

She just gave a shrug and averted her eyes. Trying to change the subject, she said to Sally. "That's a pretty color."

"Crimson sunrise," Sally replied, pleased. "One of my favorites."

"Great, you two can go to a spa together when this is all over," I snapped. "I appreciate the heads-up, Christy, really I do. I'm just not sure what to do with the rest of what Tom said. I mean, is it still safe to assume that if the Turd hits the fan (*sorry, couldn't help myself*), you're not exactly going to jump to my defense?"

She answered uncomfortably, "There is the prophecy..."

I kind of figured that would be the case. That stupid prophecy of Harry Decker's: the Freewill's return will give new life to the Icons, who will then proceed to kick the shit out of wizards worldwide blah blah blah. "Fine then..."

"But I won't act against you," she finished, catching me by surprise.

"Really?"

213

"Yes," she replied with more conviction. "My master's warnings aside, I can see that you're trying to do the right thing here. At least until this business is over..." She appeared to struggle with the words for a moment before blurting out, "you have my support."

Wow. I was actually touched ... sorta anyway. The implication, that once this was over she'd go back to trying to kill me, did put a damper on any celebrations. But still...

"Thank you," I said, meaning it.

"Isn't she great?" Tom asked, beaming at her.

"Wonderful," replied Sally deadpan. "That still doesn't help us if Turd decides to go apeshit on Bill tomorrow."

Though she had meant it seriously, her comment still caused the rest of us to break up into laughter. Unfortunately for me, she did have a point ... a potentially lethal one.

* * *

Even though none of us were in the mood to sleep, everyone was well aware that whatever awaited the next night wouldn't exactly be helped if we were all dragging our asses. As I lay there waiting for unconsciousness to claim me, I again found myself wishing that Alex had left some of his special incense behind. Never discount the theory of better living through chemistry, I say.

Speaking of Alex, I wondered where he was. I found myself hoping that he quickly finished up whatever investigation he was on so he could get back to the conference. He would probably have some bit of insight that would let us weasel out of this defilement bullshit. There had to be some loophole he knew. Of course, he also never bothered to mention the whole sacred tree business to me in his briefings. For all I knew, the dude had set me up to fail. But why? I mean, he worked for the Draculas. One didn't lightly fuck them over.

On the other hand, depending on how these talks went, François might end up being promoted to their level. Could he have maybe bribed Alex to work for him? After all, if François ascended to fill the Khan's chair, he would have the clout to keep the others off of Alex's back. That kind of made sense. Since I was an X-factor in all of this, they could both be working to throw me to the wolves.

Gah! I hated this espionage shit. It's the main reason I didn't read Tom Clancy. All of this crap went right over my head. Why did people have to try so hard to screw each other over? How much better would the world be if we could all mind our own goddamned business?

Of course, this reminded me of exactly how shaky my moral ground truly was. We kept going along under the fallacy that the vampires were the good guys here. Were we really? Hah! That was an easy one. All of that talk about global war and being a symbiotic race with the humans was pure self-serving bullshit. Even I could see that. We were like farmers trying to keep the foxes out of the henhouse, for no reason other than we wanted to eat the chickens ourselves.

Not that any of it mattered. I could sit atop as many moral high-horses as I pleased and that still wasn't going to save my ass. Jesus Christ! I didn't want any of this. All I wanted out of the world was just one actual, honest-to-god, date with Sheila. How the fuck did I wind up here?

As I drifted off to sleep, no answers to that question presented themselves. Stupid subconscious.

A Dumb Plan is Better than No Plan at All

SADLY, THERE WERE no night ... err ... daytime visitations. I had drifted off to sleep in the hope that perhaps Alex would mysteriously appear again and tell me that everything had been taken care of. No such luck. If I had fairy godparents, they sure as hell weren't reliable.

After rising, we all sat around the breakfast table – yay, more grubs – preparing. Ed and Sally double-checked their guns and pocketed some extra ammo.

Feeling a bit of weapon-envy, I said to Tom, "We should ask Nergui if he has anymore spare daggers."

"Who's this 'we' you're talking about?" he replied. "I'm covered."

When I asked what the hell he meant, he pulled something out of his shirt. It was a wooden medallion of sorts.

"What's that?"

"It's an amulet," he said. "Christy made it for me."

"+1 amulet of boners?" I asked with a smirk.

"I don't need any help for that. Nope, it's a protection thing. Christy said it was a faith charm. She told me it channels my deepest beliefs to protect me. Check it out, but don't touch it. Trust me on this."

I looked closer. It was roughly made, but upon closer inspection, I could see that there was a figure crudely carved into the center. It took me a few seconds to make out what it was supposed to be – Christy was obviously not a world-class whittler. Finally, I saw it: the plated face, the two big squares in the chest ... windows. "Is that..."

"*Optimus Prime* is back, baby!" he proudly proclaimed. "Sorta. Obviously this one ain't worth shit on eBay, but Christy said, thanks to her magic, it'll draw upon the spirit of..."

"Of your one true love?" Ed surmised. "No offense, dude, but goddamn, that is sad."

"But effective."

"And yet this girl willingly sleeps with you," Ed said with a sigh. "Sometimes I have to wonder who's really the one with the black magic."

"Fate smiles upon fools and small children," I said. "I guess that goes double for a fool with the mind of a small child."

"Are you all done jerking off to that Happy Meal toy?" Sally asked, still polishing her massive handgun. "Because we should really discuss what's happening today."

"I'm all ears," I replied.

"Not true," she countered. "You're dorky glasses and a flabby physique, too." Bitch. "But that aside, let's assume that shit is going down. I doubt the glowing moderator of death is going to let things immediately spiral out of hand due to one little slip-up. Still, it's going to put Turd in a position to demand some reparation."

"What kind of reparation?" Ed asked, sounding a little tense.

"He could very well demand your life," she said to him. "But I don't think that's going to happen because..."

"Because?" Ed prodded.

"Because you're nobody to him," I finished for her. "Why bother to use an advantage when the best it's going to get them is a few seconds of amusement wrenching your arms off?"

"I'm so glad that would be amusing for them."

"Oh, it is," said Sally. "Think of pulling the wings off a fly, except the fly can cry and scream obscenities while you're doing it."

"Thanks for the unnecessary details," he replied, deadpan.

"No problem," she said with her typical sauciness. Even in the worst of situations, Sally always got a chuckle out of making others uncomfortable. "Realistically, though, he's probably going to use it in a way where he can gain the most advantage."

"So he's going to demand *my* life?" I asked, trying real hard not to imagine being dismembered.

She shook her head. "He could, but it wouldn't be granted. I mean, it's not like you killed his whole family and then skull-fucked his Grandma just for good measure. Besides, there's no way even François can just hand you over on a platter. I doubt he'd even try with James around."

"You really should send that guy a gift basket when we get back," Tom added.

"Tell me about it."

"The most likely scenario," Sally said, ignoring us, "is going to be a challenge."

"That ritual combat thing they mentioned?"

"The same. I don't know what kind of challenge he'll make, but I wouldn't doubt it'll involve setting you up for an embarrassing ass-kicking in front of the crowd."

"Wonderful. Be sure to tape it. It'll be a hit on YouTube."

"That's where I'll come in," she continued. "Turd can challenge you, but you'll be able to set the terms. Since it's a fair bet none of François's asshole buddies will step up to the plate for you, I will."

"Fuck that," Ed replied. "We *all* will."

"No," she said, in a tone that suggested she wasn't about to be argued with. "You won't. Sorry to say, but neither of you will last three seconds in any sort of fight with these guys."

"But I have..." Tom started to say.

"Yes, I know. You have your little Barbie dress-up jewelry there. The problem is we don't even know if that shit works against the Feet. As for you, Ed, before you say anything, I will ask one question. Aside from bullshit stories, have you ever read a *real* news report about a hunter successfully shooting and killing one of these things?"

He thought for a second. "No, I guess not."

"Exactly. Just because that popgun makes you feel all manly, don't assume it'll do any good against these monsters. That leaves me."

I stood to protest. "That doesn't seem ri..."

"Can the chivalry bullshit, Lancelot. It makes perfect sense. I'm older and I've been in a lot more fights than you. I can handle myself. Besides, look at me."

We did, which caused her to let out an exasperated sigh. "My face is up *here*, dipshits."

She let the warning hang in the air for a second before continuing. "Despite the fact that every single creature watching this circus knows that size and power don't have anything to do with each other, they're going to take one look at me and assume I'm the underdog. If I win, that's great for us. If I lose, well, they'll all be expecting it, so there won't be any loss of face for our side."

"What about Nergui?" Ed asked. "Isn't he supposed to be Bill's bodyguard?"

I nodded. "He did say Gan gave him specific instructions."

"That's a possibility. But don't be surprised if there's some loophole thrown at us that disqualifies him. Like I said, they're no doubt going to want to weaken our position. Fighting with your honor guard isn't exactly going to do that."

As usual, Sally surprised me by thinking things through far better than I would have even considered. However, I did see one disturbing flaw in her logic.

"What if it's a fight to the death?" I asked.

"I'm hoping it won't be."

"But if it is?"

"If it is, then I expect you ALL to run in and save my beautiful behind. Let's not be stupid here."

* * *

None of us liked the plan. However, I grudgingly had to admit it made sense. Even if I didn't, Sally threatened to break all of our legs if we didn't go along with it. So in the end, we decided to follow her lead.

The matter settled, she excused herself to go grab a bite to eat, leaving my friends and me alone to finish getting ready. The three of us, even Tom, did so in relative silence. I think we were all rattled by how quickly things had taken a turn. Aside from a few minor bumps in the road, yesterday's talks had been nothing. Out of nowhere, though, the rumor mill was aflutter that bad things awaited us. Goddamn, I hated finding myself the meat in a shit sandwich.

Sally returned shortly thereafter, once more looking sated. Despite the fact that I wasn't too big on the concept of her feeding off the living, for once I didn't begrudge her the fact.

Unsurprisingly, Nergui was waiting for us outside our hut. I nodded to him and he fell into step alongside us. We began walking toward the proceedings and whatever cruel fate awaited us there.

Nearing the trail that led to the conference arena, as I was sure it would soon be, I saw James and his contingent waiting for us. To say he looked a little agitated would be an understatement. Can't say I blamed him. Regardless, I was glad to see him. His knowledge of these creatures far exceeded mine. Maybe he knew something that could calm the situation down. With Alex nowhere to be found, he was by far my best bet.

Unfortunately, it wasn't to be. Before James could even ask me what was going on, François swept in from our flank and stepped in front of him.

"There you are, Freewill," he said in that douchey voice of his. "There's no time to waste. Come along."

"Whoa, hold on a second," I protested as he grabbed my arm and started pulling me up the trail.

"No time for that. You're late and our hosts are quite perturbed."

James caught up and moved to cut him off. "I'm afraid I must concur with Dr. Death. I had hoped to have a minute to speak with him."

François narrowed his eyes at him. "You do not have a minute. In the future, I'd suggest you plan your little dalliances in advance."

James, however, refused to give way. "I'm afraid I must insist."

"You will insist *nothing*," François hissed. "Or need I remind you that you are only here at my tolerance?"

James looked ticked off. I started wondering if we were about to see a heavyweight throw-down. That would look bad for our cause, but who gives a fuck? I'd pay good money to watch two elder vampires go toe to toe. *Dragonball Z, eat your heart out.*

Alas, it wasn't to be. Just when the tension appeared to reach a zenith, James stepped aside. "You are of course correct, François, and I appreciate your *hospitality.*"

"Anything for a dear old *friend*," he spat and started dragging me again.

Not good. I had the distinct feeling that François was railroading me. Whatever was going to happen, he was in favor of it and wasn't about to let me get any sort of edge that talking to James might provide.

I tried to think of something. What could I do? I looked down at my empty hands and a thought hit me. Of course! It was lame, but it might work. I dug my heels into the ground. "Wait!"

"What now?" François asked.

"I need to run back real quick."

"You should have done that before you left."

"Not *that*. I forgot my drink."

François stopped and turned, a look of piteous contempt on his face. "Your drink?"

"Yeah. I left it back in the hut. I'm kinda parched, so if you don't mind..."

"I *do* mind." He looked between James and me for a moment, then grinned. "James, do be a friend and make yourself useful. You wouldn't want your precious

Freewill to face the *trials* of the day with a dry throat, would you?"

James looked like he was about to answer with something pithy, but then he simply nodded.

Oh well, it was a long shot anyway. Not wanting to give up the obvious ruse, I said, "There's a bottle on the table with my name on it. Fill it with AB negative, if you don't mind. That's my favorite."

James smiled in response. "Of course. I live to serve."

* * *

Oh, yeah, shit was definitely going down. I could tell that much the second I stepped through the ... err, anti-noise barrier, or whatever the fuck it was. Whereas yesterday wasn't exactly quiet, today was like stepping into a wrestling arena. The noise was almost too loud to be able to think over. The volume was only part of the problem, though. Its tone was what mostly bothered me. I couldn't understand all of what was being yelled, hooted, or wheezed, but a lot of it sounded angry.

As if in confirmation of this, the Sasquatches that had been stationed along the perimeter yesterday were dispersed amongst the spectators. To me, it looked like many of the factions were only a few choice words away from mixing things up with each other.

"What the hell happened?" I muttered to myself.

François immediately stopped and turned toward me, barely concealed mirth on his face. He began speaking loudly. "I implore you to reconsider, Freewill!"

Of course, much like the idiots who responded to things such as, "Asshole says what," I replied without bothering to think. "Reconsider?"

"Yes!" he screamed in a faux panicked voice, causing some of the nearby crowd to go silent and listen. "This mad course of action will only lead to war. I beg you to throw yourself at their mercy and end this insanity!"

Before I could even think of a response, his followers joined in with a chorus of cheers (*to him*) and jeers (*at me*). Just like that, the asshole had set me up and thrown me under the bus ... and I had let him.

I quickly glanced back at my friends. Sally didn't look surprised by this turn of events. Ed was doing his best to keep a neutral face. Unfortunately, Tom had to open his mouth and say, "Kick his ass, Bill."

To be fair, I hadn't been a part of too many peace summits. Still, logic dictated that when tensions were running high and people (or monsters) were in a heightened state of agitation, the last thing you wanted to do was suggest someone start a fist fight.

Almost immediately, the crowd around me started up again. Cries of outrage in a dozen different languages flew through the air. I didn't catch most of it, but I understood enough to know they weren't exactly cheering me on.

"Warmonger!"

"Death to the Freewill!"

"No mercy for the defiler!"

The insults continued and then suddenly, something wet thumped into my chest. I looked down to see it was

226

a clod of earth. There was a momentary pause from the crowd and then they apparently decided they liked that idea because I was suddenly pelted from all sides with any debris that could be grabbed. Christ, it felt like I was at a Mets game. Unfortunately, it was only going to be a matter of time before someone threw something heavy.

Before I could ponder whether to duck or run, Nergui appeared in front of me, weapons brandished. He let out a battle cry and made a few swipes at the nearest offenders, warning shots meant to scare them back. Just then, I heard a *clack* sound behind me that said Ed had just chambered a round into his shotgun. Oh crap! If the crowd didn't back off soon, it was going to turn into a full blown bloodbath with me at the center. Not good.

Through it all, I looked at François. His face held the same outrage as those around me, but his eyes glittered. The fucker was definitely enjoying this. Well, screw him. No way was I giving him the satisfaction. I opened my mouth to tell Nergui and Ed to stand down, but any words I had to say were completely drowned out by the sound that came from ahead.

A roar of pure rage rose up from below, near the center of the hollow. For all intents and purposes, it sounded as if the gates of Hell itself had been blown wide open. The bellow echoed across the entire area for several seconds, silencing all within.

I pushed forward until I could see what was going on. Standing alone at the bottom was Turd. Next to him, laid out on the conference table, was another Sasquatch. It was obviously dead, multiple wounds covering its torso. From the saggy tits hanging off its chest, I'd say female as well. Guess bras weren't big amongst the Forest Folk.

Turd looked up and saw me. His eyes locked on mine and his mouth opened in a snarl. "*Freewill, see what your treachery has wrought!*" he cried out, now having the full attention of the audience.

He indicated the body next to him, anger and sorrow both evident in his voice. "*My mate. The mother of my cubs. You defile the tree where her ancestor lay.*" He took his eyes from me and addressed the crowd. "*Such was her shame, she took her own life.*"

Gasps of shock rose from the crowd. Little by little, their eyes, or whatever they used to see, turned toward me. They did not look happy.

Seeing their reaction, Turd continued. "*Is it really surprise? Freewill T'lunta were known as conquerors, murderers. Many have legends that tell of their evil.*"

He turned toward a group of stone-like monsters. "*Terrocks, did not Freewills enslave your people long ago? Use them as servants to build their fortresses?*"

Their response was a gravelly growl of anger.

He next addressed a party of creatures that appeared to be made of living smoke. "*Wisps, you have tales of the Freewills extinguishing your eternal flame many harvests ago, yes?*"

The creatures appeared to flare up at this. Steam rose into the sky above them.

Turd then pointed to Christy's coven. "*Magi, do not your people speak of the death the Freewill brings? If he lives, the Silver Eyes shall rise and bring the end of your kind.*"

The various witches and wizards began to converse amongst themselves. A few made warding gestures and crackles of energy appeared around them. I saw Christy amongst them. Interestingly enough, her face didn't mirror the rest of theirs. She looked troubled, but if she was pissed, she wasn't directing it at me. Well, that was one plus in my favor, a minor one albeit, but at this point I'd take whatever I could get.

Turd was trying to turn the crowd against me, and doing a damn good job of it. Goddamn it! Next time, I was going to tell Ed to use a freaking bucket.

This was looking ugly. I quickly scanned the area where Turd stood. "Where's the fucking moderator?" I whispered mostly to myself.

At once, François was by my side. He lifted his wrist and glanced at the expensive watch on it. In a soft voice he purred, "Oh, did I say you were late? My apologies. We were actually a bit early. Silly me, must have forgotten to wind this thing. He should be arriving ... just ... about ... now."

* * *

With that, another jolt of green lightning flashed in the arena. When it cleared, happy doom ball was back.

229

Fuck me! I guess even glowing spheres of energy needed a break from things.

"DAY TWO OF THE PROCEEDINGS WILL NOW COMMENCE. BOTH PARTIES WILL MAKE THEIR WAY TO THE TABLE," it mind-beamed out, ignoring all of the angry commotion still rippling its way through the crowd.

"Do have fun," François said with a smirk, then stood back while his people began filtering out to their respective chairs.

Not wanting to give him the satisfaction, I turned to my friends, gave a shrug, and indicated for them to follow me. I really hoped Sally was right about her plan. I knew that she was doubtful any combat involving her as my proxy would be to the death, but the crowd sure as shit looked bloodthirsty to me.

I reached the entrance to the conference area and stood aside to let my friends go first. Nergui stopped with me, still guarding my flank. I locked eyes with each of them as they went. Tom and Ed both looked worried. Sally simply nodded to me. I mouthed, "Are you sure?" and got another nod back. I wouldn't forget this. I just hoped she knew what she was doing.

Once she passed me, I began walking again.

"Wait!" a voice called from behind me.

"THE PARTIES WILL MAKE THEIR WAY TO THE TABLE NOW," the glowing thingee repeated.

I turned and saw James making his way down the steps. Thank God. Hopefully, he had some way of turning this around. As he came up to me, I saw François tense in his seat.

James gave me a knowing smile and then a wink. Awesome, he did have a plan.

"I brought you your blood," he said, handing me the bottle. He then turned and walked over to take his seat.

What the fuck?! That was it? I was tempted to chuck it at him. He couldn't possibly be that clueless, could he?

"THE PARTIES WILL..."

"Yeah, yeah! I heard you the first time!" I shouted back, drawing a few gasps from the crowd. Fuck them! It's not as if they were on my side to begin with. I was half tempted to flip the lot of them off, but somehow managed to restrain myself ... especially when I realized I had just mouthed off to a glowing ball of lightning that could vaporize me without a second thought. Note to self: don't do that again.

Almost as if reading my mind (and for all I knew, it could), the orb said, "THERE IS AN UNAUTHORIZED OBSTRUCTION ON THE TABLE. IT SHALL BE REMOVED."

With that, it disintegrated the body. Whoa! That was harsh. I looked up, half expecting to see Turd in a frenzy of rage. However, he simply took his seat without a second glance. What the...?

Something was definitely rotten in the state of Bigfootville. I just hoped Sally wouldn't have to pay the ultimate price to find out what.

Cage Match

"*I HAVE GRIEVANCE!*" Turd shouted, bringing one meaty fist down onto the table hard enough that I felt the impact from the other end.

"VERY WELL, THE GRIEVANCE WILL BE HEARD," the glow-ball replied in a calm, almost bored, telepathic voice.

Turd went on to explain a very biased version of what happened the day before. It was his belief that having my friends shit all over his ancestors had been my plan all along. He apparently had very low standards for what encompassed a criminal mastermind. Let's just say that I don't recall Dr. Doom or Lex Luthor ever employing such methods.

He then continued, telling how his mate couldn't live with the shame. Don't get me wrong, I felt bad for the guy ... err, ape. I loved my Grandpa. If someone were to pinch a loaf on his headstone, I'd probably be a little ticked, too. Even so, I just can't see myself pulling out a noose to mark the occasion.

He went on about his motherless kids, his outraged clan brothers, and how he was barely able to restrain them from wreaking their vengeance. Turd was definitely piling it on in layers.

Unfortunately, it seemed to be working. The Sasquatches on his side of the table were throwing looks of pure hatred my way. The glares coming from François's lackeys were almost as unkind. I made a quick scan of the crowd and saw similar expressions (*at least on those with faces*). The only exceptions were James and François. François, unsurprisingly, seemed to be having the time of his life – I was half surprised that he hadn't brought popcorn.

James, on the other hand, looked perplexed. His expression was one of utter confusion. He suddenly noticed me looking at him. He gave a nod and gestured downward. What the fuck? Goddamn, I both hated and sucked at charades. Next time I got picked for something like this, I needed to remember to bring a few two-way radios.

Seeing that I wasn't getting it, he made a sipping gesture. Jesus Christ, the dude was still harping on about my fucking drink. What, did he want a medal or something?

"HOW DOES THE FREEWILL RESPOND TO THIS GRIEVANCE?"

Huh? Oh, crap, he was talking to me. I quickly looked at my friends for guidance. The best I got, though, was Sally giving me a quick *go on* gesture. Damn, I hated speaking in front of crowds.

Well, best to keep this short and sweet. I stood up and said, "It was an accident." Okay, probably not the most profound thing I'd ever said. Thinking quickly, I added, "Sorry" to my brilliant monologue.

"Way to go, Socrates," Sally whispered under her breath.

Ed, no doubt sensing I was sinking faster than the Titanic, stood up. "If I may..."

"YOU HAVE NOT BEEN RECOGNIZED," our moderator beamed out. It started to pulse angry colors. "YOU ARE OUT OF ORDER."

Ed immediately planted his ass back in his seat. I couldn't blame him. A speech that would have probably encompassed little more than, "when you gotta go..." was definitely not worth getting photon-torpedoed over.

"DO YOU HAVE ANYTHING ELSE TO ADD?"

"Oh, do you mean me?" I asked.

"YES." Maybe it was just me, but I could sense a slight condescending tone from the oversized firefly. I almost said something to the effect, but since pissing off yet another entity didn't exactly sound like a winning strategy, I decided against it.

"It won't happen again," I ended lamely.

I looked across the table, hoping Turd would accept that and maybe a friendly handshake to patch things up between us.

Instead, he turned to his bodyguard, grabbed the club from his hands, and smashed it down upon the table. The impact echoed throughout the valley. Hmm, guess he kind of liked his wife.

"*No!*" Turd bellowed. "*Not accepted. I and my people demand blood!*"

Thoughts of offering him a sip from my bottle flitted through my head, but then our moderator interceded. "VERY WELL. WILL THE LIFE OF THE OFFENDING HUMAN SUFFICE?"

Motherfucker! Ed tensed in his chair. I started to open my mouth to speak but felt Sally's hand on my arm. The meaning was clear: *wait.*

"*Human is nothing,*" Turd slobbered. "*The Freewill must die.*"

"AS MODERATOR TO THE TWO PARTIES, I CANNOT OFFER FOR SACRIFICE THE LEADER OF EITHER FACTION. WHAT SAY YOU, FREEWILL? DO YOU ACCEPT THE TERMS?"

Seriously? "Fuck no," I replied before I could think of anything more eloquent.

"THE OFFER HAS BEEN REFUSED. TURD, THE REMAINING OPTIONS ARE TO DROP YOUR GRIEVANCE OR..."

"*Combat!*" Turd screamed, causing the crowd to go nuts. Civilized meeting, my ass.

Arcs of energy crackled around the ball, silencing the crowd. "VERY WELL. THE TWO SIDES WILL VET THEIR DIFFERENCES IN ONE ON ONE COMBAT. FREEWILL, THE CHALLENGE HAS BEEN MADE TO YOU. AS LEADER, ONE OF YOUR FACTION MAY ACCEPT THE CHALLENGE IN YOUR PLACE."

"I will fight for the Freewill," a voice said from behind me. Nergui's.

Unfortunately, as Sally had surmised, he was shot down. "NEGATIVE. HONOR GUARDS ARE FORBIDDEN. ONLY ONE OF THOSE SEATED AT THE TABLE MAY FIGHT IN HIS PLACE."

This was it. No way was one of François's men putting their ass on the line for me. In fact, each of the fuckers started going through their notes as if they hadn't even heard.

"Are you sure about this, Sally?" I whispered out of the corner of my mouth. There was no response. "Sally?" I turned to look at her. She was just staring straight ahead. "Yoo-hoo, Sally. I understand if you want to back out. It's just..."

The words died in my mouth as I noticed the glazed look in her eyes. She wasn't backing down. She was under a compulsion. Fuck! Had François gotten to her after all?

I quickly turned to where he sat and found that, sure enough, he had a smirk practically wide enough to split his face. Fuck me! The asshole had set me up again.

"What's going on, Bill?" It was Ed. He and Tom had both noticed Sally, too. That wasn't good. I knew my roommates. They were good friends, sometimes a little too good.

Rather than risk going down that path, I turned and whispered, "Don't even think about it." Before they could protest, I stood up and said, "I fight my own battles."

Of course, my inner voice was quick to add, *That's why you always get your ass kicked.*

* * *

"What the hell happened?" Tom asked.

"Change of plans," I replied. "Sally's been compelled."

Ed, putting two and two together, said, "You should have let me shoot that dick when we first met him."

I nodded. "From here on in, consider yourself to have free rein to shoot whatever asshole vampire you want ... minus me, of course."

"THE CHALLENGE IS ACCEPTED." No shit, Sherlock. The moderator then went on to ask the other faction the same thing. Each and every one of Turd's little shits wanted in on the action. Unsurprisingly, though, he shot them all down in favor of handling this personally.

Oh, fuck. I could feel a quiver of fear running down my spine. My knees felt unsteady and suddenly my throat was very dry.

"What do you want us to do?" Ed asked.

"There isn't much you can do. Get Sally to the sidelines. Tom, I can't believe I'm saying this, but go see if maybe Christy can do something to snap her out of it."

"Got it," he replied, for once not adding a snide remark.

"What about you, Bill?"

"Go see if one of us packed a squeegee," I replied. "When this is done, use it to scrape what's left of me up."

"THE FIELD WILL BE CLEARED, SAVE FOR THE COMBATANTS." The ball pulsed again and then zapped the table. It began to disintegrate before our eyes. I quickly snatched up my blood bottle before it could tumble to the ground. No point in letting it go to waste.

I unscrewed the cap and chugged it down. I doubted it would do much to steady my nerves, but at least I wouldn't die parched.

"Take this and toss it..." I started to say when suddenly I doubled over. "OH, GOD!" I screamed, falling to my knees.

My roommates were both dragging Sally's still unresponsive form to the sidelines. When I went down, they nearly dropped her.

"What is it, Bill?" Tom cried.

What indeed? It felt like a nuclear bomb had gone off in my stomach. I had felt similar sensations before, but never even remotely this intense. I finally realized why James had been winking at me. He had filled my bottle with blood, all right – vampire blood.

Any vamp in the world takes a sip from another and they're going to finish the day puking their guts out. Not me, though. However strong the vampire I took a bite out of, I temporarily added their power to my own. I only knew one vamp this powerful who might take a chance like this. I had no doubt James had filled it with his own blood.

My God, so this is how he felt? Before my friends could utter another word of concern, I bounced to my feet. Well, okay, I first bounced ten feet into the air. I felt incredibly light as the blood continued to pump into my veins.

"Bill?" Ed's voice rang in my ears, several times louder than it should have. My senses were amped up, too. "Are you okay?"

I smiled, feeling my canines elongate. "I'm right as rain, motherfuckers."

* * *

Without warning, I staggered again. What the hell? Something was wrong. My body was still reacting to the blood, but it was going beyond just strength.

Oh no!

I looked down at my hands. My nails had extended into claws, albeit they seemed longer and sharper than usual. That wasn't all, though. I noticed that the hands they were attached to looked bigger, too.

Instinctively I knew what was happening. I was changing. James was at least twice as old as any vampire I had previously sampled. His blood was too powerful. It was awakening the beast inside of me. The creature, whatever it was, that had escaped only twice before – both times under extreme anger – was ripping free of its chains.

"Bill?" a voice, a human one. It was starting to get hard to think. I knew that voice ... Fred? Red? Oh, yeah, Ed. My roommate ... my delicious, human roommate. Wouldn't his blood taste ... NO!

"Run!" I yelled at him. Before he could protest, I again roared out, "RUN!"

Neither he nor Tom needed to be told twice. They grabbed Sally and dragged her from the arena floor.

I felt my sleeves begin to rip as my muscles went from flab to fab. Whatever was happening, it sure as shit beat going to the gym three times a week.

I looked up to see François's buddies still standing there, looking at me in shock. My vision began to flash red and I understood. These creatures before me weren't my betters. They weren't even my equals. They were food, plain and simple. I was the predator of predators.

And still, the changes continued.

"COMBAT WILL END WHEN ONE OF THE COMBATANTS CAN NO LONGER CONTINUE."

Combat? With these pathetic creatures in front of me? Don't make me laugh.

Almost as if sensing this, they broke and fled. Foolish prey. Did they truly think they could escape?

Before I could run them down, though, a shadow loomed over me. It was the beast with the stupid name. Odd, I remembered him being larger. A snarl was on his face, but my senses told me different. There was an undertone of fear. Perhaps the creature wasn't as stupid as it seemed.

WHAM

Perhaps not. I found myself airborne, and not of my own power. I flew twenty feet before crashing back down to the ground. The blow had been massive. It would have been more than enough to break a weaker creature.

But I was not weak. That was a lesson the brute in front of me would soon learn.

I got back to my feet and leapt, feeling the thrill of the joined battle coursing through me.

99 Bottles of Blood on the Wall

DID SOMEBODY GET the number of the bus that ran over me? What about the three before it? Holy shit, when I went on a bender, I really went all out.

I shook my head to clear it a bit, then looked down at myself. My clothes were a mess – torn to shreds and covered in dirt, blood, and whatnot. Fuck! Mom was gonna be pissed. She always hated when I came home for the weekend from...

Hold on. I wasn't in school anymore. Haven't been for a couple of years now. I blinked and looked around. It took a few seconds for the world to come into focus. No wonder why. There was a big crack in my left lens. Motherfucker! I liked these glasses. Good thing I had a spare back in ... my hut?

I looked around again, slowly remembering where I was. Creatures of all shapes and sizes sat in crude bleachers looking down upon me. Why were they staring at me? Oh, yeah. I was just about to get my ass handed to me by Turd.

What the hell happened? Did I faint? That would be just my luck. Sally's never going to let me live that one down.

Speaking of which, where was she? Hope she didn't get her hand chopped off again.

The fog in my head cleared some more. Oh, that's right. Tom and Ed dragged her away after I ... drank ... that ... blood.

Oh boy.

"FREEWILL, YOU ARE THE VICTOR. YOU MAY DETERMINE TURD'S FATE."

What the fuck? I reached up, slapped myself across the face to clear my thoughts ... and almost immediately fell on my ass. I felt a spray of blood shoot from my nose as my head rocked back from the force of the impact. Ouch! Holy crap! Guess I must've still had some residual strength running through me. Gotta watch that. Wouldn't do me any good to knock myself out.

Painful or not, it did the trick. My head finally cleared. I saw Turd lying a few feet away. Bruised, bloody, and with what appeared to be a dislocated jaw, he looked like someone had driven a freight train over him. He was still breathing, but seemed to be out cold. Thank God for small favors.

Whatever the fuck just happened, I had won ... somehow. Apparently it was just in the nick of time for the worst of the effects from that blood to wear off, too. Goddamn, that was intense.

"FREEWILL, I REPEAT, THE BATTLE IS YOURS. WHAT IS YOUR VERDICT?"

It was then that I finally noticed the sounds of the crowd again – howls, grunts, and screams. This time, though, I sensed a decisively different attitude toward me.

"Kill him, Freewill!" something shouted.

"Death to the vanquished!"

More joined the chorus, encouraging me to kill my foe.

Yeah, well fuck that. They could get some other monkey to dance for them.

I held up a hand to silence the crowd. They did, surprisingly enough. Guess people listened when the champ spoke. I could get used to that.

"We're done here for today," I shouted, partially to the crowd and partially to the glowing thing still floating above me. "Clean up Turd (*heh*) and make sure he's back at the table tomorrow."

The crowd started in again. Some of them approved of my decision. Others were quite vocal against it. I couldn't have cared less about any of them or their stupid supernatural opinions.

I scanned the audience and saw my friends. Christy was with them, apparently working some magic. Unfortunately, it didn't seem to be working. Sally still had a thousand-yard stare on her face.

I wandered over as the crowd began to disperse. Christy looked panicked for a moment, presumably over what had just transpired on the battleground. She held her ground, though. I could respect that.

"How'd I do?" I asked, looking back. Several Sasquatches were dragging Turd away.

Tom answered first. "Two words: fucking awesome!"

"I agree. That was ... something," Ed replied.

"You really are the Freewill," Christy said in a small voice.

"So they tell me." I smirked blithely. "How's Sally?"

"Whoever compelled her is really strong," Christy replied, composing herself. "She'll probably snap out of it on her own, but I'm not sure there's any way to keep her from going under again. A lot depends on what they commanded her to do."

"Fuck!" I punched a nearby stump out of frustration. To my surprise, it split upon impact. Guess I was still juiced up.

"Maybe you should take this opportunity to kick François's ass," Ed suggested.

"Hell, I'm still wondering how you were able to take out Turd," Tom said. "Have you been practicing hulking-out behind our backs?"

I shook my head and then explained the blood.

"Whoa, James did that for you?"

"Yeah. Pretty cool, eh?"

A thoughtful look appeared on Christy's face following my explanation. She leaned forward and asked, "Are all of your powers heightened?"

"I dunno. Still figuring this shit out, but I guess so."

"Then why don't you try compelling Sally to wake up?"

Hmm, I hadn't thought of that. "I don't know if it'll work. François is older than James."

"Why don't you try rather than bitching about it?" Tom suggested.

"He's got a point," Ed said. "It might work, especially since I get the impression Sally's not too fond of that asshole."

"Make that two of us," I replied. "Stand back. With the extra power in my system, I don't want to pop anyone's head off."

"Because standing back will really help with a *psychic* compulsion," Ed muttered.

"Bite me, asshole."

"Just do it already."

Jeez, no patience from mortals these days. I concentrated on trying to focus on Sally and Sally alone. Here goes nothing... "*SALLY, SNAP OUT OF IT!!*"

Holy shit! The compulsion felt like it had ten times the juice of the one I had used on Alfonzo. Sally's head rocked back as if I had decked her. However, her eyes immediately cleared. Wow, it actually worked.

"What happ..." she started to say, when a quick thought popped into my head.

"*AND DON'T LISTEN TO ANYMORE OF FRANÇOIS'S COMPULSIONS!!*"

Again, her body jolted as if from an electric shock. This time, she fell backwards, slamming her head into the rocky ground. "Ow!"

"Are you okay?" I asked.

"Besides having my skull almost caved in?" Yeah, she was fine.

"Holy shit, that was loud, Bill," Ed said, shaking his head to clear it.

"Sorry. Still kinda new at this." Fortunately, my effort to focus seemed to have mostly worked. Sally was the only one who had been knocked for a loop.

"I need to get going," Christy said, standing up. "The others are going to wonder what I'm doing."

I nodded, then added, "Thanks, Christy. I mean it. I ... owe you one. You didn't have to help."

She sighed. "I just hope it doesn't come back to bite me."

"The Silver Eyes?" I asked, having a pretty good idea of what Turd had been talking about.

She gave a single nod. "Nobody calls them that anymore, but yeah, the Icons."

"You know I'm not purposely trying to destroy anyone, right?"

"I know." She threw a quick smile at me, then a much wider one to Tom before turning and walking off.

"Well, since we're in such a thankful mood, I guess I should do the same," Sally said, getting back to her feet.

"It's no problem. Any ... URK!" I gasped as her hand shot up and grabbed my crotch in a vice-like grip.

"But just so you know; if you *ever* try to compel me again, I will rip this off and use it as a purse. Are we clear?"

"Crystal," I squeaked.

* * *

We were still seated in the now nearly empty hollow. Sally had just finished explaining what had happened. Apparently, my compulsion had not only erased François's, but the safeguards he had implanted in her mind, too. He'd caught Sally on that first morning while she was out tramping up some breakfast. His compulsion had been very specific with regards to what she was supposed to say and do. It also showed just how skilled he was. He had left it much the same way a hypnotic suggestion would work. She had no knowledge of it until it had been triggered.

"He set us up," said Ed, matter of factly.

"How?" I asked. "I mean, how could he possibly know that we were going to do something to piss off the Sasquatches?"

"Well, if he knew your track record, it wouldn't be too hard to guess."

"Thanks for the insight, Sally. There's just one problem with that: the guy *doesn't* know me."

"Well, then maybe..." she started to reply before suddenly clamming up. A moment later, I heard footsteps approaching from behind us. Guess whatever upgrade I had gotten from the blood was now out of my system. That was fine by me. That had been some scary shit back there.

I turned to find James and Nergui walking toward us. They were otherwise alone.

"I must say, that was quite impressive," James said as he approached. From the tone of his voice, he meant it. "I had no idea you were capable of that."

Nergui in turn, bowed very low to me. Apparently, whatever I had done had further cemented his Freewill beliefs.

I gave them a quick nod. Before saying anything, I looked behind them and then around us. "Where's François?"

"Oh, he stormed out of here following the fight. Oddly enough, he did not look pleased at your victory. I think he underestimated you."

"Well, you definitely fixed that one," Tom said.

"Yeah," I agreed. "I owe you. Thanks for that."

James looked confused. "For what?"

"For helping me out. That was quick thinking."

"I'm afraid you have me at a loss," he said. Before anyone could say anything else, he held up a hand, indicating we should stop talking. He quickly turned to Nergui and said, "My friend, if you would be so kind as to wait at the Freewill's tent. They will be under my protection until then."

Nergui gave a short bow, then turned and walked off.

"I thought you trusted him," I said once he was out of earshot.

"Oh, I do," James replied. "With my life and yours. Still, the fewer ears we have around, the safer things will be."

"Let me guess," I asked, sharing a quick glance with Sally. "This is a safeguard against him being compelled?"

James gave a curt nod, his expression serious. "It's quite possible that if questioned by François, he would have no choice but to tell all he heard. Nergui is no fool. He undoubtedly understands this. Now, getting back to the point, what was that about my helping you out?"

"The blood," Ed replied.

"What about it?"

"It was yours, right?" I asked.

"Mine?"

"Yes, in the bottle you gave me."

"I'm not sure what you mean. I found the bottle where you said it would be. It was already full, so I assumed you had done so and forgotten."

"That wasn't your blood?"

"No, it wasn't. Although, now that you mention it, that would have been a clever plan. I wish I had thought of it."

"What? How the hell did you think I did all that stuff out there?"

"I ... well, I'm actually not sure. The legends say the Freewills of old had hidden powers. I just assumed you discovered yours and tapped into it."

"So you're saying that wasn't your blood?"

"I'm afraid not."

"So then what was all that smiling and winking crap earlier?"

"Oh, that? I taped a note to the bottom of the bottle, asking you to meet me afterwards so we could discuss things."

"That was it?!"

"Yes."

"Hold on," Sally said. "How did you know Bill would survive?"

"It's quite simple, really. Killing the Freewill outright wouldn't help the Alma's cause. If they did that, they would force the First Coven's hand. One or more of our ruling council would have no choice but to get involved in these talks."

"So challenging me was..."

"Meant to humiliate you. Turd no doubt saw you as an easy mark. Breaking you and then showing the rest of the proceedings that you weren't even worth killing would weaken our position. Instead, though, you did to him what he sought to do to you."

"I don't know," I replied. "He seemed pretty pissed. The fact that his wife committed suicide..."

"Strikes me as odd," James interrupted, a troubled tone entering his voice. "I wish I had gotten a chance to speak to you before this whole debacle and learn what had happened."

"So you could have told Bill to turn around and march back to his tent?" Tom asked.

"Hardly. Remember, Dr. Death, I have spent time amongst the Alma. I know a little of their customs and even more about diplomacy. What your human friend did should have barely registered as even a minor insult."

"What?" the four of us replied as one.

"Yes, and in times such as these, when outsiders are permitted into their lands under truce, it is understood that small infractions are tolerated."

"Small infractions?" Ed asked. "I thought that Bigfoot yesterday was going to rip my head off."

"No offense, man," I replied, "but I can see how shitting on their ancestors' corpses might be a sore spot."

"But it isn't," James said.

"Okay, now you've lost me."

"This place is sacred to the Alma, that much you know," he explained. "The tree, was it a maple variant, if I may ask?"

"Yes."

"It holds significance to them, but in more of a spiritual manner. It's a symbol of growth and rebirth."

"So it's sacred to them, like they said."

"No," he continued. "Sacred, yes, but not in the way that, say, Hindus venerate cattle or Christians the cross. Besides, it's not like you burned down the forest. All you did was..."

"Shit on their ancestors," I repeated.

"Fertilize the ground," James corrected. "It's common practice amongst the Alma. Considered a minor blessing, even."

"You've got to be wrong," I replied. "People ... err apes don't usually off themselves due to *minor blessings.*"

"I will admit that part has me puzzled. It's almost like they purposely wanted to find offense and had planned to use your ignorance against you."

"Except it wouldn't have worked if you had warned us," Sally said, a glimmer of insight sparkling in her eyes. Not being a complete idiot myself, I put two and two together.

"Except François stopped you."

"And put a very specific compulsion on Sally," Ed said.

"And conveniently had his own negotiators handy when the Draculas' group didn't arrive," Sally added.

"And has been a major dick about everything," Tom replied, adding his own unhelpful two cents.

"I will admit that is very strange," James said. "Except for that last part. I've known François for a very long time and he has always been, as you so eloquently put it, a dick."

"Jesus Christ!" Sally exclaimed. "He's selling us out. François is working with the..."

"I will stop you there, my dear," James interrupted. "One does not lightly throw accusations at an elder vampire with only circumstantial, if highly probable, evidence. That is especially true in places such as this where there are ears everywhere."

"So what do we do?" I asked. "We can't let this asshole get away with..."

"It's quite possible you've already done enough. Judging by how quickly he stormed out of here, I'd say you made a bloody mess of his plans."

"One of Bill's specialties," Sally quipped, not unkindly.

James nodded. "As I am learning. Whatever François had planned has no doubt been put in jeopardy. It's possible that he will have no choice but to let the peace negotiations continue in the manner that they were meant to."

"That's good," I replied, feeling a bit of relief wash over me.

"Of course," James continued, "he may also become desperate and attempt to modify his plans."

"Let me guess. That would probably involve getting rid of me, right?"

"Doubtful."

"Oh, well that's a..."

"He would no doubt wish to remove you from the equation out of spite alone."

Great, just what I wanted to hear.

* * *

The five of us had been walking back down the trail toward the huts. Compared to the earlier ruckus, it was now eerily quiet. If I didn't know better, I'd have said we were the only ones in the woods for miles around.

As we walked, I had a chance to reflect upon the events of the past few hours, or at least the parts I remembered. I looked down at my ragged clothes. Damn, I liked this shirt, too.

Sally took this as cue to ask, "So what exactly happened back there? I kind of spaced out when that compulsion triggered."

"No idea," I admitted. "What did you guys see?"

Ed shrugged, "Well, we were kind of busy dragging Sally out of harm's way."

"Yeah, she's heav..."

Sally interrupted Tom with, "If you finish that sentence, you die."

"Uh, yeah," he stammered before quickly changing the subject. "After that, it was hard to say. You were moving too fast."

"Yep," Ed agreed. "You only started to slow down again after you'd kicked Turd's ass and started to change back. The best I can say is ... you got bigger."

"Hulk smash?" I asked with a grin.

"Something like that."

"What about you, James?"

"Yes?" he asked, coming out of whatever reverie he had been in.

"What did you see?"

James looked troubled by my question. "That's what's been bothering me, actually. I too had a hard time following your moves."

"*You did?*"

"I am somewhat embarrassed to admit it, but yes."

Even Sally was impressed by that. "Wow."

"Indeed. That tells me one of two things. Either our friend, Dr. Death here, is far more formidable than any of us imagined..."

"Or?"

"Or our mysterious donor is a vampire whose power far eclipses my own."

"François?" I offered, even though I had a pretty good idea what the answer would be.

That elicited chuckles from both James and Sally. "Sorry, Bill," she said. "But I doubt he'd piss on you if you were on fire, much less open a vein so you could take a drink."

"Then who?" Ed asked.

That was a damn good question. I just wished I had an answer.

Midnight Tryst

ONCE WE WERE within sight of our hut, James left us to confer with his people. That was fine by me. I needed to change and think things through. Sally claimed to have a headache from all the mucking around in her head and wanted to lie down for a while – not too surprising. Tom and Ed, well, they both said they were going to stay close to the hut. I couldn't blame them.

After I got dressed – and found my spare set of glasses so I could see again – I joined them at the table. Despite all of us wanting to brainstorm on the shit pile we had somehow stepped into, we were careful to avoid it. The walls of the hut were thin. Leaves, mud, and assorted crap weren't going to do much to mask our words if any of François's men were close by, and it was a fair bet they were.

Thus, to pass the time, we pulled out a deck of cards and decided to play a few rounds of poker. That was a mistake. By the end of the game, I was fifty bucks in the hole. What a fucking trip.

Disgusted, I decided to join Sally ... well okay, not physically join her. That would have earned me a quick downgrade to eunuch. Instead, I decided to lie down and grab some sleep. Considering what I had planned, going to bed a little early wouldn't exactly be a bad idea.

* * *

Sleep is overrated. Horrific nightmares plagued me from the moment I lay down. No, they had nothing to do with Turd, Bigfoot, or some other fairytale monster. I'm talking real horror here. My dream-self had finally worked up the nerve to ask Sheila out, and I mean really ask her out this time – none of that *is it a date or isn't it* bullshit that I've been fucking around with. Nope, this time I asked her flat out, "Would you like to go out on a date with me?"

Well, okay, my dream-self might have thrown a *please* in there somewhere. I never said my subconscious was cool. Her answer of, "No, Bill, I think of you as a brother," was horrible enough, but her follow up of, "Besides, I already have a double date planned with your roommates," caused me to wake up in a cold sweat. Fuck that noise!

I had a brief moment of waking confusion – in which I seriously contemplated killing them both just to make sure that didn't come to pass – but then my head cleared. I looked around. Both of my roommates were sound asleep. I turned toward the door and saw it was still fairly dark out. I couldn't have been asleep for long. However, then I looked at my watch and saw it was actually eight AM. Oh, yeah, I was still practically up in the fucking Yukon. Stupid Canada and its screwed up days.

I quietly got out of bed and walked over to the cooler for a drink. I lifted a pint and then stopped. Goddamn, why didn't I think of this before? I grabbed a few random packs and sampled from each. No vampire blood. Hadn't James said something about my bottle already being full when he came to get it? That meant someone had snuck in here at some point and planted it.

I was mulling possibilities when I heard Sally say, "Hey, toss me one of those." She stepped out from behind her curtain and joined me at the table.

"Couldn't sleep?"

"You snore like a chainsaw," she replied, taking a sip.

"I thought you only drank from the tap."

"All things considered, I think it might be smart to eat in for the remainder of our time here. So why are you up?"

Rather than tell her about my dreams – which would no doubt earn me nothing but grief in return – I decided instead to fill her in on the course of action I had been considering. "I'm thinking of checking out the Sasquatches."

"Playing Sherlock Holmes now?"

"Something like that. Besides, it'll be daylight soon. They won't expect me to be up and about."

"Us," she said.

"Excuse me?"

"They won't expect *us* to be up and about."

"What about you not wanting to know things in case François makes you squeal ... which, just for the record, might be kinda hot to hear."

Sally's boot connected with my shin under the table. Ouch! "I don't think that's going to happen. Whatever it was you did to me yesterday seems to have cleaned him out of my head. It's like you put up a concrete wall in my brain to reinforce my mental barriers. It's hard to explain..."

"You're saying you're safe?"

"In a nutshell."

"How do I know François didn't compel you to say that?"

She looked at a loss for that one. Hot damn, no matter the situation, I so loved when I could occasionally beat Sally in a war of words.

"I'm just kidding," I said. "I believe you. Besides, he's been one step ahead of us so far and it hasn't exactly helped him."

"You do have a way of fucking up the best laid plans of mice and men."

"And asshole Nazi vampires, let's not forget them."

* * *

Aside from our immortality and preference for blood, there is one behavior that all vampires, regardless of age or social status, share: our wardrobes are full of hooded clothing. It's kind of a necessity for those times when one must brave the unforgiving light of the sun. It might make us look like weirdos, especially in warm weather, but it beats the hell out of turning to dust. In a dense forest, such as we were in, there was much less chance of that happening, but better safe than sorry.

I pulled a bottle of high-grade sunscreen from my luggage and liberally slathered it on. Sure, it made me smell like a rancid palm tree, but that wasn't a bad thing considering the lack of shower facilities. I covered up all exposed skin, then tossed on a ski-mask for good measure.

"Are you going to spy on them or rob a bank?" Sally asked, stepping out of from behind the curtain. She was similarly, if somewhat more garishly, covered up.

"Well at least you don't have to worry about being shot by hunters," I replied, smirking at the bright pink hoodie she now wore. "You do realize they'll see you coming from a mile off, right?"

"That's kind of the point. If they catch us, which I give a pretty high chance of happening, I can just claim I was out exploring. Nobody in their right mind would be doing any sort of espionage dressed in this thing. You, on the other hand, look like you're about to take hostages."

"*Touché.* Now let's get going before the rest of the crew wakes up."

"Hold on, I want to get my gun."

"I thought you told Ed that bullets wouldn't work."

"Doesn't mean they won't hurt like hell. If I'm going down, I'm making sure every ape in the area gets a fifty-caliber kick to the groin."

I winced. "Thanks for the imagery, but I really think you should leave it. That story about being out exploring will sound a lot more plausible if you're not packing enough firepower to take over a small country."

She considered it for a moment, then grudgingly nodded. I just hoped it wasn't a decision we'd both live to regret.

* * *

We stepped outside to the rapidly brightening day. Amazingly enough, Nergui still stood guard – albeit he was now positioned under the shade of a large tree. He saw me and, despite my outfit, snapped to attention. Vampires as old as him were hard to fool, their senses being far closer to a comic book character like Wolverine. He started to step forward, but I held up a hand.

"I need you to stay here, Nergui. Protect my friends inside. Also, don't let them wander very far."

"My duty is to you, Freewill," he predictably said.

"You saw what Bill did yesterday, right?" Sally asked. He nodded in response. "He's been mastering his powers. I think we'll be all right."

Nergui appeared to consider this, but still moved to join us.

"My friends need your protection more," I protested.

Finally, Sally sighed. I couldn't see behind the sunglasses she now wore, but I was sure there was an eye-roll going on. She stepped close, putting one arm seductively around me. "My coven master and I wish to be *alone*," she purred.

For just a split second, a knowing look came over Nergui's face. He smiled ever so subtly and stepped back to his spot.

Smart. During her little adventure in New York, Gan had been convinced that Sally was my concubine – or whore, as she put it. Doubtless, she had filled Nergui in on this. Sally was using that knowledge to make him stay put and keep an eye on my roommates, as well as stay out of our hair. There was also the added benefit that if François managed to compel Nergui, he wouldn't get anything useful out of him.

That fact that her tone and gestures were also giving me a little morning wood in the Woods of Mourning, well, that was just a nice bonus.

Nergui taken care of, we continued on our way. Once we had gotten far enough that he couldn't eavesdrop, she said flatly, "Say a word and die."

I didn't need to be told twice.

* * *

Keeping off the trails that ran through the area, we bypassed several encampments. There was no point in giving ourselves away. Though it appeared some of the other creatures present were likewise photosensitive, few of them were dressed in modern attire. While they might not be able to identify us, it would be pretty obvious to any beings who saw us that we were vampires.

As we walked, a thought hit me. I had no idea where the fuck we were going. I started to say something, but Sally, apparently reading my mind, answered my unspoken question.

"Their scent is strongest this way," she said. Her voice then took on a more condescending tone. "Aren't you glad I insisted on coming?"

I mumbled something inaudible in response.

"I thought so," she replied glibly. "You really do suck at this, don't you?"

"Sorry. I didn't exactly go to ninja school, you know."

"I mean the whole vampire thing in general."

"Fuck you."

"Not even on a dare."

"Sorry, I forgot you save that privilege for guys who stick a five spot in your g-string."

"Speaking of which, how are things going with that girl you like? Have you started paying her to be seen with you yet?"

Ooh! That was a low blow.

"Listen, you gold bricking, poorly coifed, bitch of a ... UMPH!" Unfortunately, I wasn't able to finish my cleverly scathing comeback as a huge hairy hand came out of nowhere and covered my face.

Mission Improbable

"*T'LUNTA MAKE LOT of noise,*" a voice growled in my ear. Oh, fuck!

I grabbed the large fingers and managed to pry them off my head. Damn, that was a lot harder when I didn't have super vampire blood coursing through my system. The hand released me and I jumped back, taking a defensive posture or what might have passed for one in a bad kung-fu movie.

As I stood there preparing for an attack, Sally simply said, "Hey, Grulg. Where have you been? I didn't see you there yesterday."

"You didn't?" I hadn't even noticed. Not to sound like a racist asshole, but all of these things looked the same to me. I wouldn't have been able to pick Grulg out of a lineup with a half dozen of his buddies.

"Yeah," she replied. "Wasn't it obvious?" She left unspoken the part about it being obvious to non-pathetic vampires, but believe me, it was implied.

"*No speak here. You follow,*" Grulg replied, then turned and loped off into the woods.

Sally looked at me, shrugged, and then took off after him.

Knowing that no matter what choice I made, I'd probably end up regretting it, I did likewise.

Grulg took a path perpendicular to the one we had followed. If anything, he seemed to be leading us into even deeper woods. Soon, the shadows thickened as the canopy above us grew denser. Within a short while, our coverings became unnecessary even though it was the middle of the Canadian day.

Finally Grulg stopped. We were in a clearing, but the surrounding trees all leaned inward, providing the place with a perpetual twilight feel.

"*Secret place.*" Grulg gestured around him. "*Only Grulg know.*" I was tempted to point out to our grammatically challenged guide that it wasn't exactly a secret anymore, but I didn't exactly think that would endear him to me.

"So what's this about, Grulg?" I asked.

He stood up straight as he answered. Both Sally and I had to crane our necks to look him in the eye. "*Grulg honorable warrior. Live with honor. Fight with honor. Kill with honor.*"

I tried (and failed) to suppress a gulp at that last part. Maybe Grulg had led us all the way out there to avenge his leader. Even with Sally backing me up, I wasn't too sure on our odds if such was the case.

"No one is saying otherwise, Grulg," Sally said in a soothing voice.

"*Grulg know that, she-T'lunta.*"

I snickered, and she shot me a glare.

"*Grulg proud and loyal,*" he continued, ignoring our idiocy. "*If peace come, then Grulg honor peace. If war come, then Grulg crush his enemies until Grulg win or Grulg killed.*"

"Nobody wants that last part," I said.

Grulg growled at me. "*Stupid T'lunta not understand.*" Great! Now I was being insulted by a giant, shit-flinging monkey. "*Grulg not care. Grulg do as told. War, peace, it all same to Grulg. But this ... this not honorable.*"

"What isn't?" I asked.

He growled again, then walked over and backhanded a small tree, shattering it. I backed up a step, wondering if this was going to get messy. Sally didn't seem overly perturbed, though. She was one stone cold ice queen.

"You can tell us, Grulg," she said. "It's okay."

That seemed to calm Grulg down. Chalk one up to the whole beauty and the beast concept. Forget music – Sally's marvelous rack could apparently soothe the savage beast.

"*Turd,*" spat Grulg. "*He no act with honor.*"

Aha. Now we were getting somewhere. James had said that Turd's behavior was out of sorts. Now one of his own followers was ratting him out. Considering theirs was a caste-based society, it said something for Grulg actually to be speaking out against his superiors.

"Let me guess," I surmised. "This has to do with setting me up to take a beating yesterday."

Grulg gave a look that suggested his opinion of me was slipping several notches, and then actually chuckled. "*No, T'lunta. Leaders should be able to fight. Also, Turd not give you beating. I was told that you give him one.*"

"Okay then," I replied with a sigh, "but what about the whole setting me up part? Doesn't that strike you as a bit treacherous?"

This time he leaned back his head and full out laughed. He sounded like a broken garbage disposal.

"Way to make an impression, Bill," Sally whispered out of the side of her mouth. Bitch!

Finally Grulg's laughter subsided. "*Funny T'lunta. Strength, speed, intelligence ... all these things make good leader. Treachery just mean he smarter.*"

"Well, good. Now that we've established Turd's credentials as a fucking genius..."

Sally interrupted my tirade. "Grulg, what the Freewill is *trying* to ask, is what about Turd's behavior is dishonorable?"

He nodded at her. "*Grulg show you. T'lunta follow again.*"

"We already followed you," I protested.

"*Grulg lead you away because you no stop chattering. Sound like ... what you call them ... squirrels.*"

Thus admonished by a giant talking gorilla, we put our respective coverings back on and once more followed Mighty Joe Young through the forest.

* * *

"You want me to *what?*" Sally asked.

"*Jump in*," Grulg repeated.

"Why?"

"*Cover scent. Grulg's tribe not smell you.*"

"Oh, Jesus Christ," I said, pushing my way past her. "Stop being such a fucking princess." I wasn't too big on this plan either, but I could tolerate getting a little dirty if it would help us gain some leverage over Turd.

I jumped into the pungent smelling pit and began rolling around to coat myself. When I was done, I got out and walked over to her.

"See? Was that so bad? A little mud won't kill you."

Sally gave me a look that was practically overflowing with pity. "That's not mud, moron."

"It's not?"

"No, stupid."

"*T'lunta smell good now*," Grulg commented. "*Now she-T'lunta turn.*"

"No fucking..." but she didn't get a chance to finish. I shoved her in, mid-complaint. I took enough of her shit as it was. It was finally her turn.

* * *

After managing to convince Sally to not kill me, a long and painful ordeal if ever there was one, Grulg led us back in the direction of his tribe. Soon, we could see more crude huts through the trees, but I didn't see any Sasquatches wandering amongst them.

"*Others sleep now. This way*," Grulg whispered, leading us toward one end of the makeshift village.

269

At the far end was a hut several times larger than the others. Skulls lined a crude walkway leading up to it. Grulg didn't need to tell me this was Turd's place. No matter the people or the culture, there were always those who had to flaunt their swag. Grulg took us on a roundabout way toward the rear of the hut, keeping us out of sight from the rest of the village.

Once at the back, he lowered his voice so that we could barely hear it. "*Turd inside recovering from battle. Stay quiet.*"

Typically, when someone tells me there's a turd waiting for me somewhere, I'm not too enthusiastic about going, but since the fate of the world was potentially resting on this...

Grulg reached over to the wall and pulled up a loose section of leaves. It made an opening just big enough for Sally and me to fit through. I gave her a shrug, then made my way inside, hoping against hope that I would make it back out again in one piece.

* * *

Ugh! And I thought *we* smelled bad. Forget a few air fresheners – this place would require a tanker truck full of Lysol before it smelled anywhere close to habitable.

We emerged in a pantry of sorts. Crude shelves filled with wooden bowls lined the walls. I didn't bother to look in any of them, though, being pretty sure whatever they were filled with was still moving. I motioned for Sally to follow and, staying low, crept forward in the dark.

Though larger than the other huts, the construction was still primitive. We passed one foul smelling room with a large hole dug into the earth beneath it ... no doubt Turd's personal latrine. Hell, for all I knew, it could've been his bathtub, too. A partition of sticks and leaves stood in front of us. Peering around it, I saw the main living area before me. Even in the gloom of the hut, I could see fine, and what I saw caused me to grit my teeth in anger.

Peeking around to look, Sally whispered, "Damn, Turd got game."

Turd slept on a thick bed of moss off in one corner. Surrounding him, also sleeping, were several Sasquatch females. I highly doubted they were his sisters.

I turned back to Sally. "For someone whose mate just offed herself, he looks..."

"Shhh!"

"Huh?" I asked.

"Just listen," she whispered back to me.

"I don't hear..." but then I did. What the?!

I tried to focus in on the sound. It was ... *music*. Even odder, it was music that definitely did not belong here. "Is that ... Limp Bizkit?"

"Sounds like it to me," Sally confirmed. She again peeked around the divider. After a second, she pulled back and said, "Look closely at Turd."

I did as told. He still looked pretty battered from our battle the previous day. The beating he'd taken definitely hadn't done anything to make him any less ugly. However, his breathing was strong, indicating he was just asleep. A few moments later, he let loose with a rippling fart, momentarily drowning out the music.

Oh, yeah, the music. I looked closer. At first, I didn't see anything, but then something caught my eye. It was a white ... wire, it seemed. It crossed his chest, then separated into two, each one leading toward opposite sides of Turd's head. The other end led to something that was stuck in one of the skulls strapped across his chest. I strained my eyes and that's when I saw it – a little corner of white plastic in the mouth of the skull.

I pulled back and faced Sally. "Is it me, or does that fucker have an iPod?"

"And shitty taste in music," she added.

Ignoring her, I continued, "Aren't these the same assholes who are trying to start a war with us because they hate technology?"

"Yep."

"Okay, thanks. Just trying to make sure I'm not the stupid one here."

"Well..."

"Not helping, Sally," I snarled, a wee bit louder than I should have.

Make that a *lot* louder than I should have. There came a screech from the main room. I looked around the corner to see one of the females sitting upright and looking in our direction. She screamed again, rousing all of the tent's occupants.

Sally and I were covered from head to toe in Bigfoot excrement, but that didn't even begin to describe just how deep in shit we were.

The Great White North

I TURNED TO tell Sally to run but, low and behold, she was already making her way back toward where we'd come in. I took a split second to think bad thoughts in her direction before following her lead.

I emerged from the back of Turd's abode to find her standing with Grulg.

"*Go!*" he whispered.

"What about you..." I started to ask, but apparently he was way ahead of me there.

"*T'LUNTA SPIES!*" he screeched and then swung a meaty fist. It purposely went over my head and smashed into the closest tree, sending splinters flying.

I turned to run, but Sally hesitated for a moment. "Thanks, and sorry about this," she quietly said to him. Without further warning, she swung an uppercut, connecting squarely with Grulg's groin. Eight feet of solid muscle or not, you get your nuts turned into mashed potatoes and you're going down. Grulg was no exception. A high pitched keen came out of his mouth as he dropped to his knees, his hands cradling his pulverized privates. Once down, Sally grabbed his head and brought her knee up into it like a pint-sized pile driver. Grulg flew backwards and landed on his back, stunned.

"Now we go," Sally said, then took off running.

"What the hell was that for?!" I yelled as I caught up to her.

"Keep your fucking voice down," she hissed, running as quickly as the dense foliage would allow. "Just because they can't smell us, doesn't mean they're deaf."

"Fine," I replied, lowering my tone. "Why'd you take down Grulg?"

"Don't be an idiot your entire life. He's one of their warriors. There's no way they'd let him get away with just pointing and saying *they went that-a-way*. I saved his life by kicking his ass and I'm sure he knows it.

"Did you really have to nail him in the balls? I mean ... ouch."

"I do whatever works, and that was the fastest, most believable way to knock him down. Now shut up and keep running."

* * *

Some days I really didn't mind being a vampire. Don't get me wrong – if I wasn't an undead freak, I wouldn't be drenched in shit and running for my life in a frozen foreign wasteland from a pack of giant monkeys. Since I was, though, at least there were some perks to the job. Superhuman speed, strength, and especially endurance were really awesome things to have when being pursued by angry monsters.

Sally and I ran aimlessly for what felt like miles. Hell, for all I knew, it *was* miles. It's hard to tell when the only things you could see in any direction were trees and more trees. All I know is that eventually, Sally slowed down. She motioned for me to zip it, then stood there listening for a few moments. Since her senses were more acute than mine, I was happy to let her do the honors. Besides, if she made a mistake and we got caught, then at least I'd get to blame her before we were torn limb from limb. Sometimes it's the little victories that make life worth living.

"I don't hear anything," she finally said.

"Awesome. Think we lost them?"

"Hard to say. These guys can be pretty quiet when they want to be. This is their backyard, after all. The thing is, I'm not entirely sure they were ever actually following us."

"Grulg?" I asked.

"Yep."

"Makes sense. It doesn't help him if we're caught."

"Not to mention, we might rat him out to save our own asses."

"No we wouldn't."

"Speak for yourself," she said matter of factly. Say what you will about Sally, but she's a survivor. At the very least, if she's going down she's taking everyone else with her.

I took a moment to look around. Endless forest stretched in all directions. I found myself wishing I had joined the boy scouts that one summer like my parents had wanted, rather than just sitting in my bedroom playing Nintendo for two months straight. "Where are we?"

"The woods," Sally blithely answered. Yep, ask a stupid question...

"I meant do you have any idea where we are compared to, say, our camp?"

"Do I look like a fucking GPS to you?"

"Only if it stands for 'gives people syphilis,'" I snapped. "Seriously, can't you smell where the other vampires are or something?"

"All I can *smell* is shit, and since we're covered with it that doesn't exactly help us."

"Speaking of which..." I pulled off my ski mask again. Gah! It was getting kind of hard to breathe in that thing. Thank God for short Canadian days. The sky was already starting to darken, so we were probably okay. "Ah! That's a bit better."

"For you, maybe. Now I have to look at your face."

"Hey, at least they didn't see ours. Good thing we were covered up back there. Although you might want to ditch the hoodie. There's still enough pink showing where it'd probably be easy to ID you."

"I guess you're right. It's not like dry cleaning is really going to help it at this point." She stripped it off, sadly revealing herself to be wearing a shirt underneath, and tossed it into the bushes. "At least I can't freeze to death."

She did have a point. A human lost in the wilderness would be toast. A vampire, well, the worst we'd probably have to deal with would be an extended walk ... assuming, of course, we didn't meet up with another angry moose.

* * *

And walk we did. Hours passed, or I assumed they did. I had left my cell phone back at the hut. It wasn't much good out here in the land of zero bars. As for my watch, while supposedly waterproof, it was apparently not shitproof. It had stopped working not too long after we took a nosedive into the Bigfoot latrine.

We tried mostly to go in a straight line. Doubling back wouldn't help us, especially if we ran into any of Turd's group. We wound up changing direction only once or twice after Sally caught a few promising scents. It was kinda like hiking with the world's cutest bloodhound. Unfortunately, they were all false alarms. The stench coming off of us was wreaking havoc with both of our noses. Fortunately, though, smell wasn't the only enhanced vampire sense.

As we walked in full darkness, Sally suddenly cocked her head to the side. "Hear that?"

I listened. For a moment, there was only silence, but then my ears picked up a sound. It was distant, but definitely there.

"What is it?" I asked.

Of course, I got an eye-roll in return. "Did you spend your entire life indoors?"

"Oh, like you didn't," I countered.

"No, actually."

"Dressing up like Sheena: Queen up the Jungle for clients doesn't count."

"Hey, at least I've been camping before."

"Oh, yeah, when?" I demanded.

She opened her mouth to answer, but then hesitated. "Never mind," she snapped.

"Hold on. Spill! When were you camping?"

"It's not important..."

"Then I'll just assume you're full of shit."

"Fine!" She rounded on me, causing me to back up a step. "I was a ... Girl Scout, okay?"

That being answered, we continued on our way in respectful silence.

Oh, who am I kidding? I immediately started laughing my ass off.

"Sally the Girl Scout. That's great."

"It's not that funny, asshole."

"So did you go door to door selling your *cookies*?"

"Ignoring you now," she replied and trudged ahead.

"Tell me, do they give out merit badges for lap dancing?" I was just about to let loose with a tirade of Girl Scout jokes when the sound became noticeably louder. I finally realized what it was.

I caught up to Sally just as she stopped at the edge of a drop off. About twenty feet below us, a river roared past. It wasn't particularly wide, but it was moving quickly.

"This'll do," she said.

"For what?"

"Bath time," was all the answer I heard before being shoved forward into empty space.

* * *

FUCK ME! The water was cold, as in just a few degrees above freezing. I surfaced and immediately began screaming every obscenity in my arsenal (a not insignificant amount). There came a loud splash in response. I turned back and saw Sally surface about thirty feet behind me. I opened my mouth to voice my opinion on things, when I slammed into a rock. It felt about as good as it sounds. Unfortunately, before I could do much more than ponder my newly smashed skull, the current carried me into another rock, then another.

This went on for about five minutes or so, the river playing human pinball with my body. Fortunately, it's very hard for vampires to drown, that whole being dead thing coming into play. Sadly, there's nothing wrong with my nerve endings. The only good part was that I was soon too numb from the cold to feel myself being pummeled.

At last, the river became both wider and deeper. The pace of the current slackened and, within a few more minutes, I found myself treading water. The sound of the roaring rapids started to fade and silence settled in. I looked around to get my bearings and saw the shore about ten yards away. Teeth chattering, I began to paddle for it when something touched my leg.

I stopped and looked around. Nothing but quiet ... well that and a whole lot of freezing water. Must have been a...

It did it again. What the hell? Was there some hungry fish debating whether I'd make a good meal? Did they have alligators in Canada? I decided that it was best not to stick around to find out. I began to swim for the shore ... and that was when something grabbed my leg and pulled me under.

Frozen Wasteland

"GEE, BILL, I had no idea you could sound so much like a little girl," Sally said, standing at the edge of the water wringing out her hair.

"That wasn't funny," I replied, teeth still chattering.

"And yet here I am laughing. Who did you think it was?"

"I don't know, but when you've seen Jaws as many times as I have, you get a little nervous about things in the water."

"Why doesn't that surprise me?"

"Fine, so you got your little payback from earlier. Happy now?"

"You think I shoved you into that river just for some petty revenge?"

"You didn't?"

"Well, okay, I kind of did," she smiled. Thank God she looked really cute wet. Otherwise, I might've been tempted to slug her. "But, it was also necessary."

"Define necessary."

"Take a breath, genius. Notice how we don't smell like a pig pen anymore? Now I might have a chance in hell of catching a scent and getting us back."

"Hopefully you can do it before I freeze solid. Aren't you cold?"

"Freezing," she replied. "But, unlike you, I'm not a wuss."

"Good for you, ice queen."

We began to walk again. The river had completely turned me around. As far as I was concerned, we were hopelessly lost. Sally, though, didn't waver for a second before picking a direction and setting off in it. Who knows? Maybe she really had been a Girl Scout after all. Of course, it was possible she had as little clue as I did and was just faking it. Still, it beat standing there on the riverbank like two lost idiots.

"Think they started without us?" I asked, catching up to her.

"No doubt. Hell, François's men probably broke open the champagne when they saw that you weren't there to stop them from selling us out."

"Maybe Ed and..."

"I wouldn't hold my breath," she said. "They're humans. Without you around, they'll be given about as much consideration as two burritos. I'm hoping Nergui didn't even let them go. It'll be safer for them."

"Ooh, is that worry I hear in your voice? Sally and Eddie sitting in a tree ... F U C..."

"Finishing that thought would be detrimental to your health," she growled. Suddenly she stopped, so abruptly that I almost walked into her.

"Relax, Sally. I was just joking."

She turned and gave me a condescending look. "You need to try better than that if you want to ruffle my feathers."

"Then why..."

"A scent, two of them actually."

"What is it?"

"You want the good news or the bad news?"

"I'm an optimist at heart. What's the good?"

"I'm pretty sure I smell vampires."

"And the bad?"

"We'd better start walking a little faster. I think it's about to snow."

* * *

Snow was an understatement. One minute, nothing, and the next we were walking in a winter wonderland. If you're thinking it did little to help warm me up, you're correct. Fuck this shit! Once I got back to New York, I was locking myself away in my office with a week's supply of blood and a space heater.

We doubled our pace. The way it was coming down, it wouldn't be too long before we were wishing for snowshoes. Considering that Sally was unlikely to want to share body heat any time soon, that meant we had best track down the vamps she had smelled. I just hoped they turned out to be friendly.

* * *

"We're close. Just up ahead," Sally said.

I still couldn't tell the scent of other vampires for shit, but there was nothing wrong with my nose. I took a whiff. "I think I smell..."

"Diesel," she finished for me. "They might have a truck."

"As long as the heater is working, I don't care if it's a fucking Smart Car."

We moved more quickly, eventually breaking out into a full run – slippery ground be damned.

After a minute or two at that pace, Sally hit the brakes. She came to a halt and I followed her lead.

"What is it?"

"They should be here."

"Who?"

"The other vampires, idiot."

"Doesn't look like anyone is here to me." I cupped my hands over my mouth and shouted, "Hello!"

"I'm pretty sure if we can smell them, they can smell us."

"Well then, where are they? Don't tell me you led us into an encampment of the world's stupidest vampires."

"If so, they could crown you king," she quipped, taking another breath. "Oh no."

"I'm going to assume that's not a good 'oh no.'"

Sniffing the air, she walked a few yards to the right then stopped and dropped to her knees.

"So where are they?"

"Here." She bent down and began brushing snow away from an area. Within a few seconds, the slush began to mix with something black beneath it. It looked like soot or ... *ash*. "And here." She indicated a spot close by. "Four more scattered about the place, by the smell of things."

"Six dusted vamps?"

"Yep. If I were to place a bet, I'd say four negotiators..."

"And two bodyguards maybe?"

"Something like that."

"Well, I guess that mystery is solved."

"Not really," she said. "I think by now everyone assumed this is what happened. The question is not so much *what* as it is *how* and *why*."

"Can you ... err ... sniff out any clues?"

"Do I look like Grizzly Adams to you?"

"Who?" I asked.

"Never mind. And you call me pop culture ignorant," she said with a sigh. "I can try, although this goddamn snow isn't helping."

"You look here. That diesel smell is pretty close. I'm going to go check it out."

"Don't wander too far. If I have to come looking for you..."

"Yeah, I know, I'll never hear the end of it."

* * *

Fortunately, I didn't have to wander far at all. I crested a small rise about fifty yards away and saw the source of the smell down below. It was one of those big ass Snowcats, like the ones you see on the Travel Channel when they're off exploring the Arctic tundra. Goddamn assholes. They sent me a piece of shit station wagon that my grandparents could have owned, but these fuckers got a piece of prime tech. I was tempted to go back and take a nice big shit on each of their remains. Fucking Draculas!

Pushing my irritation aside, I realized that the Snowcat itself wasn't the interesting part. It was both its condition and the surroundings that caught my eye. They told quite the story, and it was pretty damn scary.

The Snowcat was lying on its side. It had somehow tumbled down into a shallow ravine. It was all beat to hell, but it didn't look like the crash had caused it all. The doors on the top side of the vehicle were completely torn off. Either something wanted out badly, or something wanted in even more urgently. Judging by the pieces of twisted metal strewn about, it seemed like that latter scenario was far more likely.

What could ... oh, who was I kidding? I knew quite well what could do this sort of damage. The wreck practically screamed that they had crossed paths with a couple tons of pissed off forest spirit. I had little doubt Sally was now coming to that same conclusion. A bunch of Sasquatches had waylaid our team, dumped the truck end over end, and then gone after the creamy center inside. The vamps, not being complete idiots, had made a run for it. However, their pursuers had...

Wait a second. Running full out, most vampires could outpace a Bigfoot. James had told me as much back when we were in Mongolia. Then how...?

Hmm, maybe it was an ambush. A few monkeys scared the vamps, then chased them right into the waiting arms of Turd and his minions. That sounded plausible to me.

I walked down to the Snowcat. It sure as hell wasn't going to be getting us back to anywhere anytime soon. On the other hand, if the inhabitants had vacated the premises quickly, then perhaps they had left some supplies behind. As I mentioned earlier, being a vampire means I'm not all that worried about dropping dead regardless of the circumstances. However, I was still freezing my balls off. Hell, I'd settle for tearing apart a seat cushion and stuffing the foam down my pants ... not that I needed to stuff anything down my pants to impress the ladies. It would be strictly for warmth, you see, and...

I let that train of thought go as I reached the vehicle and considered the best way to investigate. Oh well, when in doubt, go for the obvious.

Getting into the cab proved to be a snap. Not only were the doors ripped off, but the windows were all smashed, too. Judging by the spray of glass, they had been broken outward. Now the picture began to get clearer. While something ripped apart the door, the vamps inside had taken the express route to try and run.

Looking at the cabin – which was a lot roomier than the clunker we'd driven up in – I saw that I was correct.

The previous occupants *had* vacated the premises in a hurry. I saw bags of luggage and a large cooler stashed in the back. Suddenly I knew how my D&D character, Kelvin Lightblade, felt whenever he came across a treasure hoard. Heck, I didn't even have to kill any dragons to get it.

Yeah, all I had to do was dive in shit, run for my life, and then get swept down a river. Note to self: next time, hope for dragons.

I tore open the luggage, hoping for a few simple items that might be useful. I didn't need anything fancy. Besides which, showing up at camp all decked out in the regal finery of recently deceased diplomats might look a wee bit suspicious. I didn't relish the thought of Alex kicking my ass if that happened.

Oh, yeah, Alex. He would want to know about this.

Of course, I had no idea how. For starters, I didn't know if he was even still alive, much less where he was. Secondly, what was I going to tell him?

Hey, Alex, I found the negotiators.

Where?

Uh ... somewhere in the forest.

Oh, well, I'd cross that bridge when and if it became important. For now, I lucked out. I found a couple of coats and a few heavy sweatshirts. I stripped out of my still wet (and freezing, let's not forget that) clothing and put them on. They fit me okay, but Sally would be swimming in them. Oh, what a shame. Sally in clothing that was practically falling off of her ... *nice*.

Up next was the cooler. Much like ours had been, theirs was full of pints of blood. I knew most vamps preferred it fresh. However, large as it was, there probably hadn't been enough room in the Cat for a gaggle of human-sized snacks. Regardless, I was absolutely thrilled with the bottled stuff myself.

I bit into one. It was still fresh. The cold weather had refrigerated them, while the cooler had provided enough insulation to keep them from becoming bloodsicles. I sucked down two, then grabbed another handful along with some clothes for Sally. Never let it be said I was a bad sharer.

* * *

I came back over the rise to see Sally seated on a log. She was holding something and had her head lowered to it. What the fuck?

Hearing me approach, she looked up in my direction. I saw the telltale smear of blood on her face that told me she had been in the middle of eating ... err something.

"It's about time," she said.

"Worried about me?"

"Not so much for you as worried that you fucked something else up."

"Your concern is touching," I said. "Beware of vampires bearing gifts. Here." I tossed the bundle of clothes to her.

Though she hadn't shown the slightest outward hint of inconvenience, she quickly pulled a sweater over her head and put a coat on. She gave me the briefest look of gratitude – so quick I could have probably imagined it – before beckoning me over.

"I have something for you, too."

"Ooh," I replied salaciously.

"Not that, ass. I caught a rabbit while I was examining the area. I left half for you."

I was touched that she had thought of me ... grossed out, sure, but touched nevertheless. Still...

"Pass," I said, opening my coat and tossing a few blood packs to her.

She caught them and gave me a glare. "You couldn't have shown up with these things ten minutes ago?"

"Sorry. Didn't know the dinner bell was ringing."

"Well, thanks anyway. I hate rabbit."

"Doesn't taste good?" I asked.

"It tastes fine. I just can't stand picking fur out of my teeth."

* * *

I filled Sally in, both on what I had found and on my assumptions. She wanted to take a closer look, so we began walking back toward the disabled vehicle.

"So what did you find?" I asked, walking alongside of her.

"Nothing."

"Nothing?"

"Just six dead vampires."

"Well, I didn't expect the Bigfeet to stick around and gloat."

"That's just it. I don't think they were ever there. There aren't any giant footprints or damaged trees. There's barely any sign of a struggle."

"Ambush?"

"Unlikely. It's too clean. Also, there's no smell. I take it you've noticed that Grulg and our buddy Turd are somewhat on the *fragrant* side."

"Oh, yeah."

"Well, that kind of stink tends to stick around for a while. I mean, if I could smell those vamps, I should've been able to smell any lingering squatch-stink from twice as far away."

We crested the rise and the Snowcat sat before us. I pointed it out, although a blind man wouldn't have missed it.

"Well, whatever tore into that thing was definitely big and mean," I said. "The damn thing looks like it was hit with a wrecking ball."

"Mean, yes ... but I'm not so sure about the big part."

Her implications immediately clicked in my head. "François?"

"Yep. He might've been able to do this."

"By himself?"

"Maybe," she replied a little doubtfully. "It's hard to say. I haven't seen too many elder vamps go all out. To be honest, I'm not entirely certain what a vampire of his age can and can't do."

I nodded in agreement. Up until now, the Khan had been the oldest vamp I had ever met. Since the most action I had seen from him was shoveling food and drink into his fat face, that didn't exactly give me too many reference points. Still, I had seen James a few times. If he decided he needed to kill a truck, I don't think I would put my money against him.

By now, the snow was coming down even heavier. I was still in favor of examining the wreck and the surrounding area, but things were rapidly starting to look like the North Pole, minus Santa's merry workshop. Soon enough, we'd have a better chance of building an igloo than conducting an investigation. Besides, I barely even watched CSI. What the fuck did I know about crime scenes?

We decided that getting back was more important, especially since the victims of this massacre were all beyond our help.

"I'm open for suggestions," I said. "Maybe they have a GPS in the cab."

"The battery would be dead by now," she replied, as usual spoiling my plans with a little well thought out logic. "Follow me." With that, she walked toward the wreck.

I started after her, having no idea what she meant. For all I knew, she was planning on pulling off some kind of A-Team like stunt and fashioning a working snowmobile from the pieces. I mean, I had never seen Sally with a welding torch before ... and actually I didn't really fancy the thought of her with one. Still, that would be cool if...

Sadly, that train of thought was derailed as she came to the Snowcat and kept right on walking.

"So that's your brilliant plan ... we keep wandering aimlessly?"

"If I were as dimwitted as you, then yes. Fortunately, for us, though, I am a wee bit smarter than that."

"Well lead on then, Ms. Sooper Genius."

"It's pretty simple really. The Cat obviously rolled down this hill."

"I could've told you that."

"Yes, but what was it doing up there to begin with?"

"Well ... err ... I don't know," I admitted.

"Hence why you're following my lead. Duh."

* * *

Hot damn, Sally was right. We crested the hill the vehicle had tumbled down and found ourselves standing on a dirt road. It wasn't exactly a super highway – hell, it was barely a wide trail through the trees – but it was a sight for sore eyes nevertheless.

"I never cease to amaze me," she proudly proclaimed.

"I'd be a lot more amazed if you could tell me which way we're supposed to go."

"That way," she said evenly and pointed.

"Let me guess, you have a fifty-fifty shot of being right?"

"A bit better than that." She pointed down toward the wreckage. "The Cat looks like it rolled down the hill sideways. That means it was probably going the same way as it's facing now. Care to guess what's waiting in that direction?"

"A whole menagerie of freaky creatures?"

She tapped her finger to her nose. "All of them no doubt wondering where the legendary Freewill has wandered off to. Well, let them wonder no longer."

What Happened
While I Was Out?

I'D LIKE TO say we made good time. If the weather had been clear, we probably would have. A vampire running all out could probably beat a car on a road like the one we were on. Unfortunately, blizzards tended to be the great equalizer in these sorts of things.

With each passing mile, the snow got deeper and, even with our vampire senses, it was sometimes difficult to not wander off the trail (for me, anyway).

Fortunately, we had Sally's nose to help us along. Eventually she began to pick up traces of Sasquatch scent. We were entering their territory again, which meant we were going the right way. Soon she mentioned other scents as well ... lots of different creatures up ahead. If that wasn't the very definition of the peace conference, then I don't know what was. Good thing, too, as the weather kept getting nastier.

I was about to ask her, for probably the tenth time, if we were getting close, when she stopped dead in her tracks. Before either of us could utter a word, another voice rang out, "What are you doing here?"

* * *

I recognized it. As a shape materialized from the storm, I called out, "Alex? Is that you?"

"The same," he replied sternly, walking up to us. Unlike our mishmash of purloined clothes, he was dressed for the environment. Gone was the cloak he had worn earlier, and in its place was an outfit straight out of one of the Call of Duty Arctic missions. The dude looked like some combination of snow ninja and Navy SEAL. "I ask again, what are you doing here? Need I remind you that there is a peace conference going on..." he trailed off again, looked briefly at Sally, and then apparently made up his mind to continue. "A conference which I gave you *specific* instructions to oversee."

"Yeah, about that..."

"Instructions?" Sally asked, but then her eyes lit up with recognition. "I see. That's what you were trying to tell me the other day."

"Trying?" Alex asked.

"Sally stopped me. She was afraid François would compel her ... which, oddly enough, is exactly what happened."

Alex turned to her and inclined his head respectfully. "An impressive amount of foresight. I dare say, Sally, my people may have to keep a closer eye on you in the future. You have potential."

"Yeah," I commented. "Potential to be a..."

"But that still does not answer my question," Alex cut me off. "Is there a reason why you are out here rather than doing your duty?"

I shrugged and started telling him of our adventures from the past several hours. Since most vampires tended to be backstabbing assholes, I would normally err on the side of caution with one I didn't know too well. Unfortunately, James's hands were kind of tied in this situation. Being that my choices of who to trust were limited to François, Turd, and Alex, it seemed to be a pretty obvious choice to me.

Several times during the telling, Alex raised an intrigued eyebrow at my story. Sally, of course, had to jump in at points to *correct* some of my details or to point out my failings. Alex had to warn us back on track a few times after we broke down into our typical bickering. Finally, I finished. Thank God, too, as the snow wasn't exactly tapering off.

"I suppose I should be thankful I ran into you both *after* your little dip in the river," he quipped once we were done.

"Hilarious, I'm sure," I replied. "Can you take over now? I think we have enough here to hang the guilty parties by their bootstraps."

"Do not be so sure. You have circumstantial evidence at best against François. Elders are often given the benefit of the doubt in cases such as this."

"What about the First?" Sally asked. "Couldn't they compel him to confess?"

298

Alex shook his head. "Doubtful. It is difficult to compel any vampire over half-a-millennium in age. Even the most powerful of the First would be hard pressed to do that. Then there is the matter of the Grendel's leader."

"Turd?"

"Yes. What are you going to accuse him of? Vampires have no laws against music, at least last I checked. Besides, he isn't one of us. Any direct accusation against him would go a long way toward causing these talks to fall apart."

"I hate to break it to you, buddy," Sally spat, "but these talks are already up shit's creek without a paddle."

"Not the way I would put it, but I can see how you might think that," Alex replied.

"Wait a second!" I exclaimed. "You said direct accusation, right?"

"I did."

"What about an indirect one?"

"I'm not sure I follow you."

"That's okay, I doubt Bill is even following himself," Sally quipped.

I ignored her (despite knowing that she wouldn't go away) and explained, "I'm led to believe that the rest of Turd's tribe wouldn't be too happy to know about his little technology fix."

Understanding appeared in Alex's eyes. "Quite true. The Grendel have always shunned it."

"So I imagine their leader would be knocked down quite a few pegs if they discovered he was a gizmo junkie."

"Blackmail?" Sally asked. "I'm proud of you, Bill. You're playing with the big boys now."

I smiled back. "That almost sounded like a compliment."

"Don't worry. Won't happen again. The only question, though, is who's hooking up Turd?"

"François, obviously," Alex said, "although I am not certain why."

"Careful, that sounds a lot like an accusation."

He smirked. "I directly serve the First, Freewill. My accusations carry a bit more weight than most. Still, you are correct. Knowing *what* is not the same as *why*. That is why you must get back to the talks. Perhaps then we might gain insight into this."

"What about you?" I asked, exasperated that I was still somehow neck deep in this crap.

"I will go check on the remains you found. It's possible there is some bit of evidence that you have missed. Something that will help tie this all together."

We gave Alex directions as best we could. Hopefully he'd be able to find the wreckage, and maybe even more. Being pretty much a newborn in the vampire world, my senses weren't that great. Sally's were better, but she's not exactly ancient either. Perhaps Alex would be able to sniff out some clues that we could use to stick it to François once and for all.

We just had to be careful. If the French fuckhead caught wind of this, he'd no doubt try to stick me first ... no doubt with something sharp and pointy.

* * *

"You certainly picked an interesting time to disappear."

"Sorry, James. Sally and I took a walk in the woods ... and got lost." I shot him a quick wink. Hopefully, he got the point that I was being coy (as opposed to hitting on him) since there were others potentially within earshot.

"I see. And your somewhat interesting choice in attire?" he asked with a smirk.

"We had a bit of an accident."

"Indeed. So where is your hiking partner, anyway?"

"She refused to come here without changing first. You know how women are."

"Well, be that as it may, I'm sure you can fill me in on your adventures at another time. Unfortunately, you're a little late for tonight."

That wasn't particularly surprising, although that didn't make it suck any less. It also explained why I ran into James on the path to the meeting valley ... or whatever it was.

"They ended already?"

"Already?" James asked, surprised. "This was the longest session by far. They were negotiating for hours."

"Sorry. My watch kind of died. Unlike us, when it goes, it tends to stay dead."

"I should say so. Alma excrement is full of their fae essence. It can wreak havoc with electronics."

Now it was my turn to look shocked. "How ... did..."

"The Alma have a very *unique* odor. It takes a fairly thorough washing to completely eliminate it. I might suggest a good delousing before tomorrow night's proceedings."

"Noted."

"Come, walk with me," James beckoned me to follow. "The conference has already broken for the evening. We can take the scenic route back to your hut. It'll give us a chance to offer our proper *respects*."

"Respects?"

"Yes, one of the outcomes of this night's talks ... a very peculiar one at that."

* * *

"Does this place look familiar?"

"Yep. That's a tree ... and that's a tree. Oh, look there. Another tree."

James sighed. "I meant the area. I believe we're fairly close to where your friend..."

"Took the shit heard round the supernatural world?"

"As always, Dr. Death, you do have quite the way with words."

"Thanks, I try. Oh, speaking of my friends..."

"They're fine. They took their seats at the table and were mostly respectful ... at least one of them was. Ed, I believe his name is."

"Oh well, as long as Tom didn't get himself killed. Although I'm surprised they were there at all."

"Why?"

"I didn't think they'd go without me. I mean, I had told Nergui..." I trailed off before I said something that indicated my little adventure had been premeditated.

"Don't worry," James replied, "They never left Nergui's sight."

"Well, that's good. So, anyway, you were going to tell me how badly François's minions sold us out."

He raised an eyebrow. "I was going to say no such thing. I was merely going to tell you that François's team offered the Alma some concessions with regards to the *grave* insult from the night before."

"Uh huh. And pray tell, what concessions did they make?"

"That's the odd part," James said, continuing to walk. He seemed at ease, but I could see his eyes continually scanning the brush as well as the flare of his nostrils. If his spider sense started tingling, I was sure there would be an abrupt change in topics. "They offered up to Turd that we vampires would wish to pay homage to the Alma's dead as a show of respect."

"*We* vampires?"

"Not you or I, to be sure. To my great surprise, Turd was open to this."

"What's so surprising about them accepting a little ass kissing?"

"Am I correct in assuming that the envoy of the First brought you up to speed on the Humbaba Accord?"

"Alex? Yeah."

"Then you know that the dividing line between our territories and the Alma's are quite strict. The forests and mountains are theirs, plain and simple. Cities and towns are ours. Plains and Deserts are neutral territory."

"Glad I'm not a big fan of camping."

James waved his hand dismissively. "The occasional trespass is allowed. However, that tolerance does not extend to their sacred areas. We're here today by the Alma's invitation. Had we stepped foot into these woods at any other time, the response would have been both swift and brutal."

"Let me guess – in return, François offered to let the Bigfeet wander into our areas whenever they liked? Not like anyone in New York would probably notice."

"Hardly," he replied. "There was no such exchange, simply the offer on our part. What I also found odd was how the offer's details were settled upon. On the one hand, they're quite specific, yet they almost seem to purposely leave other aspects as vague as possible."

"How so?"

"The offer is not an open invitation. Only a set number of vampires will be allowed in, and only at predetermined times and locations."

"So when, where, and how many?"

"That was the vague part. That notion was tabled for post conference discussions, to be determined between the respective regional leaders of both the Alma and vampire nations."

"François and Turd."

"Precisely, and also exclusively."

"Exclusively?"

"Yes. The Alma have many such places of spiritual significance throughout the world, yet this is the only one that was brought up. Turd quashed any consideration for elsewhere, and François's men were quite happy to not argue the point any further."

"Because they got what they wanted."

"That is merely speculation, of course," James remarked, although the glance he gave me said he agreed.

"Of course," I replied. "Speaking of speculation, care to hear what happened after Sally and I got 'lost' together? You might be able to speculate a few new ideas from that."

Without warning, James spun to face me. "Your dalliances with that trollop are of no concern to me."

What the fuck? Did he think I was going to tell him about how I banged Sally in the woods? Don't get me wrong, I was flattered that he thought I had a shot with her. Not that I wouldn't have a shot. It's just...

That wasn't the case, though. I looked into his eyes and noticed him quickly glance over my shoulder. Not wanting to turn around and be entirely obvious, I listened. For a moment, there was nothing, but then I heard just the faintest crunch of leaves. I could have easily missed it had I still been yammering. Oh yeah, the hills definitely had eyes.

"Your loss, but let me tell you ... the things she can do with her legs, woo!" I shot back, maybe a tad over dramatically. Sorry, but I'd never been good at this espionage shit.

He let out the barest of sighs. I had little doubt his opinion of me dropped a notch every time we spoke. "Yes ... well, for now at least, you'll have to keep your adventures to yourself and your friends," he replied, dropping a hint that even I was able to pick up on.

In other words, I was on my own. What a surprise.

The Lying, the Witch, and the ... err ... Zombie?

I HAD JUST gotten back to my hut, still considering whether Sally and I might need to conduct some more "dalliances," as James put it, when I heard a cry from inside.

"Ow! You bit me!"

That wasn't exactly a confidence builder, especially when surrounded by vampires. I immediately rushed in, hoping that one of the neighboring vamps hadn't decided to snack on my roomies.

At first, I didn't see anyone. Then I heard the voice again, coming from behind Sally's curtain.

"You need to watch the teeth." It was Ed.

"Sorry, got carried away a little," a snarky female voice replied from the same location. Motherfucker!

"Get a room, you two!" I loudly announced, stomping over to my luggage for some clean clothes.

Ed immediately came running out. Fortunately for my sanity, he was still fully clothed. He did have one hand on the side of his neck, however.

"Oh hey, Bill," he said, a little flustered – a rare thing for Ed. "We were just..."

"I believe the phrase you meant to say," Sally said, also stepping out, "is that it's none of his fucking business." There was a slight smudge of blood on her bottom lip.

I glared at them for a second, until he replied, "Yeah, I guess she is kind of right."

"Men are such pussies," she commented with mock disgust.

Ignoring the hundreds of things I wanted to say, I instead opted for the practical. "Are you all right?"

"Yeah. Nothing a Band-Aid won't fix," Ed replied, taking a seat at the table.

I turned to Sally. "I thought I was pretty specific on that whole no snacking on my roommates thing."

"Oh, please. It was just a playful little nip."

I was about to make another snide comment when a thought hit me. "He's going to be okay, right?"

"What do you mean?" Ed asked, getting a bit wide-eyed.

"Social diseases aside," I continued, still facing her. "He isn't going to ... you know ... turn, is he?"

"Oh, shit, I forgot about that," he said.

"Relax, stud," Sally replied. "You're fine. I'm not exactly a newb here."

"Well, that's good. Not that I wouldn't make a better vamp than Bill."

"I wouldn't argue that," she said.

"You can both go fuck yourselves ... *separately.* Where's Tom?"

"He went off with Christy after the meeting ended."

"Figures," I replied. "James brought me up to speed on what happened. How about you, did you tell Sally or was your tongue too busy..."

"Yes, I told her what happened," he said, cutting me off. "Although, speaking of that, *thanks* for sneaking out earlier. When we saw you gone, Tom and I thought maybe Turd had dragged you both off. We were going to try to find you, but then we learned you had left Nergui behind as our guard dog."

"I already said I was sorry," Sally purred. "Besides, didn't I just make it up to you?"

"Does anyone have a stake handy, because I suddenly feel the need to impale myself on one?"

She sighed. "Get over it, Bill."

I took a deep breath and counted to ten. She was right. Getting all pissy about one of my best friends hooking up with a confirmed mass murderer could wait until we got back to Brooklyn. For now, we had bigger fish to fry. Though the possibility of all-out war appeared to be less likely, we needed to find out what François was up to and stop him before he handed Turd any more concessions on a silver platter.

"Fine," I said, getting my emotions under control. "I will, as long as you two keep it in your pants for now."

She shrugged. "We were just letting off a little steam."

"Then you should have packed a dildo," I replied.

"Well..."

"Too much information, Sally," I snarled, before turning to Ed. "No comments from the peanut gallery."

He mimed zipping his lips, although he couldn't quite keep the smirk off his face. Christ! And people complained that I acted immature. This was not the time for such infantile ... oh, fuck it!

Who was I kidding? Like images of Sally and her battery-operated friend weren't running rampant through my mind. My track record with women has never been great to begin with. Thoughts like that can definitely help a guy get through a dry spell, if you know what I mean.

Still, in times of crisis, one must be able to keep one's priorities straight. At that moment, figuring out what Turd and François were up to was at the top of that list. Jerking off to thoughts of Sally ... well, that could be tabled for a later time (and believe me, it would).

Changing topics, I asked, "Sally, did you bring him up to speed on our little adventure – assuming you weren't otherwise occupied?"

"Relax. She did," Ed said.

"Including how she and I took a bath in Sasquatch shit?"

His look told me she had left out that little detail.

"And I bet she didn't even brush her teeth before kissing you." Oh, yeah, we were supposed to be getting back to business. "But enough of that. What do you two think about this mess?"

"Even a moron could see that they're up to something," Sally said, ignoring my comment. "I just don't see what sense it makes."

"Maybe Turd's forces are even stronger than we thought," Ed surmised. "It's possible that François knows it and is doing his best to placate them."

"Sounds a little weak to me," she said. "Think about it. If I had an army at my command – one that I was just itching to unleash upon Canada – it would take a lot more than an MP3 player and an offer of respect to keep me from turning this place into the killing fields."

"I don't know. Ed might be on to something," I replied. "Why else would Turd make such a show about what was otherwise a minor offense? He could have been trying to force François's hand."

"Yeah, and maybe François has been offering more to him under the table," Ed added.

Sally shook her head. "Then why kill the Draculas' negotiators? He could have just told them what was going on and made them aware of the threat. Also, there's François himself. Every time we've seen him, he's been a smug little prick. The only time he lost his composure was when Bill kicked Turd's ass, and even then he didn't look worried, just pissed."

As usual, she had a point. François didn't act like someone who was desperate. If anything, he seemed far more like a puppet master. The only question was, whose strings were he pulling and why?

Before we could continue any further with that train of thought, Tom entered the hut with Christy in tow.

Sally shot quick warning glances to us as they came in. Tom wasn't the issue. I had known him since kindergarten and he knew more than his fair share of embarrassing shit about me. Christy was a different story, though. I was fairly sure that, regardless of her good intentions as of late, she still had a long way to go before we were going to let her join our inner circle.

"Hey, Bill," Tom said as way of greeting. "Glad to see you're still alive after you left us high and dry."

"Sorry," I said. "Places to be, monsters to see. You know the drill."

"Really?" he replied, taking a seat at the table next to Ed and pulling one of the bowls over. "Out in the woods, five hundred miles from nowhere, and suddenly you have a social life?"

"Be nice, Tom," chided Christy, once again unexpectedly coming to my rescue. "I think there's enough going on here to keep us all busy."

"If you say so, hon," he replied, scooping a handful out of the bowl and beginning to munch on it.

Before this trip began, I wouldn't have considered asking Christy for directions to my own bathroom for fear that she'd fireball my ass the second I turned my back. However, adversity makes strange bedfellows ... not that I'm into Tom's sloppy seconds or anything.

"What's going on over at your end of things?" I asked her.

She appeared to mull it over for a moment before replying, "It's a little strange. Two days ago the Forest

Folk were trying to rally us to their cause due to Ed's ... you know."

"Fertilizing their garden?" I offered.

"Yeah, that'll work. They even asked us to call up our master to discuss it with him."

I frowned at the thought of Harry Decker getting involved. I doubt he'd need much convincing to act against me. "Good thing there's no cell reception out here," I commented.

"It was via magic mirror."

"Lovely."

"But that's just the thing. They were beating the war drums when yesterday it suddenly all changed."

"How so?" Sally asked.

"Before today's session, we started hearing that peace was looking more likely."

"Really?"

"Yes. We all thought it odd, especially considering what happened between Bill and their leader."

"Yeah, you totally rocked Turd's ass," Tom said.

"I really don't want anything to do with Turd's ass, thank you very much," I replied. "Go on, Christy."

"Well, I'm sure they told you that today's mood was very positive all around." I nodded at that and she continued. "Just a little while ago, I started hearing rumors that the treaty was almost hashed out. There's supposed to be some sort of announcement tomorrow."

"WHAT?" Sally and I both shouted.

"Christy's right," Tom replied, still crunching away. "I heard them say it, too. Still freaks me out, hearing those things talk. Gives me Planet of the Apes douche-chills."

'Well, I guess that's a good thing, isn't it?" I asked, giving both Ed and Sally a meaningful glance.

Christy, unlike Tom, though, wasn't oblivious to these things. "What am I missing?" she asked.

Crap! I really needed to learn the fine art of subtlety. Now I had a choice. I could stonewall her, which would probably be for the best, but would completely erase any goodwill we had built up. Or, I could spill my guts and try to hope she kept her mouth shut.

"Dude, what the fuck are you eating?"

Or, I could rely on a convenient save.

I turned toward the sound of Ed's voice.

"What? It's just that trail mix shit they keep giving us," Tom replied.

"Does this look like trail mix to you?" Ed asked, holding out the bowl. It was full of grubs.

"Gross!" I cried out.

"What the fuck?!" Tom yelled, nearly falling out of his chair.

Ed sighed. "I was afraid something like this might happen."

Christy stepped over to her boyfriend's side. "Something like this? What are you talking about?"

"Tom didn't tell you?"

"Tell me what?"

"Before we came up here, we stopped off at vampire HQ in Boston and..." Ed trailed off.

"*And what?*" she demanded.

"Tom got bitten by a zombie."

"What?! Tom, why didn't you tell me?"

Tom, looking a little green around the gills, replied, "I kind of forgot."

"Oh, this is not good."

"I feel fine," he added.

"That," she indicated the bowl of bugs still in Ed's hand, "is *not* fine. One of you should have said something," she cried.

All three of us males gave her sheepish grins back. Sally merely shrugged, as if to say she couldn't have cared less (which probably wasn't far from the truth).

Christy grabbed Tom's hand and dragged him to his feet.

"What are you doing?" he asked.

"You're coming with me," she replied, sounding close to panic. "We can fix this. I know cleansing rituals. We'll perform them all night if need be." She began pulling him toward the door.

"But I feel..."

However, Christy was not to be dissuaded. She looked him straight in the eye and said, her voice indicating she was not taking no for an answer, "I will make this better, I promise ... even if I have to *burn* that creature out of you."

With one last look back at us, his face now mirroring the panic on Christy's, Tom disappeared through the door of the hut.

For a moment, silence reigned in the room. Then Ed leaned back in his chair and casually asked, "Can we get back to discussing the issue at hand now?"

"Harsh, man," I replied. "Aren't you worried about Tom?"

"Not particularly," he replied with a grin.

"Why not?"

To my surprise, Sally answered for him. "It's because he swapped bowls while everyone was listening to Sabrina there."

"You saw that?" he asked, impressed.

"Out of the corner of my eye."

"Why?" I asked.

"Because I figured you probably weren't ready to spill your guts to Christy quite yet."

"True."

"And also because it's fun to fuck with Tom."

Bemused grins broke out amongst us. It soon became laughter. After the week we had been having, we all needed it. Poor Tom.

Ninja Vampire Attack!

WE DECIDED THAT another midday expedition was in order. Considering our near miss the previous day, I originally assumed Turd would have his whole tribe up in arms about spies. After Christy's news, however, I thought that less likely. If there was a big announcement planned, they would hopefully be otherwise occupied.

It was a big risk either way. Still, it probably couldn't wait. If what we heard was correct, the negotiations were close to being complete. If we didn't act, François's fiendish plans – whatever they were – would be set in stone. Once a treaty was signed, the only way to undo it would be an act of war. The vampires weren't going to risk that. Hell, *I* wasn't going to risk it. On the flipside, if a treaty were signed that essentially fucked us up the ass, that wouldn't be particularly wonderful either ... especially since I had a feeling I'd somehow wind up getting blamed for it. Asshole vampires and their need for scapegoats!

Tom was still out being unzombified (and yes, it was still funny), and this time Ed wasn't about to be

317

dissuaded from coming along, so we all turned in early ... or late ... the whole nocturnal schedule thing still had me screwed up. Fucking Canadians with their idiotic short days.

The plan was to wake up during the daylight hours and sneak out again. Hopefully Nergui wouldn't give us any crap about it. I'm not sure the excuse we used the day before would work with Ed around, although I guess we could always claim that we were bringing him along as a picnic lunch. Yeah, that might work.

Part one of the plan went ... well, as planned. We rose just before the sun came up, dressed for the day, and prepared to head out. As a precaution, we left a note for Tom, in case Christy ever finished zapping him. It was purposely vague to be safe, but it would hopefully clue him in, although that was sometimes a tall order with him.

Unfortunately, as with most plans I made, part one was as far as we got before fate stepped in and took a great big steaming dump all over it.

Thus, when we finally stepped outside, it was only to be met by a trio of ... ninjas?

* * *

I was just beginning to wonder when I had stepped out of reality and into a Sho Kosugi film when realization hit. They (probably) weren't real ninjas, just vamps dressed that way for daylight operations.

When they saw us emerge, they formed up ranks, blocking our way.

"Um, excuse me, guys. I need to get past," I stammered. The good one-liners were never there when you needed them.

"I am afraid that is impossible, Freewill," one of them replied in a French accent. "Our orders are specific."

"Orders?"

"We are to keep you *safe*. It is rumored that there was an intruder seen in ze' Sasquatch encampment. We wouldn't want to put your life at risk at ze' hands of those scoundrels." Frenchy's smarmy tone suggested no such thing. I should have figured François would have heard about our snooping and done something like this.

"Thanks, but I think we're good. I already have a bodyguard," I replied. Unfortunately, a quick glance beyond them confirmed that Nergui was nowhere in sight. Oh crap.

"I am afraid that Monsieur Nergui has been called away on other *business*," came the response in that same irritatingly smug tone.

"Oh, enough of this shit," Sally said, stepping in front of me. "You have no idea who you're speaking to. If I were you assholes, I'd get out of the way before..."

ZAP

There was a crackle of electricity and she went down like a ton of bricks. Ed and I were by her side immediately. I looked up from her still twitching form to see that one of the pseudo-ninjas was holding a cattle prod. A thin trail of smoke rose from it.

"Oops," he said with a cruel chuckle.

319

"I'll give you an 'oops,' asshole," Ed barked. He ran back into the hut, reappearing a second later, shotgun in hand.

"Hold it!" I quickly said. Gripping Sally with one arm, I got back to my feet, then stepped between him and our black-clad "friends." "Let's all relax here before someone gets hurt."

"Someone already got hurt," Sally growled, beginning to shake off the effects of being tased.

"You know what I mean." Still keeping a firm hold on her – and only barely noticing that my arm just so happened to be wrapped around her oh-so-wonderful breasts – I stepped back into the hut, motioning for Ed to follow.

Only once we were back inside did I release her. She immediately rounded on me – black eyes, fangs, and all. I instinctively took a step back. Tiny as she was, Sally was not on the list of people I wanted to tangle with.

"We could've taken those..."

"Shhh!" I hissed at her. Then in a much lower voice, "Don't forget they can probably hear us."

"I don't care," she said. "I'm getting my gun."

"I'm with Sally," whispered Ed. "Three on three, and us with the boom-sticks ... I kind of like those odds."

"I don't care about the odds," I replied, half-amazed to be the lone voice of reason. "But if you two open fire like this is the fucking O.K. Corral, every vamp, wizard, monster, and blob in the area is going to hear. Think about it. Even if James shows up, he's going to have a hard time convincing everyone that we haven't gone nuts. Best case: they kick us out of here and François wins. Worst case: they kill our asses..."

"And François still wins," Ed finished for me, lowering his gun. "I hear you. So what then? We sit here and act like good little prisoners?"

I shook my head. "No, we can't afford to do that. I think we should wait them out for a while, give them a false sense of security, and then try sneaking out the back."

"There is no back."

"This place is made of shit-covered twigs. We'll *make* a back."

"Or," Sally said, walking past us, "we kill these fucks quietly. That'd work, too." She went over to the table and ripped one of the legs off. She turned back toward the entrance, makeshift stake in hand.

I quickly stepped in front of her. "You need to relax."

"No, I really don't. I have a rule about anybody who puts a couple thousand volts through me."

"Why doesn't that surprise me?" I commented. "But acting hastily isn't going to help, especially since I'm pretty sure François didn't just put a couple of schlubs out there to babysit us. I'd be willing to bet that those guys know what they're doing."

"Yeah, Bill's right," Ed said. "Getting our asses kicked by a bunch of frogs would be kind of embarrassing."

* * *

We spent the next ten minutes arguing back and forth. Unfortunately, as tended to happen with our bickering, at times we got loud enough so that I'm sure the guards outside were more than aware of every single plan we came up with. The dickheads were probably snickering to themselves, in French no less.

I will admit that thought did make me wonder whether Sally's plan had some merit after all. Back in college, during my freshman year, the third floor of my dorm was reserved for international students. Let me tell you, there is definitely a secret to uniting people of all races, creeds, and religions ... just add some French assholes to the mix. It didn't matter where they came from or what they believed: Muslim, Jew, or Hindu; Chinese, Japanese, or Korean; black, white, or mixed, they could all agree on one thing: everyone hated the French students. My God, what a bunch of smug, cliquish douchebags.

I was still caught up in this reverie when I heard a noise from the entrance. The three of us turned to see a flash of light. There was a quick grunt of surprise and then two more flashes followed. I may not be the most experienced vamp, but I had seen more than my fair share of dustings to know one. I had little doubt that there were now three smarmy piles of ash lying in front of our tent.

Before we could step out to investigate, the "who" part of the equation was answered for us. A figure stepped inside. Though covered up against the sun, the mismatched eyes were a dead giveaway.

"Well, what are you all waiting for?" he asked.

"Alex?"

"Obviously," he answered, pulling off his hood.

"What are you doing?"

"I'm pretty sure he just..."

"I know *what* he did, Sally. Now's not the time."

Alex ignored our little back and forth. "Indeed. The time for subtlety is over. François's plans are nearing fruition. The First are counting on you, Freewill. Fulfill your destiny."

Okay, that was a little heavy. Still, I guess he had a point. The fate of vampire-kind, heck potentially the entire world, was in the balance. I'd hate to go down in history as the dude who fucked it all up.

"And that involves what, exactly?" Ed asked.

"Whatever you were planning on doing, human. I have simply removed the obstacles in your path. We do not have time to play François's games any longer. Unfortunately, this place is swarming with those loyal to him. They will not take kindly to the disposal of their comrades, so you need to get moving *now*."

And just like that, our original plan was back on. That was convenient. It was nice having my own personal *deus ex machina*. I could definitely use one of those in my day to day life. Hmm, wonder if Alex would be available for hire after this whole debacle was done with.

"Are you just going to stand there daydreaming?" he asked, snapping me out of my self-important delusion.

"Sorry. Yeah, let's get going."

Ed still had his shotgun and this time there was no argument from me when Sally grabbed her own sidearm. That being done, I motioned for them all to follow me. Alex hesitated, though. What a surprise.

"Let me guess, you have other business to attend to?" I asked with a pained sigh.

"Sadly, yes. I am still gathering my own evidence. We will get more done if we split up."

Ah yes, spoken just like the victims from any of a hundred different horror movies. Oh well, it's not as if he was part of my original plan anyway.

"Fine," I replied. "Good luck."

"To you as well. May the luck of the First smile upon thee."

Yeah ... okay. Personally, I'd rather they didn't. It seems that the luck of the Draculas brings with it a flood of unwanted crap, much like giving your phone number to a telemarketer.

We all stepped out of the hut. Alex immediately took off, heading ... err ... left (it's not like I carry a compass). Within seconds, he was gone.

"Well, that was a little weird," Ed commented.

"There's a vamp after my own heart," Sally replied, kicking one of the mounds of vampire dust. "Everyone packing?"

Ed and Sally both had their guns. That left me. Thinking fast, I reached into one of the ash piles and plucked out a cattle prod. "I am now. Let's go before anyone else shows up to rain on our parade."

* * *

As before, I let Sally take the lead. Her nose was better attuned than mine. I could smell Bigfoot stink all around us, but she could pinpoint the direction from whence it originated. Even without Grulg to show us the way, I had little doubt we'd come across Sasquatch central soon enough. The only question was whether we could do so unseen. Considering that we were armed, I doubted they'd believe we were just out for a morning stroll. People (and other things) were funny that way.

Fortunately, luck was on our side ... well okay, it probably wasn't. I imagined that luck was probably waiting for just the right moment to deliver a massive kick to our teeth. What can I say? My almost-year of being a vampire had made me just a wee bit cynical about these things.

Eventually we came across a fairly well-traveled trail. The number of oversized footprints leading both ways confirmed that we were on the right track. We followed it, trying to look as non-suspicious as possible – and probably failing at it.

As we got closer and still didn't see any sign of Turd's people, my confidence in our plan grew. This time yesterday, the Sasquatch tribe had been mostly asleep. Considering the "big news" that was being bandied about for the conference, I was hedging my bets that the majority of Turd's followers would either be resting up for tonight's festivities or off preparing for it. Of course, if we wound up being wrong ... well, that would be bad.

* * *

"It smells worse than the time Tom and I went to that all-you-can-eat Mexican buffet," Ed muttered.

I had noticed it, too. The Sasquatch village was just up ahead. We decided to chance leaving the trail to perform a little reconnaissance. If things looked too hairy (hah, I kill me), we'd bug out, hopefully without being caught.

"There," Sally whispered. Sure enough, I could see crude huts ahead. All looked quiet. So far, so good.

We found a patch of dense bushes that offered both concealment as well as a good view. We hunkered down and proceeded to watch.

For several minutes, there was little of interest to see. I soon grew bored. I have no idea how cops on stakeout do it. I'd be there for five minutes, see nothing, and then radio in "Looks like he's innocent," before driving off to find a donut shop.

I was just about to suggest we either find a new vantage point or start moving in to investigate, when Sally grabbed my arm and pointed.

"What?" I whispered. "It's just a hut."

"Watch and learn, stupid."

"Fine, but I don't see ... holy shit!"

"Pay dirt," echoed Ed.

On the far side of the village, about a hundred yards away, was an oversized, but otherwise unremarkable, hut. I figured it for maybe barracks or a meeting hall, nothing really interesting. However, there was one decisively odd thing ... namely the vampire stepping out of it. It was François. He was dressed as dapper as ever, holding an umbrella to shield himself from the sun. He looked like a prissy little fuck. If he was a mega-douche, though, he was still dwarfed by the giant shit that followed him ... a shit named Turd.

* * *

"Motherfucker," I gasped.

"We got the asshole," Sally said, a wicked smirk appearing on her face.

"Yep. Ed, get a photo."

"What?"

"Take a picture."

"With what?"

"Didn't you bring your cell phone?"

"Why the fuck would I do that? If you wanted photos you should have brought your own fucking phone."

Oh crap.

"Sally?"

"Don't look at me."

"Goddamn it!"

"Relax," she said. "Look, they're leaving." Sure enough, they started walking off together.

"How cute," I replied. "It almost looks like they're on a date."

Ed remarked, "For François's sake, I hope he's the pitcher and not the catcher."

I had to cover my mouth to keep from snorting laughter. Asshole.

Finally, the unlikeable duo disappeared from sight, seemingly headed toward Turd's hut. Who knows?

Maybe François had a real case of jungle fever after all. Unfortunately, that brought on a case of the chuckles again.

"If you're through amusing yourself, let's go," Sally said.

"Go where?"

"Inside there, moron." She indicated the large hut. "There might be some proof as to what those two are up to."

Oh, yeah. I had been so preoccupied with the thought of François riding himself some giant monkey meat, I had almost forgotten about that part.

I mentally forced myself to focus. We were close. I didn't know what awaited us, but I was sure we were on the precipice of something big. Whatever was inside that dwelling was important enough for François to gamble the fate of the world over. Surely the risk to our lives would be worth it to prevent global Armageddon.

I just hoped we didn't have to find out whether or not that was true.

A Sticky Situation

WE TOOK IT slow and made our way across the outskirts of the village. No point in fucking this up when we were so close. Finally, we made it. We emerged from the brush behind our target.

I pointed toward the back of the building. "Should we make a hole?"

"No, it's clear," Sally replied. "Let's try the front door. We just need to be quick about it."

"Okay. Ed, maybe you should stay here and cover our rear."

"And maybe you should suck my dick. No way am I missing this."

I glanced at Sally. She gave an unconcerned shrug, then started forward. At the edge of the clearing, she stopped and looked around. Seeing nobody, she crouched down and waved us forward. The three of us crept toward the entrance about twenty feet hence.

I don't think any of us let out so much as a breath until we were safely inside the structure. Once there, we stopped to listen. I didn't hear any sounds, but just to be safe. I turned to Sally. She quickly shook her head, so we continued forward.

A rough curtain of what looked to be various animal pelts stitched together concealed the back entryway. I pushed it to the side and stepped through. As I waited for my eyes to adjust to the darkness within, Ed flipped on the flashlight attached to his shotgun.

It wasn't a meeting hall or barracks for that matter – thank goodness.

"It's a warehouse," I whispered.

"Or a distillery," Ed said.

Crudely made wooden barrels filled the area, save for the far end. There, a series of large cauldrons rested over a bed of coals.

"Do you smell that?" Sally asked.

"Sasquatch ass?"

"No, besides that. It smells ... sweet."

"Sugar-coated Sasquatch ass?" I ventured, earning myself an eye-roll.

She stepped up to one of the barrels. "It's coming from inside of these." It was capped, but little things like breaking and entering weren't a concern for a person such as Sally. Extending her claws, she dug them in until she found purchase, then easily pried the top off.

Ed and I both stepped forward to look. Inside was a thick, viscous liquid.

"What is it?" Ed asked.

"Sally's right. It does smell sweet."

"That doesn't answer my question," he rightly pointed out.

"True enough," Sally said. "Only one way to find out." She reached forward and dipped two fingers into the substance. "Hmm, it's sticky. I wonder..."

"Wonder what?"

Before either my roommate or I could say anything else, Sally's other hand shot out and grabbed Ed by the throat. His mouth opened in surprised and she jammed her fingers into it.

"There," she said brightly. "Is it what I think it is?"

"What the fuck?" I growled. "That stuff could be..."

"Syrup," Ed said, licking his lips – the surprise evident on his face.

"What?"

"You heard him, simpleton," replied a smarmy voice from behind us. "It's maple syrup. Now kindly step away before you contaminate the whole batch."

* * *

"So now you know," François said. He and the massive form of Turd stood there, blocking our escape. "The question is, what do we do with you now?"

"Ignoring the whole 'what the fuck are you talking about' part for the moment," I replied, "how did you know we were here?"

"*Smelled T'lunta coming*," Turd answered. Oh yeah. We forgot about throwing ourselves into Sasquatch crap to cover our scent. Argh! What a bunch of fucking idiots we were. On the upside, at least we weren't caught covered in shit. That would have been fairly embarrassing ... not to mention kind of nasty when Sally jammed her fingers into Ed's mouth.

"Fair enough," I replied, trying to buy time ... for what, I had no idea. "Now we can get back to my main point: what the fuck are you talking about?"

"As if you didn't know."

"Actually I don't," I said honestly.

"Don't try and..." François stopped and looked thoughtful for a moment. "You really have no idea?"

"Nope."

"Me neither," Sally replied.

"I got nothing," Ed added.

Turd growled and took a step toward us. "*They lie!*"

Oh crap. Even armed as we were, we stood absolutely zero chance against both of them together. François appeared willing to talk, but if Turd decided we needed to die a grisly (*and sticky*) death, I was willing to bet that François would be more than willing to lend a hand.

Thinking quickly, I decided to do what I did best when confronted by deadly hell-beasts ... bluff my ass off.

"We've already done this dance, Turd," I snarled, taking my own step forward ... coming disturbingly close to being within his reach. "You lost. Try me again and I'll chew you up and spit you out like the little shit you are."

Hold on. Did I just imply that I eat shit?

To my incredible relief, though, Turd actually hesitated. It gave Sally and Ed both a chance to level their respective weapons at him, hopefully adding to my threat.

Still, if Turd smelled us coming, I had little doubt he'd soon catch a whiff of our desperation. I needed to keep talking and hope for a break.

"Is it really worth it, you two? Seriously, you'd both risk war over ... syrup?"

"War?" François spat. "You honestly don't know what this is about, do you?"

"That's what we said."

"Turd, stand down. I don't think that will be necessary." The monstrous ape turned toward him with a glare, to which François quickly added, "Please, your mightiness. It behooves none of us to resort to bloodshed ... for now."

Mollified, Turd relaxed and stepped back. I wasn't sure if François was genuinely afraid of him or just kissing his hairy ass, but whatever the case, it worked. I nodded to my friends and they lowered their guns. This was the break we were hoping for. Now we just had to make use of it. The trick was going to be getting these two psychos to talk and then figuring out some way to make a break for it. I tried thinking back to my high school chemistry classes. Was maple syrup explosive? Nah, probably not.

"There will be no war, Freewill. There never going to be," François said in a confident tone.

"So then why the hell are we all out here in Bumblefuck, Canada?" Sally asked, not really helping things.

"*Stupid T'lunta. You here because Turd is smart. I know worth of sacred trees. Worth that others will pay dearly for.*"

"So ... you want to be a lumber baron?" I asked, confused.

"No!" François exclaimed. "My God, you are dense. I've already said it. The syrup, it's worth its weight in liquid gold."

My friends and I exchanged dubious glances with one another. I was fairly sure none of us had been expecting that. Hell, I suddenly wasn't sure that we hadn't somehow walked onto the set of some weird-ass reality TV show. This was almost too fucking surreal to be happening.

"So let me get this straight," I said, indicating the barrels behind me. "This whole thing: the conference, the threat of war, everything ... is all so you two can corner the worldwide syrup market?"

"He who controls the maple, controls Canada," François replied, an avaricious gleam in his eye.

"You've got to be kidding me."

"Foolish child, do you not know the value of that which you stand before? Why, in your country alone it's a six billion dollar market."

"Really?"

"Yes!" he cried, the crazy coming to the forefront.

"So all that shit from the other day, the ritual combat and all was a setup?" Sally asked.

"Quite true."

"But what about Turd's mate?"

At this, Turd chuckled. "*Turd have many mates. She was least favorite.*"

Ed shook his head. "Harsh, dude."

"All's fair in love and war," François replied with a sneer. "There are always bound to be pawns in any chess game. Take the Khan, for instance. The fat fool dared occupy my rightful seat on the First Coven."

"That was all part of this, too?" I stammered, not quite willing to believe a syrup-derived plot could be so far reaching. This shit would blow Scooby-Doo's mind.

"Of course. We needed a way to bring all the parties to the negotiating table. He was a more than acceptable casualty."

"And now that we know, we get to be acceptable casualties too, right?" Sally asked, gripping her gun tighter. "Just how I always wanted to check out – killed by Aunt Jemima."

"So that's how it's going to be then, eh?" I asked, readying myself for an attack that was probably only moments away.

"There's no need for that," François said calmly. "Unless you force my hand, that is. Killing the tramp and the human would be inconsequential. However, killing the legendary Freewill would lead to uncomfortable questions. I would just as soon not deal with such."

"But you have to know I'm going to rat you out," I replied.

"Will you?"

"Uh, I'm pretty sure I just said I would."

"That would be a shame. Then I couldn't offer you a share of the profits in exchange for your silence."

There was a pause in the conversation. Did this dickhead just offer me a bribe? He must've thought we had rocks in our head to...

"How much are we talking about?" Sally asked.

"What? Are you seriously..."

"I'm with her, Bill," Ed said. "Let's hear him out. He did say it was a six billion dollar industry."

"Yeah but..." and then it hit me. Ed was right. I could stand on my principles and try to fight my way out of this mess ... probably losing in the process. Or I could take a big fat paycheck, keep my stupid mouth shut, and walk out of here both wealthy, a hero, and without getting my ass kicked. Don't get me wrong. I like to think of myself as a pretty ethical guy ... but I'm not a fucking idiot.

I looked at my companions. They both nodded. Still, I had to consider the consequences of my actions. I'd be a hero, sure, but it would be undeserved. Also, there was a good chance that this asshole would get credit for the peace talks and end up winning the open slot with the Draculas. From what I had heard, they were already a giant cluster of dicks. Did I really want to make it worse by putting this douche on the ruling council, fucking over a friend – James – in the process?

On the other hand, not dying was definitely appealing. Fulfilling this would also get the Draculas off my back with regards to the debt they felt I owed them. Then there was the money. Not having to work again was a serious perk. I could buy myself a new computer. Hell, I could buy a nice car and new clothes. I could even afford to whisk Sheila away on a romantic weekend for two to someplace exotic like Aruba. But would she respect me if she knew I had done this?

Fuck it! It's not as if she would ever know. Should I ever confess my love to her, I doubt it would include a statement about selling out the vampire nation.

That settled it. Aruba, here we come.

"I think we can make a deal," I said. "Like Sally was saying, how much are we talking about?"

"Ten million at the very least," François answered with a big grin.

Whoa! Papa gonna buy himself a very nice brand new bag. "Each or split three ways?" I asked – hey, since we were negotiating.

"You misunderstand, Freewill," François said. "There will be no split. The less who know about this, the better. As I said, their deaths are inconsequential."

Uh oh.

I opened my mouth to protest. "Now wait just a..."

Unfortunately, I was a second too late. One of the barrels went flying over my head, slamming into Turd like a ... syrup filled missile, I guess. The container shattered, drenching both François and him in the goop. Unfortunately, Turd didn't budge an inch from the force of the impact.

"*Turd no like being sticky.*"

"You'll regret th..." François didn't get a chance to finish the threat as another barrel slammed into him. Sally's aim was impeccable.

"Move, *now!*" she ordered, right before opening fire. Before Ed and I could even take a step, both François and Turd had each taken a fifty caliber slug in the leg. No way was it going to stop them, but it would hopefully make all the difference in a foot race – which is exactly what we found ourselves in. Except instead of a gold medal, the prize was our lives.

French Fried Mountain Oysters

"PLEASE TELL ME you're still packing those silver slugs," I said, making it back outside.

"Never leave home without them," Sally replied with a sly grin. That was good. Silver didn't mix well with vampire blood. Right about then, François's leg should be starting to look like a giant Roman candle. Unfortunately, I had no idea if it would have the same effect on Turd.

"Think it'll stop them?" Ed asked.

A bellowing roar answered before I could. Yep, that was about what I expected.

"Sally, you take Ed and make a run for it. I'll try to hold them off."

"Really?"

"No, not fucking really! Do I look batshit crazy to you?" I replied, bolting for the tree line.

* * *

"Crippled or not, we can't outrun them at this pace," Sally stated. She was right. Our vampiric speed was one thing, but Ed was still human. Though arguably in better shape than I was, he wasn't exactly a long distance sprinter (I had once heard him say, "People who have time to jog should get a second job"). I wasn't about to leave him behind and thus had matched his pace. Sally, in a surprising show of humanity, had done likewise.

"I'm open for suggestions."

"You could leave me behind and try to find help," Ed said.

"No way, dude."

"Good," he replied with a grin. "Because if you had said yes, I would've shot you in the back."

"Asshole."

"If you two are finished verbally blowing each other," Sally growled, "we could use a real plan."

Another roar followed by a splintering crash told us that the Sasquatch leader was on the move. If we were going to come up with something above and beyond *let Turd run us down and tear us limb from limb*, it would have to be soon.

"It sounds like there's only one of them," Ed said. That made sense. As I had noticed earlier, the settlement had looked deserted. The other Bigfeet had presumably been sent ahead to prep for the day's events. Still, I would have expected at least a few guards. Was it possible that Turd was keeping his dealings with François under wraps from his own people?

Turd obviously kept some of his followers in the loop. That would explain the Squatch that accused us of being defilers. On the other hand, there was Grulg. He was obviously not pleased with his leader's antics.

The big question was whether the majority of his people knew about this. Considering the empty village, I was willing to bet the answer to that was a big fat "no." I had pretty much dismissed Turd's technology fetish, but perhaps there was something to it after all. Maybe it was something we could use.

Another bellow echoed through the woods, this one a lot closer.

Shit! I wouldn't be able to use anything against anyone if I got my head pounded into mush.

"We need to make a stand," I shouted, before I could consider the idiocy of saying so. Seems the Dr. Death persona deep within my psyche was once again feeling brave. Oh well, it was better than nothing ... barely.

"We can't outrun him in the woods, and we can't hide either. But if we concentrate everything we have, we might be able to stop him."

"I can dig that," Sally said, loading a fresh clip into her comically oversized handgun.

"No killing," I warned.

"Aw, you take all the fun out of my afterlife."

"If we do that, we might as well sign the declaration of war ourselves."

"Bill's got a point," Ed agreed.

"First time for everything," Sally replied. "What about François?"

"Fuck him," I said. "We light that asshole up like the Fourth of July."

"Ooh," she purred. "Now you're making me all tingly inside."

* * *

We got lucky and emerged into a small clearing. At the far side, we stopped and took cover amongst the trees. Sally and Ed aimed their weapons while I readied the cattle prod just in case their guns didn't stop him.

As we waited, inspiration hit (sorta). "If he doesn't go down, stop firing and try to draw him off."

"Why?"

"I'll jump on his back and bite him."

"Will that work?"

"Beats the fuck out of me."

Sally and Ed both exchanged doubtful glances. Gotta love their faith in me. Oh, well, fuck it. It's not as if they had anything better to offer.

We hunkered down and waited. The second Turd showed his ugly face, we were going to give him a twenty-one bullet salute.

Only he didn't show up. Only seconds earlier, it had sounded like he was right behind us, but now it was quiet – too quiet.

Oh, fuck! Suddenly I remembered that these guys weren't just giant, foul-smelling apes. They were giant, foul-smelling *forest spirits*. Trying to catch Turd in an ambush would be like a bunch of backwoods rednecks hoping to master the intricacies of the NYC subway system on their first try. A sinking feeling hit my gut. However, that almost immediately paled in comparison to the feeling that hit the back of my head.

WHAM

One second, I was thinking how fucked we were going to be, and the next I was sent flying, completely clear on the concept of how fucked we actually were.

I landed hard, eating dirt (I hoped) as the sound of gunfire erupted behind me.

* * *

I was lifting myself from the ground when a foot planted itself squarely in my back, forcing me down. It was way too small to be Turd's.

"You disappoint me, Freewill," said François. "Such a strategy would have been pathetic for a two-year-old, much less a being of your *legendary* status."

I tried to spit out a witty retort, but my face was pressed down into the dirt.

"What was that?" he asked, bemused. "Sorry, I didn't catch you?" The foot lifted off me, but almost immediately impacted into my side. I rolled over onto my back with a gasp of breath. François's foot came down onto my chest, again pinning me in place and cracking a few ribs for good measure.

I blinked the debris out of my eyes and looked to find him grinning down at me. "I believe you dropped this," he said, bringing up a bloodied hand and dropping something from his fingers.

The bullet plinked off my forehead (*ouch*). I looked at the leg holding me down. There was a massive gash in it, partially cauterized. Goddamn! The crazy asshole had dug the bullet out with his own fingers. This guy was hardcore.

The sounds of battle caught my attention from behind François. It was a tree splintering, followed by a cry of pain ... Sally.

I struggled to sit up, but he pressed down even harder. It was getting difficult to breathe.

"No no no, Freewill. Let us not interrupt. Turd would be ever so cross if we intervened in his fun. You really should have taken my offer. Your friends are still going to die, and now you'll be left with nothing."

"Nothing?" I spat back. "I can still rat you out."

"And who would believe you? You are the aggressor here, after all. You came to Turd's village to assassinate him. It just so happened that you failed."

"Assassinate?"

"Yes. You obviously got past my guards – probably even killed them – in your mad quest to start a war. We even have the wounds to prove it now." François's sneer grew ever more arrogant. "Why, if Turd wasn't so busy killing your little trollop, I would almost consider thanking her for setting this up so perfectly."

As he rambled, I began feeling around with my hands for something I could maybe use as leverage to get him off me. I didn't stand a chance against him or Turd, but I'd be damned if I was going to let either of these shits kill my friends without trying to do something about it. All I needed was a rock, a branch or a ... my hand closed upon something even better.

"I'll tell you this, asshole. Your plan is pretty ballsy."

"Isn't it, though?" he replied.

"Yeah ... pity that you aren't."

I brought the cattle prod up and slammed it into his smarmy French crotch.

Round Two

THERE WAS AN instant satisfying sizzle followed by a smell that ensured it would be a while before I could enjoy fried salami again, and then François let out a pained yelp. Music to my ears. He actually backed up a step, letting the pressure off me, but sadly, that was it. A shock powerful enough to put a buffalo on its ass was little more than a joy buzzer to a vamp of his age.

He swung and knocked the weapon from my hand. It was little more than a casual swat for him, but I felt at least two of my fingers break. Goddamn, this guy was tough. If only...

Jesus Christ, sometimes I could be such a fucking moron. I had this nasty tendency to forget that I had a few tricks up my own sleeve.

Quickly, before my rational mind could talk me out of it, I tried to sit up. As expected, François aimed a kick at my head. Stupidly for him, he did it with the same leg that had been holding me down ... the leg with a still oozing wound. I let him catch me square on the mouth with it, sinking my teeth into the still raw flesh before I had time to reconsider.

I wrapped my arms around his leg and held on for dear life as I bit deep into his thigh (damn, if that didn't sound a bit fruity). The force from the blow would have probably knocked me flat out unconscious had I not managed to get a mouthful of blood at the same time. I swallowed and it hit my gut like a flamethrower. I began to power up almost immediately. Time to go Super Saiyan, motherfucker!

François screamed as I dug in like a tick. His fist slammed into the side of my head and for a moment, I was pretty sure I had been decapitated. Fortunately, his blood had also kicked my vampiric healing into overdrive. I bit deeper and could feel my cracked skull knitting itself back together – quite the odd sensation. One more crunch and I found what I was looking for. A massive gush of blood washed over me as I chewed through François's femoral artery (or whatever it's called ... I left the anatomy shit to Dave). I sucked it down as quickly as I could. I was going to need the extra juice.

Finally, with one last gulp, I shoved François away before he could try and punt a field goal with my head again. He went flying back, nearly to the edge of the clearing.

I stood up, feeling his power course through my body. Suddenly a worried thought hit me. I waited for a second. However, no change came over me. A moment later, I realized why. As amped up as I was – and believe me, I felt like I could bench a truck – François's blood wasn't as strong as that which had transformed me two days prior. Heck, it wasn't even in the same ballpark.

That was a sobering thought. Somewhere out there was a vamp whose power made James and François look like children comparatively.

I was brought out of my ill-timed reverie by another of Turd's growls from off in the trees. My friends! Hopefully I wasn't too late.

I turned to where François lay. Amazingly, he was getting back to his feet. His leg was still gushing, but even as I watched, I could see the flow beginning to slacken. With the silver bullet out of his leg, his healing was starting to kick back in. Still, he had lost a lot of blood. He was currently no match for me and he knew it.

"Enjoy your friends' funeral, *assassin*." He turned and ran. Even with his mangled leg, he was gone from my sight within moments. His speed was now mine as well, though. I turned toward where I had heard the sounds of battle. The world seemed to slow as I accelerated far past my normal limits. Maybe there was still time.

* * *

Yep, there was still time.

I heard Sally's voice from up ahead. "Hurry up and fucking reload! I can't do this all day."

In the space of a heartbeat, I came upon them. Ed was busy jamming shells into his shotgun. Sally, being both faster and more durable, was playing a dangerous game of chicken with Turd – a game she couldn't win.

From the look of things, Turd had already bounced her off a few rocks. Her left arm hung at a bad angle, one side of her face was bruised almost beyond recognition, and blood flowed freely from a gash on her scalp. Still, she continued bobbing and weaving, trying to stay just out of his reach.

"*She-T'lunta give up and Turd make death painless,*" the chieftain of the Sasquatch growled, taking another swing at her. Sally backed up, but her feet got tangled in the brush. She went down.

"*Turd lie!*" he screamed gleefully, then leapt. Sally's eyes opened wide as he flew at her. Then they opened even wider as a blur of motion (that'd be me) slammed into Turd mid-leap, driving him into, then through a tree.

"It's about time," I heard her gasp.

"You're welc..." was all I was able to get out before Turd backhanded me off of him. I went flying and once more landed ungracefully in the dirt. It hurt a lot more than when he had hit me the day before. I needed to remember that this battle wasn't going to be as easy. I had François's strength, but for all I knew, I was still heavily outclassed by Turd.

Only one way to find out. I got back to my feet and faced the now extremely pissed off Bigfoot leader. I raced forward and drove a fist into his gut. He let out a heavy "Oof!" but then nailed me with his own swing, easily knocking me aside. It felt like being hit by a freight train. Once again, I felt my overcharged healing kicking in to mend bone. Still, the exchange had answered my question. I was faster, but Turd was definitely stronger.

Oh well, I could still use that. I had been in enough scrapes to know a thing or two about facing down a superior opponent.

I stood still as he charged forward, opening my eyes wide and trying to look scared (*which wasn't all that difficult to do*). He loomed over me, triumph showing on his face, and brought his two massive fists down ... onto nothing. At the last second, I had put everything I had into one quick burst of speed.

I sidestepped Turd, and came up behind him. I locked my arms around his mid-section and tried to force him off balance. Unfortunately for me, that put my head about even with his ass. As luck would have it, just then Turd let out a sasquatch-sized fart.

Holy mother of all that is unholy! Let me tell you, I have been in the presence of some nasty ass stink in my day. Hell, one time Tom ate a whole bowl of beans and then let one loose in my room while I slept. I thought I was going to die then ... but this, this was a whole new world of punishment. I backed up coughing, certain that my eyebrows were in the process of melting off. It was a mistake.

Quicker than I would have thought a creature of his size capable, Turd spun and wrapped his massive hands around me. I was little more than a ragdoll to him and he knew it. He lifted me over my head and, before I could do anything about it, I was airborne.

I must have flown over ten yards when – *RIIIP* – I slammed into something and an incredible pain shot through my body. I opened my mouth to scream and nothing but a gurgle of blood came out. No wonder. I looked down to see the jagged end of a tree branch protruding from my abdomen. I was impaled at least fifteen feet off the ground. The branch had missed my heart by inches at most, but unfortunately had gotten pretty much everything else. I felt absolutely shredded on the inside.

"Bill!" I heard a female voice yell. Hmm, she sounded vaguely familiar. Wish I could've spared a few moments of thought to remember her name. Sadly, there wasn't much room in my head for anything other than, "HOLY MOTHER OF GOD, THAT FUCKING HURTS!!"

Amidst the pain, I could feel a glimmer of red rage building up in my head.

Oh, no! Not that!

My involuntary Freewill powers were kicking in. A part of me wanted to give in to it. I knew the change increased my power far beyond what even François's blood could provide. In its grasp, my body would probably shrug off this injury. Even better, my mind would blank out and I wouldn't feel or remember a thing.

The rational part of my brain knew that would be a mistake. There was little doubt I could and probably *would* kill Turd in that state. That would be bad ... really bad. It would mean war. Even beyond that, though, I didn't trust this Mr. Hyde persona lurking deep inside me. So far it hadn't hurt anyone I cared about, but that didn't mean it wouldn't. Neither Ed nor Sally would be able to escape if I decided to turn against them. That thought sobered me up.

I brought up a hand and slapped my own face. My head rocked back from the impact ... oh yeah, I was still amped on François's blood. That's the second time I've done that. Idiot! I really needed to remember my own strength. Fortunately, it served its purpose. My head cleared a bit and I felt the rage recede back toward controllable levels.

I looked down to see Turd standing there, his arms raised in triumph. Asshole!

No, wait ... make that *stupid* asshole.

He was either too busy gloating or didn't consider my other friends to be a threat. It was going to cost him.

A shotgun blast rang out through the forest. The slug caught Turd in the side. There was a spray of blood, but the impact itself barely rocked him. It did, however, get his attention, which was apparently the goal.

Turd didn't notice that Sally had gotten back to her feet. She tackled him at the knees from behind and he went down hard. She then leapt upon him and brought her fist down into the back of his head, hitting with enough force to crack a cinder block. It was a hell of a shot, but I doubted it would do much against Turd's thick skull.

She looked up at me. "Well, are you going to hang around all day?"

You gotta love Sally, supreme bitch that she is. But, she had a point. As much pain as I was in, I wasn't dust yet. As bad as it might be, I would (*probably*) survive. It was time to extricate myself from this mess.

Pity it was going to hurt ... a lot.

* * *

Did I say it was going to hurt? Hah! Hurt would have been a pleasant vacation compared to the all-consuming agony that transpired. I gripped the end of the branch that was sticking through my front and snapped it off. Unfortunately, doing so vibrated the part still stuck inside of me, which had the effect of making it feel like someone was taking a hacksaw to my internals. Tears streamed down my face from the effort. Sadly, I still wasn't done.

Bracing my feet against the trunk, I pushed. Doing so scraped the shit out of my organs, but finally, after what seemed an eternity of pain, I was free ... free to land face-first on the hard, unforgiving ground, the only cushion being a slurry of my own bodily fluids.

"Any year now," Sally growled, still doing her best to keep Turd grounded.

"Are you all right, Bill?" came Ed's far more sympathetic voice. I felt his arm loop around mine as he attempted to get me back to my feet.

"No," I gasped through a mouthful of blood.

I looked up at my friend and realized I could hear his heart thumping away. François's power was mine, but so were his heightened senses. Even aside from all the gore I was covered in, I could still smell the blood running through Ed's veins. Worst of all, I wanted it ... *badly*.

No! I recoiled from his touch, not even wanting to consider the thought.

"What?" he asked, worry masking his face.

"Stay back," I warned in a slightly stronger voice than before. "I'm having a vampire moment here." I needed to concentrate on something else. I had never felt so intensely the need for blood. Then again, I had never gotten a six inch hole punched through my gut either. Live and learn.

I began to realize that I was indeed going to live. With every second that passed, I felt the pain continue to recede. Older vampires were stronger and healed a shitload faster than us newbs. Fortunately, François was pretty damn old. My insides were rapidly knitting themselves back together. Within a few minutes, I was going to be back in the fight.

Sadly, I didn't have those few minutes. Without warning, Turd rolled over and brought up a massive fist. He hit Sally full-on and she went flying. She landed hard, finally skidding to a stop ... unmoving, either stunned or fully unconscious.

Ed, raised his gun, but I shouted, "No!" even as I was already on the move again. It hurt like a motherfucker to do so, but I had a feeling it was going to hurt much worse if I didn't end this quickly.

Ignoring the pain, I grabbed one of Turd's big feet (hah!) before he could stand. Using my stolen strength, I began to turn, dragging the oversized monkey with me. He had no leverage save to claw at the dirt, and it wasn't enough.

I spun faster and centripetal force took over. Turd's body left the ground, just like a kid being swung in a circle by an adult ... except for the fact that he weighed half-a-ton, smelled like shit, and the landing I had in mind would be anything but gentle.

"*Let Turd go!*" he bellowed.

"As you wish!" I cried, bringing my momentum to a furious climax and letting go – damn, I really needed to watch the porno puns. Regardless, it was a hell of a toss. Turd went careening through the air before smashing headfirst into the base of a tree.

"And the shit hits the fan!" I yelled, right before losing my balance and falling on my ass.

"Nice one, bro," Ed said, offering me a hand, three of them to be precise (I'd been spinning pretty fast, after all). I eventually grabbed the correct one and he hauled me to my feet.

"Yeah," I sputtered, trying to catch my breath. "That was pretty damn clever."

"I meant the throw, not the line."

"Everyone's a critic."

"Yeah, well everyone's going to be a dead critic if we don't get moving." He dragged me in the direction where Sally still lay. "I don't think that's going to keep him down."

He was right. There'd be plenty of time for patting ourselves on the back later. We needed to beat feet before Turd got back up.

We reached Sally and I turned her over. A small groan escaped her split lips, which was good. Unfortunately, the rest of her didn't resemble any part of good. She looked like she'd been run over and then dragged by a team of horses. I could see missing teeth, a broken nose, and God knows how many other contusions, but she was alive ... at least in the vampire sense.

"Still want to bang her?" I asked Ed.

"What?" he joked. "A little makeup and you'd never notice."

"God, I hope she can't hear us," I said, hoisting her up and throwing her limp form over my shoulder.

"Me too ... hey! What the fuck are you doing?"

"Sorry, man. We need to move fast, which means you need to shut up and play the bitch." I grabbed Ed with my free arm, and tossed him over my other shoulder. Fortunately, I still had a little nitrous left in my system. I was carrying two people, but they practically felt like feathers. "Now keep your head down. This could get tricky."

Thus, without further ado, I began running – putting as much of my stolen speed to bear as I could and hoping that I was going in the right direction.

If not, it would prove to be a fatal mistake for us all.

Crossing Enemy Lines

LUCKILY FOR ME, I'm not a complete idiot. I had gotten only about a hundred yards when I remembered to use *all* of my senses. I sniffed the air and caught multiple scents. I'm not a bloodhound, so rather than try to figure out which one was what, I simply put the ass-like stench of the Sasquatches behind me and kept all of the others to my front.

"I think I'm gonna puke," Ed complained as I ran.

"Aim for Sally!" I shouted back. "I like these pants." Whether or not he heard me, I'm not sure. At the speed I was making, there was a lot of wind hitting my face. And damn, I was making good speed. Hadn't I been impaled only a few minutes earlier? My gut was still tender, but the worst of the damage had already been repaired. Hot damn, elder vampire powers were awesome. To think that one day I'd have that kind of power all the time, well, it was a little heady. Of course, that assumed I lived long enough ... a big assumption as of late.

I spotted a small ravine ahead and had absolutely no desire to go around it. "Don't look down."

"Why ... Oh, God!" came the reply as I vaulted the thirty foot crevasse.

Yep, he looked down. Oh, well, I *did* warn him. I landed on the far side with a few feet to spare then continued onward. Hopefully, wherever my nose was leading me would be friendly.

* * *

Sorta friendly counts, too, I guess. I had been hoping to emerge in the vampire encampment and maybe find James. Then I could tell him ... hmm, actually I had no idea what I was going to tell him. The whole thing was so stupidly convoluted as to sound entirely unbelievable. I mean seriously, syrup ... really?

That point turned out to be moot, though. I saw a camp up ahead and it was definitely not ours. I really didn't care at that point. I could feel the power rapidly draining from me. The impaling and the extra juice required to stitch up my innards had depleted my batteries. Ed and Sally felt heavier and I was running a lot slower. As long as I didn't emerge into the waiting arms of François and his buddies, I would be happy.

"It's the Freewill," a female voice shouted. "And he's carrying victims!"

Or maybe not.

I stopped at the edge of the clearing, not wanting to further agitate the white-robed witch who stood there, arms up in a defensive gesture. Great, of all the various life forms in the area, I had to stumble upon the magical morons who wanted me dead.

"Relax," I said, holding up my hands. "We're all under truce here." I lowered Ed to the ground. "See? No victims."

Her eyes then shifted to Sally, still lying over my shoulder. "The beast has turned on his own kind!"

Others of her coven were starting to emerge and they didn't look happy. I quickly scanned the area. Where the fuck was Christy? If she was off porking my roommate and I got fried because of it, I was gonna be a wee bit pissed at them both.

"Open your fucking eyes," Ed snapped at her. "Stupid is no way to go through life."

A confused, if somewhat insulted, look came over the witch's face as her companions began to gather round.

"Way to improve the situation," I said out of the corner of my mouth. "Help me with Sally."

I lowered her to the ground and her eyes fluttered open. "Where are we?" she weakly asked.

"About to get zapped by the mages guild ... you know, the usual."

I got an eye-roll for that. Beaten to a pulp though she might be, Sally was back in the game. I offered a hand to help her up.

"You shouldn't have come here, Freewill," an older witch said, stepping forward. "You are not welcome."

"Sorry, they're with me," a voice called from behind her. Suddenly Christy and Tom were there, pushing their way to the front. Tom didn't look so hot ... actually scratch that, he did. In fact, he kind of looked like a boiled lobster. His skin was all red as if he had been repeatedly scalded.

"They're here at my ... invitation," Christy said to the older witch. "To help ... foster ... the peace."

"They look like they just stepped out of a slaughterhouse," the other witch pointed out.

"Well, you know vampires," Christy replied in a chipper voice. "Filthy animals that they are."

"Fuc..." Sally started to say, when I clamped a hand over her mouth.

"What my friend *meant* to say was sorry about that," I quickly stammered out. "You know us vampires. We just can't control the ole bloodlust."

A ripple of tension passed through the assembled coven. For a second I was sure we were about to get fireballed. Finally, the elder witch spoke again. "Just because we are under truce, do not think our mission has changed, Freewill. You would be wise to slink back to whatever foul grave you crawled from." She waved at the others to disperse and began to walk away, but not before turning back. "The master will hear of this, Christy. You're playing a dangerous game."

"Nice to meet you, too!" I called after her before turning to Tom. "What the hell happened to you?"

"I don't want to talk about it. Let's just say I had one horrific day."

I raised an eyebrow at that, then gestured to myself and Sally.

He just shrugged and replied, "Doesn't look so bad."

I had to restrain Sally from rearranging his beet-red face. Unsurprisingly, she still had a little fight left in her. "Down, girl!"

Ignoring our antics, Christy stepped forward and asked, "What happened?"

"I don't think we have time for the full story right now," I replied. "We need to get back and find James."

"James?"

"One of the few non-asshole vampires I know. He's one of the good guys."

"Oh. Sadly, time might be shorter than you think. We were all getting ready to head over to the meeting place."

"Great, I really need to invest in one of those rugged sports watches."

"Dude," Tom said. "Maybe you should invest in a new shirt first. Showing up looking like the lone survivor of a horror movie might not exactly fit the dress code."

"So says lobster boy," I shot back.

"Enough," spat Sally, stepping in front of me. "You two can fondle each other's balls later. We need to find James before François and Turd can convince every creature here to put you on their most wanted list."

"She's got a point, Bill," Ed replied. "Time is not on our side."

"Agreed," I said. "Let's get going." I took a step and then stopped. "You too, Christy."

"Me?"

"Yeah ... you've earned the truth."

She looked surprised for a moment, but then smiled. "Thank you, Bill."

"Welcome to the inner circle," Tom proudly stated.

"Besides, Christy," I continued, "if this turns into a clusterfuck – which I'm sure it will – they can't touch you. I'd prefer that at least one person makes it out of this mess alive knowing the truth." As idiotic at that truth might be.

* * *

"Are you okay?"

"Just need a minute," I said, gasping. Nearly back to our own encampment, I had gotten lightheaded. The next thing I knew, I was down on one knee.

"What's wrong?" Sally asked.

"Nothing," I replied, getting back to my feet. "I'm just running on empty. François's blood has worn off and I lost a ton of my own back there." It was the truth. Between the fight, the trauma, and the running, I had used up everything I had. Even the adrenaline in my system was fading, leaving me wanting to do nothing more than crawl into bed for the next couple of years. It was a pity that a rest break didn't seem to be in my near future. If any fighting broke out right then, the best I'd be able to do was stand there and let the bad guys break their hands against my face.

I took a couple of deep breaths to steady myself, then turned to tell my companions to keep moving. I saw my roommates exchange a meaningful glance.

"What?" I asked, ready to spit out a pithy comment regarding their sexuality.

"Here," Ed said. With that, he held out his hand, wrist up.

"Me too, bro," Tom added, doing the same.

I looked down at their outstretched arms in confusion. "You want to hold hands with me? I'm flattered."

"Don't be a fucktard your entire life," Ed snapped. "Blood. You need it. Go ahead and take some."

"What?!" I cried, horrified – partly because I was tempted to take them up on the offer.

"You heard him," Tom said. "Just don't tell anyone about this. It would be weird."

Sally sighed, but then offered her hand, too. "Might as well count me in. You'll get more bang from mine than from the fleshbags anyway."

I was ... touched. "You'd all do this for me?"

Tom laughed. "Dude, we're you're buds ... just as long as you don't make a habit of it."

"What the meatwad said," Sally added. "Besides, if you go down, chances are I'll come tumbling after. We are partners, after all."

I didn't know what to say, but I did know what to feel. I was proud as all hell to know them. With them at my side, I could face down every single Turd that life had to throw at me.

"Thanks, guys. I mean it. If I didn't have enough to go on before, I think I do now. Suddenly I feel a lot better."

"Are you sure?" Sally asked.

"Well, maybe I'll still bite *you* ... but only if you beg me first."

"Moment's over," she declared, putting her arm down.

"Aw, you know you will someday," I joked, right before noticing Christy. She had been watching the whole thing and actually had tears in her eyes.

"I'm sorry," she said, in a low voice.

"For what?"

"For *everything*. We've been wrong about you. You don't deserve our wrath."

"I've been telling you that, silly," Tom said fondly.

"I'm going to tell Harry that when we get back."

"Are you sure?" I asked. "He doesn't seem like the type who'll take no too kindly."

"I'll be okay. He needs to know that you're not going to be our downfall. The prophecy must be wrong."

"Thanks, Christy. I mean it." A smile crossed my face and I really did find I had the strength to go a little further. I started to walk.

"One more thing, Bill," she said.

"Huh?"

She turned to Tom instead. "Hon, remember that warding powder I gave you for your apartment?"

"Yeah."

"Be sure to vacuum it up before you let Bill step over it. It ... kinda would have ... vaporized him."

"What?!" I shouted, my jaw dropping open.

She smiled sheepishly at me. "Technically our truce was only for the duration of the conference."

* * *

The vampire camp was mostly deserted. I didn't see any of François's goons, which was good. Unfortunately, I also still didn't see Nergui, which was not so great. I would've felt better if we had him there backing us up, just in case. Oh well. I knew this wasn't going to be easy.

We decided to take a few minutes to freshen up. Tom was right about showing up looking like the last survivors of a Jason Voorhees massacre.

I had just barely put on a fresh shirt when I heard sounds coming from outside. I peeked out and spotted some figures walking in our direction. It was James and his people. Nergui was by their side.

"Thank God," I said, stepping out to meet them. A smile broke out on my face. "You have no idea how glad I am to see you."

James, however, didn't return my mood. "Alas, I wish I could say the same, Dr. Death," he said with a nod to his people. They immediately moved to surround me. "For now, I am afraid that you are my prisoner."

Guilty By Association

"LET ME GUESS," I said, not entirely surprised. "I tried to assassinate Turd and François?"

"You might not wish to sound so glib," James warned. "Others might view what you just said as a confession."

I turned to Sally and Ed. "I knew I shouldn't have let that asshole get a head start."

"I'm assuming you're going to ignore what I said about watching your tongue," James commented.

"C'mon, James," Sally said, "Let's be realistic here. You and I both know that Bill is a lot of things ... but a killer? I've owned kittens that were more terrifying."

"Thanks for the vote of confidence," I quipped.

"Be that as it may," James continued. "François showed up at camp not long ago. He was gravely injured and had quite the tale to tell. He told me and any Alma that were present. He even managed to summon the moderator early."

"In other words, anyone who would listen."

"Exactly. I hate to say it, Dr. Death, but your impressive display of power against the Alma leader the other day has only fueled this speculation."

"Yeah, but do *you* believe it?" Ed asked.

James smiled. "Well, I have seen Dr. Death in action under other circumstances. To say that I was less than impressed..."

"Yeah, yeah, we get the point," I interrupted, annoyed that I was being both arrested and insulted in the same breath. "So then why this?" I motioned around us.

Sally replied, "It's obviously to keep you alive, stupid."

"As always, my dear, you are quite astute with your observations," James said, a note of admiration working its way into his voice. "I am limited in regards to my actions here. However, François could not have refused my aid without sounding suspicious. Thus, by taking you into custody ourselves, Nergui and I can ensure that you remain unharmed until you get a chance to speak your peace."

"Makes sense," I replied. "I do prefer the unharmed part. Although, speaking of which ... Nergui, where the fuck have you been?"

My so-called bodyguard remained silent. He simply stood there by James's side.

"I'm afraid he can't answer," James said. "He's been like this ever since I found him. Poor fellow standing there guarding a tree stump, most likely thinking it was you."

I narrowed my eyes as a thought hit me. "Compelled?"

"Undoubtedly. Sadly, whoever did so is stronger than me. I can't undo it."

"Then why is he here?" Tom asked. "Isn't that, y'know, a little risky?"

"A fair enough question," James replied. "I don't believe so. Nergui appears to have been given several neutral compulsions. I can't tell the details, but obviously it includes orders to not speak of it. But fear not. His honor is unbending. He is here to provide protection at his mistress's wishes. Even compelled, I believe should anyone make an attempt against Dr. Death's life that his original orders will take precedence."

"Will that work?" Christy asked.

"Yeah, it should," I said, having had some firsthand experience. "Older vamps have more resistance against these things. Also, they can be shrugged off if the emotion is strong enough."

"Quite true," James added. "And I will vouch that there is no stronger emotion for Nergui than seeing his duty fulfilled." He nodded at his men to step aside for Christy. "I must apologize for my rudeness. As a member of a rival delegation here under protection of truce, you are of course free to go."

"Thank you," she replied, then added, "What about this human?" She indicated Tom. "He was with me when these alleged crimes were committed."

"Alas, he is a member of Dr. Death's contingent. As such, they must all stand with him."

"Thanks for trying, hon," Tom said with a smirk. "It's no big deal. I'm used to Bill pulling the rest of us down with him."

I somehow resisted smacking him upside the head. Instead, I asked James, "So what now?"

"Typically, conspirators at functions such as this would immediately be put to death." I opened my mouth to reply, but he held up a hand. "However, since you are the figurative leader of our side, that's a little different. I believe you will be given special consideration and at least be allowed to speak in your defense. I will caution, though: you should choose your words wisely."

"We are so fucked," Sally mumbled. Knowing my own penchant for verbal sparring, I wasn't entirely sure she was incorrect.

* * *

Fortunately, there weren't any handcuffs or restraints added to the scenario, another perk of my current station. Marching in with my head held high, as opposed to dragged in chains, might have a bit of a psychological effect in my favor ... hopefully.

Christy left us to rejoin her own group, assuring us she'd keep them in check for the time being. It was small comfort at best. The witches were the least of my worries, though. Being torn limb from limb by a bunch of Sasquatches was my chief concern right at that moment. Of course, being disintegrated by the giant glowing ball of doom wouldn't exactly be a walk in the park either.

Oh, well, I was sure I had an ace up my sleeve ... somewhere. Hopefully I could even figure out what that was before it was too late.

* * *

In many ways, I was kind of glad that Turd had set me up as the bad guy the day before. It made the crowd's reaction to my entrance seem less surprising. I was already used to feeling like the heel at a WWE event. I could handle this.

SPPT

"Take that, assassin!"

Or not.

Eww, goblin spit. That was fucking nasty. Got it in my hair, too. Jesus Christ, when this was all over (assuming I survived) I was going to spend an entire week in a nice hot shower.

"Ouch!" Again! This time, some little six-armed pixie thing nailed me in the forehead with an acorn. It was so *comforting* to know that, regardless of species, angry mobs were pretty much all the same.

James's men and Nergui all moved closer to me. James was right – compelled or not, Nergui was still doing his duty. That was something, I guess.

Sorta, anyway. Some flying thing buzzed over us and spilled its drink on my head ... at least I hoped it was a drink.

Either way, it was clear someone had been working the crowd against me. It was pretty obvious who that someone was. François had probably made a beeline back to the conference after escaping. It made sense. After all, he had more to gain by ratting me out than by staying and fighting. He knew I couldn't kill Turd without starting a war. Conversely, if Turd won, he would have killed my friends and dragged my battered body back for the same end result. I had walked right into their trap just like a dumbass.

Sure enough, standing there in the arena was François surrounded by his lackeys. One of his legs was wrapped in blood-soaked bandages. That was odd. He had already been healing when last I saw him.

I didn't see any sign of Turd yet, but did notice an awful lot of fur. Numerous Sasquatches stood around the perimeter of the meeting area, far more than had been there on previous days. That explained the empty village earlier. This was supposed to be a momentous day. After all, it was rumored that a new treaty was to be announced. Now, though, they all had a possible execution to look forward to as well. Wonderful; two spectacles for the price of one.

James and his men marched us to the bottom of the valley. There, all but Nergui stepped aside. Rather than leave and take their seats as before, they all moved to the perimeter. My friends and I were left standing there, unshackled and unguarded. It was clear, though, that such precautions were unnecessary. Considering the vamps and Sasquatches standing all around, there was no chance for escape.

* * *

A crackle of thunder blasted forth, no doubt meant to catch the crowd's attention. However, they were far rowdier than in days past. Our floating moderator thingee actually had to do it twice to get everyone to quiet down. I was personally hoping to see whether it would do so a third time or just start disintegrating random creatures. That'd be a hell of a way to deal with hecklers. Unfortunately, no such luck. The orb glowed brightly for a moment, possibly irked that its authority had been questioned, but then settled back down to its normal weirdness.

"THIS SESSION IS NOW IN ORDER ... THE GATHERED WILL RESPECT THAT." The threat hung in the air for a moment or two before it continued. "UNUSUAL CIRCUMSTANCES (unusual?) HAVE BEEN BROUGHT TO LIGHT. NON-PARTICIPANTS IN THESE TALKS HAVE REQUESTED AN AUDIENCE FOR GRIEVANCES. IT IS DECIDED THAT THEY WILL BE HEARD BEFORE PROCEEDINGS WILL CONTINUE."

Grievances? Jeez, talk about an understatement.

"FRANÇOIS OF THE VAMPIRES IS RECOGNIZED."

François had time for one quick look of smug satisfaction before hobbling forward to the center of the area, milking it a bit for added effect.

He cleared his throat loudly (douche) and said, "Today was to have been a momentous occasion. In a show of mutual respect, my people and our honorable rivals have been meeting outside of the confines of this conference..."

"THAT IS HIGHLY UNUSUAL," the glow-ball interrupted.

"Unusual, but necessary. We wished to meet each other face to face as equals, away from the eyes of those who have sought to disrupt the peace process." He cast a baleful glare at me. The motherfucker had no doubt rehearsed this. Probably had a script in his back pocket and all.

"It was time well spent. We discovered that neither of our species wishes war and were able to build upon that mutual desire. In just a few short days, we have been able to accomplish what our ancestors took months to do. Today we were to share those results with you. Sadly, this historic undertaking has been marred ... marred by treachery."

Whispers, growls, and gurgles of "Treachery!" rose up from the crowd. Talk about playing to the audience.

"SPEAK YOUR ACCUSATION."

"Yes," said François, building up the drama in his voice. "I shall. I accuse the Freewill!" He pointed a finger directly at my face. I was tempted to bite it, but I had the feeling that wouldn't exactly help my case.

"Just a few short hours ago," he continued, "I met with the leader of the Northern Tribes. I had been told of the wonderful news – that our two races would continue to coexist peacefully. As the humble servant (*yeah, right*) of my people in this region, I wished to convey my personal thanks to Turd for his honorable actions."

A slight movement in my periphery caught my eye. All of the Sasquatches at the perimeter were standing in rapt attention to François's tale. I could have sworn, though, I saw a distinct sneer of contempt from one at the mention of Turd's honor. Was that Grulg? Damn, how I wished these fucking monsters were all wearing nametags.

Despite my momentary distraction, François continued speaking. I missed a bit, but it's not as if I couldn't fill in the blanks. "...Freewill had already shown his disdain by defiling this place. But, was it enough? No, not nearly enough to satiate his war-mongering. He and his cohorts, whether compelled or simply enthralled by him, ambushed us. We fought back, knowing that peace is worth more than either of our lives.

"Sadly, you are all well aware of the Freewill's power. I was barely able to escape with my life, sustaining grievous injuries in the process." He indicated his leg. "Turd's fate, alas, is unknown. He bravely fought on, demanding I flee and live to tell of this tragedy. I have since asked the members of his tribe to send a search party looking for him. I can only hope that he, too, was able to escape the ravenous clutches of the beast that stands before us."

Various cries came from the audience as he ended his little fantasy.

"Murderer!"

"Enemy of the peace!"

"Filthy pile of *klobagh*!"

I didn't need a translator to figure out that last one. Motherfucking François! He had played them all like a violin. It was like standing in a courtroom facing off against a masterful lawyer ... which, come to think of it, wasn't entirely outside the realm of reality. The guy was at least seven hundred years old. Who knew what kind of degrees he had?

Well, fuck that, I say. He may have had more centuries under his belt, but I wasn't exactly a slouch. I had a decade of role-playing experience and a semester with the NJIT drama society. Hell, I've even watched Law and Order once or twice. If I was going down, I'd do so swinging ... verbally at least.

"THE ACCUSED SHALL ANSWER THE ACCUSATIONS."

I moved to step forward, but Sally grabbed my arm. "Don't fuck this up," she hissed. Gee, whatever happened to "good luck" or "go get 'em, sport?"

"No worries," I confidently replied. "I got this in the bag."

I walked forward and then took a dramatic pause to scan the crowd. I made brief eye contact with as many beings as I could (at least those with eyes) before attempting to entrance them with my oratory eloquence.

"François's charges are all ... bullshit." (Did I say eloquence?) Maybe not the best opening line ever, but that was okay. I could still win the crowd over. "For starters, you're several hundred years old, correct?"

"I don't see what my age has to do with your crimes, but yes," he answered.

Now for the *coup de grace*. "A vampire of your age should heal pretty damn fast. I say you self-inflicted the wounds on your leg right before coming out here." There were murmurs from the crowd at that. Oh, yeah, his entire case was about to fall flat on its ass and I wasn't even finished with my first thought yet. "I think we both know that any damage I did to you would have healed long before now."

"Like when you attacked me earlier?"

"Yes ... I mean no! I didn't..."

"See?" François bellowed to the crowd. "He admits his crime!"

Oh crap. I turned back toward Sally. She let out an exasperated sigh and dropped her face into her hands.

"That's not what I..."

"Shall we be forced to listen to more of his lies?"

"Hold on," I cried, trying to get control. "I'll admit there was a fight..."

Cries of "Deceiver!" and "Treachery!" began rumbling through the crowd.

"But it was all François's fault. He and Turd ... err ... there were these barrels of syrup ... um."

"SYRUP?" the glowing thing asked in a doubtful tone.

"Well ... yeah."

"Must we continue this charade?" François spat. "It is obvious that the Freewill is either lying or has been driven mad by his bloodlust."

Oh boy, this wasn't quite turning out as I had planned. Maybe I should've stayed in the drama club for an extra semester.

The crowd was now in an uproar. Innumerable threats were voiced. More debris was thrown onto the field. It looked about ten seconds away from turning into the world's freakiest lynch mob. I noticed Nergui inch closer to me. Bless his insane honor. Not that it would do me any good if a hundred monsters straight out of my childhood nightmares descended upon me.

"ORDER!" the moderator demanded. Unfortunately, even he was starting to lose control. I had little doubt the disintegrations were only a few moments away.

Just then, though, the crowd quieted. A hush came over them, followed by surprised gasps.

I started looking around for the source, when one of the Sasquatches pointed and barked, "*Turd! Turd lives!*"

I looked to the far side of the hollow to see, unsurprisingly, that he was right. Turd entered, flanked on either side by two other Bigfeet. He was an absolute mess. Blood was splattered across his front and sides. Nail marks ran down his cheek and chest. The skulls he wore glistened with gore. In short, he and François must've shared the same playbook because he looked a hell of a lot worse than when I left him. I had merely stunned him, but he looked as if I had backed over him with an eighteen wheeler. Bunch of fucks.

As he walked toward the arena floor, the Sasquatches around us all broke into chants of, "*Turd, Turd, Turd!*" Despite the grimness of the situation, I had to smirk. Damn, but it was still funny.

All eyes were on his entrance, save François's and mine. Ours met and locked on each other. I mouthed the word "asshole" at him and he grinned in return. Between the two of them, they were going to bury me. Talk about unfair.

Turd made his way to the center, directly opposite me. François gave him a respectful bow and stepped aside.

"TURD IS RECOGNIZED," came the booming voice of our moderator.

"*Freewill T'lunta try to kill Turd. But Turd still lives!*" the ugly fucker screamed to the crowd. "*Freewill want war!*" he added, drawing more nasty responses from those around us. He raised one hand to point it accusingly at me. It was covered in dirt and grime. Leaves and twigs stuck to it. I could see ants and assorted other bugs scuttling through his glistening fur.

Wait a second ... *glistening!*

That was it. Whereas François had been smart enough to clean himself up a bit before coming here, Turd had merely messed himself up more. The filthy fucker hadn't bothered to wash off the syrup. Maybe I still had a chance.

"*Turd wish for peace with...*"

"Turd wishes for nothing but profit!" I yelled out, drawing silence from everyone in the arena.

"THE FREEWILL HAS NOT BEEN REC..."

"Excuse me, but this is important," I said, risking a lightning bolt to the face. "Look at him. I mentioned syrup before and this asshole is practically covered with it. Syrup ... the sap from the *sacred tree*."

That obviously meant nothing to most of the participants there, but the Sasquatches around us immediately became a whole lot more interested.

"*Freewill is...*" Turd started, but he was interrupted by another voice.

"*Freewill speaks true! Grulg smell it.*"

Taking his cue, the other Bigfeet in the arena began to sniff the air. Each of them had a nose far more sensitive than even mine. Turd still smelled like shit, but I had little doubt that to them he now smelled like sweet shit.

That caught him off guard, but he quickly recovered. He growled at Grulg, then turned back to me. "*Freewill throw Turd into sacred tree.*" Oh, crap. What if they bought that excuse?

"Fuck that!" Sally cried out. "He'd have to throw you through a dozen trees to get that sticky."

Guess her knowledge of syrup production trumped mine. Way to go, Sally.

More murmurs from the crowd. I still wasn't home free, but at least there was some doubt. Sure, being covered in syrup wasn't exactly a crime. That fact didn't exonerate me in the least. Still, hearing a little doubt from the crowd was music to my ears.

The world seemed to pause for a nanosecond as this thought sunk in. Jesus Christ, how could I have forgotten? *Music!* Turd was wearing his skulls, the same ones I had seen that iPod stuffed into. It was a slim chance, but better than none at all. I had to hope he was anal about keeping his tunes nearby.

Without any further hesitation, I dashed toward Turd. Screams of outrage flew through the crowd as I stepped up to him.

Before I could do anything about it, though, powerful arms grabbed me from behind – François's.

"No! No more bloodshed, Freewill," he implored, starting to drag me back. He leaned forward and whispered in my ear, "Thank you, fool. You couldn't have done that better had I planned it."

"Yeah, well plan this, asshole!" I reached back and slammed my fist into his injured leg. He gasped in pain and his hold on me loosened just enough for me to surge forward again.

Unfortunately, I ran straight into the waiting arms of Turd. He grabbed me with his claws, and I could feel my rib bones start to bend. Goddamn, he was strong. It didn't matter, though. I was close enough. As he lifted me, I grabbed the string of skulls from his chest and tore them off.

I threw them to the ground, right as I became airborne myself. As I flew through the air, a sound not unlike shattering pottery told me I had finished the job.

Now I just had to hope ... OOF! Okay, first I had to land.

"ENOUGH," the glowing orb declared. "SUMMARY JUDGEMENT HAS BEEN PASSED. FOR HIS ACTIONS, THE FREEWILL SHALL BE..."

"*Look!*" I heard Grulg (*I think*) shout.

I lifted my head from the ground and saw that I had been right. Lying there in the remains of a shattered skull was a now broken MP3 player.

"Get up," Sally said from next to me. She hooked an arm around mine and hauled me to my feet. "I sure as shit hope you have something else," she whispered. "Syrup and shitty rock music are pretty goddamn weak against their accusations."

Once back to my feet, I shrugged. "I'm open for suggestions."

Still, maybe it was enough. The crowd as a whole was somewhat nonplussed by my *revelations*. The meeting place floor, however, was a different matter entirely.

I Can't Hear You,
I'm Screaming Too Loud

THE SASQUATCHES AT the perimeter had begun to close ranks around us. This time, though, their attention was focused entirely on Turd and what lay before him. Snorts of disbelief rose from them (I think. Hard to tell with snorts), but they gradually gave way to snarls of anger. Grulg's voice was chief amongst the agitators.

"*You betray the spirits! You betray our honor!*" he growled. Soon, similar accusations began to fly from the others as well.

"THIS IS HIGHLY UNUSUAL," the glowing thing commented. Since he had yet to proceed with my disintegration, I had to assume he was likewise intrigued. Hopefully this would be enough to make him rethink his summary judgment – which I assumed wasn't exactly in my favor.

I turned toward François. A look of disbelief was on his face, no doubt at Turd's idiocy. I mean, jeez, who brings the *murder weapon*, so to speak, to the scene of the crime? He began to back up.

"Hold on there, Frenchy!" I called out to him. "You might want to stick around. I have a feeling this is about to get goo ... URK!"

Faster than I could even blink, he was upon me. His hands wrapped around my throat and I could feel his claws extend as they began to dig in.

My air cut off (could vampires suffocate? Good question. Never bothered to ask about that) as he quickly increased the pressure to the point where I felt my head might pop off.

My roommates appeared by my side. They each grabbed one of François's arms, but they might as well have not even been there for all the good they were doing.

They weren't about to give up that easily, though, thank goodness. Tom grabbed that dopey Optimus amulet still around his neck. He yanked it off and pressed it into François's arm. Way to go, dude!

There was a flash and one of the hands choking me out began to sizzle. Sadly, the pressure didn't let up. Who was I kidding? This vamp had already shrugged off much worse damage than that today. Oh, well, it was a nice sentiment on Tom's part.

"Die Freewill!" François snarled at me, but his voice suddenly sounded far away.

A fist crashed into the side of his head – Sally's. Unfortunately, she barely moved him. I saw blood begin to spurt out from my direction, covering François's arms. Hmm, wonder if it was mine. For some reason it didn't seem all that important.

I felt all … floaty inside. It was kind of nice. I began to wonder why everyone seemed to be fighting against the friendly man in front of me. He was just doing me a favor … letting me rest comfortably while he…

And then, he wasn't there. Another fist had entered my field of vision from the other side. It was where François had been just a moment earlier. Before I could see who it belonged to, though, I found myself flopping to the ground, gasping, and holding my now-gushing throat.

My attacker was gone, but the damage had been done. I had already lost far too much blood today. I didn't have any left to spare. The world continued graying out. It was time for a nice long nap…

* * *

Or maybe not. An angel appeared in my field of vision, a pretty blonde angel. Gee, if Heaven was populated with babes like this, I couldn't wait to get there. Rather than fly me to my final resting place, though, the angel then did something a bit *weird*. She held up her arm and tore into her wrist with her teeth … her very long and sharp teeth. Did Angels have fangs? Maybe I wasn't going to Heaven after all. Still, if she was indicative of the demons waiting for me below, that might not be so bad either.

"Don't fucking argue with me, just take this!" the demonic angel commanded before jamming her arm against my mouth.

Ooh yummy! I thought, slurping the blood from her wrist – although I could think of other parts I would rather suck on a lot more. This babe was definitely a tasty dish. I couldn't believe Sally was...

Wait, that was her name – Sally!

The fog slowly began to clear from my head. I was lying on the ground and Sally was force feeding me her own blood. That was a little out of the ordinary. My vision became clearer and I saw not only her, but the worried faces of my roommates looking down upon me, too.

How the fuck did...?

Oh, yeah. François had tried ripping my head off ... had done a pretty good job of it too, if I remembered correctly. And Sally was ... hot damn, Sally was saving my ass. She wasn't nearly as powerful as some other vamps I had mixed it up with. Still, she was more than twice my age. That meant I would get at least a minor healing boost above and beyond my own abilities.

Sure enough, it seemed to be working. I didn't feel particularly wonderful, but I could sense the worst of the damage beginning to knit itself shut.

I took one last sip, then gently pushed her arm away. She and my friends looked down expectantly at me.

"I'd have rather been breast fed," I croaked.

"He'll live," she replied with mock disgust, not even bothering to disguise the smile on her face.

"Help me up," I said, my voice still ragged and barely recognizable, but alive ... at least in the vampiric sense of the word.

* * *

Chaos had apparently broken out while I had been down. I could no longer see Turd – just a sea of angry, smelly fur as the Sasquatches converged in a group, angry growls coming from them.

My friends were standing around me, probably making sure I didn't keel over again. I turned and took in the rest of the surroundings. Our moderator hung in the air, glowing an angry green color, but otherwise not doing much of anything ... which was probably a good thing. I saw James's men off to one side in an apparent standoff against François's.

Speaking of the devils, James had the asshole restrained in a chokehold. A silver dagger was in one of his hands tightly pressed against François's back. François, for his part, wasn't struggling. Smart. More powerful or not, he wouldn't have been able to do much before James dusted him. Regardless, a part of me kind of hoped that he would try.

The only one not doing anything was Nergui. Apparently still stuck under François's compulsion, he stood there glassy-eyed and unmoving. Even with the attack against me, the compulsion was still too strong for his base beliefs to overcome. Oh, well, at least François hadn't been able to compel him to attack me. Glass half full and all of that.

"What happened to not getting involved?" I called out to James once my throat had mended enough to do so.

He smiled and threw me a wink. "Your bad habits must be rubbing off on me."

"It matters not," François spat. "I've still won."

The sad thing was, he was right. Peace was still our primary mission. Saving my own ass or not, that didn't change. Even if his little syrup scheme got disrupted, peace would still mean a significant feather in his cap. He would probably wind up with a seat on the Draculas' coven and, at that point, I'd have made an uber-influential enemy.

"ENOUGH!" thundered through all of our minds. It wasn't quite a compulsion, but it got my attention the same way an air horn to the ear would. If that had been vocal, I'm sure there would be ruptured eardrums all around.

"THESE DISRUPTIONS HAVE BEEN TOLERATED, BUT NO MORE," our moderator beamed out, again at triple volume. "ORDER WILL BE RESTORED NOW!"

I gave James a nod and he released François. It was pretty clear from the warning that if he tried anything against me, he'd wind up a pile of ashes.

"ALL WILL LEAVE THE FLOOR SAVE FOR THE LEADERS AND THEIR RESPECTIVE PARTIES." It did not sound like a request.

* * *

It took several minutes, even with the orb's prodding, for order to be restored. Even then, the crowd continued whispering amongst itself. The Sasquatches seemed more interested in tearing Turd a new asshole than listening, but at last they backed off. They resumed their former places at the perimeter, but all kept their angry eyes locked onto their *leader*. Turd's negotiators, meanwhile, had been replaced. Maybe they had been a part of the whole thing. Who knew? All I could tell was a new group now sat at the other end of the table, Grulg amongst them.

For his part, Turd looked worried. A picture was beginning to form in my mind of what his share in all of this was. In exchange for letting François's men tap their sacred trees, his gadget fetish would be well fed. Before you knew it, he and his buddies would probably be all pimped out with Cadillacs, PCs, and big screen TVs. It would be only a matter of time before more and more members of his tribe were seduced by technology. If that happened, within a few years they wouldn't be all that different from us – in a manner of speaking, of course.

"YOU ARE STILL ACCUSED, FREEWILL," the moderator said. "WHAT SAY THE ACCUSER?"

Oh boy. Turd could still drag me down with him if he wanted. Peace would be maintained, but they could still demand my head on a platter.

Before Turd could speak, though, Grulg growled something at him in a language I couldn't understand. The others at the table snarled similar vocalizations.

Turd finally spoke, his eyes downcast. "*Misunderstanding between us ... me ... and T'lunta Freewill. Accusation dropped.*"

My friends and I let out a collective sigh of relief.

I turned toward the crowd and caught sight of François. He noticed me and our eyes locked long enough for me to mouth "*Fuck you*" to him. I then turned back to the negotiating table with a smile on my face.

"THE CHARGES ARE DROPPED AND STRICKEN FROM THE RECORD," Glow-ball said, thus making it official. Oh, yeah, case dismissed with prejudice, baby! "AN ANNOUNCEMENT WAS TO HAVE BEEN MADE. SHALL THAT TOO BE STRICKEN FROM THE RECORD? IF SO, NEGOTIATIONS WILL CONTINUE."

Oh, yeah. We were back to that. Damn, didn't Alex say that peace had taken a year to hash out last time? I was really hoping, now that the drama was over and done with, we weren't going to be settling in for the long haul. I was starting to jones for a hot shower.

Grulg stood and spoke, giving Turd one last growl before doing so. "*New treaty invalid,*" he said. Yep, I'd better change my name to Tarzan and get used to living in the wilderness. "*We instead offer T'lunta the Humbaba Accord. We reinstate old treaty as was done by our ancestors.*"

Whoa! That was a surprise ... a pleasant one, too. I once more sought out François in the crowd. The look on his face was priceless. I quickly flipped him the finger. No syrup for you, douchebag. Sure, he'd still likely get a seat on the First Coven, but at least he wouldn't profit obscenely in the process. A small victory, but I'd take it.

"AN OFFER FOR PEACE HAS BEEN MADE. FREEWILL, DO YOUR PEOPLE ACCEPT?"

I didn't bother to wait for François's asshole buddies to open their mouths. Alex had told me I was running the show, so it was finally time to take charge.

"We accept," I said.

With that, the crowd went wild, except this time, it was finally in my favor.

A Small Piece of Peace

"PEACE HAS BEEN BROKERED IN ACCORDANCE WITH THE TERMS SET FORTH IN THE HUMBABA ACCORD..."

Awesome!

"THE EXCHANGE OF VOWS WILL TAKE PLACE IMMEDIATELY TO SEAL THE PACT."

Vows? Okay, I guess we needed to pledge ourselves to maintaining the peace. Not a big deal.

"AS WAS DONE BEFORE, SO AGAIN SHALL THE LEADERS OF BOTH PARTIES TAKE A MATE FROM THE OPPOSING SIDE AS A SHOW OF FELLOWSHIP."

Hold on ... What? "Did he just..."

"I'm pretty sure he did," Ed said, a smirk starting to work its way onto his face.

"Does that mean..."

"THE MATES SHALL BE SELECTED AND MARRIAGE BONDS MADE IN ACCORDANCE WITH EACH SPECIES' RESPECTIVE BELIEFS."

Tom started snickering. "Congrats, Bill. Guess you're a family man now."

"Fuck you, dude."

"Yeah, Bill," Sally added, not bothering to conceal her mirth. "Have fun staying with the in-laws over the holidays."

"TURD, YOUR CHOICE?"

Both defeat and disgust were evident on Turd's face. He morosely huffed, "*Turd's daughter.*"

One of the creatures at the periphery stepped forward. Oh my God. It was over seven feet tall, uglier by far than even my worst blind date, and had tits that drooped almost to the ground.

"That's going to be one hell of a wedding night," Ed commented.

Assholes, all of them.

"FREEWILL, WHO WILL YOU OFFER?"

"Who ... I..." A truly evil thought hit me. I turned to Sally. "Partners forever, right?"

Her eyes opened wide. "Hold on! I swear to God if you..."

She never got to finish the threat for we were suddenly drowned out by a collective gasp from the crowd. What the?!

* * *

I quickly scanned the audience and saw all eyes facing the same direction. I followed them back to my *bride-to-be*. That's when I saw it.

The hilt of a dagger was protruding from her chest. I recognized the weapon. She glanced down at it, a confused look on her apelike face, and then, without making a sound, fell backwards to land on the ground dead.

I quickly spun around. "Nergui?"

He stood there calmly, his arm still outstretched.

"What the fuck, dude?"

"The princess was specific in her orders," he said calmly. "None but she are to wed the Freewill."

Holy fuck! *That* was the thing to snap him out of his compulsion?!

"I have fulfilled my duty," he continued with a smile. "I can die with honor."

You've got to be fucking kidding me. Motherfucking Gan!

Before I could turn to address the table, an earth-splitting roar of rage caught my ear. I spun back around to find looks of outrage on the faces of each and every Bigfoot in the place. Grulg stood and pointed a massive finger at Nergui.

Ten of the creatures immediately rushed forward from the sidelines. They descended upon Gan's overly loyal minion, clawing and tearing. He didn't even put up a fight. In fact, he was still smiling when he finally disappeared from my sight. Within moments, I saw the telltale flash of fire that said Nergui was no more. Just like that, he was gone, but the beasts didn't stop there. Driven into a frenzy of rage, they continued to stomp and pound on his ashes.

Oh, crap. How the fuck did this happen? We were so close.

"Listen, Grulg, Turd. I..."

But it was too late. Turd stood, once again firmly in charge, and shouted, "*WAR DECLARED!*"

Fuck me sideways with a jackhammer.

* * *

Pandemonium erupted. Howls and cries rose up all around us. Flashes of energy could be seen in the stands as myriad creatures readied themselves for battle. In the midst of it all, I sat back down in my seat, utterly stunned.

"What do we do now?" Tom asked.

"Fucked if I know," I answered honestly. I again looked around. Aside from Nergui, there didn't appear to be much bloodshed ... yet. However, there was a lot of angry posturing.

Across the table, I saw Turd lunge out of his seat, but several of the Sasquatches present restrained him before he could dive across the table at us. With a nod from Grulg, they began dragging him away ... although whether to save him from the fight that was about to break out, or for another fate, well, who knew?

I looked up at the glowing orb of death that continued to levitate above the table while everything went to Hell around us. Maybe there was still a chance to salvage this.

"Excuse me!" I shouted to it, my voice barely heard above the din. The entity flashed once, which I took as acknowledgement to go on. "Is there any way you can..."

"A DECISION HAS BEEN REACHED IN THIS ACCORD," it interrupted. "UNFORTUNATE

THOUGH IT MAY BE, MY DUTY HERE IS CONCLUDED. FAREWELL, FREEWILL."

"What? Hold on a..."

Before I could finish the sentence, there was an incredible crash of thunder and lightning. It was both blinding and deafening. When at last it subsided, the moderator was gone. Silence returned to the area ... for a moment anyway.

"Oh, yeah? Well, fuck you, too!" I barked at the empty space it had occupied just moments earlier.

"I'm sure that'll help," Sally muttered.

"*Freewill!*" one of the creatures across the table cried. "*Kill the Freewill!*"

Another joined in. "*Kill the T'lunta!*"

Oh crap.

Before they could make good on their threats, however, a roar drowned them all out. It was Grulg. Fuck! I remembered what he said would happen if we went to war. Just like that, I once more found myself unsure that any of us were going to make it out of there alive.

Once again, though, Grulg surprised me.

"*No!*" he commanded, catching many of the Sasquatches' attention. "*This sacred place. Under truce.*" He leaned across the table and looked me in the eye. "*Truce remain until sun come up. Leave this place ... now.*"

Some of the others looked as if they were about to raise a protest, but Grulg shouted them all down. Eventually they began to back off. It was odd. Had it been my side that had the superior numbers, I'm not sure we would have let them walk away to regroup.

One by one, the Sasquatches heeded the order. They turned and left. Grulg was the last to go. Our eyes met just before he turned away. I could have sworn there was the ghost of a smile on his face. In the end, he had gotten what he wanted ... his honor. Maybe there was something to that after all.

* * *

The witnesses to this clusterfuck of a peace conference quickly took the hint. Many of them beat feet out of the area. Others disappeared in flashes of light. A few even melted away into nothingness. While this went on, I sat there with my friends, none of us speaking, just watching it happen. Little by little, the crowd dispersed until only a few beings remained. At last, a white-robed figure caught my eye. Christy was walking toward us.

Tom stood to meet her. I shrugged to Ed and Sally, then rose to join him. Christy had been supportive of me in the end. The least I could do was face the music like a man.

She gave her boyfriend a hug before turning to me. There was a momentary pause in which I wondered if I was about to get blasted, but then she said, "Just tell me you didn't plan for that to happen."

"Not for a second," I replied.

"I believe you."

"Thanks. I mean that." I took a deep breath before continuing. Unfortunately, the next part had to be asked. "So what side are you guys on in all of this? Is it safe to assume whatever one I'm *not* on?"

She looked thoughtful for a moment. "The Magi have traditionally been neutral in these affairs. But..."

"But, now I'm around – the so-called great harbinger of doom, right?"

She nodded. "There is that."

"Do you believe it?"

"Believe what?"

"That I'm actually going to bring about the rise of these ... Icons? After everything you've seen, do you really believe that I'm purposefully going to destroy anyone?"

There was no answer at first, but then she shook her head. "No, I'm beginning to think the prophecy must be wrong. Maybe we've ... misinterpreted it."

"Although the way Bill's luck seems to be..." Tom added.

"Tell me about it," I said with a sigh. "For all I know I'll open a can of Coke tomorrow ... and POOF, it'll somehow be the magical resting place of an army of infernal destruction." A little chuckle broke out amongst the group.

"Either way," Christy continued, "I'll try to talk to my coven. Hopefully they'll realize we're going to be busy enough in the days ahead."

"I appreciate that," I replied, meaning every word of it. "Not to push my luck, but could I maybe ask for another favor?"

"What?"

"Is it safe to say you'll be apparating out of here, or whatever the hell you guys do?"

She let out a small laugh. "You watch too many movies. But yes, we'll be leaving this place via magical means."

"Is there any chance you can take Tom and Ed with you?"

At that, Ed started to protest, but I held up a hand.

"Don't argue. Despite what Grulg said, this place is bound to get unfriendly *real* fast. Between the Bigfeet and the vampires, everything here is going to want to either squash you, bite you ... or worse."

"Bill's right," Sally said, showing almost a modicum of concern.

Christy nodded. "I can do that. It's pretty far, but I might be able to get a few of my sisters to help."

"Just tell them Bill tried to eat us," Tom said.

I chuckled. "Not the way you smell."

"Same to you, bro." He smiled back. "I wish we all used Dial right about now."

"What about you and Sally?" Ed asked.

"Don't worry about us. I'm hoping we can bum a ride with James." I pointed toward the far end of the small valley where I could see his and François's respective groups waiting. Neither looked particularly pleased.

"Or maybe we can find where Grulg parked our Jeep," Sally added.

"Yeah," I said with a grin. "Maybe we'll get lucky and they'll have gassed us up and washed the windows, too."

* * *

"You've killed us all. You realize that, don't you?" François spat, breaking the silence.

After seeing Tom, Ed, and Christy off, we had joined the two groups of vampires waiting for us. We were all walking down the trail leading away from the scene of the failed conference. The woods around us were almost deathly quiet. It was like Turd, Grulg, and the rest of their fun bunch had simply disappeared. It was kind of spooky to tell the truth.

"He did nothing, of the sort," James replied, stepping between us. "Alas, I fear this may have actually been my fault."

"*Your* fault?" I asked.

"Yes. I obviously hadn't thought things through. Gan's wishes, combined with Nergui's hurt honor ... I had no idea the two would prove to be such an explosive combination."

"Don't let him off so easily," François said. "Were it not for his meddling, peace would have been assured and we would have all come out of this ahead."

Sally pointed an accusing finger at him. "Yeah, but you would have come out a lot more ahead, isn't that right?"

"What of it, you insipid little slut? In matters such as these, there are always winners and losers. Now, though, we are *all* losers thanks to this inept clod."

"Don't blame me, asshole," I fired back. "This whole thing happened because of *you*." James raised an eyebrow at that, so I said. "Yeah, it's true. This French fried fuck caused it all. He somehow got the Sasquatches to attack the Khan just to set this whole thing up. All so he could become the fucking syrup king of Canada. Isn't that right?"

François stood back and sneered. "So what if it is? What does it matter? I removed an enemy and set myself up for a great reward. Don't fool yourself into thinking I'm the first of our kind to do so."

James's eyes momentarily turned black. However, he somehow managed to control himself. He took several deep breaths before asking, "You risked war over something as petty as monetary gain?"

"Have you not been listening? There would have been no war. This whole conference was nothing but a ruse. Turd and his minions were pathetically easy to bribe. The First's negotiators alone would have most likely cost a thousand times what it took to sway that lummox."

"I'm sure they would have," I said. "But you cheaped out and killed them instead."

"What?" François replied, his eyes narrowing. "Their disappearance was fortuitous, I admit, but if you are daring to imply..."

"Don't bullshit a bullshitter," I snapped. "After all this, are you seriously trying to claim you didn't have them offed?"

"Actually, he did not," a voice replied from just inside the tree line. "*I* removed them from the equation." A figure stepped out toward us. It was Alex. "The act was regrettable, but alas necessary."

"What the hell?!" I sputtered, completely flummoxed.

Did he just...? The entire thing had come from completely outta left field, catching me entirely off guard. Before I could even begin to digest this *confession*, though, I realized that Alex, Sally, and I were the only ones still standing. All of the rest, James and François included, had fallen to one knee.

"Lord Alexander!" James exclaimed from his prostrate position.

"My liege!" François likewise bellowed.

Sally and I exchanged a glance. "Did I miss something here?" I asked her.

"Don't look at me. I didn't get the memo either."

"On your knees!" hissed James. "Do you not know who that is?"

"Uh ... no."

Alex simply smiled and walked over. "Well, then allow me to introduce myself. My name is Alexander."

"I kind of guessed that," I replied drolly.

"More commonly known," he added, "as Alexander of Macedon."

The name didn't ring a bell so I just stood there, waiting for him to continue.

"Son of Philip of Macedon..."

I shrugged, still not comprehending.

Sally reached over and smacked me upside the head. "*Alexander the Great*, stupid."

"Oh ... OH!" I said, realizing whom she meant. I probably should have joined the others down on my knees. We were in the presence of a two-thousand-plus-year-old vampire. Not only that, but one of the most legendary conquerors of all time. Unfortunately, right then my mouth remembered that it had a mind of its own. Instead of saying something humble and respectful, I asked, "So was your mother really as hot as Angelina Jolie?"

* * *

There were shocked gasps from all around and I realized why. If this guy was as old as I thought, he was undoubtedly one of the Draculas ... and they were not known for their sense of humor.

Even Sally took a step back, as if afraid of getting splattered by my impending dismemberment.

Instead of annihilating me with extreme prejudice, though, Alex actually chuckled. "You do continue to surprise me, Freewill. It is most refreshing, and in answer to your question ... no. Had she been, I most likely would have never left Greece."

"Forgive him, my lord," James said. "He's young and..."

"Stupid?" I asked. One didn't need to be a master of mad libs to be able to fill in that blank.

Alex ignored me, though. He stepped over to where James still knelt. "Ah, Wanderer. It is good to see you again." He put one hand on James's shoulder. Oh crap.

I hoped I wasn't about to see the Draculas' wrath firsthand. It would be totally unfair to make James an example for my failures ... not that vampires had any real sense of what's fair.

Fortunately, rather than do something dickish like that, Alex said, "Rise, Wanderer. The First kneel to no one, not even those of our coven."

Whoa!

"My lord?" James asked, perhaps the first time I had ever heard him unsure of himself.

"You heard me. I choose you to fill your sire's place. You have proven yourself more than worthy."

"What?" François hissed, rising. "I protest. This is..."

"This is *my* will," Alex said, the threat evident in his voice. "Or would you challenge that?"

A look of fear crossed François's face. He wore it well. It suited the weasely little dick. "No ... of course not."

"A wise answer. Perhaps the only one I have heard escape your lips since this began. I must say I am disappointed, François. This is not the first time you have attempted *and failed* to betray our race, am I correct?"

"I was just..."

"Fear not. Your death shall not come at my hands. I have a bit of admiration for ambition, after all, inept though your efforts may be. Fortunately for you, there will be plenty of chances to prove yourself again in the coming days."

"There will?"

"Of course. This is your domain, is it not?"

"Yes," François replied, a little uncertain.

"Well, I dare say then, you are on the front lines of this war. When the Grendel attack, yours will be the first line of defense standing before them."

"But..."

"But *nothing*! You have much to prepare for ... **NOW BEGONE FROM MY SIGHT!!**"

The compulsion was aimed squarely at François. Such was its force, though, that the trees around us all shook as if a tremor had passed through them. I may be the Freewill and immune to such things, but I had a feeling Alex could've popped all our heads like water balloons had he felt like it. As it were, François's eyes glazed over. Without another word, he turned and walked away. His men quickly followed his lead, not wishing to risk Alex's wrath.

A recent memory hit me as I watched them leave. "I thought you said..."

"I said it was *difficult* to compel someone of François's age ... not impossible," Alex calmly replied, turning back toward me. "Now that the refuse has been taken out, I must say, well done, Freewill."

"Well done?"

"Yes. I am quite pleased."

"Um, you do realize I just started a war back there, right?" I asked. "I thought the Drac ... err ... First Coven wanted peace."

"Partly true. My brothers and sisters desired that outcome."

"I'm not following."

"What a surprise," Sally commented under her breath.

"Sally..." James growled in a slight warning tone, shutting her up.

"Though I am first amongst equals," Alex said, showing that low self-esteem was obviously not one of his vices, "I am occasionally forced to acquiesce to the whims of the other First, but not so this time. The opportunity was too ripe."

"Opportunity for what?"

"To finish what I began two millennia ago, of course. I had half of Asia bowing down before me when an unfortunate encounter in India led to my being turned. As the recently reawakened, I was forced to obey my master and step into the shadows. Helpless, I watched as my armies squabbled amongst themselves and eventually dispersed."

"Yeah, I remember reading about that in history class."

Alex ignored my interruption, apparently lost in his own thoughts. "I bided my time, gaining strength and power while removing any rivals. At long last, I became the first of the First. After all these countless centuries, I knew that it was time for our people to step forth from the shadows and claim this world as our own ... as *my* own. Alas, the others begged to disagree. It has been a point of consternation amongst us for some time now."

He stepped forward and looked me square in the eye. "When you were born, though, I knew it was a sign, a call to action, if you will. We shall rise and conquer, the wishes of the others be damned."

"Okay," I replied slowly, feeling the crazy coming off of him in waves. "So you planned all of this yourself?"

"Not entirely. Your reputation precedes you, Freewill. In such a short time, you have developed quite the aptitude for ... how do I say this..."

"Fucking things up?" Sally offered.

"Yes, that will do nicely. You really are astute, my dear. I meant it when I said that earlier. I see a great future for you."

"Thanks," she answered blithely. Bitch!

"I knew deep down," he continued, "that by putting you in a position of authority, you would find a way to fulfill your destiny."

"My destiny?"

"Have you not listened to the prophecies, boy? You are the Freewill, the one who shall lead our forces against our enemies. Well, congratulations, now you have enemies to lead the charge against."

"That was your blood," I said, beginning to understand.

"Of course," Alex admitted. "I will say it had quite the effect on you. Startling, in fact. You are everything the legends said you would be. You simply require a bit of polishing before you reach your full potential."

"But ... the world, my lord..." James stammered, still not having regained his composure.

"I already told you, Wanderer, enough with the groveling. We are brothers now. As for the world ... the world needs a good purging. It has been far too long since the last great flood or Black Death. This time we shall remake the world in our own image."

Sally and I exchanged glances. Oh, yeah, this was not good.

"This is a great day, my friends," Alex said, clapping us each on the shoulder in turn. "The vampire nation shall rise from the ashes, supreme in a world of darkness!"

Yeah ... a world of batshit crazy darkness.

The Awesomely Important Epilogue

THE WORLD OF darkness would fortunately have to wait. Work was my most pressing concern right at that moment. Our trip back from Canada turned out to be considerably faster and easier than the trip there. Once the truce had been dissolved, we didn't need to worry about the Sasquatches' restrictions on technology. After filling us in on his plans for an extreme global makeover, Alex conveniently produced a satellite phone and made a quick call. An hour later, a pair of black, heavily-armed helicopters arrived to pick us up and take us back home. I guess it's good to be king.

Alex and James departed in one, headed for parts unknown. There were preparations to be made on both sides. Despite Alex's posturing, neither faction was prepared for immediate battle, which I guess was good. I wasn't quite ready to kiss my own ass goodbye yet anyway.

Sally and I were flown back to the city on the other, being told that the vampire nation would call upon us when it was time. Essentially the fuckers set me up to doom the world and then gave me a "Don't call us, we'll call you."

We spent most of the trip back in silence, a rarity for us. I knew we were both thinking the same thing, but the vamps flying us were undoubtedly Alex's men. In such company, it was best not to voice our true thoughts on the "glorious" future ahead of us.

That being said, once back, it was amazing how quickly the whole frigged-up experience began to feel like a bad dream. Sally and I had the same top priority upon arriving home ... the world's longest shower (sadly separate). She went back to Manhattan to deal with coven issues ... although I suspected her main *issue* would involve a massive amount of pampering at the hands of Alfonzo. Note to self: stake that guy just to piss her off.

I made my way back to Brooklyn where I happily found my roommates waiting for me. Christy had made good on her part of the deal. They had even cleaned up that "disintegrate Bill" dust for me, which was awfully cool of them considering I had completely forgotten about it by then.

Upon my arrival, I filled them in on what went down after they had poofed out of there. Tom summed it up best of all.

"What a bunch of fucking cocks!"

Couldn't have said it better myself.

* * *

Our boss, Jim, was overjoyed at having us back. I was kind of glad, too, since that meant I still had a good chunk of my vacation days left. I figured there was no reason to upset him by mentioning that the concept of programming video games was all for naught since civilization was teetering on the edge of total destruction. I'm considerate that way.

Despite my status of permanent telecommuter, Jim asked if I wouldn't mind popping by the office on a day when I was feeling up to it. He wanted to have a face-to-face to go over existing projects as well as some new priorities that were coming down the pipe from the higher-ups.

He was referring to the, unbeknownst to him, bullshit cover story of my *illness*. For me, though, this meant picking a day when I wasn't likely to be turned to dust. I quickly checked the weather report (*a gamble, I know*), discovered it would be overcast on Friday of that week, and set our meeting for that day. It made sense. I could stop in and talk to him, then head over to the Office to see what shenanigans Sally had been up to.

Little did I know then, but I should have prayed for sunshine.

* * *

I arrived at the office of Hopskotchgames around mid-afternoon. My first impression was that they had redecorated. The entire programming floor had been rearranged. There was still the prerequisite sea of cubes, but several open work areas had been created.

One of the database guys, Mike, saw me standing there taking it all in. "Hey, Bill. Heard you were dead."

"What?!"

"Just kidding, man. Haven't seen you in a while."

"Oh ... yeah," I stammered. The joke shouldn't have caught me off guard, but sometimes I could get paranoid over the whole undead thing.

"Like the new digs?"

"It's definitely different. One of the VPs get a bug up their ass about the décor?"

"Nah. Upper management hired these new efficiency experts. Apparently, they made quite the pitch. They've been changing things left and right."

"More management bullshit?"

"Not really. Some of it actually makes sense. Go figure," he replied. "They're all here today. You should stick around and meet them."

"Why would I care?"

"I think you'll like them," he finished with a smug smile and said no more. I was about to pump him for more info when Jim spotted us and beckoned me over.

We spent about an hour and a half going over stuff. There was nothing really special to discuss – just your typical type-A personality boss crap: him having a near aneurysm about new priorities and me making assurances. Still, he seemed in a better mood than when last we spoke. I learned it was because he was close to hiring a new admin. The relief coming off him was palpable. Personally, I couldn't have cared less. There had been nothing wrong with the old admin. In fact, she had been perfect, as far as I was concerned.

That pretty much ended the meeting for me. Jim droned on for another half hour, but I didn't hear him.

I was stuck thinking about Sheila and how our potential future had been snatched away ... first by her quitting and now by me destroying the world.

We finished up and I said my goodbyes, preparing to head over to the coven. As I was walking out, though, I noticed a few of the executive team exiting one of the larger conference rooms. I remembered Mike's suggestion. It looked like they were wrapping up anyway, so I figured it wouldn't kill me to wait a few extra minutes. I leaned up against a wall to get a load of the jokers that were here to make us all super-efficient worker drones.

And that's when all my thoughts pretty much ground to a dead halt.

* * *

It wasn't the sight of our CEO that got me. It was whom he was shaking hands with. No fucking way! It was no wonder Mike had been so goddamn sly. I had been told that my infatuation with our former admin wasn't exactly a well-kept secret. Guess they were right. Suddenly I was glad I had listened to him, smug grin and all.

Sheila stood there talking to our CEO. Hell, just a few weeks ago, I doubted he would have recognized her if he'd run her down with his BMW. Yet there she was, looking him straight in the eye and talking as if they were old friends. I almost couldn't believe I was actually seeing her again. At the same time, though, it almost wasn't her.

It's hard to explain, but she had changed. I could tell that with a casual glance alone – not that there was anything casual about the way I was staring at her. Gone was her typical bland office attire. She was dressed in a business suit – an expensive one, by the looks of it. She held herself straight and proud, an aura of confidence about her. The shy girl who had, just a short time ago, confided in me about not believing in herself was nowhere to be seen. Standing there was a woman who looked like she could conquer anything that stood in her way.

Despite all of that, though, she was still the most amazing person I had ever seen ... just more so, if that was even possible.

I stood there gawking like a complete idiot for what could have been hours, for all I knew. She said her goodbyes and then her eyes shifted in my direction. Normally I would have picked that moment to dive into an unoccupied cubicle, but I had changed, too. With the fate of the world resting upon my shoulders, the very least I could do was stand my ground and say "hi."

When she saw me, she broke out into a big smile, and I could tell it was genuine. She was just that type of person. It could've been wishful thinking on my part, but I didn't get that vibe.

She walked over and I immediately felt my veneer of bravery collapse. It was as if the cool, confident part of my brain decided that it was the perfect time for a nap.

Guess I hadn't changed that much after all. Fucking asshole subconscious!

"So ... you're back?" I stammered, feeling sweat break out on my forehead.

"Hi, Bill," she said, the warm smile never leaving her face.

"Sorry. I mean, it's great to see you again. I didn't know if ... well ... I would ever..."

She giggled. "You can't get rid of me that easily. I've just been really busy."

"I can imagine," I replied, having no real clue. "So are you ... they said efficiency experts ... and..."

"Yes, and yes." She reached into her breast pocket (*oh, those heavenly breasts*) and produced a business card. "Check it out."

"I will," I replied, absentmindedly sticking it into my own shirt pocket. That could wait until later. No way was I wasting a moment of our time together staring at a stupid business card.

We stood there in awkward silence for a few moments. Could it have been that she was as nervous as I was? Nah, not the way she looked. She was probably just thinking of a way to escape from my...

"You know, it's weird running into you here."

"Yeah, the whole work from home thing..."

"No. It's just that ... this is going to sound a little bizarre, but I had the strangest dream about you the other night."

"Really?" Please let it be a sex dream.

"Yeah. You were in the woods and these things were *chasing* you. Weird huh?"

I blinked stupidly at that for a moment. "Uh, yeah ... weird." Holy crap, hadn't I dreamt of her too just a few nights back? Well, okay, I tended to dream about her all the time. Still, maybe this was the sign I was looking for, the one that proved we were connected by fate. Yeah, I liked that. Worked for me.

"So, anyway," she continued, "were you on your way out?"

"Um, yeah ... just popped by to see Jim."

"Well then, I guess luck is with me twice today." It was? "That was my last meeting. Maybe you can walk me to the train."

Maybe? *Maybe*?! If Alex, Turd, and François all appeared and said that I could do so, but only if I fought them all first, I'd dive right into that shit without a second thought.

So of course, I answered, "Okay, I guess so."

* * *

Someone pinch me. I must've been having a dream. No, fuck that! Don't pinch me, because I didn't want to wake up. The walk to the train didn't end there. We kept talking and laughing ... and, well, just kept going. Eventually it turned into me walking her home. Holy fantastic fantasies, Batman.

Along the way, I learned a few things. Sheila's little efficiency operation wasn't quite so little. Hopskotchgames was just one of her clients. In a short time, she had used her contacts to get a foot in the door at several other companies all across SoHo. She now had a small staff and had even managed to secure a modest amount of venture financing.

"...and it's mostly because of you," she finished as we neared her apartment. We had been walking for a while, taking the scenic route so to speak. The sky was fully dark by the time we approached her stoop.

"Me? Yeah, I doubt that."

"Don't." She stopped and looked me in the eye, dead serious. "You said it yourself. Sometimes we need someone else to believe in us before we can believe in ourselves. You're the one who gave me that push."

"You would have gotten there yourself..."

"That's the thing," she interrupted. "I don't know that. My other friends, my family..." she trailed off. "It's hard to explain, but I know what I believe."

"Oh," I replied stupidly, coming up with absolutely zilch as way of answer.

"I just wanted to say ... thank you," she whispered, stepping closer, now edging into my personal space. Every *wuss* instinct in my body, of which there was no shortage, screamed at me to run.

No! I wouldn't do that this time. There might never be another opportunity like this, especially if we all ended up enslaved by Bigfoot.

"You're welcome," I said, leaning in closer – barely believing I was doing so.

This was it. Time to go for the kill, figuratively of course.

We continued to approach one another (*Oh, yeah, T-minus seven to kissy face!*). I looked deep into her eyes. I still couldn't believe how much she had changed since last I had seen her. Everything about her was different, more confident: her demeanor, her attitude, her clothes, even her eyes seemed to have changed. Gone was the subtle grey they had been. Now they seemed to sparkle, almost like silver.

Our lips were about to touch. YES! This was it...

Wait a second ... *silver eyes?!*

KER-BLAM!!!

One second I felt all tingly, almost like I was on fire. The next, I actually *was* on fire.

An explosion of white flame flared around me and I catapulted backwards. The next thing I knew, I was lying in a pile of trash all the way across the street. Flames covered the front of my body, but through them, I could see her. She stood there in shock but completely unhurt. A soft white glow surrounded her body. No fucking way!

Unfortunately, it wasn't over for me. My body subconsciously reacted to the pain. I felt my eyes blacken against my will. My fangs and claws both extended as she started crossing the street toward me. But, I wasn't finished yet.

Oh, no! Not now!

Whatever dark power flowed through a Freewill such as myself began to assert itself. I could sense the beast inside me pushing its way out. I was starting to change.

"Stay back!" I warned.

But, Sheila continued to approach, a mixture of confusion and fear upon her face.

"What are you?" was the last thing I heard her say before I stood and ran like my life depended on it. Both of ours may have.

* * *

"What the fuck happened to you?" Sally asked, taking the cucumber slices off her eyes long enough to give me the once over.

The worst of the damage had already healed, but I was covered in soot and my clothes were charred tatters. Fortunately, the change had subsided before fully taking hold. Getting away from Sheila had apparently been the key to that.

"She's the Icon!" I shouted, near hysterics.

"Alfonzo, can you leave us for a moment?"

The effeminate little douche made a sniffing noise but did as told. He walked from Sally's office and shut the door behind him. Once we were alone, she sat up and gave me her full attention. "Now say that again."

"Sheila is the Icon."

"Who?"

"That girl I like."

"Oh, her," she replied offhandedly. "How do you know?"

I gestured down at myself. "She blew me across the street."

"She blew you on the street?"

"*Across!*"

418

"That *is* a bit different. How did it happen?"

"I tried to kiss her."

"Really? You dog you."

"Not funny, Sally."

"Sorry." She held up her hands in a placating manner. "Well, it could have been worse."

"Worse?"

"Yeah, you could have been banging her."

"Not helping." I got up and started to pace, scores of thoughts racing through my head, none of them good. "It's all coming true."

"The prophecies?"

"Yes! Me leading our armies in battle, and now this. Despite what I said to Christy, I actually did it. I created the Icon!"

"I'm sure you didn't create her."

I trudged over and explained everything. How I had believed in Sheila and how that had somehow sunk in and caused a chain reaction. At last, Sally's eyebrows raised in surprise.

"I take it back. You did create her. Damn."

"Damn is right."

"I'm so sorry, Bill," she said, losing the attitude.

"So am I."

"No, I mean I'm *really* sorry."

"Why?"

"You have a thing for her, don't you?"

I sighed. "You have no idea."

"Well, I've been doing a little digging. After that whole situation with Decker and Gan, I had Colin send me any information in the archives about this."

"Really?"

"Yeah. Sorry I didn't tell you, but it all seemed like bad fairy tale bullshit."

"What did?"

"The Freewill and the Icon ... you're archenemies."

"Historically, yeah. I know that."

"No, *eternally*," she said, dead serious. "There are more prophecies about this than you know ... hell, probably lots more than I could uncover. But, they all say the same thing. You're either going to kill the Icon, or the Icon is going to kill you."

"Are you sure?"

She nodded once in response.

I had no answer to that, not even a clue. I leaned forward on her desk and lowered my head, not wanting to think about it. As I did, something slipped out of the remains of my vest pocket. It fluttered down to the desk.

It was Sheila's card, somehow undamaged. Perhaps enough of her aura had remained to protect it. Whatever the cause, Sally picked it up and read it.

"No fucking way."

"What?" I asked despondently.

She flipped over the card so I could read it, too. I knew she was talking about the title, but the tagline did it for me. It confirmed what I already knew – that this was entirely my fault. I had done it. In trying to be supportive of my dream girl, I had somehow turned her into my greatest nightmare.

Iconic Efficiencies

We believe you can do better

-Sheila O'Connell, CEO

No fucking way, indeed.

I sank back down in the chair opposite Sally. Sometimes when life decided to shit all over you, it took a mega-dump. I had seen some dark moments since becoming a vampire, but this was the first time when I could see absolutely no hope on the horizon. Damn. To say that it sucked to be me would be the understatement of a lifetime.

"I have no idea what to do."

"Same here," she said, sitting across from me. After a moment, she added, "But we'll figure out something."

"We?"

"Of course. Partners forever, right?"

"Seriously?"

"One-hundred percent."

To my surprise, I actually smiled. "You know, Sally, for all the times you're a complete bitch, I could really hug you right now."

"You could try," she replied with a smirk, "but I'd kick your ass."

I couldn't help but laugh. It was a good feeling. I decided to enjoy it because it would most likely be the last real laugh I was going to have for quite some time.

THE END

Bill Ryder will return in:

Holier Than Thou: The Tome of Bill, part 4

Can't wait for more Bill? Follow his ongoing misadventures on Facebook at:

www.facebook.com/BilltheVampire

Author's Note

Hi, once again. As usual, it is my extreme pleasure to see you here. This time out, we can ignore all the usual crap and get straight to one main point: I had a ridiculous amount of fun writing this book. There, I said it! There really isn't much more to it than that. Don't get me wrong; *Bill The Vampire* and its sequel, *Scary Dead Things*, were awesome. Now that the origin story is done, though, and the stage has been set, it was time to coax Bill out of his shell and into a much wider world than he's used to (or ready for) ... and that, well it's a hoot.

This is my third major foray into Bill's world (ignoring short stories or his and Sally's ongoing Facebook adventures) and it's really coming alive for me now. It's getting so that I wouldn't be half surprised to be walking through SoHo one night and notice a quick flash of fang from the mouth of a pretty (if sarcastic) blonde.

Isn't that what it's all about, making the characters real? I, for one, think it is. Is there anything more entertaining (or frustrating) at times than reading a book and imagining yourself there alongside the characters? What would you do? Would you help them? Hinder them? Maybe smack them upside the head a few times? Ultimately you might do all the above, but that doesn't matter. What matters is the feeling that you're reading the adventures of someone you could imagine meeting on the street, no matter how unlikely you know that actually to be.

That right there is the awesome part, because right at that point the adventure continues in ways that I, the lowly scribe, could never even begin to imagine.

If you ever happen to find yourself wandering down that imaginary path with a nerdy vampire named Bill by your side, I wish you well and hope that you have quite the adventure.

Rick G.

About the Author

Rick Gualtieri lives alone in central New Jersey with only his wife, three kids, and countless pets to both keep him company and constantly plot against him. When he's not busy monkey-clicking out words, he can typically be found jealously guarding his collection of vintage Transformers from all who would seek to defile them.

Defilers beware!

Rick Gualtieri is the author of:

Bill The Vampire (The Tome of Bill - 1)
Scary Dead Things (The Tome of Bill - 2)
The Mourning Woods (The Tome of Bill - 3)
Holier Than Thou (The Tome of Bill - 4)
Sunset Strip: A Tale From The Tome Of Bill
Goddamned Freaky Monsters (The Tome of Bill - 5)
Half A Prayer (The Tome of Bill - 6)
The Wicked Dead (The Tome of Bill - 7)
Shining Fury: A Tale From The Tome Of Bill
The Last Coven (The Tome of Bill - 8)
Bigfoot Hunters

To contact Rick (with either undying praise or rude comments) please visit:

Rick's Website:
www.rickgualtieri.com

Facebook Page:
facebook.com/RickGualtieriAuthor

Twitter:
twitter.com/RickGualtieri

Bonus Chapter

Holier Than Thou
The Tome of Bill, Part IV

THEY SAY MAN is the ultimate predator. Should he not also make the ultimate prey? It's a thrilling concept. Imagine taking that to the next level, hunting a predator that's even higher on the food chain. There's a fitting reason it's called the most dangerous game.

Running through the thick forest, I felt truly alive. The woods were pitch-black, but that wasn't enough to slow me down. My supernaturally attuned eyes cut through all but the darkest gloom as I sought out my target. She thought she could evade me, perhaps even turn the tables and win. She would soon find out how wrong she was.

As I pursued her through the forest primordial, a small voice reminded me to be cautious. She was far more dangerous than the others. I indulged myself in memories of the ones already dispatched – two humans, frail and weak. In another life they had meant something, but not out here. The one called Ed had been the first to fall. She had seen to that. Tom was next, by my own hand. I had sensed his impending betrayal and been the first to act. He had begged for mercy, but received none – such is the way of my kind.

I stopped and got my bearings. Sounds, sights, and scents filled my very being. It was tempting to throw back my head and howl primal defiance at the moon, but that would be foolish. She might be listening. Though I felt no fear at facing her, I had no intention of giving her any edge.

There ... a scent, *hers*. It was intoxicating – awakening a deep need – but I pushed those thoughts away. I was here to hunt and would not be distracted quite so easily. Her smell played out across my hyper-sensitive nostrils for a moment before I bounded off into the darkness once more.

I savored the feel of the weapon in my hand. It would do nicely. She would never see it coming. It would be quick and clean ... if I wanted it to be. But I didn't. She needed to know who had hunted her down. The look upon her face as she realized who had vanquished her would be too much of a prize to turn down. I smiled in anticipation and quickened my pace.

Victory was mine for the taking, as was fitting. Even amongst predators, I am at the very apex. My name is Bill Ryder and I'm a vampire, an immortal beast of the night – but that's not all. I am the legendary Freewill of vampire lore. The others speak of me and my coming in hushed tones. A great destiny has been foretold for me. Much honor and glory shall be laid at my feet one day.

Feh! Let them keep their prophecies. I do not exist for them or the future they proclaim for me. No, I live only in the here and now ... and right now I was closing in on my prey.

* * *

There! A lesser being might have missed it, but not me. The fabric of her jacket peeked through the foliage. She was lying in wait, hoping for an ambush. She was a smart girl, but sadly not smart enough.

I circled her position, keeping outside of her range. None, save perhaps another of my kind, would have been able to sense my presence. Therein lay the challenge. Though not of my lofty status, she had skill and power of her own. She might well be able to sense that I was advancing upon her.

I bent low, picked up a few pebbles from the ground, and held my breath as I counted to ten. The ruse would only fool her for seconds at best, so it would have to be fast.

Now! Pebbles rained down from the sky, disturbing the area where I had been only moments earlier. Before the last of them had hit the ground, I was once again on the move. Bringing all of my speed to bear, I raised my weapon and advanced upon her hiding spot.

She never saw me coming. There was no movement from the bushes, so intent was she on waiting for me to fall into her trap.

"It's over, Sally."

* * *

Holier Than Thou
Available in ebook, paperback, and audio

Made in the USA
Middletown, DE
14 July 2017